# CAPITAL OFFENSE

# CAPITAL OFFENSE

## THE MERCHANT PRINCE

Volume III

Armin Shimerman

POCKET STAR BOOKS
New York London Toronto Sydney Singapore

An *Original* Publication of POCKET BOOKS

A Pocket Star Book published by
POCKET BOOKS, a division of Simon & Schuster Inc.
1230 Avenue of the Americas, New York, NY 10020



ISBN: 978-1-4767-3067-7

First Pocket Books printing December 2003

10 9 8 7 6 5 4 3 2 1

POCKET STAR BOOKS and colophon are registered trademarks of Simon & Schuster Inc.

Photo illustration by Jae Song

Printed in the United States of America

For information regardng special discounts for bulk purchases, please contact Simon & Schuster Special Sales at 1-800-456-6798 or business@simonandschuster.com.

# CAPITAL OFFENSE

# PROLOGUE

FROM THE DAY BOOKE of John Dee, Doctor, in the Year of Our Lord 2101:

*I have heard and also seen it set forth in divers printed books that after the passing of certain persons, which in their lives were of great distinction, tales were misconceived to cause these honest men untoward calumny and eternal slander. Therefore I deem it fitting that I should now in my leisure here in this future realm reveal to you, the reader, some part of the proceedings of my ascending and descending curious estate. It is my fondest hope that the world might learn of what peril it was in and how my cohorts and I averted it. My tale, despite its giddy events that may trouble the minds of men of wisdom and discretion, I vow is not fantasized but is as true as the testimony that will be reported of me when I stand in judgement on the final day of reckoning.*

*I am old, but let this not upset you. As of this 18th day of February 2101, I am possessed of 574 years, having come into this world on July the 13th day of 1527, just outside the northern wall of London, the astrological coordinates being 4h2' P.M. Lat. 51° 32'. I thank God that I was born in England and was once of Elizabeth Regina's court, a philosopher, scholar, mathematician, and dabbler in the arcane arts of mysticism, whereby I aimed by rational processes mathematical and astronomical to seek the influences of celestial objects on sublunar lives. I vehemently bent to study the new learning that was to be had from Pythagoras, Erasmus, Frisius, the scholars of Arabia, and others of like-mindedness. For this upright and commendable study, I became greatly renowned both as practitioner and teacher and oft was sent for by Her Grace to her screened-off apartment, there in matters of astronomy, geometry, cryptography, mathematics, and such like faculties, and sometimes of her worldly affaires to sit and confer with her. There made I the acquaintance of her trusty and wise royal Principal Secretary, Sir Francis Walsingham, who with Her Grace's blessing, thought me sufficient to be put in authority and trust to perform acts of embassy whereto I should also endeavor to uncover divers secret acts of intelligencing so as to procure weighty secrets of State. The very word "secret" sounded in my being like a clarion call to battle and I never wavered from the challenge nor dwelt on personal safety but like a good hound was tireless after my prey. Oft for my Queen, I entered into this enterprise and oft found the means to gather intelligence though many was the time it chanced that my dagger and quick wit served me in better stead than my eloquence.*

*Proceeding thus in Fortune's blissfulness, which every man knows is but a turn of the wheel, it chanced that I was dispatched to Venice to seek out what perils that State and her abundantly perfumed prince, Francesco Foscari, had conceived for our blessed England. There neither my wit nor luck nor blade nor England's authority prevailed and I was walled up for my transgressions and left with neither nourishment nor light to perish as if encased in my coffin. I assayed to do all I could to free myself from this living death but in no ways could find a means of escape, so cut off from all help was I. In the end, I accepted all the terrors and deprivations that were mine and made my peace with God while awaiting the moment of His eternal grace.*

*But I was in grievous error and such is the power and mystery of the Supreme Good, that I was rescued by that which at first I conceived to be the very devil himself, for such was his form and girth that I could not believe but that all my hopes of Heaven were dashed and I was in the presence of a monstrous messenger from Hell. My saving angel streamed through the tower wall as unobstructed and undeterred as might a river through a feeble dam and, within scarce a breathing while, seized me as an eagle does a mouse and lofted us both up into the heavens upon his leathery grey back and wings. The height was perilous, but there beneath a cloud sat the creature's vessel which welcomed us both into its hold. There was I treated as a guest and given healthful nourishment and there I mended and slept.*

*Masters, by my honor, it is no lie I tell you that I slumbered undisturbed for five centuries, when I awoke to find myself yet aboard this alien vessel of the air whose mission to our world now had concluded and was eager to journey back to its home port. This argosy was crewed by creatures entitled Rocs and their captain was the self-same basilisk that had been my grotesque saviour in Venice. His name was Dyckon and he was but a stripling of three thousand years. The embassage of captain and retinue had been secretly to chronicle our world's history and make report of us back to the center of their league of worlds, a place an endless count of suns beyond our sun that they entitled the Collegium of Worlds.*

*It harrowed my brain to think what sophists my generation and those before me had been and of the error and ignorance of the ethereal upper spheres that we had magnified a hun-*

*dredfold, not knowing God's limitless glory and accomplishments. To these foreign scriveners, I was but a bit of ballast to be jettisoned ere they departed and left with me the news that our planet was soon to be trampled by a barbaric horde of other-worldly heathens that would leave us all ensnared and enslaved leaving this goodly orb to be a field of Golgotha. Rather the sun should burn all and leave not a rack behind ere such a calamitous undoing should ever come to pass. I pleaded with mine governor for some stratagem, some rescue, with a plague of woeful sighing and lamentation, but cold comfort gave me none and I fell into an unwholesome desolation. At last, taking some pity on me and imparting unto me gifts of an implanted device that translated all the languages of the Earth in mine ear and an alchemical marvel that could transmute the divers ores of the world into gold, the creature-captain left me to return to my world—albeit in as strange and godforsaken a place as fancy could surmise—to remedy what I could with the knowledge he had bestowed upon me.*

*For a year I panted after success exceedingly helped by the sudden untold wealth my alien gifts achieved for me and in the process discovered a pretty pair of stalwarts of honor and of courage who allied their stout spirits with mine own. For your understanding know you that my chief comforter and lieutenant is a great blackamoor named Morgan d'Winter and as worthy a friend and military man as can be found in the histories of Homer. I love the watchful villain. But, my heart belongs to his comrade, Kelly Edwards, a woman of infinite grace and mental fierceness. Her hair is a cascade of curling red love-locks that tumble down to shoulders the whiteness of Dover. She has a skillful cunning for matters technological and is an adept at many a modern weapon. I was truly blessed in both their acquaintances. Together we triumphed in squashing the bug that threatened our existence only to be re-visited by my guardian demon, Dyckon, and informed of a greater controversy. That of a disobedient Roc, one Fawg by name, who aspired to be sole emperor of our world. Like Satan, the supreme lie, he had the magic to assume what form he so desired and chose to present himself as our beloved Saviour, Jesus Christ, nee Yeshua Ben David, and in this infernal godhead enacted divers miracles to seduce and sway. One mortal touch by this scurrilous miscreant and the virus he carried would overmaster a man's will, and this same leprosy would strip the infected of what rein they held over their outward manifestation and change their appearance.*

*My friends and I, with the help of an army of rodent-like men (O wondrous Nature that can make vile things precious), overthrew this impious demon in the hills of Angel City and sent him to the flames of Hell whereto he belonged. But as I pen this, we have but scotched the virus—not killed it—as there be other Rocs, menials of this Fawg, who likewise threaten us all with this altering contagion.*

*Though I would fain rest here in the city of my birth from our travails, yet occasion enforces us to obey necessity and so we continue on in our pursuit. But, by my eternal soul, it is not only the virus and its carriers we seek, but also a means to carry me back to my times where I may be reunited once more with my proper chapter of History. I am sick at heart at the loss of it and like a courtier out of Regina's favor, I will do all to be reinstated. Dyckon of the Rocs has sworn that by finding the source of the plague I shall land upon the other and so I seek them both and pray continually for our success.*

*For the nonce, the world knows little of me and nothing of their peril. For the death of Fawg, though first heralded throughout the world by the queerly named Strategy Brooks, has been covered hugger-mugger by the world's High Sheriff, an international authority known as NTSA. It likes not the idea of a general panic infecting the ear of the world should the rumor of the Roc be proven true, moreover everyday I eschew their vigilance as they hunt for any who carries not their universally required identity chip which serves as key and password for many a closed door. Being not of this time, perforce I want not the device and rely on the good offices of my stalwarts d'Winter and Edwards to make my way through this much-changed world.*

*Who lists to read and consider with an indifferent eye my unvarnished testimony may behold the wondrous permutations of Fortune and the piteous case in which we all partook.*

# CHAPTER

# 1

UNHAPPY, JOHN DEE SAT in his straight-backed wooden chair on a terrace of his upper-floor bedroom. He marveled at the view: a vast panorama of Metropolitan London. The city was unrecognizable to him. It had grown so tall and so uninviting. The sun turned the clouds the color of diseased fruit, and the pall the light cast over the smoking expanse of buildings was enough to sour anyone. That, Dee supposed, included him. He had stayed in his hilltop aerie at St. Albans for three months, but he knew that he was not accomplishing half of what he had set out to do. He needed to find the other Roc to put an end to any threat of worldwide plague. The Roc might also be the key to Dee's going home. Back to a time when London was manageable. He ached to go home. The village of Mortlake was only six kilometers away, but it was no longer a village and it was no longer home.

"Doctor," called Kelly Edwards from the kitchen. "Do you want some lunch?" Under the guise of providing him protection, she had shared living quarters with him since he had arrived in London, and their relationship was developing into something more than either of them had expected—not a romance so much as a fond symbiosis.

"What are you offering?" he asked as he came in off the enclosed terrace, one brow raised suggestively. The terrace was shielded by spiderglass; it was impenetrable.

"Sprouts and technomeat in basil sauce," she said, smiling at him. She was dressed in a neat jumpsuit with three weapons clipped to the belt. A year ago, Dee would have found this military mien unfeminine and off-putting, but now he saw her as attractive and wholly female. His redheaded Brünnhilde. He came up to her and kissed her cheek. "What's news from d'Winter?"

"Nothing today. He's still looking for the Roc you think must still be here," she said. "But even though Rocs work in groups, isn't it possible that the Yeshua Roc was some kind of loner?"

"Dyckon was not of that mind," said Dee. "He is as certain as I that an attendant Roc must be in hiding on this planet. Waiting." Dee remarked as he took the plate and sat down on the kitchen stool in front of the counter. "Is there naught to drink?"

"Tea and wine. The wine's Romanian." She had gotten down glasses. "I'm having the wine."

"As shall I," declared Dee, and accepted a glass filled with a pinot noir. He lifted this in toast to her and began to eat.

Kelly took the stool opposite his and launched into her lunch. "Anything planned for this morning?"

"I am to be engaged in diverse research," he said obliquely.

"Can I help you with it?" She waited a moment, then

added, "I'll have to stay with you, in any case. You might as well keep me busy."

"Marry, then," said Dee. "You will needs come with me to the British Museum at its Montague Street entrance. The museum guard will bar your coming unless you accompany me. I am possessed of a research pass which will grant admittance to me and my assistant, but only if we arrive at the scholars' door at the same time."

"I'm your bodyguard, Doctor," Kelly pointed out as she took a sip of her wine. "I have to remain with you."

"For which I praise my stars and am grateful." He paused. The visit to the museum reminded him of lost opportunities. "I would have greatly desired to have had so majestic a collection in my time. It is the eighth wonder of the world." Dee swirled the wine and watched the liquid languidly slide down the curved glass. "I made petition to the court of Elizabeth to give me leave and a royal grant to pursue just such a scholarly enterprise. To gather the lost works of scientific antiquity." The Doctor grew more wistful, "Such a preservation of monuments and antique writers would have made England the envy of the world. But alas, it was not to be." He shook his head resignedly. After the reckless post-Reformation looting of Catholic property, he had been forced to spend years of time and much of his own money to gather books of ancient learning that had been foolishly discarded by an angry populous. Doctor Dee was reputed to have once had the largest library in Britain. Scholars from all of Europe and Asia came to stand in awe and admire his wealth of mathematics, astronomy, and the mystical occult. "Acquistion of knowledge was my quest and true understanding my prize. Burghley and Elizabeth never saw the country's need."

"The First," said Kelly conscientiously.

"Aye, the First," Dee chuckled, and added, "I am still at pains to think of her that way."

"I would be too, in your shoes," said Kelly with a burst of sympathy that made him feel awkward. Continually, he strived to seem informed on the six centuries of history he had missed. To his surprise, he found that only the world changed, not the passions of men.

"By my soul, although I would with all my heart return to her realm, I should miss you, and the creature comforts of this time." Dee busied himself with his food for the next ten minutes. "How long before you'll be ready to set forth?"

"That depends on you, Doctor," said Kelly. "What kind of protection do you need for the museum?"

"As is my wont," said Dee. "You or Callaghan, light arms you're licensed to carry, as we've done before. I have my suit."

"This is Callaghan's day off," Kelly reminded him.

"So 'tis," said Dee. "Perchance he has returned to Limerick for the day?"

"He has," said Kelly. "He's getting worn out, you know. Ever since we brought him on ten weeks ago, he's only had four days off. That's barely legal, and really expensive."

"Oft have I desired you to employ another sentry while d'Winter's abroad, if you deem it wise," said Dee. "You don't have to saddle all on Callaghan. So long as my true identity remains a secret."

"We'll get someone" she said. "We need to do a thorough check on anyone assigned to you."

He stopped short of asking her why, knowing that she hadn't told him because she wanted to protect him.

The thought bothered him slightly, and he absentmindedly asked again, "How long before we depart for the museum?"

"Twenty minutes, if that works for you," she said. "I have to secure the place and summon our private skimmer."

"What you will," he said, resigning himself to the long security check on the house. "Will you repair to secure the roof, or shall I?"

"I'll do it," she said. "You can shut down the record-room, and pack any notes you're going to need."

"Will do," he said, astonished at how much of the modern parlance had crept into his speech in the time since he had arrived in this century. Still, he reminded himself, he had often acquired local regionalisms on his travels in his own era, so there was no reason to be surprised.

"Then off you go," she said, checking her sidearm as she put their lunch dishes into the cleaner. She watched him leave the room, thinking as he went that she was too much involved for her own good—or for his. She finished cleaning the countertop, then took the spiral stairs to the roof where there was a long railing around the hydroponic garden, all but isolating the place like an island.

The roof made her nervous; it was too exposed. All that would be needed to breach it was a flyer and hand weapons. This alone made her very careful while she checked all the monitors on the roof, turning them up to their highest settings. As she turned back toward the stairs, she heard one of the surveillance units shriek a warning, and she ducked. An instant later the primrose next to her left shoulder disintegrated. The guard-beams were already swinging around in the direction from which the shot had come, their lasers poking into the air in the direction of a flyer that abruptly banked away from behind the belltower of a nearby cathedral.

Securing the roof door, she hurried down the stairs, trying to figure out how much she should tell Doctor Dee. At the base of the steps, she armed all the protective programs to fire their various weapons upon intruders. Adeptly, she ran a check on all the exterior windows and the recording devices that would keep visual files on anyone who approached this tall, narrow house on Tower Hill. Lastly she punched in the code on her wrist-vid to bring their flyer to the door.

"I've got my notes," said Dee, coming up behind her with an old-fashioned attaché case.

"You're not taking your palmtop?" She decided to say nothing about the shot on the roof.

"Harp not on that matter again," he retorted sharply. Immediately, he was slightly embarrassed by his strong admonition. They had had this discussion before. It was one of the few times they had argued. "They can be spied on too easily."

"Only by someone who has the right codes," she gently reminded him as they started toward the door. She felt him bristling at her side.

"That's enough to give me pause," said Dee as they ran out to the extended porch to meet the incoming flyer.

# CHAPTER 2

THE BRITISH MUSEUM SPRAWLED over six city blocks from Great Russell Square to Southampton Row to Great Russell Street to Tottenham Court Road to Bedford Square. Its architecture was as massive and impressive as that of any of the buildings of the lost civilizations it now housed; it had gobbled up part of the University of London and two small parks in its expansion process. It was every inch a testament to mankind's desire to grasp the past. The Montague Street entrance, tucked in across from Great Russell Square, was an unprepossessing doorway manned by only two armed guards and two I-Dent techs at their computers.

"That could be a problem," said Kelly.

"Not at all now," Dee shrugged. "D'Winter programmed a jammer into the earring he gave me to wear"—he touched the small jewel in his lobe—"The sentries haven't stopped me for want of an identity chip, and surely they would have, if the gewgaw hadn't worked."

"D'Winter is good at gadgets like that," Kelly allowed as they got out of the flyer. Her employer was always saying that he'd been born under a lucky star, but for the two years that she had spent with him, he'd been able to live unquestioned by the authorities about his lack of an implanted ID chip. It was an inexcusable breach of law enforcement protocols. Everyone in the world had an ID chip, and it was monitored by the National Terrestrial Security Administration (NTSA) of each nation. Automated systems everywhere clicked, computed, and accounted for every individual's whereabouts. Worldwide treaties and universal, official approval validated this invasion of privacy. You couldn't leave home without one. But somehow, miraculously, John Dee could. No matter how good Kelly Edwards and Morgan d'Winter were at circumventing sensors, their long string of luck with Dee sometimes made Kelly wonder. Unconcerned, Dee just took it for granted. As he said, he'd always been fortunate. She put the flyer's system on Return When Summoned without specifying a time, and went up the shallow steps to the scholars' door to the British Museum, calling out to the guards as she went, "I'm the Doctor's assistant."

Dee was waiting for her in the admissions alcove, a nervous little smile on his broad features. "You need to present your chip for them," he said loud enough to be heard by the museum guards.

"Of course," she said, permitting the I-Dent tech to scan her.

"Right you are, Miss Edwards," said the tech as he handed her a scholar's pass. "Wear this in view at all times in the museum." He then turned to Dee. "Take the moving sidewalk to Bloomsbury Hall, and then—"

"I know—the lift to the fifth floor and then on to the registration desk." Dee signaled Kelly to come with him.

"This is a rabbits' warren if ever I saw one. It's a ten-days' wonder that a man can pick out his way."

Keeping up with Dee as he threaded his way through the crush of badged men and women pursuing research in all directions, Kelly said, "True enough." Most of the Doctor's ornate elocution was easy to follow—once you attuned your ear—but she hadn't the faintest idea what a "ten-days' wonder" was. Kelly knew that if she asked, he'd only tell her to look it up.

The moving sidewalk carried them toward Southampton Row; they stepped off at the bottom of a high atrium that was filled with full-grown trees and tall flowering shrubs. The glade's existence inside the building still thrilled Dee. He found it as amazing as the modern perfection of perpendicular walls and unchanging light in windowless buildings. It was as architecturally thrilling as the canals of Venice the first time he'd seen them.

"The lift is there," said Dee, pointing to a bank of pod-like cars running up and down a thick core of power slots.

"How many times have you been here?" Kelly asked as she followed him.

"Twice. 'Tis an easy matter to remember your way if you hold fast to the memory of where you have been." As he stepped into a lift car, he held up his museum badge. "It would be best to bear yours aloft, Kelly."

She did as he recommended, and heard the door close. "Which floor?"

"Fifth," said Dee, and the car moved upward quickly. "What meant that scuffle on our lodging's roof?" he asked casually.

Kelly was surprised by the question. "What scuffle?"

"I heard a to-do of some kind," said Dee in a tone that warned he wouldn't be put off.

"You did," she improvised. "I mis-set one of the alarms."

"That isn't like you," said Dee.

"Not usually," she agreed. "But I occasionally overlook the readmission command. When I started to come inside, the monitor took it as an unauthorized entry. I had to scramble to avoid being targeted. I shouldn't have been so careless."

"Do you conclude that was the reason for the disturbance?" Dee asked, innocently enough, but Kelly sensed that he was testing her.

"I don't know for sure." She was glad that the lift was slowing down, and she was happy to be distracted by leaving the elevator car.

"Well, keep a watchful eye," Dee recommended. "I would not lose you to mindless mischance." He hurried on toward the reference desk, holding up his museum badge as he approached. "I was here a few days ago."

"I remember," said the tech behind the counter. "What'll it be today, luv?"

"Same as before," said Dee.

"Industrial investors, patent holders, boards of directors, developmental financiers, product lists," said the tech, reading from the tiny frame suspended in front of his right eye. "Anything else?"

"As much as you have on international development sites," said Dee as calmly as he could.

"The list'll be up in a nano," said the tech, and reached for a plastic sheet that emerged from a slot in the counter. "Here it is. I need you to initial it and impress it with the code on your badge."

"Will do." Dee then claimed a copy of the list.

"Take Booth 67D. You can have it until eighteen-forty,

and then you must surrender it and vacate the building by nineteen hundred."

"I am aware of the conditions," said Dee, taking his authorization chit from the tech.

As they made their way to the research booth, Kelly asked, "Doesn't it worry you that they have a record of everything you've asked to see?"

"It troubles the mind. But I content myself that any protests from me would only invite unwanted attention and conclude with the suspension of my privileges."

"You have a point," she said.

"Employ the machine. Discover all that you can upon the list."

"What am I looking for?" she asked as she set to work.

" 'S'truth, as to that I am in the dark. But I shall know it when I see it."

# CHAPTER 3

BETWEEN MARKOVO AND UST'-BELAJA the four interconnected domes rose in the narrow valley, not unlike huge onion domes of a fantastic arctic cathedral, but without Orthodox crosses atop them. Outside, the rugged mountains were filled with wildly blowing snow. Inside, the air was warm, a strange collection of plants flourishing as if in spring. The nine hundred people fortunate enough to live there tried not to pay any attention to the hourly weather reports that revealed that the rest of central Siberia was buried under several meters of new snow.

"You say Dee is still in London?" Theon Celsus turned to his assistant, Maxim Vadimovich Izevsky, and pointed his first two fingers at him. They were thin and arthritic.

"As of this morning he was, sir," Maxim said a bit too eagerly. Theon Celsus awed him, and part of his awe came from fear.

"Is there any indication that he is going to travel soon? Any reservations, or other indications we can monitor?" Celsus stepped closer to Maxim, underscoring his point.

It was mid day, and the room was washed with milky sunlight from the glowing orb far to the south. The sun would be visible for another ninety minutes or so, then it would set for the next twenty-one hours.

"None that my . . . your . . . operatives can discover," said Maxim. "He has been spending his time at the British Museum. We've been monitoring his palmtop. It doesn't provide much."

"Ah," said Celsus. "No doubt he is trying to stumble upon his past, to find out if he ever returned to his home." He tsked, a smirk marring any sympathy he might have implied. "I wonder why he bothers." The gnome-like man shook his head condescendingly. "He must realize it's just not there anymore. We've moved on."

"The computers at the museum are more difficult to break into than the ones for the Houses of Parliament," Maxim confided. "God knows we've tried."

"Don't bother for now," said Celsus, uninterested. "Time enough for that if he begins to become interested in us." He strolled over to the triple-glazed window and looked out at the expanse of white desolation. Celsus was dressed in a lightweight silken caftan, reminiscent of the doctor's robes he had worn in his own age, but much more comfortable. The vista brought back memories of his childhood in Switzerland. "I want daily reports on him."

"Shall I keep the spies after him?" Maxim asked, trying not to hold his breath as he waited for an answer.

"Yes. Watch him closely, but nothing else. I don't want him hurt or on the alert more than he already is." Celsus came back from the window. "How's everything in our little community in Irkutsk?"

"Going well," Maxim said with a lesser degree of certainty than before. "The analysis of the virus is progressing. Now that we have the data. You have the reports on your desk."

"They tell me about progress, not about morale," said Celsus smoothly. "What can you tell me about the morale?"

"It's good, very good."

"Max, Max," Celsus chided him gently. "I am not on the moon. I have ears other than yours."

Maxim ground his teeth. "All right. Some of the men are annoyed, and others are upset. They think you're keeping them in the dark."

"And so I am. They are not ready to live in the light," said Celsus.

"They know about your black-market deals. That doesn't bother them—in fact, they expect it of you." Maxim began to gather steam. "But they want to know what you're up to, who the men are who come here in the dead of winter. I can't tell them anything, so they guess, and that makes trouble."

"What is the prevailing theory?" Celsus inquired as if the answer had little importance to him.

"They think you're designing illicit drugs for the Big Three"—by which he meant the three largest multinational corporations in the world—"in order to raise venture capital for a new pharmaceutical company. They think you're moving out of the petrochemical business." Maxim tried to hold his boss's gaze.

"Do they?" Celsus chuckled loudly. The sound was like gunfire.

"Others think you're double-dealing, giving some of your mining technology to the Big Three and some to

Eastern European marketeers to take advantage of the artificially high prices." Maxim rubbed his hands together. "You can imagine how much they want to believe you're getting away with something."

"The love of larceny in the human soul knows no bounds," Celsus marveled. "If my vision were so small, I would deserve to be caught." He tapped his thumbs together. "If only Dee weren't in the picture, I would be bolder. But he alone could appreciate my secret aspirations."

"How?" Maxim liked nothing better than to listen to Theon Celsus ruminate on his schemes, for it honed his own sense of resolve.

But Celsus shrugged. "I have to think about this, Max. I don't want to make any mistakes with Dee. I was afraid I might, but—"

Maxim waited for Celsus to go on. When the silence between them stretched to almost five minutes, he coughed diplomatically. "Would you like a cup of green tea?"

"No, not just yet." He smoothed an eyebrow, then ran his fingers through the tufts of hair that surrounded his tonsure. "I am expecting a visitor. I will freshen up."

"Oh?" Maxim didn't recall seeing anyone's name on Celsus' appointment register.

"Coming in from Irkutsk. Herr Boris Michailovich Shevyenetz, who runs a hotel and has been a mainstay of the regional black market for twenty years."

"I don't know him," said Maxim uneasily.

"No," Celsus agreed. "You don't."

# CHAPTER 4

STRATEGY BROOKS WAS DESPERATE. Ever since her coverage of the attack of the rat-soldiers and the Yeshua debacle, she had been floundering. The executives, who had been thrilled with her only a few months ago, now looked on her as an embarrassment, a one-trick pony. Further, Global News Network execs had walked into diRocelli's office and removed all the master vids of the Yeshua coverage. No reason was given. Unceremoniously, they had transferred Strategy and her producer to the wasteland of Salt Lake City. There were even rumors rumbling that the *GNN Brooks Nightly Report* might be moved to the overnight. If she couldn't come up with something—anything—that captured public attention the way Yeshua—or whatever that lizard-thing's name was—had, she was sunk. Her contract was up for renewal in three months. She could lose it all. Strategy paced the length of her corner office, swearing under her breath and doing her best not to bite her banana-yellow fingernails.

"Hey, Strategy," her new assistant, Hernando, called

from the doorway. He was good-looking, slick, and ambitious. She didn't trust him any further than she could throw him, and looking at him now with his camera-prefect smile, she decided—nowhere near that far.

"Hi, Nando," she said with false cheerfulness.

"I have downloads of all the foreign webnews sites. You want to have a squint at them?"

"Sure," she said, going back to her desk. "Lay 'em on me." The enthusiasm she forced into her voice was for his benefit. She was certain he told her superior, diRocelli, and corporate everything she did. He was such a kiss-up, always sporting something with a GNN logo on it.

"They're coming through."

Brooks braced her elbows on the table and stared at the display. Hurricanes in the south. *No.* Avalanches in Switzerland. *Puh-leeze!* Coral contamination at the Great Barrier Reef. *Done to death.* Flooding in the Seychelles. *Nobody cares.* Prisons on the moon. *Too far away.* Pakistani refugees in Iran. *Too messy.* Nothing about aliens or modified-body soldiers. There was a story about clones turning out to be troublesome. *Old hat.* She ran back through all the excerpts and felt the all too familiar wash of discouragement overtake. This was ridiculous. Something major had to be happening somewhere. There had to be a story that would get her back on top. There had to be. One that she could track for a while before her broadcasting competition started a feeding frenzy. She had to grab America's attention. She shoved herself out of her chair. "Nando!"

"Yo!" he called back from his cubicle across from her office.

"Cast a wider net!" She clapped her hands for emphasis.

"Yes, boss," he said, and began to manipulate all manner of track-balls and infostix, filling the dozen screens around him with a montage of images and the air with a barrage of words.

"Now, Nando," she ordered.

"I'm nowing, I'm nowing," said Hernando.

More displays appeared on her terminal. She scrutinized them, all but quivering in anticipation. "I need times and newswire hits on all these."

"Will do," said Hernando.

Strategy pondered all she saw, afraid that she was missing something, something obvious, something that would be as big or bigger than the Yeshua story. She was beginning to despair when she saw an item on a Russian site, a little squib about a private installation in eastern Siberia, a mining outpost according to the records, but Siberia was played out . . . a mystery. It was a long shot, but it was better than sitting here in downtown Salt Lake waiting to be fired. "Nando! Schedule with the travel department for passage on a long-distance flyer."

"Yes, boss," said Hernando, trying to sound charged up.

"Get provisions for artic weather. A couple of snow-cats. Food and heat units for me, you, and the camera-man." It felt good to be issuing orders again. Orders made you feel as if you weren't running on empty.

"Where are we going? Antarctica?"

She scoffed. "Everyone and his cousin's gone there. No, you and I, Nando, are going to Siberia."

"Siberia." Baffled, he listed on his wrist-vid all the requisitions for their journey. Last, he sent a private memo off to diRocelli—after all, he had a career of his own to think of.

# CHAPTER

# 5

MORGAN D'WINTER ARRIVED BY old-fashioned cab at Dee's London townhouse shortly before midnight. It was a clear, frosty night, with a waning moon in the eastern sky. He had a case full of data and his palmtop was all but bursting with transferred files. The various perimeter security devices cleared him to enter, and finally Kelly opened the door to his coded ring.

"Hi, stranger," she said as she stood aside to admit him.

"Hi yourself," d'Winter countered, feeling oddly put-upon. He clumsily returned her hug. For a moment, Kelly was lost in the folds of his overcoat. "Sorry it took me so long to get here. There was a riot at the Karachi airport, and the tower wouldn't clear me for five hours." He headed for the living room, his step impatient and his determination showing in every line of his body. "It's bitter cold out there. And I'm frazzled."

Kelly followed after him. "What did you find out?"

"I bagged a lot of material. I'll stitch it together with help from you and the Doc. Where is he, by the way?"

"Up in his apartment. He's been reading about the Big Three and all their interconnected ventures. He claims that there is something hidden in all those overlapping, interlocking businesses that will shed light on the attacks being made on him. He's been in a funk for two days." Her voice dropped. "I was on the roof day before yesterday and someone took a shot at me. Had to be someone up in the air, and I saw two flyers in the vicinity."

"What about the old cathedral tower two blocks over?" d'Winter suggested as he sank onto the nearest of a pair of sofas.

"It's condemned," said Kelly.

"That doesn't mean much."

"You're right. The shots came from the direction of the tower. Didn't think."

D'Winter set his case on the central table. His fingers quickly manipulated the keypad on the lock. He spread out an assortment of files and vid-recorded artifacts on the table in front of him. "Want to give me a hand?" He blew at his fingertips abruptly. "Jeez, my hands are still frigid." He rubbed them together to improve the blood circulation. "Damn, but I hate the cold. Is there anything to eat in the kitchen?"

"Technomeat, some salami, some onions, celery, almond butter, and a lot of leftover curry," she said. "The Doctor isn't fond of curry." Kelly was slightly befuddled by that. "I thought the English loved curry."

"That's a later period in British history. The Doc was around for the Essex rebellion of 1601, not the Sepoy Mutiny of 1857," d'Winter pointed out. Morgan saw history purely from a military battle point-of-view. He ambled off in search of supper, leaving Kelly to begin sorting the files in front of her. She perched over d'Winter's cache of materials and started arranging the documents by date. "Make yourself some Celebes coffee," she shouted out to him. Kelly was half done with her work, and an aroma of cooking was coming from the kitchen, when she saw Dee come along the corridor.

"I thought I heard d'Winter. Has the prodigal son returned?" Dee looked exhausted; there were dark circles under his eyes. He had lost weight in the last week and was beginning to look gaunt rather than lean.

"He hath, my lord," Kelly teased, waving at the files in front of her. He didn't seem to take notice. "He's making supper."

"Um. It's good to have him back amongst us," Dee said perfunctorily, and then dropped into the high-backed grandmother chair he favored. Motioning his head to indicate his recent reading upstairs, he scowled. "It's a hard matter to resolve. Too hard a knot for me to untie. So complicated." Kelly could hear the frustration in his voice. He tugged at his lip. "I would give all of Wiltshire for a counsel with Hagecius on the astronomical significance of what is happening."

"Consult your computer," said Kelly.

"I like not to do my thinking on anything that can be spied upon or monitored." He held up his hand. "I know. Your security devices are well-nigh unbreakable. It's that ambiguous 'well-nigh' that troubles the mind. I'm loath to hazard our safety even on so small a risk."

"Hiya, Doc." d'Winter came into the living room, carrying a bowl of chicken-flavored technomeat mixed into the last of the curry, steam rising from the bowl. "Maybe you won't have to."

"What mean you?" Dee asked.

"Well, you say you worked in codes when you served

Elizabeth the First and that guy, Walsingham," said d'Winter. Thomas Phelippes, chief secretary to Francis Walsingham, and John Dee had devised several numerical and hieroglyphic word substitutions to baffle the supporters of devilish Queen Mary of Scotland. One afternoon before he'd left, Morgan had sat in perfect joy learning the rudimentary elements of what Dee called his secret writing. "I was thinking about that on my way back here. The codes aren't at all complex compared to what we have today. I figured that could be to our advantage." He swallowed some of his food. "Your codes are so simple, so outmoded, that most of the cyber-watchdogs won't be programmed to red-flag them. If nothing else, it will ease your mind about lurking hackers looking over your shoulder. I tell ya, Doc, it would ease things for Kelly and me if you would work with your computer instead of your quill." He stopped to gobble down some more food.

"Do you think that could work?" Kelly asked, impressed.

Dee was worrying a cuticle, transfixed by the obviousness of it. "Aye, it 's a trick worth pursuing."

# CHAPTER 6

ANYONE LOOKING AT DYCKON saw a tall, bulky man wearing large dark glasses, dressed in a loosely fitting suit of shiny flannel that scintillated where the sun struck it. He was adept at projecting this illusion and used it now as he made his way down the second-level walkway in Boca-Miami, the huge city sprawling along the eastern coast of Florida. It was a humid July day, the kind the state of Florida never advertises. Dyckon felt like he was swimming in a bowl of *ekbra* soup. The bright pastel colors seemed to him to be dripping off the ornate fifteen-story buildings. The salty Atlantic air stung at the corner of his eyes. It was a perfect day. He had struggled to attune all his senses to be alert to the presence of another Roc. He assumed that Yeshua had not acted alone. Tiring though it was to maintain his human illusion, it was preferable to being seen for what he was—a living gargoyle disguised in cheap clothing.

After a costly bargaining with a disgruntled communications officer of Clan set-ut, he had obtained the coordinates of ten messages sent to Earth. Eight of them had gone to Angel City, two had been sent to Waco, to an apartment house in the Pakistani part of town. What Dyckon had found there had sent him in the direction of Boca-Miami. There might be nothing to it, as there had been nothing to the story of Yeshua reappearing in Tulsahoma three weeks ago. But he felt he had to follow his only lead. Another Roc on planet Earth meant the chance of containing the uncontrollable quicksilver virus was impossible. But his continued presence on Earth was a political danger to himself. If his interest in Yeshua was discovered, the existence of John Dee, who had orchestrated Yeshua's death, would eventually be revealed. The existence of Dee would attest to Dyckon's meddling in humani affairs, and that would destroy the Roc's credibility at the Collegium of Worlds. Many millenia ago, the Collegium had assigned Rocs to be the watchers and historical chroniclers of new civilizations. They were forbidden to make their presence known, since that would unduly influence the worlds they were meant to study. No watcher team had been discovered for untold centuries—a feat every Roc held as a testiment to their methods and honor. The sole exception to that record were the Fawg's Clan set-ut, who had grown tired of being passive onlookers.

"Hey, watch it, buster," said an old man, who was making his way precariously along the walkway.

"Sorry," said Dyckon, the word coming out as a rumble. He kept walking, taking care not to encounter any more of the people, or "humani," as he thought of them. Finally he reached the Housing Office and went inside, adjusting his face so it appeared to smile. "Good afternoon. It's a lovely day."

A harried young woman looked up at him. " 'fternoon," she responded suspiciously.

"I'm an investigator, Dick Rocco." He flashed an identity icon that looked more official than it actually was. It had a caduceus in one corner and a public health seal in the other. "I'm looking for a Corwin Tarlton, formerly of Waco, Texas." He broadened the smile, making it as winning as he could. "I was given a lead that he might be here."

"What's he done?" The young woman questioned him, liking neither his musty smell, his foolish clothes, nor his official's attitude.

"Nothing at all. But he may have been exposed to an infectuous microorganism at his last place of residence, and we need to run a few scans on him, to be sure he isn't contagious." His smile turned to concern, as he thought about the shape-changing virus that would wreak havoc among the humani if it were ever released. "He's not likely to be a danger to others," he lied, "but he could be ill and not know it. National Health wants to be sure he's checked out."

"So," said the young woman with a cynical wink. "The government doesn't want to be sued."

"No, it doesn't," said Dykon. "Any help you can give me would be appreciated."

"How much?" she asked.

Five hundred years of observing humani behavior and humani greed had never changed. "Fifty dollars' worth?" he offered, holding up the bill in good faith.

"Cash," she marveled, her eyes shining. "Don't see much of that these days. All right. How far do you want to search?" She had gone to the display on her desk.

"As far as you can," said Dykon.

"All of south Florida?" She was already pushing buttons, a directory materializing in the air above the desk. "Spell the name for me."

"First name: C-o-r-w-i-n. Last name: T-a-r-l-t-o-n. He moved from Waco about twenty-five weeks ago, according to his landlord." The time was approximate because Hamil Azzahzi didn't know precisely when Tarlton had left. Due to the reptilian infestation five months ago, so many of his tenants had all gone at once. During the renovation that followed, Azzahzi had found Tarlton's apartment was neat, clean, and empty. He wished the other tenants had shown such human decency. He had no reason to doubt that Tarlton would be coming back, although he secretly hoped he wouldn't.

The young woman studied the display. "Nobody by that name. There are six Corwins, last name, and fourteen Tarltons, last name, but no Corwin Tarlton, and none of the twenty have moved in less than six months ago. 'Course, lots of people have come and gone since the space alien scare." She snickered and added, "Which turned out to be a bust. Do you want copies of this information? Just in case? He might have relatives he's staying with." She looked at Dyckon speculatively. "Another twenty'll get you the list."

"Okay," he said. "I'll want it in my wrist-vid." He laid two new tens on the counter.

"My pleasure, and you are right, it is a lovely day," she said, grinning at the money. She beamed the data into Dyckon's wrist-vid from her display. The transfer was almost instantaneous, and the two bills vanished almost as quickly. "Hope you find him." She offered him a slightly sweaty hand and he made some pretense not to shake it. "Stay out of the sun with those clothes. If you don't mind me saying so, you're sweating like a pig."

Dyckon glanced at his hands and realized his bio-shield aura was wavering. Most humani would mistake the effect for profuse perspiration. Too much stress he thought. "Thanks. I hope I find him too," Dyckon said, and hurried out of the office. There hadn't been much chance that Tarlton's movements would show up in Boca-Miami records. After all, without an implanted ID chip, the marooned Roc was pretty much invisible to the bureaucracy. Still, being a centuries-old cultural scholar, Dyckon was inured to pursuing every avenue to its eventual conclusion. No matter how long it took. He found an alcove where he could use his phonelink without being overheard. He punched in and was immediately in communication with his spacecraft. His serpentine double tongue making a sound that translated into English as "diary," Dyckon started dictating his findings. "I'm in Florida. I haven't found any records of what I'm looking for. No leads as yet, but we must start somewhere. If Tarlton is here in Southern Florida, he may be one of the Clan Fawg. His complete absence on the humani scans would indicate that." There was a slight pause, and then his split tongue flicked, "Bio-shield has a slight malfunction. Make note to do a diagnostic. End transmission." Dyckon rang off to continue his search for a disguised ophidian in the crowded jumble of tropical south Florida.

# CHAPTER

# 7

DEE LISTENED TO THE report d'Winter provided. He stared vacantly over the steeple of his fingers, sunk in thought. "So naught's done?"

"I wouldn't say that," d'Winter remarked as he shut off his wrist-vid. "But we need to start looking for some new avenues of inquiry."

"Aye." Dee paused, staring straight at his second, and then made his point again. "Naught's done." He got to his feet and began to pace. He hated inaction. It only reminded him that he was standing still. Sometimes, he was overwhelmed by this time's complexity and technology. So much strangeness to evaluate.

But d'Winter refused to accede to his employer's dark mood. "Not yet. We have to change directions, shift our focus, compensate for parallax."

"How?" Dee asked.

"I've been trying to figure that out all the way here. The last thing I want to do is alert the Roc—assuming there is one—that we are on to him, because who knows what he'd do. And then, I don't want to make it easy for the men who've been after you to find you. Doc, you do make my work tricky."

Dee bowed. "Not for all the world would I have you bored."

"No fear of that. The trouble is, anything we do, it can be tracked by anyone if they really want to. Kelly and I can't block our ID chips forever. We're going to make mistakes."

"Then, like a Lincoln fox, we must find the means to throw them off the scent," said Dee. "We must direct attention away from us."

"How are we going to do that? Even planting a false trail leaves ways to be tracked, and there's a risk of being found. There must be people still asking questions about Angel City," pointed out d'Winter. He tried not to yawn. "I've been up nights with this."

"Small wonder," said Dee. "Even the messages we've sent out have most likely been waylaid and read." He didn't like admitting so much. But to assume otherwise was to underestimate your enemy. That was always a grevious mistake.

Kelly glanced at Dee, then gave her attention to beginning the encryption of the latest message for Dyckon before her. "I'd like it if we had a more secure way of sending messages."

"Wouldn't we all?" said d'Winter.

Dee clicked his tongue in exasperation. He'd been in a foul mood all morning. "By Jesu, why can we not employ the ciphers that I was schooled in when I served the Queen's business. Master Phelippes gave me a goodly number."

"The code you described to me yesterday?" Kelly asked a little too patronizingly.

"Aye," Dee pointed out, "they were elegant and functional, and harder than hoops of steel to break without the key. What more need you of a code?"

"You described it to me, as a two-number key, and you would incorporate the code into the text of unexceptional letters." From her tone, you could tell that Kelly was skeptical.

"Yes," said Dee, "minus the key, the letter is nothing so much as an ordinary by-your-leave letter. We often used pages of predetermined pamphlets to identify the key, or chapters and verse in Cranmer's *Book of Common Prayer*."

"Let me make sure I have this right: the page number is the key. This is page 72, so it's every seventh word, and in that word, the second letter spells out the message. Have I got this right?"

"Aye," said Dee.

"What if you don't have a key?" Kelly asked.

"Then, in theory, you can't extract the message. That was the point behind the code, but with our adversaries' machines to work on it, I'd wager that it wouldn't go unbroken long, once the underlying schematic was identified. We had a monthly code, but sometimes, if a letter was delayed, I'd have to use an earlier key. A great many men used this kind of gematria in my age, and I understand it was in common use right up until the twentieth century.

"If we altered the key more frequently, then I think it would be possible for you to make the secrecy of it live a while longer." Dee cleared his throat. "I've cudgeled my brains about this, and I do believe that if we employed a rotating key—one that altered for each line of text?—that it might be sufficient to slow down any deciphering of it, even with a computer to do the work."

D'Winter shook his head. "Once the pattern was figured out, the whole thing would be shot."

"But would they have the wit to look for a device like that? Say the sum of coded words on a line should signify the frequency of the coded words in the next, and the number of the letter would be fixed by another formula?" Dee suggested. "It's hardly foolproof, but it would take much meddling to come to terms with." He tried to sound amused, but that failed terribly. "Verily, I have not the mind for codes the way you do, there's the trouble. We employed grid codes and counting codes—'tis not the manner of thing you do any more."

"And that could be helpful," said Kelly suddenly. "You're right, Doctor. Those old codes aren't usually part of the new programs. I think it might be worth the risk."

"So long as we don't have other pre-Enlightenment minds around, you may be right," d'Winter agreed.

"Very droll," said Dee caustically. "From what I've learned of your Enlightenment, it imposed empiricism on everything, even where there was no call. Not all manner of things can be weighed by the standards of those Continental wits. Science is not only about that which can be known and quantified. Science must also accept what man senses in Nature. It is fault to Heaven to accept only that which is verifiable. Inner contemplation must play a part, as does Faith. For the light of inner contemplation and of Faith is nothing other than reason itself. For from where else does contemplation and Faith flow but from Divine Reason. All knowledge, repeatable or not, subject to qualification, not quantification, is science."

"That's very . . . Elizabethan of you," said Kelly. She had rarely heard the Doctor so metaphysical.

D'Winter wasn't sure that he had followed the Doctor's last words, so he nodded in silent agreement. His mind raced back to the idea of Elizabethan code. "There is something in what you say. And it might be worthwhile, if for no other reason than that it's apt to force those watching us to tip their hands." He rubbed his chin. "I think you may have hit upon something, Doctor. Not what I expected, but still . . ."

"You think it could work," said Dee, allowing himself to hope.

"I think it's worth a try." D'Winter looked over at Kelly. "We need to do a trial run. Nothing too complicated."

"All right," she said. "Who do you want to attract with this exercise? Do you have any idea what could be at stake here?"

"Not enough of one," d'Winter grumbled.

"Hold," said Dee. "This smacks of pushing a stick into a hornet's nest. Methinks we should reach Dyckon and inform him of our plans."

D'Winter frowned. "The trouble is," he said, "that we have two puzzles to unravel: the present location of a possible second Roc, and the identification of the person or persons who have made repeated attempts on your life."

"There is also the matter of returning me to my own time." The unlikelihood of his journey home had been in the Doctor's thoughts since he'd gotten up that morning and looked out on an unfamiliar London. Where was the Thames? Where were the tolling church bells?

"Yes, there is that as well," said d'Winter. "But, if you don't mind my saying it, that's for after we've taken care of the first two. Don't you agree?"

Dee shrugged, trying to ignore the surge of homesickness that welled up in him. "Aye. I know you have the right of it. But you cannot imagine how tempting it is, just to dally with the notion of sailing home at the first opportunity that presents itself."

Kelly did her best to smile, although she wasn't much in the mood for it. "I'm going to hate to see you go."

Dee met her eyes. "And I shall miss you as much as anything in this strange future of yours."

D'Winter cut in before he too became maudlin. "We can talk about that later, when we've found the way to get you back. Right now, there are more pressing matters to deal with." He gave Dee a measured look. "Are you prepared to travel?"

"Where?" Dee asked.

"I'm about to find out." D'Winter picked up his palmtop, thumbed it into life, and began to enter an array of numbers into its electronic innards.

# CHAPTER 8

THE ROC WHO HAD been disguised as Corwin Tarlton now took on the shape of a portly Greek merchant as he made his way through the International Mart outside Chicopolis, an urban hub that had sent out tentacles from Illinois into Michigan, Indiana, and Wisconsin. Its population topped eleven million, and rising. He bustled as if on an important errand, which kept other people in the Mart from impeding his progress. An eighteen-acre open-air mart, the space was briskly air-conditioned, which chilled him to the bone. It was not as pleasant as arid Waco or steamy Boca-Miami. This was a fine spot to plant one of the vials of virus, for it would spread through the tens of thousands of humani who came here to purchase all manner of goods from all over the world. In a matter of hours, the contagion would be on its way to every continent on the planet, and the subjugation of humankind would have begun. He made his way to the biggest of the food courts, a three-acre expanse surrounded by booths offering every possible cuisine. The conflicting odors of spices and herbs made the air seem dense. He looked around as if searching out his favorite food, but in reality looking for a booth dispensing tea and coffee as the most likely place to begin his campaign.

"Who are you?" asked a small child who had stopped beside the supposed Greek merchant. He'd first been intrigued by the man's bushy mustache, which tumbled over the man's lip like a caterpillar, but now he was caught in the fascination of his own reflection in the strange man's dark mirrored sunglasses.

"Go away," said the Roc.

"You look funny," the boy announced.

"Go away," the Roc repeated more forcefully.

"Tell me," the child insisted, pointing at the Roc's nose.

"I am Petros Costas," said the Roc, choosing the name he had seen over a Greek grocery store. "Now leave me alone."

"That's a funny name." The child, then raised his voice. "Hey, mom! I found a funny man."

"Be quiet," said the Roc. "It's very rude to shout, and it's very impolite to push yourself into other people's lives."

"He's strange!" the child crowed as he clung to the Roc's trouser leg.

The Roc struggled to break away from the child, resisting the urge to kick the pet in the stomach—humani didn't like having their young attacked. "You are a very ill-mannered little boy," he grumbled.

The youngster laughed merrily. "Strange, strange, strange," he sang and watched himself in the Ray-Bans, waggling his head and making faces.

As the Roc tried to back away from the nuisance, the youngster clutched at the man's thigh. The "Greek" grabbed for the boy's shoulders and arms. "Let go of me!" the child said loudly. A number of people swung around to look at him. Out of the corner of his eye, he caught sight of a blowsy woman in her early thirties rushing forward.

"Release my child! Get away from him, you freak!" she shouted. "Brody Wayne Hatley, you come here to me right now!"

Tolerance for strangers had diminished radically since Yeshua's death had been vidded in Angel City. For a week, the media had been flooded with stories about invading space aliens. The nation had kept a tighter hold of its children's hands. But in the weeks that followed, as much of the GNN footage was debunked by authorities, the fear quotient slipped from five to two. Still, American xenophobia didn't need much excuse to flare again, and anyone out of the ordinary could engender agitation. The child shrieked, and the food court erupted in alarm. Patrons left their meals to come to the rescue of the child, many of them trying to get hold of the old Greek.

The Roc shook Brody free of his leg and struggled to flee. It was hard to hold on to his shape, but he did his best, keenly aware that he wasn't doing as well as he ought. He could tell his skin was too shiny, and his body was shifting in too-obvious ways. But he headed into the center of the confusion, trying to lose himself in the chaos. Shoved and pummeled, he made it out of the food court and into one of the broad corridors that led off through the Mart.

"What happened?" Brody's mother shouted. "Did that strange man do anything to you? Did he try to?"

"He was just strange," said Brody, all his fun ruined.

The mother ran up to the nearest uniformed security

officer. "Some foreigner tried to abduct my boy. You've got to find him. You've got to arrest him." Others in the crowd pressed closer, exhorting the officer to act quickly.

The security officer sprayed the crowd with tranquilizer, then turned to the woman. "Can you give me a description?" He'd been through three mandatory crowd control seminars since Angel City. Every population center had gone on maximum alert; the nation needed to feel safe again.

"Foreign," she said. "Fat. Greasy. You tell him, Brody."

"He was strange," Brody mumbled.

"See?" his mother exclaimed, turning on the officer.

"Yes, ma'am," he said. "We'll get his image from the tapes and put out a bulletin on him." He signaled his office on his palmtop. "We'll get him, ma'am. Don't you worry." He said it automatically, certain that the miscreant was long gone, if he knew what was good for him.

Indeed, the Roc had already left the enormous building using an underground tunnel. *This was a disaster! How could it have all gone so wrong so quickly?* he asked himself as he found a commercial refuse bin in which to hide. What had seemed such a good idea half an hour ago was now dangerous and foolhardy. He would have to find another place and another way to infect humanity; he relaxed back into his Roc shape and did his best to recompose himself. Now, he would have to wear another appearance, which meant finding another false identity, and another jammer for identity chip scanning machines. All these things were expensive and time-consuming. He began to feel irritated and put-upon. At least things would be much better when all this was over and humanity was fully in Roc control. No more intrusive little boys, no more outbursts, no more lack of purpose, or cross purposes. Humani had such lovely potential for providing vast amounts of labor of all sorts. Finally that potential would be realized. Those who survived the shape-shifting virus would be as docile and tractable as lambs. With that prospect to lull his anxiety, the Roc finally drifted into an uneasy sleep, dreaming of a new leader to rise and command the army he would deliver.

# CHAPTER 9

"CONCERNING FAWG'S CLAN, WHAT persuades you this deed was of their making?" an unconvinced Dee asked Dyckon. The Doctor was alone in his Holbern Road apartment while d'Winter and Kelly were out for the evening attending the theater in Covent Garden. On the monitor display, the large reptilian was presently in his human form—a less intimidating and much more pleasing shape than his real one. Dee had insisted upon the disguise; it was necessary in case of any breach in their security. "A riotously public disturbance seems not like a Roc undertaking. You are by nature a discreet people keeping to the leeward side of care."

"The food court is in one of the largest shopping marts in North America. It has daily traffic in excess of ten thousand people." Dyckon paused for an inordinately long time. It was getting harder for him to concentrate. His mind seemed muddy and over-taxed, as though he were laboring on a heavy-atmosphere planet. "I saw the surveillance tapes. I'll patch you in to them.

Watch the man with the little boy holding on to his leg. Watch him closely."

"Why?" Dee asked, feeling impatient.

"Just watch," said Dyckon wearily. The Roc thumbed his desk-vid. A half-second later the display in Dee's room showed a crowd becoming unruly, milling around a stocky man and a boy of about seven. Dee studied the images, wondering what he ought to see. Then he noticed something about the temples of the stout merchant, a shininess at the hairline that made him blink. There was a subtle transformation at the base of the throat as well. His height seemed to shift in comparison to the child's.

"Scales," Dee whispered. "His body is misshapen and degenerate." He switched the display back to Dyckon. "All right. You have convinced me."

"Have I? I hope so," Dyckon said, just a little superciliously. "Because I think he's still in North America."

"Why so? After the failure in Chicopolis, would he not flee to another country where he was unknown?" Dee could not entirely quiet the apprehension he felt. Tracking his prey was proving harder and harder. More and more, preventing world contamination seemed impossible.

"Honor," said Dyckon.

The sense of honor was variable in men's characters, Dee thought. When in distress, those destined to do lofty deeds would follow its call to death, but baser men would quickly shake it off as a cumbersome burden. Fawg, the clan leader, might have obeyed its silent dictates, but it was hard to believe a foot soldier would be so inspired. Dee decided that he didn't have the knowledge of the character of the Roc to make an educated assessment of the subject. After all, Dyckon's kind were a different species and certainly must have traits and impulses that he, Dee, would never begin to understand. Dyckon, who had spent centuries with members of this rebellious sect on his mission to Earth, must be relied on for the psychological profile. "Nay then," said Dee. "Let us presume that you are in the right." He paced down his room, flexing his intertwined fingers, a sure sign of mental restlessness. "You must anticipate what action he is likely to pursue."

"Theoretically," Dyckon said hesitantly, "I have some suggestions on that point."

"I was never in any doubt but that you would," said Dee, his expression unreadable. If he was aware that his friend's thoughts were less linear than they had been, Dee covered it well. "You were in the right about Chicopolis, and in like ways you may have been in the right about a fugitive sojourn to Florida."

"I wasn't," said Dyckon irritably. "It was a guess, and not a very good one. His landlord in Waco thought Tarlton said he had family in Florida." He made a derisive sound. "Half of North America has family in Florida, as far as I can tell."

"Marry, and Arizona," Dee sighed. "Forget not Arizona. Wrinkles forbid."

"As you say," Dykon agreed, frowning a little, as he momentarily lost his train of thought. "I wonder . . ."

"What?" Dee queried at Dyckon's second uncharacteristic hesitation.

"The Four Corners Corridor Mall," said Dykon slowly. "Outlet stores for companies from all over the world. It would be another good place to attempt to infect humans."

"You're still certain that's their intent," Dee said.

"Fawg set-ut has been belittling your kind for the last one hundred and fifty years. In planning to bring humani to heel, he hadn't access to any armies so he most surely needed to plan a different attack. Infection seems to be the most likely way. He had access to a quicksilver virus."

Dee stopped his pacing and stared hard at the monitor. The alien's incongruous reiteration of a history lesson stating the obvious was both startling and upsetting.

Suddenly Dyckon turned inexplicably defensive. "I cannot support anything that puts more contagion into the environment, any environment. Such things are too risky. Who knows what mutations might occur, quite spontaneously, that would lead to chaos for both our species?" He made the Roc equivalent of a sigh. "Wouldn't you agree?"

"Aye, I follow your point," Dee said politely. He had spent much of the last month reading up on genetic theory. He disagreed with much of it, but he had to acknowledge that the potential for damage described in the theory was very real.

"If there is a mutation here on Earth, it might convince the Xifo to return to this solar system and reconsider their takeover of the planet. Their new acquisition of mutated humans would be reported to the Collegium of Worlds. Questions would be asked and the truth would soon be discovered about Roc interference. That scenario is unacceptable to me or any well-bred member of my species. Fawg set-ut and his three clansmen were under my command. Ultimately, I am responsible for the members of my ship—both to the Collegium and to my people. I must undo what Fawg has started."

Being well schooled in the responsibilities of command, Dee nodded. "What think you must be the next step?"

"I think I must go to the Four Corners Corridor tomorrow. If you can join me there, with Kelly and d'Winter, we may be able to search more efficiently." He paused. "I know it might not be entirely safe for you to come back to North America just now, but I ask you to think it over. I believe your coming out of hiding is worth the risk. You can't hide forever."

"It is perilous to me and mine if we are caught, but I will think on it. I will talk to Kelly and d'Winter of the need when they return," Dee said. "That done, I'll impart to you at what hour you may look to find us, and where."

"You don't have to come, if your guards think it's too dangerous," said Dyckon. "But if you do come, tell your people very little."

"Mayhap I will not venture forth. It is a perilous risk." Dyckon's reminding him of his own lack of active participation in the last few months pricked at his conscience. "But the search would only take longer without us. The world's safety can little afford the luxury of our wasting that time. As you yourself guess, I and mine may have to visit other market centers eventually. I will honor your privacy and keep your secrets from them as best I can." Even as Dee made the promise, he felt uneasy. It bothered him to keep anything from his friends. He guiltily changed the subject. "You cannot be certain that the attendant Rocs will choose to attack Four Corners Corridor and none other. You cannot act alone."

"No, I cannot. Nor could Fawg." Dyckon was certain Fawg had accomplices to his bold plan to enslave the humani. But who? The plot was nearly inconceivable—Fawg would have needed time to convince anyone, even one of his bellicose clan, to provide unqualified assistance. Fawg's megalomania was so far outside of accepted Roc behavior that only someone familiar with mankind and its way of thinking would have entertained its possibilities. So, it had to be one of the Fawg clan members on Dyckon's ship. Yes, his tired mind thought, there was no doubt that help had to have come from the Earth mission. Two of the clan members were on new planetary missions. Only Mattik's presence was unknown. Mattik, the religious scholar of the mission, who had seemed to worship the vainglorious, charismatic Fawg. Who better to help Fawg with his impersonation of a reborn Messiah? But there was no concrete evidence that Mattik was involved, he reminded himself, and Roc society forbade publicly accusing another without absolute proof. In the long Roc lifespan, there was always time to validate your suspicions.

"I feel positive he will be there tomorrow," Dyckon said. "It is a very good place from his point of view, though not quite as good as Chicopolis. Fawg set-ut made his attempt in Angel City, and this Roc—if there is but the one from Waco—will want to emulate his efforts, to prove it can be done. To do less would mean dishonor to the Fawg clan and to the memory of Fawg set-ut. The number of people traveling through Four Corners is high enough to make it attractive and therefore the probable target. The crowd of people offers you a modicum of safety from the authorities. The more help, the better likelihood of capturing him and securing the timeslip device."

"Have you given thought to what divers other places they might lay siege to?" Dee asked, not satisfied with Dyckon's reasoning, but teased by the prospect of the time travel device and going home soon.

"I'm preparing a list," said Dyckon. "I think I should have had it done before now." There was self-reproach in his voice

"Aye, 'tis not like you to be so unprepared." Despite his recent vow—or perhaps because of it—Dee decided to tread in a sensitive area. "For that Kelly is expert in the world of commerce, when your particulars are complete, provide a report to her that she may proffer you some unlooked-for help. She may have goodly opinions that as yet are unthought-of by you. She is an able general and possesses as worthy a mind as one would wish. Young in limbs, but old in wisdom. I have ever been fortunate in her advice."

"Possibly," said Dyckon darkly, his doubt giving that single word vast implications. In the last few minutes, he had grown more convinced that the long search would be over tomorrow at Four Corners Corridor mall. It was a hope unconsciously bred out of his utter fatigue.

"Nay, you are a fool to refuse any expertise. Though you have walked among us for untold years and studied us as one would scrutinize ants, this imminent peril is hazardous and you needs must look to us for assistance. Verily, to prevent that you do not falter and lose this world, you must betake yourself of the best of this world. Be not too proud nor deaf to good counsel. Surely to turn away is to take the reckless path to frustration and risk loss of all. For, as you have reminded me, time is against us."

"Yes, time is running out," said Dyckon. With strong reluctance in his voice, he added, "But I dislike having so many people be privy to my mission." The need for privacy was the hallmark of his people.

"All of us have reason to keep your confidence," said Dee. "On the Queen's business I have spent enough time that I have long since come to terms with the need for secrets, and Kelly Edwards has professional reasons enough to comply with your requests and mine." He recalled, belatedly, that Dyckon had a touchy sense of honor even when he wasn't this exhausted, and he sought to restore some of their lost amity. "We'll do what we can to offer help, but we shall not act against your orders."

Dyckon seemed mollified by this offer. "Very well," he declared. "I'll expect to hear from you with your decision regarding your joining me before this time tomorrow. After that, I'll be at the Four Corners Corridor Mall to meet with Fawg's man alone."

Dee saw a haggard face on the monitor. One that had grown so since Dyckon had first revealed Fawg's disobedience of the cardinal principles of their society. "Aye, so you said." He risked more of his friend's irritation. "Have a care, you must rest. To worry the memory of a mischief that is past and gone is the best way to draw a new mischief on."

There was no response from the Roc. "I shall have an answer for you before you depart," Dee promised, and broke the connection. He stood for a few minutes, reviewing all the potential danger in returning to North America. He remembered the contagion in Angel City and the hideous mindless corpses being ripped sacrilegiously from their hallowed graves. He saw the exhausted visage of the gargoyle commander who could not forsake his responsibility for the Pandora's box that had been opened on his watch. When he had gone over every permutation on his thoughts, his duty was clear. He went to the closet, pulled down his travelcase, and began to pack. D'Winter and Kelly would see it his way.

# CHAPTER 10

STRATEGY BROOKS HURRIED UP the slick steps of the NTSA building in D.C.'s north quarter. Hernando followed behind, determined to participate in everything she did. A gentle snow had been falling for the last two hours, giving Washington a picture-perfect patina that covered up the city's grime. Most citizens of the United States pictured their capital this way—hushed and reverent. The solemn buildings, daubed by the mixture of storm and dim morning light, seemed larger than they were. More stately. Landscape lighting bathed buildings like the NTSA in a theatrical halo. The equidistant trees, now devoid of their leaves, were spectral; the neighboring bushes were beginning to look like clumps of white chocolate. The trip from Utah had been easy, although they had been a little stacked up at Reagan International. Now the snowflakes stung her ears and stuck to her mascara. God knows what it was doing to her hair.

And for what? she thought.

The United States National Terrestrial Security Administration was thirty years old. It had grown from a group of fifty concerned scientists and twenty military theorists to a bureaucracy that employed over two hundred thousand people worldwide, operating under the auspices of ninety-four treaties that gave the NTSA access to all eighty-nine countries that were signatories to the Terrestrial Protection Treaty of 2083. All agreed to forgo recognition of national borders if there were an interplanetary attack. This enormous building with its rows of Ionic columns was the heart of the NTSA, a monument to the power it had attained.

Hernando and Strategy walked through the great wooden doors at the top of the steps and stepped into the hushed marble lobby of the vast building. Footsteps echoed softly from unseen halls and passageways. Portraits of great scientists of the past lined the aisle to the reception desk. They removed their gloves and scarves. A security team scanned their implanted computer chips, then politely allowed them to pass.

"Where's the office of Reed O'Neal?" Strategy asked as soon as she was through security.

"May I help you?" said the large black man seated behind an imposing granite desk. Pale flickering light from an array of security monitors embedded in the desk illuminated his blocklike face.

"I'm here to see Reed O'Neal, the Director of NTSA." She hoped that the mention of the Director's name would get the guard to quit the vid-game he was playing and focus on her.

"Do you have an appointment?" He kept playing.

"Yes," she sighed, going through the obligatory dialogue, "eleven A.M."

"Your name, please."

"Strategy Brooks." She waited for some sort of recognition, some acknowledgement of who she was. Even an oaf like him must watch the news. "And this is Hernando Carrasco."

"One minute." The guard spoke into his headset, rattling off a series of numbers, then pausing before giving another series of numbers, obviously an extension and a password. A name, a pleasantry, a repetition of their names, and then another pause. Strategy turned to Hernando with the universal look of exasperation at security precautions.

Finally the guard looked up at them. "Miss Brooks, Mister Carrasco, someone will be down to show you both upstairs. In the meantime, I will need to scan you for ID."

Strategy was about to protest that they had already been scanned, but decided to manifest her displeasure with a profound sigh. She hopped from foot to foot, waiting impatiently, while the guard aimed his bioscan. Almost immediately, he presented them with individual security passes, which would allow them only into the areas where they were expected. Any deviation from the allowed route would set off all sorts of alarms. Hernando attached his to his jacket. Strategy stuffed hers into her coat pocket.

"Great," said Strategy, "maybe now we can get to our meeting." Her sarcasm was lost on the guard, who had already returned to his vid-game.

A pert young woman named Maggie eventually took them upstairs. On the fourth floor, Strategy and Hernando followed their guide to Wing D, and continued along to Corridor J. Office 1287 was at the end of Corridor J, and boasted a tall window that looked out on an inner courtyard. The snow had barely touched the protected enclave. Maggie left them there with a pale secretary who served as door-dragon. She officiously took note of Hernando's security pass and pointedly asked to see Strategy's. She took her time consulting Reed O'Neal's schedule to confirm their appointment before admitting Strategy and Hernando to the inner sanctum.

Reed O'Neal was waiting for them, seated behind a massive desk calculated to intimidate all but the most confident of his visitors. The room had a Venetian fireplace, a Napoleon wingchair, a Newtonian coffee table, and Louis XIV chairs: in sum, an imperial reception room meant to impress. But, in Strategy's mind, the room was redundant. Director O'Neal had rugged good looks that outdazzled his office. Though he was in his late fifties, he looked ten years younger. He stood a little over six feet and had beautifully chiseled features. His ancestry was certainly Scandinavian. He was preposterously vertical, with shoulders that never sagged. It was obvious he exercised every day, and Strategy remembered that there was often footage of O'Neal and President Marino working out at the White House gym. He looked better in person. The reports of his physical daring—he was a skier, a parachutist, a wind racer—were a source of wonder to the nation. He attributed it all to his previous career in the navy. He didn't smile, nor did he rise, but Strategy didn't miss his subtle, but appreciative, once-over as she approached the desk.

"Good afternoon, Miss Brooks." He made sure she had to reach across the desk to shake his hand. His fingers were long and elegant. He wore an Annapolis ring.

"Good afternoon, Mister O'Neal," she answered, a little in awe of his beauty and his military bearing. Strategy noted how his sandy hair going gray and his pale blue eyes made him look like a movie-star version of a president. In fact, O'Neal would have been pleased with that assessment. He worked at it. The press privately called him "Apollo." Not so much for his good looks but for the fact that he thought of himself as a god. His political aspirations were legendary, although it was said that he was extremely happy with his directorship at NTSA, where he had served under two administrations. There were whispers of a run at the vice-presidency should Dorn step down.

"Thank you for coming to see us on such short notice," he said genially.

Strategy wondered if there were more people coming to the meeting.

"We like to maintain good relations with the NTSA," she said brightly, looking back at the dragon-lady who was closing the door. But the brightness lasted only a moment; her curiosity got the better of her. Her Southern impetuosity and her reporter's brusqueness blended into a rather direct, "Why are we here?"

His ensuing smile lacked sincerity, but he did his best to maintain it. He had practiced since his twenties. "I hear you're planning to go to Siberia."

"Yes," she admitted, a bit surprised that the NTSA would pay attention to her travel plans.

"On a story, I must assume, as the travel request is a formal one, and through your company." A visit to Siberia required a visa from the Secretary of State's office. It was standard practice for a network to do all the paperwork for their news teams prior to sending them out. Rarely were there any problems. Strategy couldn't understand why her visa application would be kicked over to NTSA and, moreover, why it would require her to have a private interview with Reed O'Neal. Did his mention of the "company" mean GNN had had something to do with this? She had lost ground there since the other networks had attacked her reportage of Yeshua's true identity. She wondered if the company was working with NTSA. She wondered if Hernando was NTSA. O'Neal went on as if he had read her mind, still smiling. "And your associate is going with you?"

"So he is," said Strategy.

"Given the work you have done in the recent past, I can't help but think you may be following up on your Angel City story. Your so-called alien invasion."

"You mean Yeshua," said Strategy.

"Of course. What else would I be concerned about? The hysteria that still surrounds your little trick has made an impact on our activities. That shouldn't surprise you, with all you did to make everyone think that you had found a real alien, and an army of humanoid rats living in Angel City. That sham nearly caused a national panic. I'm told there was an eighteen-percent surge in church attendance. But polls now show that the public has grown bored with it." He paused. "Your ratings have fallen off considerably, an eight-point-six share, haven't they?" He tilted his chair back and looked at her along his nose. "Would you like to sit down?"

"Not unless we're going to be here for a while," said Strategy bluntly. She hoped she would have a chance to repudiate his statements about the events at Angel City. She couldn't argue about the share. She had always assumed that the rival networks had attacked her because of her scooping them. But NTSA might have used their political muscle to squelch her reporting of space aliens being on Earth. Either way, it was no secret her viewership had tumbled. Strategy met O'Neal's confident gaze, her mind racing—you'd think that he'd want to prove the existence of extraterrestials. Beltway mavens were opining that NTSA might take a $10 billion budget cut in the next fiscal budget. The importance of NTSA's existence had been questioned since the last election. A confirmation of space aliens would surely catapult the NTSA into the limelight and generate the need for even more funds. It would certainly make O'Neal's name a household word. All things being equal, she and O'Neal should be on the same side, she thought.

"That's going to be up to you," said O'Neal, gesturing to the Louis XIV chairs, his smile turning to a grimace. He'd held it a long time, she thought.

"I think we'll stand," said Strategy. She put her hand on her hip, daring "Apollo" to interfere with her work.

"Tell me then—what are you going to Siberia to find?" O'Neal asked, unable to conceal his impatience.

"A mining installation," said Strategy.

"A mining installation. Not imaginary aliens." O'Neal's tone remained skeptical. His eyes were icy.

Strategy and Hernando both shook their heads.

"Any idea what you're looking for? Or are you just location scouting for a sequel to your last movie?" He looked them up and down with a scowl that distorted his attractiveness. Made it ugly. Strategy glanced away, no longer eager to go toe to toe with the political bully she'd glimpsed.

"Just following up—you know how it is. A fresh lead on the new territories." This was close enough to the truth that Strategy was certain that any scans of her speech would process as truthful. In an office like this one, she knew that everything was monitored. Hernando was no fool; that's why he let her do all the talking.

Strategy suddenly realized she had nothing to hide. She was really and truly only going to Siberia to investigate a mining installation. Why should O'Neal and the NTSA even care? If anything, this was State Department business. Why were they even there? It was a nagging question that kept her unsettled.

"What do you mean, 'fresh leads'? Why should your diRocelli over at GNN send you off on nothing more than hints? Are you sure you haven't got some information we should have?"

"All we have is hunches, nothing more," Hernando blurted out before Strategy could continue.

"You do know that concealing knowledge of extraterrestrial activities is an international felony," O'Neal said pointedly.

"Yes." *Again,* Strategy thought, *Siberia and extraterrestrials. What's his problem? Where is this questioning leading? Is there something happening in Siberia that the government doesn't want me to know? Is that why we were brought to Washington?* Suddenly, like a clue in a crossword, it made sense. *We're close to something,* Strategy realized. *Something in Siberia. Why else rattle our cages?* She immediately took a less aggressive posture.

"If we find out anything that the NTSA is entitled to know, we'll file a full report, just as we're required to do. Didn't I do that after Angel City? I cooperated in every way I could. You know that, and I know that. Perry Courwitz in your Angel City office will tell you everything I did." Solving the riddle of O'Neal's concern made her bold. "If you ask me, I think you think we told you too much."

It was O'Neal's turn to be caught off guard. He didn't like being outsmarted, especially by the little people. After all, he had always charmed the public with his seeming knowledge of history and his good looks. The unsuspecting world assumed beauty equaled truth. He always seemed so sure of his power and of his facts. He threw both of them around so well.

"I have copies of your reports, of course, and our own inquiries, as well," O'Neal said smoothly, his practiced smile returning. "You were very helpful to bring this to our and the world's attention. Although our experts over in National Center for Contagious Diseases found your prophet's features were actually distorted by a mutant bio-germ, the man was as human as you or I."

The director continued, "Still, it is imperative the nation stay alert to the dangers of alien terrorism. Your country is grateful."

*This is such bullshit,* Strategy thought hotly. *What about the dead rising from their graves? What about the giant lizard that Yeshua morphed into?*

"With all due respect, you weren't there." Strategy fought to keep her temper in check. "Perhaps the government assumes that its citizens will wholeheartedly embrace your techno-crap explanations, but you shouldn't be so sure about the press." Here's to the fourth estate, she silently saluted.

"Techno-crap or not, it was your investigation that allowed us to inform the public. I want to be sure such helpfulness will continue before I allow you to leave the country." The Director smiled, again.

"That's a State Department decision," Hernando spoke up again.

"Certainly," said the Director, "but the Secretary likes to stay at my cabin in Vail. The skiing is so good there. Now that you've been reassigned to Utah, you should try it." He let the barb hang for a moment, then rearranged his shoulders and relaxed his face. What came next seemed like a rehearsal for a future vid-op.

"If you're planning a stunt to improve your ratings, I'm telling you not to do it. The people of our great country don't need to be unduly frightened again. Alert, yes. But you misled millions. You do a disservice to the American people by beguiling them with nightmares of phantom space creatures. You do a disservice to your profession by not substantiating your facts before you carelessly broadcast science fiction. You do a disservice to yourself by lying to the American people with Hollywood special effects. Don't travel to Siberia only to give us another hoax like the one in Angel City." He seemed to like the sound of what he had just said and looked sharply at Strategy and Hernando. "Don't you think that we'll scrutinize everything you do?" He tapped his fingers impatiently. "You can't imagine how inconvenient that chimera has been. Your government wouldn't look kindly on another one."

"We showed you what was happening as it happened. It was honest reporting." Strategy permitted herself to raise her voice a little and to glare at him. Even to her own ears, her defense sounded flat-footed. The Director was right—she lacked facts. She lacked tangible proof. She lacked something to beat that superior smile of his into a bloody pulp. Strategy took a deep breath. She knew what she had seen. A pompous air of authority and an opulent office couldn't melt her conviction. But the Director's personality could very well convince others. Maybe he was playing this for Hernando, she realized, and through him, the people Hernando reported to. "Scrutinize all you want. I welcome it. The truth will out."

"Watch yourself, Miss Brooks. We won't tolerate any more of your foolishness," said O'Neal. "The world is safe. We don't like anyone telling the people we aren't doing our job."

"Well, you aren't," said Strategy. "I saw what I saw. The whole world did; it was all over the vids. You know as well as I do that what we aired was accurate. You may spread disinformation through your links with other networks, but right here in this room in the heart of the NTSA, I know you know what's real."

O'Neal fixed her with a hard stare. "All right, for the sake of argument, let's suppose what you showed was real. Just for the sake of argument, you understand." She nodded. "Now let's stop pretending that you are doing this for the good of the nation. You're a reporter—you live and breathe news. And you have created a very tough act to follow."

"How do you mean?" Strategy couldn't keep from asking.

"You have a reputation to salvage, and you'll do anything to restore it, won't you?" His smile had a rictus quality. He tapped the flat of his hand against the edge of his desk. The bottom of his ring clicked rhythmically against the wooden surface. "You've started off on this alien infiltration story, and you've been roundly criticized." He waved away her urge to respond. "And now the only way to regain your credibility as a respected newscaster is to prove that you're right. This rush off to Siberia is a desperate ploy to make sure you have a new sensation to put on the air. A new proof. Or at least . . . new footage."

"I'd have to be more than desperate to run off to Siberia on a fishing expedition," Strategy said, aware that was precisely what she was doing. "Besides, I tell you, I'm investigating a mining installation." It sounded so lame. The lie detector would validate it as the truth, but it still sounded so lame.

O'Neal shot back, "You're desperate. You're off to Siberia. A godforsaken place where few Americans visit or would travel to verify anything. How convenient. That's the end of it. The NTSA will—" He caught himself. "The State Department will deny your visa."

"And what if you're wrong?" Strategy asked, her self-possession returning.

O'Neal laughed a little too quickly. "I'm not." He was never wrong. He tilted his chair back again. "You're trying to restore your position on the news, and you'll do anything—anything—to achieve it. We're fully monitoring Siberia, all the new territories. There is not even a whisper of anything out of the ordinary. You're a threat to national stability."

Strategy refused to rise to the bait. "Was there a whisper in Angel City? Why do you refuse to admit what's right in front of you? Aliens reached Earth, and you didn't find out about it until we announced it on the news. All your plans failed. All your precautions failed. The NTSA has spent billions of the taxpayers' money on what? Not intelligence. Not protection. On what?" The question hung in the air like a weather balloon.

"So you resorted to scare tactics," O'Neal added pointedly, diverting the subject.

"Oh, come on, Director." Strategy leaned forward as she sometimes did to rattle someone she was interviewing. "I can't believe you don't understand how Washington works. The NTSA failed to protect this country from an alien menace, and if—no, *when*—that becomes part of the public debate, someone else will be sitting in this elegant office. Marino will have no choice."

"A clever diversionary tactic," said O'Neal, once again attempting to reclaim the direction of their talk and appear unruffled. No man could have sounded more detached.

"Diversion from what?" Hernando asked suddenly. O'Neal had almost forgotten he was there.

Strategy looked sharply at her assistant, annoyed to find him now perched on the Louis XIV chair. "Yes. Nando's right. Diversion from what?"

O'Neal achieved a genuine smile. "Your paucity of facts. Vids are doctored every day. News is entertainment. It's common knowledge." He glanced at Hernando, "You know Miss Brooks has done this before—on several occasions." If in danger, lie. It was an old principle. Besides, it was a plausible lie. "No one's going to believe you, and we'll take care of the rest. You're a clever woman. You've parlayed your mendacities into hours of air time."

And of course, she had. But then, so had everyone else. Still, that would be no defense if O'Neal brought the full weight of the NTSA down on her. The government had ways of curtailing careers, abolishing liberties, changing clearances in the bio-chips they implanted in prenatal heads. Without a spotless set of credentials, Strategy would be forever barred from Network newscasts. She was going at this all wrong In a minute she had revised her game plan.

"From Siberia? Come on, Mister O'Neal," said Strategy, slipping into her broadcast persona. "We're making this all much too complicated." She took a page from his book and bestowed on him a saucy little smile of her own. She actually sat down and crossed her legs. She tried to get them on camera as often as she could. "Think about what I have at stake here. Why would I undermine the very credibility I've worked so hard to create? I don't want you and the NTSA as an enemy. I have admitted that I made a mistake with Yeshua. I accepted him at face value, and so I was suckered." She looked down at her hands. The moment had played so well on the vid-cast. "I've said as much to the whole world, and taken my lumps for it. I don't want that to happen again."

"Very touching," said O'Neal. She was very pretty, he realized, in a big-haired sort of way. "You don't mean to say that you haven't made the most of your supposed mistake, I hope?"

Strategy had heard very much the same complaint many times, and it no longer fazed her when someone brought up her poor judgment. "I should have looked more deeply. I know that. But he was really persuasive, and I let myself believe. I'm not about to be fooled again. Sure, I want to find out if there are others of his species on Earth, and where they're hiding. But not at the risk of my career—or the risk of national security. Besides, really, that's not why I'm going to Siberia." She started to unbutton her coat and saw his incredulity. She leaned forward. "Really."

"Really? Miss Brooks, *please!*" O'Neal exclaimed, pretending conviviality but probing her eyes. The tone in the room was shifting.

"Really." Strategy allowed just a touch of Texan drawl.

"So, you've come across something that makes you think a visit to Siberia would be worthwhile. A mining installation?"

"I said so," Strategy reminded him.

He didn't like being interrupted. "So . . . you're going

looking for that, and nothing else?" O'Neal spoke precisely, stressing the last three words.

"Yes," she said coyly. "And if I don't find any story, then, no story. But if I come across something, I can say you helped me."

"What do you mean?" O'Neal was looking at her with confused suspicion now.

"I mean that if you'll give me my visa, I'll check out my private sources. If anything *interesting* should come up, I'll make sure NTSA gets credit for what we find." She was making this up as she talked, but the more she offered, the better she liked it.

O'Neal conintued to scrutinize her as he slowly nodded his head. "I think you and Mister Carrasco better pack extra silks. It's very cold in Siberia this time of year."

Strategy rose to don her coat. Hernando followed. O'Neal rose to say goodbye. The negotiation was over. Both sides thought they had won. Hands were extended. Thank-yous were exchanged. The Director moved toward the door to usher them out. Hernando walked out to make a phone call. Strategy took advantage of being alone with the Director to say, "You will allow me to have exclusive coverage if anything does develop."

"By the way, I love your program." He took her hand. "Oh . . . something else."

"What?" She regarded him with cynical mistrust.

"If you don't find anything, this meeting never happened."

She almost smiled. "Done."

# CHAPTER 11

NOT REALLY KNOWING WHAT he was looking for, John Dee studied the screen at the front of the flyer, his full attention on the landscape revealed beneath them. He was still feeling apprehensive, knowing that he was in danger now that he was in American airspace. His thoughts whirled as he tried to anticipate all the risks, knowing there were risks in this century he was not even aware of. With all the flyers and other traffic around them, Dee hoped d'Winter was right, and they could slip through in the confusion.

"The NTSA will probably have an alert out for you, now that we're back in America," d'Winter said. "We have to assume that they will know who we all are."

Dee did his best to appear self-possessed, but could not suppress the surge of excitement mixed with apprehension that roiled through him. "Bear a fair presence, though your heart be tainted." God bless old Sir Francis; he was a master.

Kelly had reminded him as they boarded the flyer back in England. "The NTSA could take you captive in almost any country in the world. But if they can convince the Foreign Intelligence Surveillance Act court—"

"FISA."

"FISA . . . that your name belonged on a warrant, while you're here in the States, they could lock you up as a suspected threat to national security and throw away the key. No trial, no lawyer, no habeas corpus. You'd simply disappear. NTSA has treaties with every nation on earth but two."

"Then the want of a name is useful," Dee had responded. Now, looking down on the edge of the prairie snuggling up against tall mountains, he wondered if he hadn't been a bit precipitous in coming to America. The Four Corners Corridor Mall was less than twenty minutes ahead, its landing field as massive a complex as the international discount mall that occupied thirty-four acres under three gigantic, tent-like roofs. The mart's seven stories housed every conceivable shop, storefront, and warehouse, along with restaurants featuring cuisines from every corner of the world. The parking structure was five stories high, and covered another twenty-two acres. It was serviced by a cloverleaf tramway that ran from the airport and into the center of the mall.

"You'll have to walk into the mall—there're scanners on the tram—and your lack of a chip will be picked up at once." D'Winter brought the flyer into the landing pattern. He'd been against this meeting since he'd first heard of it. Too much could go wrong. The mart was swarming with security devices; moreover, it was in the United States—a country no longer safe for Dee and probably not for any of them. D'Winter was sure the NTSA would love to interrogate his employer. "You and Kelly should go in together—couples are less obvious than a man alone. I'll take care of the customs work." He signaled Kelly, who was dozing in the narrow bunk at the back of the little cabin. "Time to rise and shine."

"What time is it?" Kelly asked as she sat up and rubbed her eyes.

"Local time, about twelve-thirty. It's the busiest time for the mall. It's Presidents' Day, the busiest shopping day of the year. That's in your favor. There's a real crowd down there." D'Winter toggled the landing beacon, and prepared to follow it down to the ground.

"Mayhap it is the more perilous with so many people about," said Dee.

D'Winter shrugged. "Could be," he allowed. "Where are you going to meet?"

"Main floor, Sector G," said Kelly.

"That's a lot of territory," said d'Winter. "Anything more specific?"

"That's what his last communication said," Kelly reminded him.

"Keep your head down, Kelly. You know the NTSA will be scanning for us as well." Getting through the chip scanners in Customs would be tricky, but there were ways to avoid them if you knew where they were. Morgan did. It was an old game for him. Kelly would be new at it.

"How long until we dock?" Dee asked, still unable to calculate the speeds at which people traveled in this world.

"You mean 'land'? Ten minutes, maybe fifteen, depending on how many other private flyers are ahead of us," said d'Winter.

"I have to do something about my clothes," said Kelly, looking at the rumpled fabric of her jumpsuit. "I have a change in my duffel."

"Better get to it," said d'Winter.

"Tell me when we're almost on the ground," Kelly said as she went into the closet-sized bathroom.

"What about you, Doctor?" d'Winter asked. "Do you think you ought to change clothes?"

"Is that a recommendation?" Dee studied his clothing, thinking it was too bad he had no brocade for a proper doublet, and superfine wool for leggings. But these days, such clothing would stand out as much as his chipless head. He brushed at the metallic weave of his clothing. It gave him the appearance of a lunar worker. He'd seen many such jumpsuits on the moon. That seemed ages ago. "Will this not do?"

"You might want to step into the refresher," d'Winter suggested, pointing to an alcove like an upright coffin. "You'll look less conspicuous."

By that Dee assumed he needed to shave. The fashion of the times was to face the world clean-shaven, a convention he'd been hard-pressed to accept. A man without a beard was a boy, a peascod, a gelding. The loss of his neatly kept triangular trim was a constant reminder of all he'd lost. "As you wish," Dee said, and went to step into the refresher.

D'Winter adjusted a few toggles on the dial and said, "You're going to have to be very careful. This place is going to be dangerous." This whole trip is ridiculous, he thought; it all could have been done in England, in Latvia, in Nigeria. Anywhere but here.

"Do all employ this aroma? Is it a common practice?" said Dee as he emerged from the refresher, his clothing looking restored, his hair neatened, his face as bald as an egg. The scent of something from the forest was wafting about him.

"When they have the opportunity," said d'Winter. "It's only polite."

"What about you?" Dee asked.

"I'm landing the flyer," said d'Winter, pointing at the display before him.

"Good enough," said Dee, and heard the warning buzzer to strap in for set-down. He scrambled into the harness he had been provided.

"You sure you want to go through with this? It's going to be tricky in there." Kelly asked as she hurried to buckle herself into her seat, her concern much less pronounced than the pilot's. She was now wearing a neat ensemble of wide-cuffed trousers and a tulip-sleeved tunic with an embroidered hem. Her face looked radiant and her hair was shining. Her shoes were cushion-soled, appropriate for walking the long corridors of the mall, and she had a handsome satchel large enough to hold a two-day-old calf, or so Dee thought as he looked over at her. She smiled at him. In her lap rested a festive cap with a large brim, which was newly lined with a leaden substance that would block an ID scan. The brim would throw a shadow over her face. Though a disguise, it would make her look enchanting.

"I must go and meet with danger now, or it will seek me in another place and find me worse provided. The readiness is all." Dee replied. "You look marvelous."

"Thank you." She managed an encouraging smile just as the flyer set down and was signaled by the landing squad to taxi to Row 19, Slot 84. "Here we are. Too late to turn back now."

"Yes, we can," mumbled d'Winter, loud enough for his employer's ear.

"Dyckon has named the place, I cannot but say

'aye,' " Dee said as he loosened his harness. "This want of a chip misgives me though. I'd feel better if I knew specifically where this Sector G is situate. This is as huge a place as I have seen; it dwarfs cloud-kissing Dover." He rubbed his chin, again ruing the sacrificed beard. "I trust he'll find us."

"Are you sure of that? What about this other Roc?" They had come to think of Fawg's backup as one Roc, though they knew there might be more. It made their search seem easier, their hopes more attainable. "What if he's here too and finds us first?" D'Winter shut off the flyer in its assigned spot and got out of his landing harness.

"It is a throw of the die and we must hazard the throw," said Dee, trying to conceal his concern about this possibility. "How far must we travel?"

"About five kilometers, more or less." D'Winter locked down the display panel and rose from his chair.

Dee frowned, calculating the distance in furlongs. "Half an hour or forty minutes should find us inside, if we are not prevented."

"Remember we have to go in through the parking structure. And don't get on the tram or the shuttle." Kelly slung her satchel strap over her shoulder. "Here's your hat." He'd almost forgotten it. He'd wanted to forget it. It looked like half of a cannonball but weighed but a hundredth of one. Like Kelly's cap, it was lined with a thin strip of lead. The hat too was of the lunar variety and matched the workman outfit Morgan had prepared for him. But John Dee was never partial to hats; they overly accented his large ears.

"Aye, I am expert," said Dee, eager now to get started. "You've made me well acquainted withal." With that, he donned his helmet. His face took on a theatrical scowl. Then in as deep a bass as his tenor voice would allow, John Dee did an excellent imitation of Morgan d'Winter, "Let's move."

Kelly smiled, amused. "Very good."

D'Winter merely gave him a look that questioned his intelligence."Don't take any chances. If you think you're being followed, get the hell out of there and we'll find another way to make contact," d'Winter said. He cocked his head. "This is a very risky day at the mall, Doctor."

"Good sir, 'twas my occupation to take risks and 'tis no great bother for a man to labor in his occupation," Dee said. "You must trust in my skill, my dagger, and my faith. I am well schooled in your arts." The archaic language coming from under the lunar construction helmet was a bit laughable.

D'Winter shook his head, refusing easy comfort. "I know you're courageous. But there are hazards here that didn't exist in Elizabeth the First's reign."

"And tediously you do remind me of them," Dee said with a hard sigh. "You have my word I'll heed Kelly's alarum if there be aught I don't perceive."

"Just make sure you remember that when the time comes," said d'Winter, unable to let it go.

Dee chuckled dryly. "Aye, I have"—and here he purposefully stressed his words—"on occasion ignored your worship's wisdom . . ." The first part of the sentence hung for a moment in the air, waiting, then, "And I acknowledge it." A slight bow. Then the humor was gone and there was a gravity. "But Dyckon—my benefactor, he that rescued me at Death's door—has taken as great a risk as we in coming here. If it is folly, then it is folly. But a friend must bear his friend's infirmities. Moreover, he is wiser and knows our prey, and we must learn what he has to tell us."

"That's why we're here," said Kelly, reaching to open the hatch. "You ready?"

Hefting the sack at his feet and holding on to the oversized hat on his head, Dee said, "I am at your service," and prepared to follow her.

# CHAPTER 12

THE FLYER PARKING AREA was a broad expanse of plasticrete, shimmering from the harsh sunlight and heat. More than two hundred flyers were lined up in herringbone ranks, U.S. Homeland Security stickers on their wings showing they were secure. Homeland Security, the branch of the government that oversaw the FBI, the Coast Guard, and the U.S. NTSA, was responsible for national defense and immigration. No pilot was allowed to operate a vessel in American airspace or a ship in American waters without up-to-date credentials from the Bureau. But perfectly policing a country as expansive and as commercially robust as the United States was inevitably a losing battle. America for a century had thrived on exporting technology and pop culture while importing cheap labor and refurbished ideas. The very small trickle of unwanted people and black market commerce that came through the national ports of call along with legitimate cargo was part of the cost of being America, Inc. England in Elizabeth's time had been no different. There were fortunes to be made.

Stepping down onto the pavement, Dee was struck by the heat, and, a moment later, the wind that rushed in from the west like the swat of a hot hand. He glanced at Kelly. "Wither?"

Kelly pointed to the nearest five-story rectangle. "That's the parking structure."

"Is it?" It was an uncomfortable walk in the heat and with a helmet. "All the arches and the roads lead there," said Kelly, then added, before he had the chance, "like the roads of Rome." They shared a smile. To an unsuspecting passerby they were a pleasant couple off on a shopping spree.

They started toward the parking garage, walking quickly but not so quickly that they would attract attention. They kept up their light banter. Passing four flyers with Russian stickers on the wings, Dee marveled, "They come from as far off as Muscovy to shop?"

"That or to make deals with merchants," said Kelly. She had put on dark glasses, making it difficult for Dee to read her mood. The brim of her cap helped shield her eyes from the sun as well as her hair from the arid air from the west and the roaring wind from the jet engines. The ensuing turbulence was aggressive and overly personal. For John Dee, the jet transports seemed like royal pennants. Their personal styling and foreign inscriptions were lions rampant. Each ear-splitting engine roared its owner's privilege and authority, intimating a special relationship with Heaven.

"I suppose this must be a fine place to be a merchant. With so many people coming to buy—well, there is money to be made," Dee said as they neared the mall with its boastful, fifty-foot banners in nine languages proclaiming that there were 2,840 outlets inside, twelve food courts, and seven floors of bargains. The buying power of money had inflated to seventy-five times its Elizabethan value. He had never had enough back then, what with the bills for the Library, scientific equipment, travel, and taxes. The upkeep of Mortlake had been a constant struggle. For all his exploits and contributions for the Crown, Her Grace had been miserly, never giving him the sinecure he rightfully deserved. He blamed that mostly on Lord Cecil, the Lord Treasurer. Dee had often been forced to juggle and borrow. But that didn't keep him from investing. He had jumped at the chance to join Frobisher and Lok in an attempt to find the lucrative Northwest Passage. Then, a few years later, he inveigled himself into a promising venture to own the rights to brass-work mines in Devonshire. The wars in the Lowlands had broken out again, and there was great demand for metal for cannon. But neither a route to Cathay nor a quest for ore ever paid off. He had blithely shrugged his shoulders and scrambled on to find wealth somewhere else. Now he was richer than Croesus—even if that legendary king's wealth had compounded annually for the three thousand years since his death. But in the transition, something had been lost—the joy of acquiring something you couldn't afford. The struggle to stay financially afloat had been life affirming.

"The storefronts go for more than a quarter of a million here, and thousands compete to get one," said Kelly. "When I did promotional work, I saw all the statistics. The right advertising can make or break an outlet." It seemed ages ago when that had been her life. When snatching up a major advertising account was all she hoped for. All she prayed for. Who would have guessed those circumstances would lead her here?

"That's enough money to buy kingdoms—a royal exchequer's worth."

"They make it back quickly." Kelly pointed to a broad arch ahead of them. "That's where we're going." Dee glanced around for the security patrol, and took note of landmarks should a hasty retreat be necessary.

They crossed the last stretch of plasticrete and entered the shadow of the parking structure. Despite the shade, the adobe-white building radiated heat and bounced the wind back at them. They were forced to hold on to their hats and speak louder. "Where is the nearest entrance?" Dee asked.

Kelly shook her head. "Shouldn't go in the nearest door. It tends to be more closely watched." Her companion mutely acknowledged the wisdom of that. "It's better to go up a level and in the next door." She saw the thin line of sweat on his upper lip. "It's another quarter mile," she shouted. Kelly pointed in the direction of an escalator tower. "Let's go up there."

"Lead the way," Dee said with a hint of resignation. She was perfectly in the right. He wished he'd worn Dyckon's suit—he would have been a lot cooler.

The escalators were broad and quick, crowded with eager shoppers—some whole families among them—riding up. They reached the second floor without a hitch and entered the mall at a door conspicuously labeled 2 H-North, which indication Kelly murmured into her small clip-on communicator. The air-conditioning, a blast of welcome arctic air, came rushing at them from the mall's entrance. There were more than twenty people headed for the small doorway and its slow-moving turnstile. Kelly shoved Dee toward them. "Go through the scanners with them.

Cram in with someone else when you go through. I'll be right behind you."

"Aye," said Dee, keenly aware that he was safest in a group, but not liking being shoved.

There was a flurry of confusion as they funneled toward the door. He once nearly lost his headgear as the crowd jostled for entrance. He felt people's body parts smashed against his arms and back. The smell of sweaty humanity filled his nostrils. Morgan, of course, had been right about the refresher. People crushed and pushed to get through the turnstile. His short stature made him a target for every taller person who wanted to get to the door ahead of him. Worst of all, his translating device was unable to decipher all the foreign words that rattled in conversations around him. The high-pitched feedback from the overload hurt his ears. But people's body language was unmistakable: parents reached for children, arms pointed in the direction of certain stores, mouths twisted in admonitions about not shoving. He thought to look around for Kelly, but he was too short to see past the men behind him. Besides, they were all jammed up against the turnstile, all wanting to get in, to get their shopping started. He couldn't swivel his shoulders. As though caught in an undertow, he was being pulled toward a scanning device that might immediately do him in. But he managed to squeeze in with two very tall, very hefty African men who in their native Kenyan chirped away about the jewelry they were wearing. No alarms sounded. Being short had its advantages. And then he was in a broad gallery lined with brilliant storefronts, and with a huge skylight five stories overhead. Elongated red, white, and blue banners and bunting, streaming down from the tall ceiling, wafted in the air-conditioning. It looked like High Street on the Queen's Coronation Day.

Dee struggled out of the crowd in front of a store calling itself Toot Ansam, showing fashionable clothes for children in its window displays. His father, a mercer, would have loved the uniqueness and variety of the materials. He looked around for Kelly and caught sight of her about thirty feet away, in front of Industrial Strength, an outlet for carpeting and flooring. Starting toward her, he stayed alert for security patrols. Petty constables were so easy to spot in this era; they all wore identifying uniforms. Though his helmet wobbled on his head and the translator was giving him a headache, his senses heightened as he made his way through the throngs of shoppers. The noise of the marketplace was constant, a hive-like buzz as loud as a high-speed train, and it made him jumpy. It was like being in the Shambles, a long Yorkish alley overcrowded with hanging meats, barking dogs, mewing cats, bellowing shopkeepers, and blathering commerce. You could lose your life there as easily as your wallet and never hear yourself scream. Where the Devil was Sector G?

He reached Kelly, who, pointed toward the high railing at the edge of the gallery. "There're escalators over there. We can ride down to the main floor, and then find Sector G."

"Fine," said Dee, trying to conceal the grumpiness that all the jostling had caused. "How many people would you say are in here?"

"The traffic statistics say that seventy-five thousand shoppers visit this mall daily. 'Course, this is Presidents' Day. It could be double."

The number astonished Dee. He still had the capacity

to be shocked by the staggering number of people living in this century. In 1570, there had been only 120,000 in London, and that included Southwark and all the other outer parishes. And London was the most populated city in Europe. "Little wonder the shops are so dear here."

"This is the third largest mall in the world."

"There be larger ones?" he exclaimed.

"Aye." She took a momentary pleasure in his provincialism. At times, he could have all the wonder of a small child. "Northwestern India, Rio de Janeiro, and Xinqun. Xinqun has more than a hundred thousand shoppers a day."

"Think what mischief a Roc with the virus could do in those places," said Dee.

"I'd rather not," said Kelly.

"Why would a Roc choose this mall if he could go to a larger one?"

"Probably because the other three don't have as much international traffic as this one has," said Kelly as they started down the escalator. "Could also be closer to home."

"Why so much international traffic here?" Dee asked.

"Better tariffs and Homeland protection," said Kelly promptly. "You're less liable to be bombed here."

Dee thought about this as they reached the ground floor. "Was that why he went to Chicopolis?"

"Who knows?" Kelly said, and pointed toward the two-story-high letter G with an arrow angling off beneath it. "We go that way. We'd better split up again."

"Fine," said Dee, relieved to see the sign. Maybe they would find Dyckon after all. He turned in the direction that Kelly had pointed out, not happy in the least about the wave of humanity coming toward him from that direction. Where were they all going? Why were they all so tall? Kelly seemed to melt into their midst.

A gaggle of youngsters in school uniforms hurried by, the girls giggling, the boys practicing their struts. If the Roc virus should touch them, their days of enjoyment would be over forever. Dee thought this terribly sad, and he determined that it would not happen.

Always ahead of him, Kelly skillfully threaded her way through the crowd, glancing over her shoulder from time to time to be sure that Dee was behind her. D'Winter had planned it this way. There were scanners throughout the mall doing random checks. One person alone with a scanproof hat might alert security. Two walking together was asking for trouble.

Dee studied the shoppers as discreetly as he could. Dyckon must have assumed an appearance different from the one Dee had seen on the monitor several hours ago. Then, he'd appeared as a tattered homeless man with oily matted hair, looking very much like a begging "counterfeit crank" that haunted the Queen's highway. That identity would be unacceptable here in this teeming ocean of merchandise and prosperity. Dee thought to look for a stranger with dark sunglasses who might be concealing the unmistakable red reptile eyes that were unchangeable in a Roc's transformation. But thousands of shoppers had not removed their glasses after coming in from the harsh sunlight. No, he and Kelly would wander Sector G until Dyckon found them. In the meantime, they were like sitting ducks out in the open where the scanners could find them.

# CHAPTER 13

LAKE BAIKAL SHONE LIKE a long, metallic blade under the wings of the flyer as Strategy Brooks flew into its international airport. Below her, banks of snow seemed to dam the water to keep it at bay. She turned up the collar of her fur vest, preparing for the weather. "Nando," she said, her eyes gleaming, "we're going to get back on top with this. I feel it in my bones."

Hernando's grin was lupine. "You just tell me where to point my gear."

"Siberia is a big place, but Irkutsk is the hub of the area. Almost all traffic passes through here. We just need to find who to bribe." She rubbed her hands together, preparing them for the cold. "You should make arrangements with the Celsus mining installation to set up an appointment for an interview. We'll need to start there. Assure diRocelli, we're here doing the job we signed on for."

"That's a big lake, isn't it?"

"Don't be so glum, chum," she said. "The NTSA is up to something out here. Maybe they're hiding another alien. Maybe they've got a whole Roswell military base out here." She acknowledged the landscape outside the window. "They could have a whole terrarium of lizards on ice out there."

"Roswell?"

"About a hundred and fifty years ago, many Americans believed the government had a special hangar, hangar 18, at the air force base, in Roswell, New Mexico, holding E.T.'s in refrigeration. It never panned out. But it became a widely held American myth. Check out the History Channel sometime."

"So, you're still hot to trot for aliens."

"Nando, you weren't there in the Hollywood Hills." Maybe the glibness and the directness of the question and the six-hour transit ride had gotten to her. Maybe she was too stiff, too bored, or too tired to carefully guard her emotions. Failing to observe her own ethics of professional wariness she said, her voice quivering, "You don't know. I spent weeks with Yeshua in Angel City—in *very* close quarters. I know that he performed miracles at the drop of a hat, and believe me, there were times when he had me convinced he was the Second Coming, but it never occurred to me—not once—that he wasn't human. Christ, he didn't just look human; he was beautiful. But, when those rat-men strafed him and he lay dying transformed or morphed or whatever into this huge bat-lizard thing, I knew this thing wasn't from our neck of the woods."

She fought back a tiny memory of fear, replacing it with a growing anger. "Now, you figure this has got to be the biggest news since the L.A. quake in '39, before it was named Angel City, and for a while GNN let me run with it."

"You had the world scared shitless," Hernando said.

She clicked her harness into the locked position. "Yeah, for two weeks, the Vatican was ready to beatify me. *Newsweek* was talking to me about a cover. But then, *Viacom News and World Report* and Bertelsmann and Liberty and everybody the fuck else started shouting 'hoax.' Claimed I remastered the vids. That I had done it for better ratings. As if I needed better ratings at the time."

She shot a glance at Hernando, who nodded his support. "GNN never came to my defense. DiRocelli tried to find out why. But according to him, nobody from the Black Tower answered his calls. Except that one call from Corporate that reassigned all of us to Utah and scheduled us into a two A.M. time slot. No explanations given. Now I can barely get an interview. But, Nando, I know what I saw and what I reported was the facts. My vids didn't lie. There was a God's honest space alien that died in L.A. that day, and for all we know there may be *more* around. And I'll bet bagels to Bosnia, the NTSA put the squash on me when they didn't want the world to believe it. I've got a real good feeling that O'Neal knows about some others, and they're right here in this butt-end of the world." She took a deep breath and looked out the window. "We just got to smoke them out."

"That's why we became journalists," said Hernando with mixed admiration and bewilderment.

"Yeah, well," she said, slightly mollified. "Buckle in—we're landing."

The airport, despite its recent improvements, was in chaos. Travel-weary groups of sports enthusiasts, petro-engineers, natives, religious fanatics, and airline personnel crammed huge traveling bags through X-ray machines. Check-in clerks argued with tour guides and double-checked on headsets with their invisible bureaucratic bosses. Incomprehensible loudspeaker warnings competed with the conversations of tired passengers on their phones. Innocents abroad looked lost and confused as bored policemen waited for lunch. Strategy and Hernando cleared customs and security through the media line, and were outside the terminal in less than half an hour. A limousine, grimy with snow, was waiting for them at the curb. A driver in a uniform with faded gold braid stood outside by the rear of his vehicle, the exhaust from the running engine keeping him from trembling. At chest level he held the side of a raggedly torn carton box with the word "Brooks" on it. Together they all tossed the luggage into the yawning trunk, eager to get into the warm car. Despite a slight tug-of-war with the driver, Hernando refused to release his camera case and took it with him into the safety of the large limousine. Strategy settled herself on the suede seat and spoke to the driver in acceptable Russian, "Take us to the Sheraton Irkutsk. I need a bath."

What was normally an hour's trip was made longer by slow-moving traffic and icy roads. The long limousine fishtailed several times during the trip, but Hernando never lost hold of his camera. The Americans, having taken seats on either side of the car, rarely spoke but fixated on the view of large mounds of snow pushed to the side of the road. The countryside that had looked so pristine and white from the air was hardly that at eye level. Their route passed half-finished construction left fallow until the spring, the unprotected floors piled high with hillocks of snow. Beyond the roads were battered hovels with yards littered with wreckage and refuse. Many of the cars that passed them were of a vintage that had not been seen in the States for decades. They were dented and rusted; some had cracked windows. Hatless stragglers in threadbare coats trudged along the road to menial jobs. When the wind wasn't blowing, they would sometimes stop to watch the long limousine, as rare an oddity to them as a flying carpet, bounce along the potholed road. In their reaction was unmistakable wonder mixed with resentment. The fact that Strategy and Hernando were now in a third-world country was not lost on them.

"This country needs help," Hernando reflected.

"Yes," agreed Strategy quietly, privately wondering whether it was really so terribly different from conditions in Angel City.

The Sheraton in Irkutsk was a four-story building with two wings that faced away from the nearby railway station. In keeping with the gentrification of the area, it had been newly remodeled, though not very well. The lobby was warm, however, and furnished with overstuffed chairs and sofas. Ignoring the long line of people waiting to check in, many of whom were from the same flight, Strategy headed for a manager type at the counter.

In passable Russian she inquired about their rooms. She withdrew her passport and visa, as did Hernando, and handed them over to be examined. The man, fortyish with a long cigarette hanging from his mouth, pointed at the long line and informed them that they were not next. He suggested that they return to the back of the line and he gestured to the next in line.

"Perhaps you don't know who I am?" Strategy raised her voice so that the entire lobby could hear her. In an undertone she added, "My network might not be so interested in promoting your modernized hotel if they knew about my difficulty with management." With an appraising glance at the GNN credentials Strategy presented, the manager took them aside. Strategy frowned as he checked his computer. The hotel manager now switched to English, "I'm afraid you don't have a reservation, Miss Brooks."

"What? That's not possible."

"There must be some mistake," echoed Hernando.

"No. No. There is no mistake. I have no Strategy Brooks or Hernando Carrasco on my reservation list for tonight. You are expected, however, to arrive next week. You have arrived too soon."

"Next week!" Strategy vowed to kill the twenty-something assistant who had made the reservations. "All right, no problem, just give us two rooms. We'll be here on an open-ended stay."

"I'm afraid I can't do that. We are totally booked up for the week with a convention of Illuminati. They have come for a religious retreat. All space has been reserved. In fact, most of the good hotels are all full. It is the high skiing season. I'm so very sorry."

Hernando withdrew his wallet and took out a hundred. He laid it on the faux marble counter between them. "Perhaps you can find some rooms you've forgotten about."

The cigarette came to attention in the clerk's mouth and he rechecked his computer, but there was nothing. The three of them argued for another five minutes before the clerk got on the phone and made a brief call in Russian. He hung up and reached for the hundred. Strategy slammed her white hand over his olive-skinned one.

"I have arranged for two very comfortable rooms over at the Majestic on Fedeyov Street, two blocks north of here. Boris says you may stay the week and then, if the accommodations are not to your liking, the Sheraton Irkutsk would be happy to have you return here and we will put you up in the Taras Bulba suites at half the going rate. We are disconsolate at your inconvenience."

"What if we don't like the Majestic?"

"Oh, but you will. You will," he reassured them with all his worth. "It's old-fashioned but comfortable. Done in the grand manner—brass and velvet and stuffed animals. Boris keeps a good table. And I believe there are some other Americans there." The manager looked from them to the line, which had grown appreciably. "I am most sorry"—he mustered a grieved look—"but for you there is nothing more I can do."

Snatching the hundred from the counter, Strategy sent Hernando to fetch their driver , and tell him about their change of plans. "I'll be out when the limo is warmed up," she snapped.

Strategy watched as the bellhops took other exhausted travelers to their properly booked rooms. The prospect of staying in some run-down, old-world hotel in Irkutsk evoked feelings of both dread and rage. What the hell had she gotten herself into?

# CHAPTER 14

THEON CELSUS LACED HIS fingers together and rested his dimpled chin on them, smiling like a well-fed cat. "So that newswoman is in Irkutsk." His garb today was reminiscent of Russian caftans of the sixteenth century, a long robe of red-and-gold brocade that hung to his ankles, worthy of a tsar.

Maxim looked at the vidscreen, where an image of Strategy getting out of her limousine was frozen. "Does this worry you?"

"Why should it? She's a minor annoyance, like a gnat." Celsus pursed his lips. "If she becomes inconvenient, she'll be gone."

"How do you mean, gone?" Maxim asked, although he already knew.

"All manner of accidents can befall someone in Siberia. It is simply a matter of choosing the most effective," said Celsus. "She may prove useful, of course."

This seemed more sinister to Maxim than the prospect of a killing. "Useful in what way?"

"Ach, Max, Max, don't worry," Celsus admonished

him as he moved back in his chair, dropping his hands into his lap. The image of repose. "It is prudent to have access to the media, and she may be the very link I've been searching for."

"That may be," said Maxim, still worried. "How do you know if you can trust her?"

"I don't know that I can, yet." Celsus shook his nearly bald head. "It is intriguing, having her here. The universe, as always, must be telling us something."

"Irkutsk isn't here," said Maxim.

"It's much closer than Angel City, and we must assume that she is looking for something, or her assistant wouldn't be with her, with all his equipment," said Celsus, chuckling. He rose and walked to the window, staring out at the vast expanse of forest that was just beginning to lose its mantle of snow. Theon Celsus, seeing his face reflected back at him in the window, pondered the need for rational authority over chaos. The massive power of Markovo's treeline was awe-inspiring, but such power was impotent unless it subordinated itself to Man's will. Harmony, both in Man and Nature, could only prevail once Nature was subdued. That was divine Heaven's plan. One had only to look to the opening pages of Genesis. He studied his reflection and thought of his fellow voyager. "I wonder what Dee is up to. He's so restless, I'm certain he must be trying some desperate ploy. I was impressed by all he did in Angel City, weren't you? Such derring-do! He thinks he's still in Walsingham's service."

Maxim had become accustomed to Celsus's abrupt switches in conversation. "What are you planning to do about him?"

"Nothing yet. I have to find out where he is, and then I

can decide how to proceed." Celsus made a gesture of annoyance. "Dee is a brother. And like a brother, he can be a bother. If I knew what Dyckon's role in all this was, it would be easier for me to arrive at a plan." With the heel of his hand, he cleared the fog from the window where his breath had collected. He sat back to admire the light on the snow.

"Why is Dyckon so important?" Maxim was baffled.

"Max, certainly I've told you this before. He's important because he brought me into this time, and Dee as well." Celsus snapped his fingers impatiently. "He collected two men from the past and . . . I don't know how much he's planning to do about . . ." His voice trailed off as he took a step closer to the window and became characteristically lost in a new, intruding thought. "I'm not privy to his confidences, so . . ." Something outside distracted him. "Is anyone scheduled to come out today?"

"No," said Maxim.

"Then what is that Ranger Multi Terrain doing at the gate?" Celsus demanded, pointing at a dark spot near the high fence. His finger began tapping on the glass pane as if this faint sound might get the Ranger's attention.

"It's their usual patrol routine," said Maxim, with a surge of irrational relief. "They drive the perimeter every three days."

"Just so, just so. I hadn't realized it was time for another run," said Celsus, and turned away from the window. "I believe I will arrange to go into Irkutsk in a day or so."

"What on earth for?" Maxim envisioned all manner of disasters. "Are you tempting trouble?"

"I don't think so," said Celsus. "I would prefer to think that I am forestalling it."

"Then you intend to see the reporter."

"Yes. The question is, will I permit her to see me? I'll have to speak to Boris Shevyenetz about that, for he'll be able to advise me. If I know Boris, he'll have the whole of her plans out of her before she's finished the shashlik." Celsus rose and strode down the center of his office, his kaftan brushing the glorious Bukhara carpet with sensuous whispers. "If I had the opportunity to speak to Dyckon, none of this would be necessary."

"Then why not try to reach him?" Maxim suggested hopefully.

"I have no means to," said Celsus curtly.

"Well, have you tried?" Maxim asked.

"Reason, Maxim, reason." His tone of voice was icy. "If I haven't the means, how can I try?" His testy manner warned Maxim that Celsus was seriously displeased. "Originally, we spoke often while I adjusted to this century, but then, when I became established, he left me to my own devices. Since I built this place, Dyckon has contacted me only once since he first returned to Earth. Though, granted, that was a very important visit. Preferably, I would not have him looking over my shoulder. But the death of Fawg makes circumstances unusual, and we have so much work to do in so little time."

"Then don't you think Dyckon will know it, and will—"

"Max, don't be foolish," Celsus reproached him. "For all I know, these developments are of Dyckon's making. I don't want to do anything that could be detrimental to whatever he is doing, if he is actually doing anything." He stopped pacing and swung around to face Maxim. His mind made another mental jump. "Make the arrangements for a trip to Irkutsk."

Maxim sighed and summoned up another argument. "Why not have Boris come here?"

"He's not the kind to keep secrets, ergo I would prefer to keep him at arm's length," said Celsus. "Boris is very useful in his way, but I don't see that it would benefit me to show him how to find me."

"Then use the vidscreen." He pointed to the vidscreen that was just now showing a riot in southern India. "You've done so before."

"That I have," said Celsus.

"Then do so now," Maxim urged him. "With that reporter on the prowl, who knows what would happen to you once she found you? She might discover who you are or what you don't have. If news got out, the international NTSA would surely want you for questioning. Can Boris Shevyenetz protect you? Isn't it more likely that he would barter your safety for his advancement?"

Celsus reached out and patted Maxim's shoulder. "Poor Max—so cautious!" He reached out to gently touch his associate's temple. There was a paternal warmth in the gesture. "But at least, now, you are using your mind. Don't fret, Max. I won't do anything foolish. But I would much rather have the element of surprise on my side than cower here, worrying about what might happen."

Maxim gave up. "All right. I'll arrange for a transport to take you to Irkutsk."

"You'll come along, of course," said Celsus, half-smiling. "To guard me."

# CHAPTER 15

PEERING THROUGH THE CROWD, Dee prayed that Dyckon could see him. The constant confusion and noise made him edgy, and the unrelentingly insipid music piped through the facility was maddening. From time to time he lost sight of Kelly, each time experiencing a disconcerting feeling of being lost. He'd known the same sense of dispossesion when Dyckon had left him aimlessly to wander Angel City. Even the moon had been less disorienting than this mall. The intermittent feelings of abandonment added to his ill temper.

Up ahead, Kelly suddenly popped out of the crush and reached for Dee's wrist. "Look at the old-fashioned automobile. Isn't it marvelous?" she enthused, wrenching him around to face a display showing President Roosevelt motoring around the Grand Canyon in a holiday hologram. She seemed idiotically rhapsodic about the Studebaker, but under her breath she cautioned, "Careful! There are scanners in the arch!"

Involuntarily looking above the exhibition, trying to

see what Kelly had noticed, he started to speak, but she tightened her hold on his wrist. "What?"

"Security seems to be particularly interested in faces today," she said, keeping her voice low in spite of the loud hum of conversation around them. "Look." With her head she motioned behind Dee at a group of mall security who were checking their hand monitors and then looking up at people in the crowd.

"I understand," said Dee, quickly turning around and lowering the brim on his helmet. "This is a damnable situation."

"I hope Dyckon finds us soon," Kelly said as they walked briskly away from their pursuers.

"Amen," Dee exclaimed, and sidestepped a rushing squad of seven-year-olds, who came hooting and hurtling along the corridor, adults scattering ahead of them.

Kelly pointed to a coffee shop a short way ahead. "There's a balcony. We can sit there and let Dyckon find us."

"Won't we be discovered?" Dee asked.

"It's possible, but we may be discovered almost anywhere in this mall," Kelly said.

"Then let's do it," said Dee, coming up beside her and stepping out of the chaotic flow of shoppers. "I'd be glad of a glass of sack, I would. It might subdue my choleric humour."

"Tea or coffee is what you'll get. And can you drop the Renaissance?" said Kelly with a nervous laugh. "Just till we're out of here." They went into the coffee shop and up the three steps to the balcony. "There's an empty table at the far end. There by the service door."

"Good," said Dee, and headed toward it.

"I'll go in and get us coffee. What do you want?" Kelly offered.

"You know my wont . . . my taste. I leave it to you," Dee said as he went to sit down. He chose the chair that gave him the widest view of the area and inconspicuously began to take stock of his surroundings. At the next table, four young women in scanty cellophane attire chatted about fashion and entertainment. The next two tables had couples with children, then there was an empty table, and three more with more families. Next was a table with two well-dressed men each consulting their wrist videos and talking to the communicators in them. The last table had a pair of old women hunched over tall glasses of coffee and froth. All of them seemed likely disguises for Dyckon, but Dee impatiently kept searching. The Roc would be alone.

Kelly appeared with two oversized tankards. "This is their mead coffee—they say they have mead in the mix. I thought that sounded Elizabethan."

Dee was dubious, but he held his tongue. "Thank you," he said, careful not to say "gramercy," which sprang to his mouth as he slid the tankard toward him. "The foam is—?"

"Whipped cream. They claim it's the real thing, but who knows?" She sat down, not looking at him, but studying the crowd below them. "I shouldn't sit here with you long." He imperceptibly nodded understanding. "See anything important?"

"Not yet." Dee made a tentative move toward the tankard, then decided it was too hot to sip.

There was a flurry of excitement in front of a Supplies and Buys store as a speaker blared out an announcement of featured savings inside. Several dozen shoppers bolted into the store, and many others slowed to see more of what was going on.

"I feel we're too exposed out here," Dee said as he studied the shifting mass of people.

"No more so than anywhere else," said Kelly. "Drink your coffee."

"Drink yours." Dee took hold of his tankard and prepared to drink.

Kelly sat back and lifted her tankard. "All right." She took a long sip. "Why?"

He took up his tankard. "Not drinking would be conspicuous." The taste was strange, but he managed two good swallows before he put it down again. He decided that indeed there might be mead in the coffee; it was sweet enough. He looked over the crowd as if disinterested, and said, "I hope Dyckon isn't sitting in a similar window seat somewhere in this sector, waiting for us to come by."

"Do you think that's possible?" Kelly asked.

Dee was about to answer when he noticed a blocky, square-headed man surging toward the coffee shop. He stared hard at the man, wondering if this could be Dyckon. Certainly the assertive manner was like the Roc's.

"Excuse me," said a well-modulated voice behind them. "But is that chair taken?"

Dee started looking back over his shoulder, he saw a man of medium height, dressed in a beige sweater, closing the service door, he had just slipped through. There was nothing remarkable about the man, not his hair color, not his clothing. "We're expecting someone," he said, thinking he should investigate what escape might lie behind the door.

"I think that you're expecting me, Doctor," said the ordinary man, and pulled out the chair.

"Dyckon?" Dee asked, surprised. Next to him, Kelly sat a little straighter.

"Yes. I didn't want to stand out, not even in all this." He put a large, white cup on the table and sat down.

Kelly was careful not to stare. "Have you found the other Roc?"

"Do you mean Mattik?" Dyckon asked, nodding his head as if making the acquaintance of Dee and Kelly. After making brief eye contact with Kelly Edwards, he looked away uncomfortably. The old Watcher had qualms about having an uninitiated humani acknowledge him in person. He had spent centuries purposefully hidden from any such interaction.

"Is there another we are looking for?" Dee took another drink.

Dyckon nodded. "Yes. You make your point."

Time was of the essence. "What do you have to report?"

"Very little. But I can tell you that Mattik is looking for another opportunity, and this place is a likely target, particularly after Chicopolis." Dyckon's sigh didn't sound quite human, but not so strange that others would notice. He glanced at Kelly, his features unreadable. "And there is so much of this place. So many humani."

"That there is," Dee agreed. "And like it or not, he could be here, infecting everyone who comes in contact with him."

Kelly took the hint. "I'm going to excuse myself for a little while," she said, taking up her satchel. "Don't stay seated here much longer. I'll keep you in my eyeline," she counseled her employer and, then nodded curtly to Dyckon, "Nice to have met you."

As soon as she was gone, Dee looked around, then

hissed, "You've put us all in a very vulnerable position bringing us here, to this mall, to America. And just to tell us this is a likely target for Mattik. What were you thinking?"

The Roc, taken aback by Dee's vehemence, answered defensively, "I'm sorry, my friend. I had no idea the authorities would be so eager to find you, nor did I know how much their technology has progressed in the last few years."

"Since the death of Fawg and my appearance on that blasted news program, Kelly and d'Winter and I have been hunted without respite. The government's lawful ruffians, the NTSA, crave to know more about you and your sort. The Devil take you, I should just let them have their way and let them pinch us; you've made their job so much the easier by witlessly beguiling us here."

Dyckon spoke urgently. "I'll be brief. I'm going to have to leave the planet soon. My bio-shield that maintains both my altered image and the membrane that prevents contagion is breaking down, and soon I'll be dangerous to humans. I warned you of this when I first showed you the gel. It's bad enough that one Roc is probably spreading the virus. I can't make it worse, which I will if I stay here."

"How soon must you leave?" Dee tried to conceal a sudden stab of emotion. He was being left alone again.

"I will be gone as soon as we're through here," said Dyckon. "I'm sorry to abandon you at this crucial time, but it would be wrong for me to remain. We Roc are historic observers; we must never interfere with your history. That would diminish our credibility with the worlds of the Collegium."

"Oh. Musn't have that," said Dee archly.

"Truly," said Dyckon, seemingly impervious to the sarcasm. "But I must tell you that I have to do all that I can to protect your species. You must find Mattik and Fawg's viruses as quickly as you can. My career in the Collegium depends on it."

"Finding him is difficult," said Dee pointedly, reminded that for Dyckon, saving humanity was merely a political expediency. "I had hoped that for our coming here you would have provided something substantial that would have helped in the search. I'll rely on you to advise us *on something* before you go. Perhaps we should rise and move about for a while."

Dyckon's hands shimmered weirdly. "I don't want to take any more chances in all that confusion. If anything happens to my bio-shield, the whole mall will be exposed, not to mention the pandemonium of seeing me. I'm struggling to maintain this form. Being among so many humani makes it difficult for me to focus. It's less risky sitting here than trying to fight my way through the crowd. Besides, there are security agents approaching."

"How can you be sure?" Dee looked over the crowd again.

"Their communicators make a distinctive squeak that I can hear." Dyckon lowered his head. "It may be more difficult for you getting out than it was getting in."

"And it wasn't easy to get in," said Dee witheringly. "Was it all for naught?"

"I'm afraid so," Dyckon said, shrugging. "I'm sorry I brought you here. It was unwise. I can only attribute it to my frequent use of the metamorphosing gel while hunting for Mattik. I warned you that it breaks down the mind."

"Then we'd best be even more careful." Dee drew a long breath. He had come out of traps before.

Dyckon finished his coffee and slowly rose. "You go. I'll find my own way out the back."

"I'll come with you. Kelly will follow us." Dee volunteered, his anxiety heightened.

"Not unless the two of you can transform yourselves into very heavy rodents." He nodded toward the service door. "That only leads to a utility closet . . . with a rathole."

Dee, no longer capable of sitting on his anger, spat, " I understand. You had no thought of our peril, but took pains to provide a safe retreat for yourself, leaving us to fend for ourselves. How considerate. What a wretched, rash, and ungrateful old fool you are. As I am for trusting in you." He rose from the table. "Kelly and I will try for the parking structure. D'Winter is waiting in the flyer. If we should fail, make use of yourself in informing him."

"I will," said Dyckon.

Dee caught sight of Kelly making her way toward him. "Just in time," he said. Without a second glance at Dyckon, he strode to meet her.

# CHAPTER 16

REED O'NEAL LEANED FORWARD so he could see the display from Four Corners Corridor. He was smiling. "At last," he said to the empty room. He toggled the communicator. "Move in carefully. He may be armed. We don't want a firefight."

The agent in charge of the mall search replied, "Don't worry. We'll get him. We've narrowed him down to Sector G."

"How large are the sectors?" O'Neal asked.

"Three and a half acres," said the agent promptly. "We should complete our sweep in forty minutes. We've got sixty agents on the floor, all searching. Assuming he doesn't move out of the sector, we'll have him. He won't be able to make it out any of the doors, so it's just a matter of time until we catch him. There's no way he can escape."

"He's avoided capture before," O'Neal reminded him.

"Yes." The agent's chagrin came through as loudly as an explosion.

"We don't want that to happen again, do we?" O'Neal

sounded falsely concerned, but he made no apology for his manner.

"No, sir, we don't," said the agent devoutly.

"Get him and you'll be promoted," O'Neal encouraged him.

"And if I fail, I'm out and I'm fried," said the agent.

Bristling at the man's tone of voice, O'Neal considered reprimanding the agent for his insubordination, but changed his mind. He was much too close to victory to spend any time in spiteful digs at lower life-forms. He decided instead to empower his troops. From his desk's lowest drawer the Director retrieved a silver ewer of extra virgin olive oil, a white terrycloth towel, and a small white porcelain bowl. Carefully, he placed the bowl in front of him, the cloth to the right of the bowl, and the ewer above. He removed his Annapolis ring and in a reverent, sonorous key intoned, "Through this holy anointing may the Lord in his love and mercy help us with the grace of the Holy Spirit. May the Lord who frees us from sin save us and raise us up."

He anointed his hands carefully, allowing the thick oil to cover every bit of skin. He did this slowly and reverently, and when he was satisfied with his ministration, dipped a corner of the towel in oil and daubed his forehead, his eyelids, his lips. With elbows on desk and fingers steepled, he prayed for success and the safety of the planet.

A few moments later, the monitor glowed as if in answer to his prayers. He clicked on the interoffice link and said, "Do we have detention quarters prepared?"

"Yes," came the answer.

"Two- or three-room suite?" O'Neal asked, picking up the towel to wipe his hands.

"Three-room," said the man on the other end.

"Fully monitored? Sound, sight, heat, movement?"

"Yes."

It was hard not to gloat, but O'Neal did his best not to be too obvious about it. His hands felt young and smooth. "Very good. What about transport?"

"It's all arranged. There's a prison flyer standing by at Four Corners."

"Excellent. Carry on, Mitchells," said O'Neal, and gave his attention to wiping his forehead and watching the monitor. "Mitchells, you still there?"

"Yes, sir."

"What about medical personnel? Do you have sufficient people there to see to the wounded in case there is a firefight? I want experts there from the Centers for Disease Control. Understand? We have no idea what contamination this man may carry. I don't want the press screaming we went in half-cocked."

"Sir, we'll put Doctor Armstrong and his team in the air in the next fifteen minutes. From CDC, they should be here in thirty minutes, tops. We have three dozen infantry personnel, doctors, and lab techs from Fort Hood stationed outside the mall, and we have established a live hookup with the Centers in Atlanta. A laboratory transport is en route from Dugway." Mitchells obediently waited for any further directives; there weren't any. "It's going to be an important day, sir," said Mitchells before he rang off.

The display from the mall showed a mass of humanity, jostling and bustling—a bit too crowded for easy scrutiny. This was bad for the security forces looking for their quarry. O'Neal put his hands on his desk and leaned back straight in his chair to watch, as if the hunt would go better if he was the picture of command.

"We think he's moving again. He may be on to us," said the agent in the mall.

"Then fan out. You can't afford to let him get away." O'Neal wanted to imbue every word with determination in the hope that the agent would take his cue from his superior and redouble his efforts.

"We think he has someone with him," said the agent.

"A hostage?" O'Neal slapped his hand on his desk. "That's all we need."

"It could be an accomplice," the agent ventured. "Someone's been helping him all along."

O'Neal nodded. "Very true," he said. He scanned his desk blotter for stray droplets of oil. "Make sure you bring the person with him in as well. We'll have a suite prepared for him too."

"Or her," the agent suggested.

"All right. Or her." O'Neal broke the connection abruptly.

# CHAPTER 17

D'WINTER STARTED AS HE heard a warning squawk from his communicator on the encrypted frequency. He hesitated before answering it. "Yes?" he said cautiously. He rarely got messages on this channel, and he was wary of what might be in the scrambled signal.

"Mister d'Winter," said an unfamiliar voice. "This is Dyckon. I am very much afraid that the NTSA has seized the good doctor and his companion."

"What happened?" D'Winter's tone did not betray that his worst fears had been realized.

"There was a force of them in the mall. They were coming for Dee." He paused. "I think it would be wise for you to leave, and soon."

He took it like a bullet. He couldn't really hear Dyckon's words over the flood of emotions cascading through him. When his power of speech came back it was in an angry torrent. "Coming here was bullshit. You screwed him. You betrayed us all. You snake-assed bastard. What the hell were you thinking? You gave us up!"

"I had no idea how dangerous . . . I am sorrier than you can imagine."

"I don't give a flying feague how sorry you are! Where are they? Did you see them taken?" He clung to a shred of hope that Dee and Kelly had eluded their pursuers at the last moment. "Did you see them taken?" he repeated wildly.

"No, but I heard the government transmissions, and the Doctor and the female are definitely in custody. You must—"

D'Winter flipped off the encrypted wavelength and over to the local news link. He listened to the excited report on the capture of foreign aliens at Four Corners, the media implying that there was dangerous smuggling going on, and declaring the operation a triumph for law enforcement.

". . . a harsh reminder of how vulnerable we can be. In these days of easy travel, the activities of smugglers and other criminals have become rampant." The reporter sounded personally affronted by this. "In spite of everything the customs force and the Coast Guard have undertaken, dangerous products are slipped into America by unscrupulous merchants, and our security is threatened with every one of them. The two detained today"—the brief grainy vids definitely were of John Dee and Kelly Edwards—"may be only the first wave of what is supposed to be a major assault on America and Americans."

D'Winter's first impulse was to rescue them. But that was a fool's errand, he told himself. The NTSA wouldn't let him anywhere near them. No, rescue was out of the question. He connected back to Dyckon.

"As I was saying, Mister d'Winter, you must leave now."

"I'll get out in the next five minutes. I'll head for Edmonton. I have a place there."

"Canada might not be safe enough," Dyckon warned.

"Possibly," said d'Winter. "But they'll have to find me first." He was already turning on the various systems of the flyer. "Where are you going?"

"Off planet," said Dyckon. "I'll try to keep in touch."

"Yeah, you do that. And hey, thanks. Thanks for squat," spat d'Winter, and flipped off the channel with a vengeance. "Shit," he muttered as he signaled the tower for clearance to taxi, "I knew this trip would screw us."

"Stand by for a security scan," the tower advised him.

"Where shall I go for that?" d'Winter asked, making sure he didn't sound as vexed as he was.

"Runway 4, the security station at the north end of it." The controller was talking a bit too rapidly. "It shouldn't take long."

"Thanks," d'Winter said, and released the brake on the wheels. As the flyer started to roll, he saw a wedge of security Multi Terrains coming out from the mall, hood-lights blazing, sirens whooping, as they made their way to a security transport waiting on Runway 6. The likelihood that his friends were in one of those and he was powerless to act ate away at him. Of course, they would be coming for him next. He stared at the All Terrains, waiting for something—a sign, a sight of his friends, anything that would give him cause to act.

"Pull over," said a security officer as his air-skiff came alongside d'Winter's flyer. "Just off the runway."

"I know. The tower told me." D'Winter complied with just enough ill grace that he appeared to be like all the other flyer pilots. Was this it? Should he resist?

Another security officer rode up on a skimmer, his

Klaxon sounding. "Prepare for scan. Prepare for scan," the electronic voice announced.

"Scan away," d'Winter said, doing his best to seem slightly bored and reaching for his artillery.

A whiny hum filled the air, and then the electronic voice said, "Scan complete."

"Can I go now?" d'Winter asked when nothing more was announced. He was getting very twitchy waiting.

The security officer in the air-skiff provided the answer. "You'll be allowed on Delta Runway in about five minutes. There's an NTSA transport on Delta now that has priority liftoff. As soon as it's cleared secure airspace, you may depart."

"Thanks," said d'Winter, certain now that Dee and Kelly were in the hands of the NTSA, but unsure if skimmer patrol was faking him out. If he did make it out, if someone had made a royal mistake scanning him, he would have to make the most of his liberty. As for his friends, he reminded himself, they'd been separated from him before. They could take care of themselves. Where there's a will, there's a way, he'd heard Dee say often enough. Then he remembered that it wasn't just freeing his friends but continuing the search for the Roc and the virus that mattered. There was a lot he would have to do in the next twenty-four hours before Kelly and Dee completely vanished into the maw of the NTSA. In a moment of self-recrimination, he flayed himself for having brought them here and not protected them.

"Flyer cleared to leave," said a tinny voice in his ear.

D'Winter didn't need another offer. As hastily as he could without appearing suspicious, he set the flyer hurtling into the sky. He flew on, trying to decide whether to go north or south or west; he was uneasily aware he was being monitored, but was unaware of the most significant watch being kept on him, a surveillance that was relayed almost halfway around the world.

The transport telecommunications system in Theon Celsus' private room pinged.

"Mister Celsus, this is Maxim. Forgive me if I am disturbing you, but just now you received an encrypted message from Dyckon. Shall I forward it now?"

"From Dyckon, most certainly."

It was the audio recording of the conversation between the alien and Dee's bodyguard, Morgan d'Winter. John Dee had been arrested by the NTSA at the Four Corners mall in America. At the end, he heard the old Roc saying, "Philippus, I thought you'd like to know." No one had called him by his real name for a very long time.

# CHAPTER 18

BORIS MICHAILOVICH SHEVYENETZ GAVE Strategy Brooks his very best smile, recognizing her from the many times he had seen her news-vids. "Welcome to Majestic Hotel," he exclaimed, his big burly arms open and wide as the Siberian sky. He bustled from behind the check-in counter, all but bowing her into the lobby. "Thank you for choosing my establishment for your stay in Irkutsk."

Strategy returned his smile. "I'm told you keep a fine table, and that your courtesy is very Old World." She was flirting, but in the practiced, professional way that had become second nature to her.

"How gracious," he said with his hand at her elbow, firmly but politely guiding her to the registration desk. "I need to impress your passport number here," he said exasperatedly but with a twinkle, as if all the government formalities were such a nuisance, "and the voucher of your credit line for charges."

Hernando searched about in his thick coat for his documents. Strategy had both these things ready, and handed them over with something close to a flourish. The innkeeper's playfulness was infectious. "Kind sir, my assistant and I have been traveling all day. Can we get a meal quickly?"

"Most certainly," Boris said, waving his hand as if it were nothing, all the while taking care of recording the material she had given him. "You shall eat soon and you shall eat good," he said as he returned her passport and voucher to her. Taking Hernando's identification, he scrutinized it briefly. "These are seeming in order." He double-checked the nationality. "Many thanks." Dismissing Hernando, he focused his full attention back on Strategy. "What accommodations would Madame prefer?"

"A suite, of course," she said. "With two bedrooms and a sitting room. And private baths, of course."

"Of course," he agreed, acting surprised that he hadn't guessed. "I have three such, and despite the season, two are presently vacant."

"I'll assume you're reserving the better of the two for me." She very nearly batted her eyes at him.

Boris ducked his head. "But of course. That will be the corner suite. It is called the Aral Suite. I took the liberty of lighting a fire. You like fires, yes?" Hernando and Strategy both smiled. "The Caspian Suite is occupied, as I said, and the other suite, the Azov Suite, is vacant. Should the Aral Suite not suit you, then you may move to the Azov Suite. I make fire in there, too. No problem. But from the Aral you can see the Sukachev—the art museum. Two centuries old!" He came out again from behind the counter. "I'll tell the kitchen that you will order a meal as soon as you come down from your suite. The dining room is to the right as you face the main staircase." He touched a buzzer and a skinny kid in a kind of nineteenth-century uniform scurried up to the desk. "These bags to the Aral Suite. Quickly," he said in Mongolian. He switched to English, "Can't you see these are honored guests?" Boris shook his head and looked to Heaven as if the boy were a curse and Boris's perpetual cross to bear.

The teenager reached for the suitcases on the hand trolley and hefted them with surprising ease. He headed for the cage-like elevator without speaking a word.

"Which floor?" Hernando asked.

"Third floor; the corridor on your left," said Boris. "Are you very famished? I have a side of venison that is burning on the spit just now. It will be ready shortly. If you have a bowl of soup and a bit of vodka, the wait shouldn't be too big."

"That sounds lovely," said Strategy, even though she disliked all manner of game meat, Boris's charm was irresistable; he was like a Siberian Santa.

"I'll attend to that while you're getting settled," said Boris with a wink.

"Let's walk up. After all the sitting we could use the exercise," Strategy suggested to Hernando, glancing at the tall, stuffed bear in the case near the registration desk. "The staircase is too grand to miss."

"If you like," said Hernando, who really didn't care.

"Come on, then," she said, and began a stately ascent up the dark-red carpeted stairs, all but posing on the landing. "Maybe we can get some shots of this place. For atmosphere, you know? An interview with Boris? Some local color."

"Sure," said Hernando, who had expected this was coming.

"This is really something," Strategy approved as she climbed past a cluster of stuffed animal heads.

The suite was surprisingly spacious, and the furniture,

although far from modern, was in excellent repair. A long couch with rolled, overstuffed arms and back dominated the sitting room. Three chairs, a desk, and a table completed the furnishing. A large, mahogany-framed architectural design by Vasilyev hung above the couch. A wall-sized vidscreen was embedded in the faded red wall. Across the room, a bank of windows looked out on the street, where they indeed could see the snow-covered art museum with its fine wooden filigree. To the left of the window was a gas fireplace with imitation taiga logs and a fire blazing.

Strategy handed the bellboy a ten-dollar coin and watched him leave. "I think this'll do," she said as she warmed herself in front of the fire.

"I need the bathroom," Hernando said, and chose the most likely door.

Strategy draped her parka over the metal firescreen, a puddle of water forming on the marble hearth floor. Her feet thanked her as she released them from their tightly bound snowboots and rubbed them to restart the circulation. She took a little time to look around the suite. She chose the bedroom with the nicer furnishings, and looked into the mirror to straighten up after the long, rumpling demands of travel. She was just finishing her repairs when Hernando appeared in the door behind her.

"Ready to eat?" she asked.

"I haven't had venison—not real venison—before. Just the technomeat that's called venison," he said, sounding more wary than pleased.

"My daddy in Austin used to hunt buck, but I haven't had any since I was this high. Where's your sense of adventure, Nando? You might not have this chance again." She flicked her comb through her hair one last time. "Let's go. Do you have the code for the door?"

"Yep." He shrugged into his charcoal-leather jacket as she brushed past him to find more comfortable shoes in her bag.

The dining room was dark and seemed huge. There were three other people in it that Strategy could see, a well-tailored woman wearing a mink, who occupied a large booth all alone, three platters laid before her and a second, unused dinner plate at her left elbow. Something about her hairstyle said American to Strategy. The other two men were Mongolian, by the look of their clothes, and they huddled in a secluded booth as if intending to be invisible.

"I guess we just choose a table," said Hernando, looking about for a maître d'.

"I guess," Strategy agreed, and selected a large table not quite in the center of the room. Its chairs were upholstered in deep-red velvet, matching the wallpaper with its flocked scrolls. The china was white with blue-and-gold borders, the silverware antique, and the napery of thick, soft linen. "This place is quite a find. So much more real than the Sheraton."

"In Irkutsk—who'd've thought it?" said Hernando in disbelief. "I haven't seen anything like this outside of Old Prague."

Before Strategy could say any more, Boris came bustling up to them, large menus in embossed leather covers held out to them.

"And you're the waiter, too," Hernando quipped.

"When we have special guests." Boris beamed at Strategy. "The venison is just done. To begin I have soup with pelmeni, and then shashlik. The venison will be main course, with marinated vegetables."

"What kind of soup?" Strategy asked, to keep him talking.

Boris raised both hands to his full cheeks as if the very thought of the soup's ingredients were an ecstatic experience. "It is made with fish stock made from *omul,* then herbs are added for flavor and fortification. Last, little dumplings, pelmeni, made with pepper and cheese inside them, go into the soup, and they simmer together for half an hour, until the dumplings are cooked but not soggy." He exhaled with gusto. "It is ready now. Let me bring you each a bowl of it. Hit the spot."

"Fine with me," said Strategy, and glanced at Hernando, who was studying the many-paged menu with real curiosity.

"Do you really have bear steaks?" he asked.

Boris shook his head. "Not tonight. If you would like to try, give me a day or so, and you shall have as much as you want."

Hernando shook his head. "No, thanks anyway."

"As you wish. I do have some wild boar in the freezer. I could make a steak for you tomorrow, yes? In a sauce of port and bittersweet chocolate with shallots. Or, if you like better, I could buy some"—here Boris did a bad impression of an actor from an old John Wayne movie—"western imported barbecue sauce. You decide while I go fetch soup." With that, he bolted away.

"Well?" Hernando asked. "What do you think?"

"I think he's got something to hide. He's being much too genial," said Strategy.

"Isn't that a bit cynical?" Hernando asked, although he agreed with her. "Maybe he's just got a crush on the vid-star?"

"It may be," said Strategy. "But I wouldn't bet on it. Still, he is charming."

Hernando lowered his voice and his eyes. "You saw who's sitting in the booth, didn't you?"

"No, who?" Strategy motioned Hernando to tell.

"Leeta O'Conner."

"You're dreaming." She swiveled her head to stare at the lady alone at the table. "She died in the fire." All Strategy could see was the woman's back. The fur masked her body type.

"Then this woman is her twin. I got a good look at her face when Boris just went over. Why don't I go ask her?"

"Not now." Strategy moved Hernando's menu aside so she could stare at him directly. "For one thing, I'm telling you she died in the fire, and for another, I'm hungry. I want to eat. We can investigate later." Strategy turned again to stare, her mind working. "The truth is, the body was never found."

"You think she knows you're here?" Hernando asked.

Before she could answer, Boris marched out of the kitchen holding a wide, beautifully painted tray with two basin-sized soup bowls from which fragrant steam arose. "I hope you have good appetites," he said as he set the bowls before Strategy and Hernando. "I'll bring you a bottle of wine, Hungarian. I have Bulls' Blood and a dry Tokay."

"You know the food. Bring us whichever you think is best," said Strategy as she picked up her soupspoon. "By the way, is that woman"—she gestured toward the lone diner—"a guest here at the hotel?"

"Yes, she is. Bon appétit!" And Boris was off again, calling to the restaurant staff as if they were a team of reindeer.

With a grateful sigh, Strategy dug into her first meal in Irkutsk.

# CHAPTER
# 19

ALL THE LIGHTS ALMOST blinded Reed O'Neal as he faced the media gathered on the steps of the NTSA headquarters. The reflection from the recent snow made the glare worse than usual. He briefly shaded his eyes, not wanting to appear to be concealing anything, not even his face. "Ladies and gentlemen," he said, using the old-fashioned phrase to catch their attention. "Please. I only have a short time—" He waited for the various reporters and vid-ers to jockey into position. He heard his name being called by dozens of photographers, all trying to get his attention and a full shot of his face. Made obdurate by the blinding glare and the cold, he refused to give them the satisfaction. He upbraided himself for not leaving this announcement to Anders; the media would have made less of the occasion. Although he secretly liked seeing his name and photo in the papers, he asked himself again how anyone could stand to face these vultures all the time and only for the dubious privilege of getting elected. He'd rather walk through radioactive slag than have to deal with the media every waking hour, always looking over your shoulder in case someone might be watching, and having to answer for everything you did to any fool who had ever cast a ballot. As the crowd came to order, he looked at his prepared notes one more time. "There's been an arrest made at Four Corners Corridor mall by the NTSA, and the detained parties are being brought to our headquarters," he said a bit stiffly.

The volley of questions that erupted after this announcement was deafening and incomprehensible.

O'Neal held up his hands. "Please, please. Let me finish." He waited while the sound diminished. "We have no more information just now. We know that the networks covered the removal of the arrested parties, and we want to reassure the world that there is no reason for worry. The National Terrestrial Security Administration has a duty to this planet to contain any potential hazard, but we also have a responsibility not to cause undue alarm, and until we determine the level of risk the arrested parties represent, if any, I won't speculate."

More questions burst forth as the reporters strove to be heard. Bits of questions came out of the babble: ". . . any danger to . . ." ". . . why did you arrest . . ." ". . . who is it?" ". . . how many people did you . . ."

O'Neal let the questions continue for a short while, then cleared his throat.

"Mister Director!" one of the media people bellowed. "What's this really about?"

"We don't know yet. That's why we've detained . . . the persons we've detained. They may provide a critical intelligence resource." Deciding that he sounded evasive, he held up both hands for silence and continued. "Let me make this perfectly clear: so far as we know now, the persons arrested present no immediate danger to the world, but we believe they may have crucial information that could be important in terms of terrestrial security."

"How do you mean?" shouted a well-known reporter from one of the Viacom networks.

"I can't discuss this yet. As soon as we learn what we need to know, you'll be informed." He hated this part of his job.

"Who did you arrest?" another reporter yelled.

"No comment," said O'Neal bluntly.

"You know who it is," a handsome man in the front row accused him.

"No comment," said O'Neal.

"Not American, is that it?" another called out.

"Again, I cannot comment on that," O'Neal insisted. He turned away from the temporary podium and prepared to go back into his headquarters.

A ragged chorus pursued him. "Mister Director! Mister Director!" The flashing lights assured him that the next day's newspapers would be filled with photos of his back, straight with purpose, as he headed inside to do his job.

Inside the enormous lobby, O'Neal stopped at the security desk. "I'm not in to anyone but Senator Havers," he said to the imposing black guard.

"Only Senator Havers—yes, sir," said the guard as he cleared O'Neal around the security checkpoint. "And the President?"

"Yes, of course," came out less brusque than he had wanted.

Riding up in the elevator, O'Neal let himself think about the capture of the chipless man. Who was he, and how had he contrived to avoid being chipped? No one on Earth had succeeded in doing that for more than forty years. This problem gripped him like a hand to his throat, and the more he thought about it, the more it troubled him. When they had first lost him in Angel City, Courwitz had speculated in a debriefing that he'd become dinner for the Untouchables or gone into the caves with Piper and his rat people. His whereabouts were an unsolved mystery for more than a year and a half before surveillance picked him up again on a train heading for San Luis Obispo. He managed to elude the NTSA again, and his escape gave a black eye to the FBI. The Bureau would have insisted on a crack at him if O'Neal had shared intelligence. But he'd be damned if he would do that; the absence of ID chips was most definitely under his jurisdiction. The cipher's appearance days later in close proximity to the alien shape-shifter made him the Bureau's number one priority. It had taken months, but now they had him. The gnawing questions were: Who was he? What did he know? And what could he tell them about an alien threat? As he emerged from the elevator, Margaret Gris was waiting for him, a notebook open in her hands. "What news?" O'Neal asked her.

"They'll be landing shortly. We're setting them down at our private field in Oxon Hill and we'll bring them in under armed escort," she said, a tight little smile on her face.

"What have they said so far?" O'Neal asked.

"No information on that," Margaret admitted as if embarrassed by her lack.

"Have we got a pharmaceutical warrant?" O'Neal was almost to his office, but he halted and stared at Margaret.

"Not yet," Margaret hedged. "It may have to go all the way to the Supremes."

"Oh, shit," said O'Neal. "That's going to take time, and that is the one thing we haven't got to spare." He resumed walking, letting Margaret struggle to keep up with him. "I'm going to need to talk to Havers before the day is out."

"Shall I arrange a call for you?" She held her wrist-register at the ready.

"Not quite yet. I want those two in the detention suites before I talk to anyone outside of this agency. Is that clear?" He fixed her with a hard stare.

"Yes, sir," she said, and moved away from him as he waved to dismiss her.

Lois Middleton, his executive assistant and official door-dragon, handed him a memo-chip. "Thirty-nine inquiries," she said as he swept past her.

"Yes, yes," he said, taking the memo-chip as he reached his door. He shut it behind him and crossed the carpet to his desk. For once his luxurious surroundings didn't please him. What was the use of being the power behind the throne if he was to be subjected to the same scrutiny politicians were? He sat down and reached for his antique palmtop. Using the stylus, he tapped in a secure number and waited while the connection was made.

"Vassili," he said when the call was answered.

"Reed," said the head of Russian Central Security. "What can I do for you?"

"It's more a question of what I can do for you," said O'Neal in impeccable Russian.

"Ah?" Vassili Illych Dorokin did his best to sound only mildly interested. "And what might that be?"

"There is a newswoman in Siberia, currently in Irkutsk on assignment for GNN. She says she is looking for mining installations, but she may have other plans." O'Neal enjoyed the sudden rush of satisfaction that came over him.

"What sort of plans?" Vassili asked.

"I leave that to you to find out," said O'Neal, and broke the connection. He sat for a short while relishing what he had set in motion. Then he sighed and asked Lois Middleton to get Senator Nathaniel Havers on the phone.

# CHAPTER 20

THE SPRAWLING CITY OF Oxon Hill lay beneath the descending flyer, the lights of the airport reflecting off the thin mantle of snow. There being no windows in the plane, Dee and Kelly were unable to appreciate the view. The carrier banked around to line up with the runway, then touched down with hardly a bump.

"Stay in your seats," said the nearest guard, looking from Kelly to Dee and back again. Diagonally across his chest, he gripped a massive rifle that appeared more appropriate for hunting elephants or tanks than shooting men. Each of the NTSA troopers held one. The weapons' size held a secret, Dee thought, one that bore deciphering. "And don't move until you're told."

"Aye," Dee sighed. Soldiers still gave the same orders as they did five hundred years ago. But at least, this one had said *something*! He had been feigning sleep for the last half-hour, striving for the opportunity to think his way out of their dilemma. He had hoped to hear some mention of what their fate was to be, but the men on the transport had been as silent as stones. He and Kelly had exchanged no more than a dozen words since their capture, knowing everything they said would be monitored and recorded. Sleepily he rubbed his hands over his eyes and brow, "Even should we escape from this flyer unharmed, how far could we fly? There are half a score of you and two of us and there are sentries at the border of the airfield. The odds are in your favor." Dee was disappointed when he saw no reaction on the faces of the men. Since their capture, he had frustratingly learned nothing at all.

"That's an odd accent you got there," suddenly remarked another of the guards, unmistakably from one of the deep southern states. "Where you from?" They wore NTSA uniforms but with no name badges or rank designations.

"My lad, you are as open as a book," said Dee. "You'll have to do better than that."

"When are you going to let us call our attorney?" Kelly demanded, facing the guard who sat beside her. There was a jittery sound to her voice. The air in the military transport was at a moderately cool temperature, presumably to keep the guards at maximum attention, but she was dressed for the torrid heat of Four Corners, and the lightweight materials of her short-sleeved tunic did nothing to keep the nipping air from prickling her skin and making her teeth chatter. She had asked for a blanket but had gotten no response. Dee, making an attempt to put his arm around her, had been slammed back in his seat. Her guard made no effort to answer but continued to stare at her as he had all during the trip.

"That there's being decided," said the talkative scarecrow from Dixie in front of Dee. His grip on his cannon was a little looser than the others'.

"We have a right to call our attorney," Kelly insisted.

"And y'all will get your call," said the guard, delighted with his self-importance.

"When?" Kelly glared at him.

At that moment, David Hudson, the officer in charge swung his thick torso around in his seat and looked at the southern boy. It was a look of reproach filled with censure and loathing—one that Cosimo de' Medici would have been proud of. The boy slunk away a little farther down the fuselage. Dee silently cursed. Hudson turned back to Kelly with a patronizing grin, his chins doubling. "Miss Edwards, you know as well as I that the NTSA can suspend such privileges—"

"Rights," she corrected him. Her jaw locked in a spasm of cold.

He paid no attention to her interjection or her distress. "—when it deems it necessary for the safety of the earth."

"In other words, you're suspending our constitutional rights," said Kelly.

"I wouldn't put it that way," said Hudson.

"Why doesn't that surprise me?" Kelly asked with heavy sarcasm.

Dee could see that the bulldog was becoming garrulous, and he decided to speak up. "Where are you going to take us? Can you tell us that, at least?"

"The NTSA has secure facilities."

"We're going to prison," Kelly said, explaining the obvious in an excoriating tone. "Without any charge filed against us, or public notice of where we're being held. You won't even let us call our families." If we had any, she purposefully neglected to say.

"You're going to secure facilities," the officer repeated,

and signaled to his men. "Up." He nudged Dee's shoulder. "You can unfasten your harness now. You, too," he added to Kelly.

"I guess the transport has arrived," said Kelly, none of her defiance faded.

"Three of them, and an escort of patrol cars," said Hudson even while he was actively listening to his new orders on an imperceptible earpiece. At least that was informative, thought Dee.

"Oh," said Kelly as she stood up. "We must be very dangerous." She raked a contemptuous glance over the leader of the guards. "Ten of you, and all the troopers outside."

The nearest guard hefted his weapon. He didn't need to speak. The threat of the gun was obvious. But it seemed to Kelly that his unsparing stare was more unnerving than his oversized weapon. He was so creepy she instinctively backed away. Hudson, misunderstanding, rattled her cage, "Lady, we ain't gonna kill you, just take out your legs."

Kelly shrugged. "I'm terrified," she said, summoning sarcasm to hide her all-too-real fear.

Dee unfastened his harness and rose slowly. "We're not going to do anything foolish."

"That's certain," said the hill of flesh as his large hand reached for the metal door latch. "Three of us will go out first, then you"—he pointed to Kelly—"then one of us, and then you." He pointed to Dee. "Then the rest of us. You'll find Federal marshals waiting below, and the airport security guards all on alert."

Aha, thought Dee, d'Winter had been right about airport security. Perhaps he had been right about other aspects as well.

"You've made your point," said Dee. He briefly considered d'Winter's safety. He had heard nothing to make him think that d'Winter had been captured, but then he'd heard so little. Perhaps Dyckon, that cowardly dragon, had at least had the courage to warn Morgan before slithering away.

As the large sliding door slammed open, Dee's reverie was blasted by the shock of winter air that assailed them in the transport. He immediately looked at Kelly and watched her standing body cramp into a quasi-hunched position, her knees and shoulders visibly vibrating, her unprotected arms crisscrossed over her chest, her head ducked down against the onrush of wind. Without a word, the southerner yanked her up and thrust her toward the door of the plane. She stumbled. Dee could do nothing but bark his disapproval.

They got out of the flyer just as the guard ordered, and shortly they and four of their guards were in a heavily armored all-terrain transport, lights flashing and tires squealing as they barreled out of the airport, their escorts around them. Dee held fast to his seat each time they rounded a corner. The loose material of Kelly's wide trouser legs flapped with the turns. The guards were never off balance in any way.

"Are you all right?"

She nodded vigorously. The vehicle was slightly heated, but it would take a while for her to unclench her hands or loosen her jaw. Her exposed skin had an almost bluish color, and he thought he saw a wetness around her eyes.

"How far do you think we have to go?" Dee asked Kelly when they had been on the road about ten minutes.

"If we're going into Washington itself, we'll probably

be there within the hour. If they've got another prison, who knows?" she said, no strength now in her voice. The cold, the rudeness, and the fear of the unknown had taken their toll, and she had lost her anger and begun to panic. She caught her lower lip between her teeth.

Dee half-expected the guards to order them to be quiet, but they didn't. They just stood as they had before, like monuments, hands firmly gripping their weapons and continuing to stare, intently focused on their two captives.

"What sort of gaol have they?" Dee asked. He had been in cells before, and he wasn't looking forward to being in one again. He hoped they wouldn't manacle them—the numbing of the hands and the feet, that was the hardest to bear. Impossible to stand or hold anything for days after the release. He didn't want to picture Kelly Edwards helpless like that—not when he was guilty of putting her there.

"Officially they don't. The NTSA is very secretive, and Reed O'Neal likes it that way," she said bitterly.

"Who is he?" Dee asked, hoping to dislodge that lip from between her teeth. The need to answer questions could often take one's mind off fear.

"He's the Director-General of the NTSA. Presidents have less power than he," said Kelly, and looked at the nearest guard as if expecting a rebuke. None followed.

Dee thought back to the various members of Elizabeth's Privy Council, especially Burghley and Walsingham, and nodded. "One of those who plies his trade in the shadows."

"Yes," Kelly agreed as she stared at her unkempt reflection in the darkened window. "One of them."

# CHAPTER 21

MATTIK WAS IN HIS Corwin Tarlton form again, but with a distinctly Latin look. His skin was browner, he was more thickset, his face rounder and fleshier, his shoulders a little more stooped. He stood in a kiosk outside the enormous Mexico City mall along with fifty shoppers. He was hot and nervous, trying to decide if he should risk entering the mall. Mexico City, with its forty-four million inhabitants, was a wonderful target for his mission—so many shoppers—and the mall added another three-quarter million humani from all of the Americas to the mix. Ordinarily he would not have hesitated, but almost instantly since the world's discovery of Fawg, security had been universally increased tenfold. A half-dozen NTSA Federales were methodically scanning lines of people as they entered the center. He knew he wouldn't be able to get inside the huge glass walls, not without a humani chip. After Chicopolis, his jammer had been useless and, despite several attempts, he hadn't been able to secure another one. Remembering that the work ethic was more easygoing here than in the States, he had come to Mexico expecting easier access to a megamall. Under a sweltering sun that heated smoggy layers of thin air, he was utterly amazed to find that he'd been wrong. Speakers blared out instructions for shoppers in six languages, with assurances that the extra guards were there for the safety of the public. The security here was tighter than Boca-Miami or even Waco.

His bio-shield was holding up quite well, but he knew if he removed even a small part of it in the mall, with the merest touch the virus he carried would spread rapidly, bringing spontaneous shape-changing to anyone infected and then a soulless loss of self. He knew also that continued contact with the virus was affecting his mental abilities. It was getting progressively harder to reason.

"Step into the shuttle from the left and exit on the right," the speakers intoned as the shuttle approached the kiosk.

"You getting in?" the driver asked Tarlton in Spanish after all the other waiting shoppers had climbed aboard. His universal translator hissed the meaning into his mind. Though he appeared to the Mexicans like a citizen, the Roc was incapable of speaking the language, he just shook his head and mutely waved to the driver, hoping he'd drive away. Instead, he got a kindly warning, "It's twenty minutes until the next shuttle comes."

Mattik shrugged his shoulders and pointed at his watch in the manner he had for centuries seen so many male humani make when they were forced to wait for their forever tardy wives. Understanding, the shuttle driver saluted in sympathy and Mattik stepped back from the shuttle. The driver looked up at his rearview mirror, smiled at him, and closed the doors, leaving Mattik alone in the kiosk. The humani had so many languageless communications. Over the course of his visit to Earth, his responsibility had been to study its religions; the study of language had been left to another. He regretted that now. Turning around and seeing hundreds of people file through the wide doors, Mattik watched in frustration and forgot to sweat.

For ten minutes Mattik stood, lost in thought. He could go into the heart of the city and walk along the street with his bio-shield off, but then his disguise would be lost and he might be caught, which would make for more trouble than he wanted. He shoved that choice away quickly. The ugliness and cruelty of Fawg's annihilation played over and over again in his mind as it had endlessly replayed on his vidscreen that day in Houston. This world had seen a Roc, and their instinctual fear prompted them to mindless murder. More than murder. Massacre. He saw again the army of misfits riddle his master with dozens of oozing holes and heard again the thundering explosion that scattered parts of him everywhere. It had been unimaginable, unthinkable, but—after close observation of countless generations of humani—utterly expected. And now this frightened world was looking for him. With no one to turn to for guidance or leadership, Mattik chafed at being alone. He had trusted his master to always be there for him. A flailing feeling of panic rose in him, like the horror of becoming untethered in weightless, airless space. In his thoughts, Mattik listened again to the calm commanding voice—Fawg had always spoken so well—precisely instructing him how to release the virus in gigantic malls. The memory of his clan leader's orders soothed him. Mattik grew proud again as he recalled Fawg describing the glory that their actions would bring to Clan set-ut.

It was a testament to Fawg set-ut's training that Mattik

never had the creativity to waiver from his master's plan of invading the humani centers disguised as anything other than a man. It never occurred to him to crawl, slither, or fly in. Nor did it then occur to him that after succeeding in his mission and converting humanity into a mindless army, he would have neither Fawg nor a clan leader to transfer them to. He had neither a ship to get off-world nor a communications device to beg rescue. He certainly didn't think himself capable of leading a world alone. When he thought about it at all, he assumed Fawg in his wisdom had made plans for this contingency. Thus, thwarted by security and utterly on his own, Mattik reluctantly walked away from the kiosk into the maze of the three hundred acres of parking. Retracing his route to the cargo transport that had brought him, he retrieved some food, his travel bag, and the cold storage unit that maintained the vials of virus. Looking for another of the all-terrain transports carrying goods to the mall, he hoped to steal a ride to another population center. It was far too dangerous to travel any other way. He searched the rows of transports for signs for international companies, and found one from the All Asia Trading Company with travel decals for the Bengal Link. This would give him a chance to leave the continent. For the last three hundred years, he thought, the Asian subcontinent has not kept up with the technological advances of the West. And there were certainly more humani living there. Asia would solve all of Mattik's problems, he resolved. Cautiously he went around the transport, checking the cargo hold. Finding it open and empty, he climbed in, changed his shape to that of a large stack of packing padding, and settled down to wait for the pilot to return.

By sundown he was on his way to Acapulco and the Asian shipping lanes. He returned to his natural Roc form and made himself as comfortable as he could in the confines of the transport and settled in for the long journey from Acapulco to the Bay of Bengal.

While in transit, the panic attacks returned.

# CHAPTER 22

THE DOOR DIDN'T CLANG shut, it sizzled, reminding Dee of the first kindling of the heretics' pyres that had blazed in Queen Mary's reign, as well as Elizabeth's. There were no bars, nor visible locks anywhere; the walls were translucent, high-test plastic that sealed seamlessly, making Dee feel that he had been caught in a large box of unusually solid fog. When Dee pushed on the place where the door had been, nothing happened. He tapped at the wall, but found no difference in the tone of it anywhere. It was like being in an alabaster sarcophagus, and many men might find it claustrophobic, but John Dee, who had been in far less accommodating prisons than this one, didn't find it so. He had been confined in dungeons, towers, wells, and pits made to hold wild animals. Most had been dark and damp, and all had been cold enough to freeze his marrow and wrench his guts. The cold palsies had often left him a wriggling loathsome worm of a thing. But this warm, light chamber was better than what most monks enjoyed, and Dee settled into it with guarded optimism. The one thing he missed was a window. He would have liked to see his old companions, the constellations. He'd long since learned that a modern city's lighting eclipsed that of the stars and that the night sky was devoid of any heavenly bodies. It was, sadly, to his mind an inverted bowl of dark loneliness. Perhaps not having a window was preferable, he decided. Without a view, he could persuade himself that the world he had been stolen from was still out there, just out of sight. Just as he knew God was out here. Just as he knew that Morgan was most assuredly out there and would do all in his power to rescue him and Kelly. His faith gave him the assurance that neither his Lord nor his servant would desert them.

The cell was six strides by seven-and-a-half strides, or about eleven by thirteen feet—generous dimensions considering what Dee had endured before. The floor was green and looked like marble or blue cheese and, like marble, was slightly cooler than the air around it. A sink and a toilet occupied one corner, with a single towel and a tissue dispenser ready for his use. He made note of them and studied the other updated penal accommodations. A platform bed shaped itself to his form when he stretched out on it experimentally, warming and shifting with his every movement. There were three pillows, of a pliant substance that modified shape to suit him. Aside from the bed there was an overstuffed chair of the same green as a Norfolk marsh; it, too, adjusted to his body when he sat in it. The upholstery was worn and faded, suggesting a great deal of use but made of a durable fabric, unknown to the doctor, that allowed no smirch or stain. There were initials and other, less savory things scratched on its elephantine legs. Had he any instrument that would help him to do it, Dee would have added his own graffiti to what was there, but all items with an edge on them had been taken from him upon his imprisonment.

Looking up, he saw suspended from the ceiling a vidset with segmented displays showing the range of channels the vidset could access—all of them devoted to the news form of entertainment. "GNN," he said. He followed the instructions beneath the monitor and watched for a while, seeing two versions of Reed O'Neal's brief announcement of his—anonymous—arrest. The event palled quickly, and he ordered the vidset back into wait mode. He preferred the company of his own thoughts to the nattering on the screen.

Over the next hour or so, his curiosity prompted him to reactivate the vidset. Part of the presentation featured vid-clips of Yeshua/Fawg's battle in Angel City, the rat-soldiers swarming up the hills. There was no mention that Yeshua might be an alien, in spite of the sheen of scales on his face. Instead there was talk of disguises and projected distortion fields, and various assurances that no alien could possibly visit Earth without quickly being detected. Dee listened to the glib explanation of the rat-soldiers: virus-spawned skin conditions, or perhaps some sophisticated facial appliance. The battle in the Hollywood Hills was old news, and he knew official obfuscation had done its work on the case. Misdirection was an old game. When the Privy Council had publicized the contrived Babington plot to murder the Queen, England had been swept by wild talk and half-truths. Englishmen, filled with wine and fears of Catholic rebellion, believed Rome threatened them all. Irrationality and rumor had prevailed. Dee sighed and ordered the vidset off again.

At another time he might have prayed, but in this

place he worried what prayers might reveal to listeners other than God. From what Kelly and d'Winter had told him, eavesdropping was one of the principle activities of the NTSA. This being their prison, that must mean every breath he took was monitored. He consoled himself with the near certainty that d'Winter had escaped. So long as d'Winter was free, he had hope, for it meant he had an ally beyond the walls. *Si fortuna me tormenta, spero contenta.* D'Winter had a dozen hidey-holes in various places around the world, and he must have reached one of them by now. If only Dee could get in touch with him, he could use his Enochian code to supply d'Winter with needed information. To do that end, he would have liked a writing tablet, but knew it would be foolish to put any of his cipher on paper as it would surely be seized and, in time, decoded. The stratagem would die aborning; nevertheless, he painstakingly worked out the letter substitutions and the details of a message in his head. The mental exercise kept darker thoughts at bay. It took him almost three hours to compose the coded message revealing limited details of his confinement. When it was done, he laughed at all his pains. But he had passed the time, and he had enjoyed doing it.

A musical buzzer announced the arrival of food, and a moment later a slot opened in the wall and a covered tray was slid in, a large mug of coffee and a bottle of mineral water accompanying whatever was under the lid. Dee went to take the tray, wondering if the food was safe to eat. It smelled appetizing enough—a distinct improvement on the meager fare he had been given in the dungeons of his own century. Then, he had feared poison, now he was on guard against drugs put into food that would drive one mad, or cause one's tongue to wag beyond remedy. Reluctantly, he pushed the tray away, not knowing how many times in the future he'd be able to do that. Like a fervent *religieuse,* he chose to mollify his hunger with spiritual meditation. Eventually the slot opened again and the tray was removed. Momentarily sorry to see it go, he was soon relieved not to be further tempted. The prayer helped. His thoughts circled back to the recycled air. Though he had learned that such air was dehydrating, he had not dared to drink the coffee or the bottled water, deciding that he could risk the sink. The quality of the water might not be the best, but it was more apt to be free from drugs. He stepped to the sink and looked for spigots or other means to turn it on. Suddenly a stream of lukewarm water gushed out, splashing the front of his jacket and surprising him. He jumped back and the water ceased to flow.

"Ah," he said, allowing himself that much of a reaction. He went back to the sink, and, prepared this time, cupped his hands and put them under the spout, prepared to catch as much of the water as he could. When his hands were full, he bent and drank from them, then repeated the process until his thirst was gone. After an interval, he dutifully revisited in his mind the encrypted message for Morgan and found happily that he'd had no loss of mental dexterity. So far as he could tell, he had suffered no ill effects from the tap water.

Lying down on the bed, he felt it begin to warm. It wasn't an unpleasant sensation, but he found it unnerving. A short while later, he sat up and put himself into a trance-like state of mind, the sort of discipline he had used when scrying. For that, he had focused on an "angelical stone" to conjure up what he had thought were heavenly beings, but had learned were really holographic communications from Dyckon. How proudly he had reveled in those manifestations and the glory of genuine intercourse with the Unseen, but his pride had betrayed him. Now if he thought of the Roc at all, he thought of slitting his fleshy throat and ripping out his black deceiving heart. By dint of will, as he sat on his bed, he put aside thoughts of revenge. With no crystal stone, he fixed on his breathing and the positive powers of his psyche. He focused on being one with his soul, with what he had been taught was God's angel in man. This mental discipline took him back over the centuries to his own time, to Mortlake and the pleasures of his library. He transported himself through the rooms, lingering to bask in the remembered mellow sunlight that fell in through the heavy draperies on the east side of the house. In a remote part of his mind he wondered if perhaps his servants might perceive his misty outline and report that the building was haunted. Heaven knew more than haunting was believed of him in England in his own century.

An unexpected screech from the vidset announced that four hundred shoppers at the Four Corners Corridor Mall had been put into quarantine because of possible exposure to an unknown toxin. This alarmed Dee, and he came out of his trance to watch the flashy reporter declaim, "The NTSA has released a statement advising everyone who has shopped at Four Corners in the last seventy-two hours to report to their local NTSA field office for a screening. The test is painless, brief, and free to anyone taking it. The purpose is to avert a possible public health crisis. The National Centers for Disease Control ask that anyone with an unexplainable rash or other sudden skin condition report to one of their field offices as well. The toxin in question can cause serious secondary problems and may spread to others."

"Oh, wickedly cunning, they will bruit it about that Kelly and I are the source of the contagion," Dee said to the vidset, and looked around, certain he had been overheard.

"While there is no reason for public alarm," the reporter went on smoothly, "there are public safety concerns that need to be addressed."

Dee shook his head at this temerity. "Tomfoolery and mischief."

A fizz from a place in the opposite wall warned that the undetectable door was opening, and a moment later a tall man came into the cell. "What mischief?" he asked in his colorless voice.

The readout on the television read 3:00 P.M. The visitor, his first since being locked up, was in his fifties, with a kind face and a determined look. This gave Dee hope. But there was also a twinge of fear in his eye, but fear of what? To gain the advantage, Dee told himself he would have to learn that quickly. In his right hand, Dee's uninvited guest carried a machine that the Doctor recognized as a recording device and a stainless steel cup. In his left was a thin folder with not much in it. The badge over his coat pocket read DARYL ANDERS and, in smaller letters below it, NTSA. The agent peered at Dee for an extended moment as though he didn't know where to start.

So Dee took the initiative, "God bless your worship. How does your worship this fine day?"

The pleasantry seemed to rouse the keeper to his task. He turned on the recording device. "Good afternoon. My name is Special Agent Daryl Anders. I am with the United States National Terrestrial Security Administration." He looked down and read a card that sat on the outside of his file, "I am here to start the questioning regarding your lack of an internationally mandated bio-chip and any and all connections you may have had with alien intelligence. Primarily, you have been found in violation of United Nations Resolution 102005, which makes it mandatory that all citizens of the world have bio-chip identification implanted in them. The lack of such a chip is punishable by placing said person into the custody of the government that discovers the violation. Secondarily, we have reason to believe that you have been consorting with alien intelligence. Therefore, you are hereby remanded to the federal facility in Arlington, Virginia, under a warrant from the United States Foreign Intelligence Surveillance Act court. You are in custody until either NTSA or the court deems it fit to have you released. You are under suspicion of being an agent for a hostile alien power whose intent is to commit acts of terrorism. FISA has found you to be an enemy combatant."

"If you are saying I'm a terrorist, you're wrong."

Agent Anders looked up from his reading, seemingly relieved to be done with stating the obvious. "That is immaterial. You are being detained simply to allow us to gather intelligence on the hostile that was discovered in Angel City as well as to answer questions concerning a confirmed sighting of an alien spacecraft over nearly the same area two years before. As well as one on the day and in the place that you were taken into custody. Your innocence or guilt of the charge has nothing to do with your being detained. "You are here on matters of national security, and we have the right to question you."

John Dee was not totally surprised by Agent Daryl Anders's statement. Both Morgan and Kelly had taken pains to educate their employer on what the scenario might be if he was arrested. "To be held as an enemy combatant, I must be a soldier in a war sanctioned by the United States Congress. What war is the United States engaged in?"

The gangly man was unabashed by the question and with a very straight face answered, "The War on Terrorism by Extraterrestrial Hostiles. Congress approved the war status sixty years ago at the founding of the NTSA. It is a founding tenet of our Charter." With the priggishness of a schoolmarm, he wagged his index finger at Dee. "And . . . we both know you don't have a chip."

There was no denying that was true and readily provable. Dee decided to reserve any further legal squabbling over jurisdiction until later. Instead, he followed another line of defense from his lessons, "I should like an attorney."

"I'm afraid as an enemy combatant you are not permitted legal counsel, as you are primarily here for questioning. Legal counsel inhibits the flow of information. As to the matter of the bio-chip, when the government decides the severity of the matter, a trial will be set up, and then you will be permitted a lawyer."

"Nay, but you may not hold me against my will. I have rights."

"I'm afraid sir, in cases of terrorist enemy combatants, habeas corpus and peacetime civil rights are suspended."

"Then may I be allowed to have access to my friends?"

"No, sir, you may not. You are held incommunicado."

"I am a British citizen and demand to talk to the English ambassador or a member of his staff. That is my privilege under the Vienna Convention."

"I will report that to my superiors. However, in the meantime, I must ask you for proof of your right to make such a request. Could you tell me where and when you were born and how it is that a bio-chip was not implanted in you at that time."

"I was born in London"—Dee hesitated warily—"in '57."

"That would make you 45? Right?"

Give or take several centuries, Dee thought, "Yes," he said aloud. "As to the missing chip, I know not why it wasn't implanted. You'll have to inquire of my mother's obstetrician. I was a babe at the time and knew not to insist on having one."

"As to that, sir, do you have any living relatives?"

"No."

"Friends of your parents still living?"

"None that I know of."

"Is there anything concerning the missing bio-chip or the alien appearances that you would like to comment on at this time?"

"I have not a comment, but rather a question," Dee retorted. "Where is Kelly Edwards? Is she all right? May I see her?" Anders did not answer the questions.

"Sir, as part of the questioning, you must urinate into this container."

"To hell you say! Wherefore?"

"I'm sorry? Wherefore?" Anders seemed genuinely lost at the meaning of the word. In ignorance, he pointed at the bottle in his hand. "Right here."

"Speak you not the Queen's English, man? What an ass thou art! Wherefore must I?!" shouted Dee as if he were speaking to the deaf. "Do you not ken the word *wherefore?*" An exasperated sigh. "*Wherefore* meaneth 'why'. Wherefore, or, in the vernacular, *why* must I piss in your blasted tin cup?"

Agent Anders continued in the same frank tone. "So

that we may analyze your DNA and see if it corresponds to human DNA."

They are not sure I am human, Dee realized. "You think I'm a Roc with the virus," he snorted. "Why, man, I have searched for half this year trying to flush them out. You whoreson ass, I am as human as thou art. Here, feel!" Dee extended his hands to the man. Anders quickly backed away, eager to avoid contact.

The comic aspect of the retreating scarecrow lifted Dee's spirits. "Come, man, come. Give it me. Give me your piss-pot and I will prove to you and your physicians that I am a man."

Though the captive appeared to be a small man, Anders by no means was going to allow himself to get within Dee's reach. Even at three feet away, the NTSA agent was not at all sure about his own safety. If this was an alien hostile, it might morph into a gigantic nightmare at any moment. Plus, his prisoner—whatever he was—kept blathering about a virus. Was there a threat of alien contagion? Anders had seen the vids of Angel City and now thought both scenarios astonishingly possible. Further, the prisoner now seemed agitated. Capable of unprovoked acts. Anders spoke as calmly as possible. "Sir, please lower your arms and back away to your bed."

For a moment, Dee saw the look of trepidation in the man's eyes and could name Anders's fear: the dread of a superior prisoner overpowering his guard. How many times had Dee seen that look? And how many times had his agility proved the fears justified? His laughter subsiding to a chortle, he backed away. Anders, never taking his eyes off Dee, carefully bent down and placed the urine sample bottle on the floor near the cell door. "Now urinate in it, sir."

"Now?"

"Yes. I must witness the process so as to prevent any break in the chain of evidence."

Dee shook his head in disbelief and began to fill the receptacle. What a timorous pigeon-livered mouse, his keeper was. His masters must be cruel men indeed, he thought. He'd been imprisoned many times in his career, but this was the first time he'd been asked to make water. With a flourish, Dee completed the contribution and presented the filled steel container back to the scarecrow. He grinned mischievously as he set it on the floor and immediately danced away from the specimen. Anders, making sure not to make contact with any of its surface, secured the container into a clear plasticine pouch. He relaxed when the process was complete. His bureau chief had thought getting the sample would be impossible if the suspect was indeed an alien.

"Wouldn't want to trade that for a small beer, would you?"

"I must inform you that in addition to a DNA analysis we will do a brainscan to check your synaptic connections as well as a full neuro-psychiatric examination. That will start tomorrow."

"*Cave quicquam incipias, quod paeniteat postea.*"

"Excuse me, is that Latin?"

"Be careful about starting something you may regret."

"That's not a threat, is it?"

"No," Dee said passively, shaking his head. "No."

Daryl Anders dutifully checked inside his folder for anything he might have missed. A man such as this, thought Dee, might be bribed. But then he realized there would be cameras everywhere. He studied his keeper and hoped to find out his weaknesses. "I will ask you once again, is there anything concerning the missing bio-chip or your vicinity to the appearances of alien spacecraft that you would like to comment on at this time?" Then he remembered something. "You said 'Roc.' What is a Roc?"

"It is what the monsters are called. It is what they name themselves. Just as we are dubbed humans."

"How do you know that?"

Dee realized there was no answer for that but to explain Dyckon and their relationship. He knew, too, that information was often a valuable commodity. The NTSA agent pressed harder and asked the question again.

"In the battle, when I was hard upon him, I heard the monster call his kind that." Dee decided to be generous, "He called himself Fawg."

The polygraph would later indicate that the first statement was false and the second one true. Anders and the experts at the Bureau would evaluate that evidence for weeks. In the meantime, the NTSA agent had finished his interview, but had two last questions. One was a formality: "What is your name?"

"John Dee, Doctor of Philosophy and Medicine."

The other question had been on Anders's mind since the beginning of the interview. "Why do you talk as if you're a character from Shakespeare?"

Doctor John Dee stared at his interrogator in confusion. He didn't understand the question. For surely he was not an actor in a scene from *Henry VI*. He was, quite simply, a man in captivity.

# CHAPTER 23

MAXIM HESITATED A MOMENT outside the philosopher's room before knocking. It was always a challenge to be in the man's company, as he was brilliant in so many matters and disapproving of so many more. When he entered, he found Theon Celsus quietly sitting on a hard chair and fixated on the space just above his cupped hands that covered his nose. As Maxim closed the door, the little man with the large head switched his focus to quizzically stare at Maxim as though he, Maxim, had the answer to some inexplicable riddle. That, of course, was utterly impossible, as Maxim was quite aware of his own minimum ability to catch the unspoken, the implied, the crux of any problem. Sheepishly, the aide looked away. Why Celsus even tolerated him was a mystery. But Celsus' trust and companionship honored him, and it was the brilliant man's respect for him that so bound the lumbering man's loyalty.

"Have we cleared customs yet?" Celsus inquired, as if that was the sole question he had been contemplating. Maxim dutifully gave details of their schedule, then left, closing the door behind him.

Shortly, Celsus joined Maxim and they disembarked. The car that had been ordered met them at their plane and drove them off the tarmac into Irkutsk. Theon chatted politely, making a few pithy comparisons between wintry conditions here and those at his homes in Switzerland and Germany. He reminded Maxim that he always found himself so nostalgic in Irkutsk, attributing the feeling mainly to the intricate and delicate wooden carvings that decorated the Irkutskian homes. Then he lapsed into silence, leaving Maxim to study the bleak landscape flashing past the tinted windows of the car.

"Maxim, I have decided to meet with Strategy Brooks." Celsus spoke abruptly.

Maxim turned his gaze to his employer. "Do you think that wise?"

Theon Celsus just smiled and patted his bodyguard on the knee. "I cannot tell, but I must be obedient to what Providence deals me."

Maxim had hoped there would be an explanation, but Celsus lapsed back into thoughtful silence.

Strategy and Hernando had found their lunch superb and the icy vodka to be exquisite, completely extinguishing any residual feelings of cold and fatigue. Boris had stopped by during the meal to recommend the Siberian custard with cloudberries. It sounded mouthwatering, and they had readily agreed to wait for it even though it took thirty minutes to prepare. They were reveling in it when two men wearing black scarves wandered up to their table.

"Miss Strategy Brooks of GNN?" The men had distinctive Muscovite accents, very different from the more rustic Siberian ones of the area.

At the end of the dining room, the far-off conversation between the two Mongolian men suddenly stopped. The lady in mink quickly got to her feet and exited through the kitchen, never turning her face toward anyone. Hernando was instinctively on his guard, but Strategy was not rattled in the least; celebrity had taught her to expect fans anywhere. "Yes." She smiled up at the strangers, giving them her best angle.

"We are from Russian Central Security."

"You are a little out of bounds, aren't you? This is the Siberian New Territory. You have no jurisdiction here," she said, her Russian a little sloppy from the vodka.

"NTSA."

"Ohhh, I see. Checking up on us already, are you? Well, we've just arrived and have come across nothing untoward . . . except a very large bear at the top of the stairs. Perhaps you should investigate." She leaned over, conspiratorially whispering, "I don't think he has a chip." She didn't wait for a response, but continued as if at a cocktail party. "How rude of me. Allow me to introduce my comrade and cameraman, Hernando Carrasco." The two turned to Hernando. "Nando, these two men . . . are from the NTSA Moscow." Strategy looked back at them, wrinkling her nose in mock disapproval. "Some of . . . Vassili's men. I'm sorry, I didn't get your names?"

"We must ask you to come with us. Both of you," the taller of the two said in passable English, putting his hand on the back of Hernando's chair. "We have some questions about your intentions regarding—"

The Russian never finished his sentence, as Theon Celsus stepped up to the table. "Excuse me, Miss Brooks, may I be of some assistance? I believe your dessert has been interrupted."

"We are NTSA, and we have reason to believe that Miss Brooks and Mister Carrasco have information that would be valuable to our ongoing investigations." The agent took a step toward Celsus, but stopped abruptly as Maxim put himself between the man and his employer.

"Well," said Theon, "as you are obviously not Siberian NTSA, our American friends are not required to follow you anywhere. Moreover, as they have traveled to meet me here for a business meeting . . ."

Strategy, startled, began to demur, but Celsus reassured her. "Miss Brooks, I am truly sorry I have you at a disadvantage. My name is Theon Celsus of the Aurum All Chemical Mining Company. This is my aide-de-camp, Maxim Izevsky. I am here for our interview." He gallantly raised her hand to his lips and lightly kissed her knuckle. Turning toward the surprised Russians, he continued, "I suggest that you ask your questions here while Maxim and I remove our coats. I'm sure they have nothing to hide. Maxim, why don't you go find Boris and order some of those cloudberries and some black tea. Gentlemen, would you care for anything?" The NTSA agents shook their heads in confusion. Hernando opted for another vodka.

As Celsus and Maxim moved away from the table, the NTSA agents questioned Strategy and Hernando about their visit to Irkutsk. Strategy responded that they had come to do an in-depth piece on the Aurum All Chemical company which had numerous mining and oil rights in Kazakhstan, Mongolia, and Siberia.

"As you know," she said, her tone as patronizing as possible, "the company has grown quickly in the last few years, primarily due to the development of an inexpensive process to desodiumize oil. The profits from the monopoly on this technique have gone into acquiring thousands of acres of property, allowing the company to diversify into the mining of silver, gold, and lead. Theon Celsus—who you gentlemen just met—has gained a reputation as a new-age thinker who advocates returning to nature and finding eternal secrets." Strategy paused, allowing the agents an opportunity to stop her. When they remained silent, she continued her lecture. "I have sources who tell me that Aurum All Chemical is about to get a large stake in the lucrative oilfields at Tengiz. There are also rumors about illegal oil swaps on the black market. I'm sure you gentlemen will agree that all of this points toward a potential feature story."

"What about the connection between Aurum All Chemical and extraterrestrials?" one of the agents asked bluntly. Strategy and Hernando exchanged a glance at the ham-handed approach.

"Gentlemen, I assure you, my interest in Aurum All Chemical is strictly from a business point of view." Strategy looked up as Celsus and Maxim returned to the table. "Perhaps you would like to speak with Mister Celsus about his business—or his relationship with aliens."

The agents glared at her. "That's NTSA business, ma'am," one finally said.

"Then take it back to Vassili," she snapped. "I've answered your questions."

The agents turned away scowling. They had nothing, and Vassili would surely express his displeasure. Strategy smiled in satisfaction and gestured for Celsus to take the chair beside her.

"Now, who are you?" Strategy asked. "Really."

"I told you—Theon Celsus of Aurum All Chemical."

She gave him a wary "don't kid a kidder" look, and he added, "Really."

"Well, diRocelli sure set this interview up in a hurry."

"Despite the vastness of the steppes here in Asia Minor, news travels quickly in the New Territories." Celsus said, by way of explanation.

"Not that fast," murmured Hernando.

"No, you are right, Mister Carrasco, not that fast. But, Miss Brooks's—or may I call you Strategy?—reportage of things alien has reached even our far-flung communities, and we are all impressed by the excellent coverage and insights she gave us." Turning his attention back to the GNN anchor, he continued, "Surely, you must have learned a lot from spending so many days with the alien when he was in his human form?"

"Mister Celsus—or is it Theon?" Strategy said in a mischievous, flirting tone. He brightly acknowledged the reciprocity. "Nando and I are appreciative of your gallantly coming to our rescue—not that we needed it—but that doesn't immediately make you my best friend. So let's skip the niceties, and you simply tell us why you're here. From what I've heard of your reclusiveness, you don't strike me as the kind of guy who is beating the bushes for publicity."

Theon Celsus turned to his aide. "You see, Maxim, how well her mind works. I was right to have come. Miss Brooks, I don't know why you want an interview with me, but I know divine Providence often brings disparate people together for excellent reasons, advantageous reasons. I am quite certain we were destined to meet. Just this morning, I made up my mind to try to find you, and while I was on the way, I learned of an event that the world must know of, and of course you are the perfect person to tell it."

Strategy ruefully smiled and turned away, shaking her head.

"Is there a problem?"

"No, Theon, it's just that the last time someone said something like that to me, I ended up befriending a guy who swore he was Christ and turned out to be a living gargoyle."

"I assure you, Strategy, I am completely human, but your instincts are partially correct. What I am to tell you does indeed have to do with a space alien—one of the same breed as the one in Angel City. I want to play you something that I just received today. May I?"

"Yeah, go ahead." Strategy kept her guard up, though her curiosity was piqued.

Swearing her to secrecy and making much of her keeping her news sources privileged, Celsus activated his wrist communicator and replayed the vid of Dyckon's conversation with Morgan d'Winter. Strategy was unimpressed, but Celsus was not to be so easily dissuaded and explained that the unseen voice was that of another alien, named Dyckon. Moreover, he told her that Morgan was the personal bodyguard of Doctor John Dee. He was genuinely surprised that neither she nor Hernando seemed to know the name. Theon pulled at his ear and tried again. "Dee's the fellow in your vids, the unknown man who fought Yeshua and was part of bringing him down."

With shocked recognition, Strategy instantly started asking questions. All her attempts to find and/or identify that intrepid stranger had been futile, she complained. She had begged her audience to help locate the man. GNN had even offered a handsome reward. To her amazement, no one had come forward. His complete absence as a credible eyewitness had been used to discount the footage as a hoax. "You must take me to this John Dee immediately," she demanded.

"Have you seen the news since you left the States?" Celsus asked.

"Of course." Strategy wondered why he would ask such an obvious question.

"Then you know about the NTSA's arrest of two enemy combatants," Celsus said.

"Don't tell me," Strategy said. "One of those nameless prisoners is this John Dee."

"No one is confirming this information," Celsus said. "But I have had John Dee under surveillance since your Angel City vid-clips alerted me to his whereabouts. He knew too well this lizard creature, and I fear he might be partnered with others. I cannot present my findings to the government officials—my trading partners in the petroleum black market would find that an untenable relationship."

"Why come to me with this?" Strategy asked, flattered but skeptical.

"This conversation seems to indicate an alliance with alien agents," Celsus said, gesturing to the vid. "Now he is locked away, with no chance of sharing his testimony with the people of the world."

"Can you prove that the Dyckon voice was unregistered with any of the world's citizenry?" Strategy asked. She couldn't allow herself to be fooled by special effects—not again.

"I see that you must have something more—for want of a better expression, a smoking gun. Something that will convince you of my authenticity. And the thing is, I have such a proof and I should have told you about it at the beginning, but regrettably, it slipped my mind. First the hair," he said self-mockingly, patting his large bald scalp, "then the mind." His hand slipped down to tug at the fringe of hair that skirted the back of his head. "During our investigations in London, we uncovered to our absolute astonishment that Doctor John Dee has no identity chip. This makes him rather unique, don't you think? It's another reason why we originally kept him under surveillance."

"That's not possible," blurted Hernando.

"Oh, but it is," Celsus countered. "I suggest you use your GNN sources to verify the truth of this. That is, of course, if NTSA allows you anywhere near him. You will find that in today's briefing, they didn't—and in my opinion, will never—admit that the man they are now holding has somehow avoided the universal implant. The world supposes that to be impossible. Perhaps after investigating, when you prove that my revelation is true, you will be convinced that my vid is equally true. John Dee knows quite a bit about our friends from outer space and there is a story to be told here.

"I am sure, Miss Brooks, that we shall meet again." Celsus and Maxim stood up from the table and faded out of the dining hall just as quickly as they had entered.

Strategy looked at Hernando and asked, "When Celsus first sat down, didn't he say something about 'Providence' and 'advantageous reasons'?"

"Yeah."

She mulled it over for a moment. "So what does he get out of all this?"

# CHAPTER 24

EXTRACT FROM THE DAY BOOKE of John Dee, Doctor, in the Year of Our Lord 2101:

*Knowing not whether History nor Justice shall ever hear tell of my part to satisfy my duty, it were a profitable exercise here to set down what hath befallen me and how I chanced to be gaoled here. It was ever my practice to set down notable things, that negligence and long continuance of time may not make them utterly to perish. Thus, here I chronicle what before my mind passes on this first day of my imprisonment as far as my poor wit and capability serve me, here truly will I rehearse unto you my innermost thoughts. It is my great wish that I be not prevented to continue in this practice every day of my imprisonment so that I may better distill my thoughts and school you of the truth of my purpose. When that I have previously been mewed up, I have known no greater joy than scribbling my thoughts and, thereby, sharpening them. I blush to say it, but it has ever been my vice. I am come hither without my own deserts and against my own will, but I trust that God of his goodness will discharge me of my care and that most quickly.*

*For that the space is commodious and well provided, I find no cause, thank Heaven, to reckon myself in worse case here than in a goodly neighbor's house. But my mind likes not the thought that while I rest here as a charge of the government, the virulent Mattik is preparing for such a calamity that the world knows not the remedy. Our search for the caitiff was scotched by that interfering fool, that nameless he from Terra Incognita who, spurred by some unknown daemon, treacherously led us into a trap that proved our undoing. I pray God that Morgan either was counciled in time or ware of our peril by some other means and so quit the field and 'scaped the net that hauled us in.*

*It befell of this time yesterday, a little afore noon, after a beverage at a café to slake our thirst, a report came to me by one, whose name I will never utter, that sheriffs of the realm, those of the NTSA, pursued my companion and me. Not of a mind to be taken and well aware for what reason we were in danger, we made our leave by quietly pressing in amongst the throng that streamed through the internal square of Four Corners. We had hopes of returning to our coach wherewithal to find safety and rescue. Kelly Edwards, in whom I had not want of trust, struggled to guide me away from our pursuers, but alas, to no avail. At every turn, they seemed to be stationed in abundance and in their possession had such devices that made their hunt for us and the recognition of us the more convenient. With every breath, I cursed myself and the witlessness that led me to abandon d'Winter's wise council to remain in London and risk all for the chimera of a fainthearted friendship. My feigned friend, that served and served but packed when it chanced to storm, left me and mine in the tempest to buffet on our own. For the better part of an hour, like Actaeon's hounds, our pursuers dogged our every step and no amount of knavish cunning on our part kept them from pick-*

*ing up our scent. At last it was my opinion to abjure from flight and stand down and be taken. What remedy had we else? One, Hudson, a man of great girth and height, with all his watch made up to us and short of breath declared, "You are a prisoner of the United States government." I demanded, "For what offense?" He made no reply but discourteously made gesture and upon that six of his under-curs rushed upon us, treating Kelly with unmannerly abuse as one would truss a trull. I was of a mind to strike, but a swarthy youth with the help of his fellows seized my dagger, which I had secreted in my sleeve, and cuffed me for good measure. And so we were apprehended but with so little art or expertise that Hercules would have wept to see it.*

*After we had been rudely restrained, this same Hudson pretended such friendship towards me and told us both that the NTSA was a good and gracious thing and had a mind to treat us fairly. This same master lieutenant did wish me to be of good cheer and think on him as a friend. In a voice as honeyed as his own, I answered him back that if I should not do so, then would he kindly thrust me out of his custody. He liked not mine answer but turned his sway and attention on my compatriot. Neither Edwards nor I listened to his guile but steadfastly spoke not a word. He commanded us to be ferried with such a band of silent sentinels that methought that we had quit this world and were in company of that melancholy ferryman that leads the dead to Erebus. But, alack, our final destination was not Elysian fields but a solitary room, where now I sit and while the time till I am summoned forth. Here may all men note the chances of Fortune who follows some whom she is pleased to promote, and even so to some her favor is contrary, though they should travail ever so much with urgent diligence and blessed purpose.*

*Kelly is I know not where. It is a sore affliction unto me that I know not what state she is in, but, by Heaven, I shall be ever valiant with my Keeper in my efforts to obtain license to see her. I must find a mean unto d'Winter to acquaint him with what has befallen Kelly and myself. Yet that path is gated, for here I have no friends for mine help nor way to announce myself to the unsuspecting world. For the NTSA, that hath committed me hither, refusing me either attorney or council, are loath to give out that I am taken. The want of attorney, friends, admission of my arrest, and habeas corpus are egregious faults against the common laws of the world. Nay, they are faults to Heaven for they play false with a man's rights and freedoms. The agency's secret statutes and ordinances give them liberty to hide all from public view. And forasmuch as I am by the Foreign Intelligence Surveillance Act court scurrilously condemned (and yet not condemned for I have not been attained nor convicted) for an evildoer concerning the want of a device that I alone seem to be bereft. A fault certainly not of my own making and therefore not malicious. For where there is no malice, saith the Law, there can be no offense.*

*That this realm, these United States, being but one poor member and small part of this great world, might make laws disagreeable with the general law of mankind is naught but wickedness. Just as Angel City, being but one poor member in respect of the whole realm, must not make a law contrary to the laws that bind the whole realm for that would be flat rebellion against the commonwealth. So it is that the law that names Kelly and me terrorist and strips us of aught that she and I would most enjoy is contrary both to the culture and rights of civil liberties of the as yet unrepealed principles of these United States. Moreover, our captor's behaviour is contrary to the principles of the Magna Carta on which the laws of this American nation are grounded. And over this, I cannot think that so many worthy men, so many wise personages of this Nation who labored long and mindfully to till the soil of Christian jurisprudence ever meant to have mortally punished any man or woman in whom there could be found no malice. Therefore by their own culture and principles are they unable to justify our imprisonment. Liberty is given by nature even to mute animals. And surely it is a great pity that any Christian nation should by flexible government banish their own uprightness and culture built up for centuries, but for a whim and a surmise of procuring intelligence.*

*Whilst I tarry, I cannot help but think that the monster waits in ambush to poison the wide world with his contagion. Since none but we are privy to his existence and his master's true desires, must I not do all to tutor my keepers to what great calamity waits to ravish them? Yet am I loath to do so, as that weighty knowledge is the great jewel of intelligence in my coffer. To squander that is to despoil us of the chance to barter for our freedom and mayhap find my path back to Mortlake. Perforce, like the sun in the last of twilight, the time for my private enterprise has faded and, like a weary traveler, I must forgo the dream of making it home. I am at sea as to what to do. It grieves me mightily that the sands of time drain through the glass, which is naught but to the creature's advantage. Yet must there be a scrupulous policy in my tutelage to the authorities of the matter, for who that is not a madman would heed or countenance my very being? Would God that Kelly and I be permitted parlay soon that she might council me on how best to couch my words and make them judge me not a fool.*

*I cannot think but that the end of days is near at hand, and my mind is racked with many dreadful questions. Where is the hand of Divine Providence? Man is God's most beloved creature, more beloved than the Angels, proved by the Savior's death insomuch as He died for us and not for Lucifer. Why then has He forsaken his chosen in surely our hour of need? Have we so shrunk from His word that in His displeasure He hath called the day of wrath upon us, when Heaven and Earth will quake and rise, when the trumpets will awaken all? Am I alone, poor miserable creature, Heaven's servant and like Lot alone have the power to intercede with destruction? If this be so, I faint with the burden as I have done oft these two years. Moreover, Lot was befriended by a divine angel that guided him in his task and led him out of Sodom. Why has my celestial angel in whose faith I trusted betrayed me to mine enemies? And I should fail? Will I not be thrown into the deepest circle of Hell? I, a most cunning caitiff, hath passed the whole course of my miserable life most sinfully and God must think me not worthy to come to eternal felicity, for He yet leaves me here in the world an impossible while, further to be plagued with mischance and trial. This misgiving sickens my soul.*

*But I must not despair, but will remember my Savior who gave up His life in the battle for our souls and was victorious. He was resurrected from Death and bathed in Glory, for indeed to fight and to struggle is to follow on His pathway. He who is slain and remains on the battlefield has won the victory. That one alone who has been smitten carries off the victory. He alone has stood his ground. The undefeated may escape with his life, but what honor has he? Therefore, I, in despite of hardship and bondage and eternal loss of home and hope, must valiantly persevere; for I see now my way is to push beyond my petty skills and desires and follow the path that He has given me. Why else have I been stolen from my home and Time to walk this Earth, but to do His singular service and shoulder the cross that I have been given. Come what will, I must see it through.*

*But, even now my thoughts betray my honorable sacrifice and return to Mortlake, that right fair house, with my library, my books, my gallery, my garden, my orchard, and other necessaries handsome about me, where I might be merry and content and conclude my life. There do all persons know my mind and share in my delights. Happy I was to gaze upon the stars and read my charts and have discourse with the learned of the day, never dreaming another day would come when I, playing Methuselah, would want their company and their world and find myself at the edge of the doom that much we postulated. What fate imposes, that must men abide, for like the wind and the tide it is bootless to resist. But in despite of reason, that cozener hope flatters evermore that I might gain the Timeslip device and once more return there. To Mortlake. To home. It is a bitter cup to make so hard a choice 'twixt the health of the world and where my heart lies.*

*Whatever my stars, I pray God to impart to me the gifts and graces of His Holy Spirit so that with prudence and wisdom I may treat rightly of the things that are yet to do.*

# CHAPTER 25

STRATEGY BROOKS GOT INTO the hired rover and glanced over at the driver. "Do you speak English?"

"Of course. It is my second language," said Sergei Valerievich Platov. "May I say it is an honor to drive you, Miss Brooks?"

"You may," said Strategy, who was generally immune to flattery. She dug into her satchel and pulled out two views of the so-called mining installations. "See these?"

"Most impressive," said Sergei. "Is that what you want to explore?"

"Yes, please, and with as little fanfare as possible." This last was a warning. "I want to get as close to the Celsus site as possible."

"Of course," Sergei said again, smoothly. "Nyet problemy."

"Easy for you to say," Strategy snapped, and turned around in her seat to see if Hernando was properly strapped in. "Everything okay back there, Nando?"

"Everything's fine," said Hernando. He pulled out a hotcup filled with the vodka-laced coffee Boris had prepared for them an hour ago. The coffee was almost cool enough to drink, and Hernando tasted it carefully, getting a froth of cream on his nose for his trouble. He was glad he was in the backseat. His boss seemed a little crankier today than usual. Maybe a sip of his spiked coffee would help.

The bells in the Orthodox churches were chiming nine. Irkutsk was gray under leaden clouds, the promise of snow by afternoon in their ominous sag. Following the main street to the edge of the city, Sergei kept up a steady, informative chatter about the history of the area. He informed them how Irkutsk merchants were always great patriots and philanthropists. They had dedicated themselves to rebuilding the city after the Black Year of 2079 when a deadly retrovirus had been cultured in the industrial waste dumped into Lake Baikal. Carried on the black smoke that emanated from the Selenga pulp-and-paper plant, it had wafted its way to Irkutsk, where it attached itself to the respiratory system of most of the local inhabitants. The death count had been in the thousands, but the city fathers had spent billions on a regional promotional campaign to brag about the lake's beauty and the winter sports. Celsus mining had bought the malignant paper mill and spent a fortune converting it into a pharmaceutical plant.

"The Siberian Railroad made Irkutsk important, that and Lake Baikal. The interest in the lake came after the railroad made it accessible to travelers. Then, of course, world skiers discovered how accessible we were by transport. We have the best snow in the world. It is our cash crop—that and our timber and minerals." He pointed out three huge hotels between the airport and the city. "Very good places, very expensive."

"I like where we are," said Strategy. "More authentic."

Sergei laughed. "In so many ways."

"How do you mean?" Strategy asked, deliberately turning up the charm.

"Everyone knows that the old black market is still very much alive, although the goods have changed over time. Boris Shevyenetz runs a thriving business in illegal furs and uncut gemstones. He deals with the Mongolians and the Manchurians as well as Russians and Siberians, and he supplies America and Europe with these rare items—for a price, of course. He's probably socked away a fortune by now. His business has increased since that American widow came to help him. She can travel for him—unimpeded—in ways New Territory Siberians cannot." Sergei grinned. "Is there a story in this?"

"Probably," Strategy said with more candor than she usually showed. "But just now there is a difficulty."

Sergei's expression fell. He had bribed two other men to get this assignment. The American newscaster woman was famous; she must have thousands to pay for stories. "How do you mean, a difficulty?"

"Well, just now we're on another assignment, but it would be very useful if you would give me an interview, with the understanding that I might need some time before I could work on it." She gave him her best sideways glance. "I'd also need you to be ready to give me more interviews if the story panned out."

Sergei was not immune to her deliberate charm. "I will use the time to gather more information," he promised her, and engaged the six-wheel drive as he turned off the main highway and took a narrow track through the spindly forest. "There has been much overlogging in Siberia this last century, and the forest will need decades to recover."

"That's too bad," Strategy said, because it was expected of her.

"It has been disastrous to the economy of the region," said Sergei. "But we will recover. We always have. Siberia makes it necessary." He pointed up ahead. "We'll have to pull over. There's another vehicle coming this way."

"How can you tell?" Strategy asked, peering into the white and green ahead of them.

"A signal on the road sensor. We have to have them, or there would be real trouble out here. There was a time when drivers carried pistols to fight for the right-of-way. I myself have seen my life pass in front of me several times."

"Sounds like the Wild West," said Strategy with the suggestion of a laugh.

"Oh, very much so. The Wild East, in fact," said Sergei, chuckling at his own joke. "It wasn't safe to be out on these roads alone. There are times it still isn't. But now, at least, we are all equipped with sensors. They tell me a satellite reads our ID chips and forwards our whereabouts to an early warning agency." He looked for a sign for a turn-out and pulled over as soon as one came into view. He backed into the spot, careful not to allow the exhaust pipe to be swallowed by the snowdrift. Too many tourists had died of hydrogen gas poisoning that way.

"How long will we have to wait?" Strategy asked.

"Not long. Perhaps twenty minutes at the most." He swung around and glanced at Hernando. "If you want to take any vid, now is the chance to step out for a shot."

"I don't think so, thanks," said Hernando. "I'd hate to be out in the snow if heavy equipment comes whipping over that crest." He pointed toward the road ahead of them. "Besides, I don't want to overly expose my equipment to the wet and the cold. I'll stay right here, thanks very much." He took a long swallow on Boris's doctored coffee.

"You have a point," said Sergei, and offered a hotcup to Strategy. "Mocha with good European brandy. I got it as a tip from a patron last month. It's very good."

Ordinarily Strategy would have refused, but she was feeling nervous and cold, so she said, "Thanks," and took the hotcup.

Ten minutes later, a large, balloon-tired Multi Terrain churned past them, throwing up vast amounts of slushy snow as it passed. Hernando was grateful he'd stayed inside. The Multi Terrain had kicked up enough snow to gave their vehicle a sizeable barrier to penetrate in order to regain the road. Two attempts, and Sergei's rover plowed through. He muscled his car back onto the road and followed in the wide tracks the Multi Terrain had made. The undercarriage of the car flattened out the snow collected between the treads. To the American passengers, the thumps were disconcerting. As the car bumped along, Hernado moved his vid bag to his lap. He held it tightly, hoping none of the sensitive camera connections would rattle loose.

"They've made it easier for us," the Siberian driver remarked.

"That was quite a transport," said Hernando. "Electric and hydrogen?" Back home, you rarely saw anything but electric and petroleum. Pollution of air and water was much lighter at the beginning of the twenty-second century than it had been in the last, when holes in the ozone layer had threatened to raise the median temperature of the world. American manufacturing had finally been reined in ecologically by a string of progressive presidential administrations that had stressed alternate fuel consumption and by-product responsibility. The oil companies no longer ruled the roost, but they were still a force to reckon with in the States.

"Most of them are completely pollutant free. That one is probably one of the new solar powercell rigs. It may have come from the Celsus mining compound." Sergei guided the rover around an outcropping of partially exposed rock.

"You mean the place we're going?" Strategy asked.

"Yes," Sergei told her. He wondered if there was money to be made in a story about solar engines or mining transports or unplowed roads. American programming seemed to be always expert at making something out of nothing. He just needed to find the hook into grabbing these Americans' interest.

"Well, why didn't you say so?" she demanded, sliding around in her seat to try to catch a glimpse of the Multi Terrain.

"It's long gone," said Sergei, shrugging. "Is it important, that you see that transport?"

Strategy thought it over. "No, I guess not. Not yet, anyway." She took a second, long sip of her mocha. "I wonder who was in it?"

"Who knows?" said Sergei. "But I could find out."

# CHAPTER 26

KELLY LOOKED TIRED BUT not injured, which Dee had feared most. He held out his hand to her. Instead of taking it, she embraced him and laid her head on his shoulder. There they stood for the better part of a minute, locked in unspoken communion, sharing their fears and their loneliness. Much against his will but for propriety's sake, he offered, "Let me help you to a chair." She looked up and nodded. They were alone in the exercise court of the detention center, a large, square room twenty feet on a side, its high ceiling punctuated with large skylights that revealed nothing more than a stretch of cloudy blue. There were three exercise machines, a round table, three chairs, and nothing else in the room—no clocks, no access to other parts of the building. The sliding doors were somewhat translucent, but showed nothing but an occasional vague movement beyond them. They had not seen each other for four days. Alone in their respective white cells, it had seemed like four months.

"They're monitoring us," said Kelly listlessly.

"Aye, I do not doubt it," said Dee.

"Just keep it in mind," Kelly warned him as she dropped into the nearest chair.

"My mind harbors naught but your good safety. You are faint with care."

She shrugged. "I'm extremely hungry, but that's not important." She yawned suddenly as though she were unscathed by their predicament. She grinned sheepishly. "I haven't slept much. What about you?" Her behavior astonished him; she was trying to buoy his spirits. She had the heart of a lion. Never was there a woman like her.

"I'd have to say the same," he responded, longing to hold her again. The flush was gone from her cheek, and her mane of red hair was listless and needed a washing She was imprisoned, and her very existence was in jeopardy. All for following his instructions. She had put her complete trust in him. He feared now that she hated him for that. "Has anyone talked to you?"

"You mean that puppet, Anders?" She laughed tonelessly. "Yesterday, probably not long after he talked to you."

"Dare you to hope . . ."

"They can hold us forever," she said listlessly. "The Sixth Amendment does not apply. The NTSA won't file criminal charges or give any reason for our detention. They don't even have to admit to anyone—not anyone at all—that they have us. They don't have to respect any of our Constitutional rights." She put her hands to her eyes but didn't cry. "Centuries-old international law regarding enemy soldiers out of uniform gives them that power."

Dee volunteered nothing. He couldn't get over how pale she looked. He'd seen such women in the Tower, already halfway to Heaven, counting the hours before their scheduled beheading. And the impact of her frailty was so violent, so accusing, so indicting that for a moment he lost out to his insecurities. "Please forgive me."

She touched his arm gently. "You sweet man, there's nothing to forgive."

He leaned in close and folded himself around her shoulders. His embrace said so much more than any of his great vocabulary and lyrical witticisms could ever hope to do. Together, they drew strength from each other, and when they separated, much had been communicated that O'Neal with all his eavesdropping would never know. The absent flush was back in her face. His sense of isolation abated.

"Think you that they'll keep us incommunicado forever? For one such as I, 'forever' is a little longer than most."

"They'll probably try." She laughed shakily. "You worry them."

"They like not my want of a chip, that's certain," said Dee, delighting in her refound mirth.

"We already knew that," Kelly said, looking around the blank walls. Her will to survive was beating back the despair.

"So we did," Dee agreed. He patted her hand. "But I've wormed my way out of worse. In my time, I was infamous."

She held up her hand to silence him. "Never mind that."

"Well, truth is truth," said Dee.

"But it's best to keep such things to ourselves," she said with more emphasis than she had intended.

"I think so, too," Dee concurred. "But I'd be a fool to leave off trying."

"What are you doing?" she mouthed before saying, "I guess we all need to hope."

"And those with friends have more reason to hope than those without," Dee said, a bit defiantly. He wanted to tell Kelly he was putting the NTSA on notice that he and Kelly could not simply vanish without consequences, or so he hoped.

"You can't count on such things, not in here," Kelly said.

"The miserable have no other strength than hope," still playing on the word, then adding clearly, "and allies."

"Well, don't make things any riskier than they are," she suggested.

"I shan't," he promised her. With that, he explored the room looking for weak points or objects that might be turned to weapons. The skylights were unattainable, the furniture was bolted to the floors, and the exercise machines gave him more than a moment's worry.

"Prithee instruct me for what purpose are those devilish devices employed?" He pointed with revulsion to the exercise equipment. "Belike your NTSA is cousin to our Topcliffe, who before he made his prisoners taste the rack, brought them to his chamber to give them full view of his hellish instruments. There was no more mercy in him than there is milk in the male tiger."

"That one is for swimming," she said, a little incredulous of his seeming ignorance. Like a stewardess, she cheerfully described the equipment. "That one is for stretching, and this one is for strengthening the back and legs. Those pulleys give you resistance and the bench flexes. Do you want to try it?"

"By Heaven, no!" he exclaimed with a vehemence born not so much of fear of the machines or the unthinking blitheness with which she described the racking, but of horror at a devious culture that would trick a prisoner into gladly volunteering for torture.

"The swimming machine is kind of fun," said Kelly. "It does half the work for you. It's actually quite relaxing. Would you like me to demonstrate it for you?"

"No, thank you," he said. But she walked toward it anyway. "Whilst thou swims, I will stand here upon the shore and dig my toes into the sand. Have a care not to drown."

"Well, you might like to know about them. You'll need to do something to keep in shape while we're in here. I'm going to use the swimming machine." Saying this, she lay down on it, fitting her arms and legs into long supports. As she started the motor, the supports began to move, taking her through a number of movements that might have been a kind of swimming, Dee admitted to himself, if he used his imagination.

"What has Anders learned of you?" Dee asked casually after watching her for a while.

"Just that I know that he's detained us illegally and that I question his authority." She changed her position and the machine changed the way it moved her arms and legs.

"Will that carry weight, do you think?" He smiled.

"I hope so. I figure it's on record somewhere." She turned off the machine abruptly.

Dee sighed. Even now, she still could not completely believe her country would abandon her—as if Heaven's will required it to keep records of her complaints. He knew governments enjoyed flexing visible power, especially over the powerless. No nation on earth, no matter how tied to the Church, allowed mercy to overrule necessities of State. Opponents of government with grievances of whatever sort quickly became enemies and were dealt with accordingly. But if Kelly had a flicker of hope, so would he. If Kelly could in some small way believe in the sanctity of America's laws and lawmakers, so would he. Perhaps, for once, the law would provide his escape.

"The NTSA can't afford to look as if it's abusing its power, because that's the one way it could be curtailed." She looked over at Dee as she disentangled herself from the tethers of the machine. The new thought made her hope bolder. "We'll find a way out of here. Don't doubt it for a second, Doctor."

"I shall do my best to obey you, madam," he assured her, and kept his misgivings to himself.

# CHAPTER 27

"THEON CELSUS CALLING," THE high, slightly accented voice said to the young Colombian who answered the call. "I'd like to speak with Franklin Swink, please."

"Mister Swink is abovedecks just now. Shall I take your number and have him return your call or shall I see if he is available? It may take a while for me to find him."

"I'll wait—but please hurry. I am calling from Asia. You can tell him it is an urgent business matter."

"I will, sir."

The young steward toggled the hold switch and climbed the stair to the top deck. He had to hold tightly to the stair rail, as a choppy sea was buffeting the ship. Under a threatening steel-gray sky, the eighty-foot yacht *Knight Errant* bucked and sidled through the large swells thrown up by the Gulf of Mexico. However, Franklin Swink, its owner, sat calmly in his custom-made recliner with his feet braced against the mahogany stern of the boat. The breeze tore at his lightweight jacket, whipping it in all directions. Swink concentrated on the sea, scanning regularly for marlin. He was deep-sea fishing, and the day hadn't been very productive. Swink was in his eighties, but age hadn't slowed him down. He was a ruthless litigator, racking up an impressive record of wins against various governments. It had been three years since he'd forced the Vatican to change their policy on their dress code and he had won billions of dollars for the clergy members of the class action suit. His fee had been very impressive, almost enough to match the gross national product of a small third-world nation. Certainly enough to enjoy a most comfortable retirement.

But the inactivity of the past three years had not agreed with him. His psyche itched for a battle, and he regretted permanently stepping down. It was not entirely his own choice. It was a promise he had made to his wife when she was near the end. The freedom from caseloads had allowed him to devote his every waking hour to her. They had taken the venerable Orient Express to exotic locales, and he had never seen her look happier. He had attended to every detail, every side-trip itinerary with the same focus and energy he brought to his most renowned briefs before the Supreme Court. His wife had died peacefully in Singapore, and Swink had been left with his grief and no outlet for his obsessive need to take charge. His energetic mind bridled at a life of newsvids, magazines, and golf. At first he had lectured and he had congratulated himself for getting large honorariums from legal-convention planners eager to have him as the guest speaker—a little work for a lot of money. The preparation of speeches and the research had taken his mind off his loss, but in the last few months he had become tired of hearing himself speak.

"Yes. This is Franklin Swink. Can I help you?"

"Mister Swink, thank you for taking my call. My name is

Theon Celsus. I'd like to talk to you about taking on a client, a rather—"

"Mister Celsus, I'm sorry, but I don't practice law anymore. I suggest you look elsewhere. Thank you." D. Franklin Swink made a move to toggle off.

"Mister Swink, give me five minutes of your time. I promise you this is the case of a lifetime."

"Such a deal," said Franklin—it was a favorite expression of his. "Okay, Mister Celsus, my rate is two thousand dollars an hour, you're on the clock."

"I am the CEO and CFO of Aurum All Chemical Mining Company. We are a one-point-five trillion dollar company."

"Mister Celsus, my expertise is not corporate law."

"I am fully aware of that. Mister Swink, you are the world's foremost—"

"I *was,* Mister Celsus, *was.*"

"You were the world's foremost authority on international law. Aurum would like to hire you to represent two recent detainees of the U.S. government. Perhaps you saw yesterday's news on the NTSA arrest of two persons at Four Corners?"

"No, I've been at sea. Has the government brought criminal charges?"

"We don't know."

"What did your 'detainees' do to merit such attention from Reed O'Neal?"

"I'm afraid I can't answer that either."

"You don't know much for a man willing to spend a chunk of money."

"I am familiar with one of the detainees. He is not a terrorist . . ." There was a moment's pause, and the attorney thought he'd lost the connection. ". . . but a man of mystery."

"Mister Celsus, you sound like a penny dreadful."

"I'm sorry, I'm not familiar with that term. But I do know you are a man who spent his life advocating the rights of individuals against oppressive regimes. I do know that you never back away from a fight. I do know you are no friend of the NTSA."

In 2093, Swink had brought a motion before the international court to rein in the NTSA 's international alliance and its power to trespass on the world's privacy. It had been one of his most ignominious defeats, and O'Neal had used the opportunity to label Swink a milquetoast liberal and a traitor to his own country. Although this had transpired years ago, when O'Neal was a freshman at the NTSA, Swink's anger had never abated. He was good at holding a grudge.

"Mister Celsus, all that may be true, but that was another life. I am retired now. Speak to Cora Hazeltine at Wood, Stephans, Hazeltine, and Baxter. She's very good."

"Sir, you and only you are the man for the job—"

"I don't think so." Swink looked at his watch. "You have thirty seconds left."

"Then perhaps I should tell you that one of the detainees doesn't have an ID chip."

"That's not possible."

"Take the case and see for yourself."

Against his better judgment, Swink was intrigued. The very premise was impossible. Every child was impregnated with a chip, even those from the remotest regions. Swink's legal mind considered the challenge of arguing the constitutional, if not the moral, question of a human being forced to be constantly monitored and shackled to a device that informed governments where they were. It was an infringement of personal liberty that had bothered him and others for years. There was the added pleasure of revisiting a 150-year-old executive privilege that allowed the suspension of habeas corpus. Only three presidents had invoked the rule since its inception, but no one had taken them on.

"It's an unusual case," he said slowly.

"I doubt there will ever be another quite like it," Celsus said mysteriously.

What Swink said next surprised even him. "Captain, come about and make back for Galveston. Mister Celsus, you've just hired yourself an old country lawyer. I'll be in D.C. by tomorrow night. Please wire my up-front fee to me by Tuesday."

The line disconnected and Franklin leaned in and gripped the back of the captain's chair as he heard the engines grind. He stared at the instrument panels and watched their gauges wavering like tall aspens in a gale as the bow switched directions. The analogy was not lost on him, and he announced to the crew, "I'll be in my cabin for an hour. I do not wish to be disturbed." He needed to present his breach of promise brief to his dead wife.

# CHAPTER 28

THEY HAD FOLLOWED IN the deep tracks to the shore drive along the edge of Lake Baikal, the deepest and oldest of all inland waters. The lake, seventy kilometers wide, froze so completely solid that drivers like Sergei could use it as a road south to Mongolia. Both Hernando and Strategy were amazed at how blue everything was. The icy lake, the distant mountains, the sky. Every other color seemed washed out, as if blue were the only coloring the local authorities allowed. Perhaps it was different in the summer, when the taiga, Siberia's immense forest, added shades of green. The factory sat on the lake where the Selenga River emptied into it. A laser fence sandwiched between two tall chain-link fences kept strangers out, and its blue emanations seemed in keeping not only with the scenery but also with the shamanism that used to reign there.

"Whatever they're doing in there, it sure as hell isn't mining—not any kind I've ever seen before. The ice and snow aren't enough to explain those reinforced buildings," Strategy said as she peered through the high, barred gate at the domes and steeply pitched roofs of the Celsus compound. "If he's doing mining here, where is the highwall? The overburden? If this is a working mine, even with the best of reclamation, there should be mounds of scree.

"Look at those!" She pointed at the chemical and biological warning signs hung every fifty meters on the blue force-field fence. "Why are there biological warnings? Are you getting this? It's better than anything we could get on satellite relay."

Hernando had climbed out of the Multi Terrain as soon as Sergei had stopped and was already vidding the place. "You can say that again." He kept on until the cold began to make his recorder run poorly. "I'll get back inside and warm this baby up again, and have another go at the place."

"Don't bother. Save it for when we get inside the gates." Strategy heard Sergei gasp. He unconsciously lifted his hand to cover his nose and mouth. "Well, I didn't come all this way to stand outside in the cold, that's for sure. I want to see what's going on in there."

"Go ahead," Sergei said in a tone that suggested she was insane. "Then go have a stroll through the Kremlin treasure vaults."

"I just might do that," Strategy said, getting back into the Multi Terrain. Strategy had been very intrigued by what Theon Celsus had told her, but she was damned if she was going to take it on face value, especially since his wasn't a pretty face. She was too good an investigative reporter not to want to do a little poking around to see what made the suave Theon Celsus tick. He was after something besides goodwill, of that she was certain. Immediately after he had left the Majestic, she had tried to contact the research department at GNN in Salt Lake. But there was a fourteen-hour difference, and only the night staff was up. She'd accessed the Internet, but she found only the routine stuff—facts and figures about Aurum All Chemical's bottom line, pretty pictures of land reclamation, and the company's diversification into petroleum and pharmaceuticals. Under Celsus himself, she found public relations drivel about Theon being an ardent environmentalist and a recluse. But Strategy, undeterred, found a secondary source; Boris as usual had been a rich vein of information. He'd provided the pics of the factory and told her where to find it, and then he had tried to dissuade her from going.

"In the meantime, is there a guarded gate anywhere? Some place I could ask to talk to someone inside?"

"Not really," said Sergei. "This is the only gate, and, as you see, no guard. There are monitors everywhere. They know we're here. They're probably listening to everything we're saying right now." He looked about nervously. The protectively cupped hand was still at his mouth. "I don't think we should linger." With unconcealed fear, he craned his neck to peer down the side of the barricades on either side of the gate.

"Why not?" Strategy demanded.

"Because there's supposed to be a pack of genetically modified bear patrolling the grounds. At least, that's what everyone says." Sergei was uneasier now. "They're supposed to be trained to attack—"

"Fairy tales to keep the peasants away," Strategy scoffed. This was almost as incredible as a man without a chip, she thought. "Really. Genetically modified bears!"

"Maybe. Who wants to find out for sure?" Sergei said, looking up toward the main dome. "Besides, this place isn't safe. This is the plant where the germs came from in '79."

"You mean the Black Year?"

He spit on the floorboard and nodded. She pumped him for information. This complex had been a cellulose plant, a final destination for the area's timber harvest. But the pulp products and the mulch dumped into the lake had become the breeding ground for microorganisms that caused respiratory asphyxiation. International medical teams had saved many, but the inhabitants of the Lake Baikal district had always grumbled that it had been too little, too late. Celsus' mining company had bought the site in 2080 at a rock-bottom price and then had spent millions cleaning up the problems. But who could be sure it was really safe again? After all, Theon Celsus was known to rarely visit the area. Maybe he didn't trust his cleanup crew. No one knew exactly what he was using the plant for now either, but some whispered drugs. Downwind in the very early mornings, the air was pungent with the smell of agar.

"So the biological warnings could be a scare tactic, too," she said turning to Nando.

"They could also be left over from '79. A requirement from the cleanup."

"Those postings don't look that old." She stared at them, trying to put the puzzle together. "And," she said, pointing back over her shoulder toward the compound, "they could be doing biological tests or drugs that have nothing to do with the cleanup." She turned back to the Siberian, remembering he had put them on this line of questioning. "Do you know all this for a fact, or is it just rumor?"

"I don't bring others here," Sergei admitted. "They say it's not safe."

"Then why did you agree to bring us?" Hernando asked.

"I thought I could be part of your story. Be seen on American TV maybe? Maybe sell you another story?"

"I don't believe this." Strategy narrowed her eyes.

"Also, I *was* interested." He shrugged good-naturedly. "It would be sensible to have a look at the compound for myself. And you've given me a good excuse to be here, if we're asked any questions by their security . . ." Sergei smiled and indicated Strategy. "I was following orders. Besides, I can tell my friends that I've seen this for myself, and that will—"

"Bragging rights," said Strategy with a laugh, cutting him short. "Wait a minute. Didn't you just tell me this was the only gate and there were monitors everywhere? How could you know that if you've never been here before?"

Sergei winced. He gave his most ingratiating smile. "I lied."

She couldn't help but melt at his temerity. After all, she was not averse to a little truth-bending herself if it got her what she wanted. "You get us into the compound, then you'll know you can deserve to brag," she said, leaning back against the vehicle's door.

"Yes. Look. At the top right corner of the small wooden building, you can see a security camera." Sergei said, pointing to an older structure two hundred meters away and slightly to their left. They must have a lot of surveillance posts. They must keep track of everything."

"If that can get us inside, then let's attract their attention," said Strategy, getting out of the Multi Terrain and beginning to walk along the road beside the force field. She waved her arms as she approached the gate, and called out, "Hey! You inside! I want to talk to someone in charge! I know your boss!" She repeated herself in Russian and Chinese, then stopped and waited.

"She's foolhardy," said Sergei to Hernando, who was almost finished warming his battery pack.

"Yeah, but she needs a big story." He squinted at the domes made dazzling by the brilliant sunlight. "I didn't think this would come to anything much, but now, I don't know. She's got incredible instincts," he said, watching her out in the snow hopping and waving her arms.

Sergei coughed. "It's risky, chasing such stories."

"Yes. You should have seen what she covered in Angel City," Hernando exclaimed. "Now, that was something. The execs had to admit she was more than a pretty face good at reading aloud. But that all came tumbling down around her. They think she faked it. That left her pretty low. She needs something with juice so she can regain face."

They watched as Strategy began throwing snowballs at the blue laser barrier. "I was beginning to think it wasn't going to happen, but this just might turn out to be another cover story," Hernando continued.

"*If* she gets to file it," said Sergei.

"Oh, don't worry about that. She'll file if she's in traction at the bottom of a well. She's that kind of reporter."

Sergei watched Strategy, who was now walking up and down in front of the gate, shouting in three languages. "Somehow," he said to Hernando, "that doesn't reassure me."

# CHAPTER 29

FRANKLIN SWINK HAD IMMEDIATELY swept into action. Through contacts with old colleagues, he first acquired a suite of rooms at a rather large Washington-based law firm and set up shop. By Thursday he had called a press conference with the major media outlets at the Jefferson Memorial speaking out against the unlawful treatment of the newly arrested detainees by the NTSA. It was a good-sized crowd. Almost as many came to see the old boy back in action as came to cover the statement.

He thanked them all for coming and started in on the events six days ago at the Four Corners Corridor Mall. He spoke to them about liberty and America and what this country stood for. For his own personal satisfaction, he let slip a few choice epithets about the moral ambiguity of Reed O'Neal who, he said, was misappropriating executive authority, perhaps for his own political gain.

A whiz-kid court journalist reminded the advocate that the Director had decades of precedent to back up his clandestine arrests—precedent unquestionably upheld by the Fourth Circuit Court of Appeals. Franklin quickly conceded that throughout American history the judicial branch had given extraordinary power to the executive branch regarding claims defending national security, but then parried that these claims had all turned out to be hollow when the threat had passed. He gave them chapter and verse of eight-score years of Justice Department failures, going as far back as World War II and the internment of Americans of Japanese descent. As to tyranny, depriving uncharged men and women of their right to a speedy trial was manifestly a direct attack on the unalienable rights this country held so dear.

The cynical men and women of the press corps snickered slightly at Swink's high-flown rhetoric and choice of site for the announcement. The Jefferson was a little too obvious—a little too on the nose. The older guys reminded the younger ones that Swink had always been "a wee bit theatrical." Quickly Swink delivered his sound-byte.

Pounding the podium for emphasis, Swink roared to the gathering, "I find Reed O'Neal's actions on behalf of the NTSA unacceptable. Citizens must be able to confront their accusers."

With the message out of the way, the "counselor from Galveston," as the press had long ago dubbed him, laid out his plans to submit a writ of habeas corpus. His hope was that the Fourth Circuit would order the NTSA to produce the detainees in court so that a judge could decide the legality of their imprisonment. He then took questions.

"Mister Swink, how many people were arrested and what are their names?"

"The government has not announced that, and I am unable to provide that information for you. I am here representing a principle as much as the human beings imprisoned."

From the middle of the seats, a twenty-year-old from Viacom news shouted, "It's the NTSA. What makes you so sure they're human?!" Laughter rippled through the press.

"A point well taken," Swink joked back. Then, with a twinkle, "but even if they aren't, this country promises them 'unalienable rights.' " The crowd, thoroughly enjoying this, laughed and thundered, "Boo," back to the podium. Franklin waved his hands in apology, loving the old give-and-take. "Next question."

The news conference continued for another half-hour. By the end of it, he was pretty much shot. He had answered complicated points of constitutionality, executive war powers, FISA, "enemy combatants," *Marbury v. Madison*, the Fourth and Sixth Amendments, due process, and the political ramifications for President Marino. He indicated one last question and called on Nola Owensmouth of the Dallas media magazine.

"Mister Swink—"

"Nice to see you again, Nola."

"Nice to see you, sir." She smiled at the familiarity. "For the past three years you have repeatedly stated you were retired. What changed your mind?"

Swink had expected this one, too. But his answer was more for himself than the media, "My wife, Anne."

Nola, who had known the late Mrs. Swink, was not allowed a follow-up question. Instead, Franklin's aide and old friend, Norm Lewis, took the microphone and thanked them all for coming. He turned around to see Swink off to the side in the company of some of the beltway pundits that both men had known for years. It was obvious he was thoroughly enjoying himself, taking the questions and the congratulations with a sweet sense of comeback. Norm beamed. Franklin was in his element and he had work to do. What could be better?

When Lewis was finally able to get Franklin into a waiting limo, he saw how tired his friend looked. "You up for this?"

The counselor from Galveston took a long hard look at what lay ahead and merely shrugged his shoulders. The mental fatigue he now felt reminded him that he was eighty-two. Being an advocate was work for the youthful, he thought, but he wanted to taste one more challenge, one more high-stakes clash of wills. "Norm, I want to use whatever contacts you have to find a man called Morgan d'Winter. He may be hiding somewhere in Canada, but that's only a maybe. From the little I know, he's good at hiding. When we get back to the office, I'll want any pertinent court cases, check with lexus-nexus, get me a calendar date for the Fourth Circuit, and . . ." He leaned back, exhausted, into the soft leather seat. ". . . and an old-fashioned cigar."

As Swink emerged from the antique glass elevator, he was met with a round of applause by the staff and lawyers of Bush, Geffin, McGuire, and Sucke. The news conference had already played more than once on many of the news outlets. He graciously accepted their appreciation and made his way down the long corridor to the quadrangle of rooms Bob Bush had made available to him. He closed his office door on the world and reached for the Havana that Norm had already left for him. He didn't light it; he'd given up smoking long ago. Moving around to his chair, he sat and savored the taste of the unlit cigar, its earthy redolence. He rolled it in his mouth, revisiting his performance of that morning. He started to put his feet up, when Norm buzzed from the outer office, "Lin," which is what his nearest and dearest called him, "you won't believe this, but I've got Morgan d'Winter on a weak private channel."

"Such a deal!" He removed the cigar. "How'd you get him so quickly?"

"Says he saw you on the news-vid."

"Well, put him on. Put him on."

Norm's connection faded, and a very grainy image of a brawny black man took its place. A very mistrusting d'Winter glowered for a moment and then spoke. "What the hell are you doing?"

"Why the hell should I tell you?" Swink growled back. "What's your relationship to the detainees?"

"What's this case mean to you?"

"I was hired by an interested party to look into the matter. An anonymous party."

"Dyckon?"

"Who?"

"Never mind. You've dealt with the NTSA before," d'Winter said.

"Successfully, I might add," said Swink with great confidence.

"So I have discovered. You've represented twenty-nine groups of clients and you've prevailed seventeen times."

"You checked me out. Good. It saves time," said Swink. "You must have some idea what we're up against if you've done that much."

"The NTSA," said d'Winter succinctly.

"That means Reed O'Neal. I should warn you, he hates being put on the spot. He has always denounced my abuse of due process, and many of my clients and their friends have had their pasts scrutinized." Swink glowered back at d'Winter. "It only makes me angry and it should make you careful."

D'Winter searched the octogenarian's face, not liking the age of the man and doubting the old warrior's competence. The truth was, even if Swink had been much younger, Morgan wouldn't have felt more sympathetically toward him. He shared his employer's basic mistrust of lawyers.

Swink spoke again. "So tell me why your associates are of such interest to the NTSA. How many are there besides John Dee, and what are the others' names?"

D'Winter hesitated. Swink hadn't mentioned Dee's name on the news-vid. How much more did he know? "I would prefer to speak with you face-to-face. I can send a flyer for you and bring you to where I am—"

"I'm not comfortable with such an arrangement," Swink said without apology. "After my morning's announcement, Reed will have a detail of NTSA agents watching my every move. I'm told you are in hiding and I don't want to lead them to you."

Morgan was still suspicious, but the reasoning sounded right. He didn't want another clandestine meeting to end up like Four Corners. He'd go along with this old man until he saw a reason not to. "I've only got a minute left before this hookup gets compromised. Listen up. There are only two detainees: John Dee and his business assistant, Kelly Edwards. She's American, He's . . . British."

"Why is the NTSA holding them?"

"We've been after a biological terrorist. I got to assume the NTSA think it's us." D'Winter saw the look. "It ain't."

"Do they have any criminal records?"

"Kelly doesn't, for sure. Dee . . . maybe, way back in the past."

"How far back?"

"Long enough not to count."

"What put you onto the terrorist?"

"A tip we got."

"Why'd you go after the terrorist by yourselves?"

Morgan bit his lower lip in slight frustration. He'd seen the Swink conference twice. No mention of missing chips or Angel City or gargoyle aliens. There was the one gag about "alien rights," but Morgan would have bet Swink didn't suspect the deeper connotations.

"It was personal."

"That's awfully vague. If I'm to be your lawyer, you've got to tell me everything."

"Hey, you ain't my lawyer . . . yet. And as far as I know, you ain't Dee's."

"Is it true John Dee doesn't have an identity chip?"

"Why do you ask that?"

"Is it true?" Franklin Swink insisted.

"I gotta get off this channel."

"How do I reach you in the future?"

"I'll do all the reaching. Who's the anonymous Mr. Moneybags?"

"I told you I can't tell you that."

D'Winter looked at his running chronometer. Damn. Five seconds left. "Got to go. Get them out soon. Before its too late."

"I'll do the best I can. You have my word." Morgan d'Winter broke the connection before Franklin Swink could ask, too late for what?

Swink leaned back in his chair, returned the cigar to his mouth, and stared at the diamond pattern in the ceiling. He catalogued the facts he had gained from the brief conversation: Mr. Morgan d'Winter most definitely was in hiding. Furthermore, d'Winter seemed unaware of Theon Celsus' involvement. There was someone else involved named Dyckon.

He rolled the cigar, sucking on the sharp leafy taste. D'Winter's evasion of the big question completely convinced him that this John Dee was indeed chipless—an amazing phenomenon. He had a past, but that was long ago. Perhaps that was when he managed to wriggle out of his ID chip. He was British, not from some far-flung remote region—he had to have had one.

Franklin rose from his desk and slowly walked toward the window. He was a little closer, he thought, to knowing why NTSA wanted them. The three or four or five of them may all be somehow mixed up in bio-terrorism, a perfectly understandable reason for the Agency to get involved. As he pulled back the drapes to spot the agents who by now were surely watching him from the street below, he framed the legal question he would address: how will this affect my protecting their civil rights?

# CHAPTER 30

"I KNOW YOU FROM the news," Dee said, matching his tone to O'Neal's and keeping his eye on Agent Anders, who sat silently beside him.

O'Neal made a grimace of distaste. "I dislike having to explain NTSA business to the public. They're easily panicked and they don't understand our function."

"Nor do I," said Dee.

"I don't owe you an explanation," said O'Neal. "You owe me one."

Five minutes before, a fizz from a place in the opposite wall had warned the Doctor that the undetectable door was opening, and a moment later, Reed O'Neal and Daryl Anders had come into the cell. Dee was ordered to remain on his bed at all times and not to approach the two men. In turn, the men of the NTSA had stood rooted with their backs to the invisible entranceway, keeping their distance. O'Neal stood militarily straight, his arms and hands parallel to the sides of his body. A commander of armies out of uniform, Dee thought. As before, Anders had a recording device and his file, which was noticeably thicker now.

"But why must I answer you?" Dee asked. "What gives you such sweeping authority?" He knew the answer, for all spymasters, from Throgmorton to O'Neal, saw themselves as masters of more than their own domain.

"The President has entrusted that authority to me. You would have to know about the old Central Intelligence Agency and its modern cousins, the National Security Council and the Defense Intelligence Agency, agencies that have tacit permission and unaccounted budgets that enable them to work covertly all over the world. They laid the groundwork for what became the National Terrestrial Security Administration. But you don't know about that, do you?"

"Very little," Dee lied, remembering everything he'd been told. "As you intend. Care to elaborate?"

O'Neal didn't take the bait. "You're a puzzle to me, do you know?"

"I think, rather, that you believe I'm a danger . . . to you," said Dee boldly.

Anders's eyes flicked to the Director, who seemed unconcerned. "To me, little man, you are hardly anything so important. But you and your alien trespassers pose a long-term threat to this country, to the world. We were obliged to take you into custody in a very public way. You forced my hand, and I dislike that. You have made it necessary for me to use Senator Havers and our friends in the media to repair the rift in the public confidence your presence has created. I dislike having to employ Senator Havers more than absolutely necessary. If he speaks out too much on our behalf, we come under scrutiny, which is what we wish to avoid. Having to reveal our activities plays into the hands of the enemies of this country."

"And how comes it that I am to be entitled with the name of 'enemy'?" Dee asked with feigned innocence.

There was a slight hesitation before O'Neal answered. What right had this traitor to question the judgment of his betters, of the American government? He should thank his lucky stars the Turks or the Aussies had not arrested him. He'd be bagged and tagged by now. "You must know that you're the only person on this planet without a chip."

This was an argument Dee had prepared for. "Are you certain? Mightn't there be a lone wayfarer in the jungles of Africa or the wastes of Siberia or the deserts of Arabia or the remote isles of the South Seas who has not been maimed with a chip? Have you really accounted for all ten billion of mankind?"

"Of course we have," O'Neal said brusquely. "What makes you think we haven't?"

"Just that even now there are diverse, distant places, and enforcing your temporal sway upon them all, perforce, is a Herculean labor and just as fantastical." Dee shrugged. "If a driver of camels in Mongolia is in want of a chip, how might you ever know? A baby born upon the far side of the moon? You want the power of Heaven to have knowledge of all."

"We would know," said O'Neal. "All governments subscribe to the program. No one gets housing or food or medical treatment or education without a chip. No one travels on any public transportation, no one is admitted to a public building without one. No one is exempt. It is a necessity for today's world. A necessity for every country's national security. Plus, it is the most dependable census mankind has ever devised." He shook his head in aggravation. "Why am I debating this with you?"

"For it appears that in seasons past I have evaded your grasp," Dee said, goading him deliberately.

O'Neal scowled. The man's smugness and vernacular were maddening. "And by the look of you, for years and years. You're what? Forty? Forty-five?"

"My age is of no matter," Dee said, becoming wary again.

"Your age is part of the puzzle," O'Neal said, for the first time looking over at Anders, who handed the Director Dee's medical results. "Certain combinations of errant genes substantiate your claim of being from England." He flipped through an array of findings. "All the chemical and genetic profiling indicates that there is nothing alien about you."

With that, John Dee politely nodded thanks to Agent Anders, who had taken the sample. But O'Neal's military mien was not to be interfered with, and he continued on in his precise, colorless voice. "At least nothing our tests can detect. There are, however, antibodies in your blood to"—he read from a list—"smallpox, scarlet fever, influenza, tuberculosis, and bubonic plague. Diseases that were totally wiped out longer than fifty years ago."

Though the medical results were puzzling to the NTSA doctors, their presence had sealed the argument that John Dee was not a creature from outer space. It was ridiculous to believe that a chameleon-like creature, comparable to the one in Angel City, would add to his disguise by replicating ancient antigens in a world that had not seen them for a half a century or more. No, the red-cell team argued, he was human all right. The real question was, where and how was he exposed? The secondary question being, could his unique antibodies have helped in the removal of the ID?

"Your x-rays show evidence of deep scars to your head, abdomen, shoulders, and arms. I think you must have had a chip and then had it removed. And you survived the procedure. Learning how you survived is reason enough to hold you."

"Think what you like," said Dee. "I am not your problem."

For the better part of a minute, O'Neal said nothing. "You were in Angel City."

"That I was," Dee said, and volunteered nothing more.

"You took part in the riots there," O'Neal said, adding, "Our first awareness of you was in connection with a UFO we spotted a year and a half before. During the interim, our research has shown you amassed a very healthy fortune selling inexplicable technology to rogue industries. Yet neither we, nor the Brits, nor anyone else has any tax records on you for the years before the UFO in Angel City. The only explanation is that you were abducted and programmed to work for off-world beings. I've seen you on the vids Strategy Brooks provided. Your proximity to the creature indicates it had some sort of familiarity with you. It certainly allowed you to get closer to it than anyone else. She thinks I discount them as nothing more than sensational effects, manipulated and morphed to make the event more spectacular, but you and I know that isn't the case, don't we?"

"I know not what you mean," said Dee, concerned about the amount of facts they possessed about him. Perhaps, he thought, he could add some misinformation. "I saw a riot, I saw men who appeared to be rats, and a creature as much dragon as man. But that may only have been an illusion."

"So the world believes," O'Neal said with a hint of smugness.

"Then why do you bother with me? What can I, one man, do to topple your towering organization?" Dee asked with genuine curiosity.

"You are a problem because you have no chip. You have appeared as if out of nowhere and you have been up to real mischief." O'Neal tapped his palm where the implant held his communication screen. He turned to his associate. "Mr. Anders, please turn off your recording device. Mr. Dee, no one can see or hear us. I've turned off the monitors in this cell and Mr. Anders works for me and is utterly loyal. You can talk to me one-on-one. Tell me about the aliens."

"I doubt that would be wise," Dee said steadily.

"You don't believe me?" O'Neal asked.

"By this hand, I have every reason to doubt you."

"You could spare yourself any amount of trouble. The same goes for your colleague."

"She has done nothing wrong. She is in my employ, and her behavior must be on my head."

"Oh, very noble," O'Neal approved sarcastically.

"Responsible," Dee corrected him. "She has obeyed my instructions and done what I've bid her. You cannot hold her to blame—"

"It isn't a matter of blame, it is a matter of association. The NTSA has the right to detain those suspected of collaborating with alien influences on the same authority as we have for detaining aliens themselves. It's in our charter. We have extralegal powers we can invoke in times of crisis, which this is."

"And have you ever detained an alien?" Dee inquired politely, secretly hoping that they had somehow seized Mattik. He decided to tell them everything if they had.

"You know the answer to that better than I," said O'Neal.

"How do you reckon that? Have you not but presently told me that your file there proves otherwise about me? Sir, have you taken an alien creature?"

It was plain that the NTSA hadn't. There was concern in Anders's face and obvious disappointment in the Director's. It was clear O'Neal had hoped Dee was an alien in disguise. "Perhaps," O'Neal hedged. "But let us continue to discuss you. We will run some further tests," he said grimly.

"What more tests do you need?"

"You have an unaccountable propensity to use words and syntax from the Elizabethan period. It bears looking into."

Anders finally spoke. "We believe it's a code of some sort."

"Or a sign of a mental aberration. A weakness." O'Neal couldn't tolerate weakness in himself and despised it in others. "Agent Anders, see to it that the prisoner has a complete psychiatric and neurological evaluation. And that journal of his that he hides behind the monitor—have it analyzed. See if there really is a code." Moving to the place where Dee kept the diary hidden, Reed O'Neal himself moved to retrieve it. It was a lesson to prove nothing was hidden from him.

"You whoreson ass. I am a man who speaks what I think. Verily, I *am* an Elizabethan as you term it. Aye, a loyal subject to Her Grace, Elizabeth Regina," he exclaimed, making a daring grab for the book. "I speak not code, but the Queen's own English, and not the mincing of words and scraps of sentences that your time calls English, that has neither grace nor music in it." The loss of his diary with all his inner thoughts was a severe blow. Recklessly, he had said too much. Secrets had been revealed.

The directness and absurdity of the statement took both NTSA men by surprise. The Director gave the Doctor a condescending, contemptuous smile. Anders's eyes widened in unfeigned astonishment. Not sure if his boss had been only bluffing before about the listening devices, he looked down immediately and made sure that he was starting the recorder correctly. The profilers had been right, though. Exploit the weakness and it will crack the prisoner's defenses. The journal was added to Anders's growing file.

"I think Ms. Edwards will tell us something different. What do you think?"

"I think only poltroons impose the might and dread of their authority on loyal servants, or stoop to prey on terrified women," said Dee. He finally got to his feet and took a step toward O'Neal. Immediately in response, Anders stepped forward and produced a taser. Its presence didn't deter John Dee—he didn't know what it was and he had a point to make. "If aught is done to harm her—anything—you'll have no help of any kind from me."

"Why would you suppose I need your help?" O'Neal said with a sneer.

"Because you're here," said Dee. "That must mean you want something, something you—and not Anders—can glean only with my cooperation."

"I don't make bargains with criminals," said O'Neal.

"Are you sure that's what I am?" Dee countered.

"You haven't got a chip. That's illegal," he said with pleasure.

"That's the heart of it for you, isn't it?" Dee challenged. He slipped into old ways. "You desire to know how it falls out that I lack one. You relish not the thought that your precious system might be fallible. You aspire to Heaven's powers but like proud Lucifer know not that you have overreached. Like a greedy publican espying a well-fed vagabond, you pant to know how I've made it through all your security traps and checks and am not apprehended until now. And when I impart to you God's honest truth, you leer at me as if I were a monkey."

"You've had help," O'Neal said flatly, tired of the hyperbole. "Someone has put Franklin Swink onto your case. Not that it will do you any good."

"Of course I have." Dee quickly agreed. He studied O'Neal for several seconds. "But not any kind of help you know about."

# CHAPTER 31

AFTER A COMMUNICATION FROM the clerk of the court, Franklin Swink toggled onto his vid-screen, where the decision on his appeal to the Fourth Circuit Court was posted. The decision was written by Chief Justice Littlehorse and circuit judges Sekyla and Ash. He began to read:

> Kelly Edwards and John Dee filed a petition under 28 U.S.C. 2241 challenging the lawfulness of their confinement by the National Terrestrial Security Administration in the Langley Naval Brig. The appeal by the petitioners questions whether a declaration by the Director of the NTSA setting forth what the government contends were the circumstances of Edwards' and Dee's capture was sufficient by itself to justify their detention.
>
> It is to be noted that in response to the filed petition, the Defense Intelligence Agency (DIA) with the National Terrestrial Security Administration (NTSA) have filed a response, and motion to dis-

miss, to the petition of habeas corpus. Attached to its response was an affidavit from the Deputy Solicitor General, Michael Scott, which confirms the material factual allegations in the petitioners' petition—specifically, the absence of a mandated ID chip, seizure of Edwards and Dee, Kelly Edwards' position as chief aide and employee of John Dee, the designation of "enemy combatants" by our government, and the ultimate incarceration in the Langley Naval Brig. Moreover, the government contends that allowing counsel for "enemy combatants" in the absence of charges would interfere with the detention. A hindrance to the interest of gathering intelligence would be created, by establishing from the onset an adversarial relationship with the detainees. That issue is not presented in the Edwards and Kelly appeal. Therefore we did not take it up.

In February 2101, Franklin Swink filed a petition of habeas corpus, naming as petitioners both Kelly Edwards and John Dee. The petition alleges that Kelly Edwards is a citizen of the United States and that John Dee is a citizen of the United Kingdom. This court has previously determined that Franklin Swink is a proper "friend" to the detainees and may file petition for them. The petition alleges that Kelly Edwards as an American citizen enjoys the full protection of the Constitution, as is also the right of John Dee by virtue of the Montevideo Conventions #65902 ruling, granting citizens of all signatories to the treaty equal protection under each nation's laws. The petition further alleges that the government's current detention of them in this country without charges, access to judicial tribunal, or the right to counsel violates the Fifth and Fourteenth Amendments to the U.S. Constitution. By way of relief, the petition asks, inter alia, that the court 1) "Order Respondents to cease all interrogations of Kelly Edwards and John Dee, direct or indirect, while this litigation is pending"; 2) "Order and declare that both detainees are being held in violation of the Fifth and Fourteenth Amendments to the U.S. Constitution"; 3) "To the extent Respondents contest any factual allegations in the Petition, schedule an evidentiary hearing, at which Petitioners may adduce proof in support of their allegations"; 4) "Order unmonitored immediate access to Edwards and Dee"; and 4) "Order that the Petitioners, Edwards and Dee, be released from Respondents' unlawful custody." Further, the petition demands a speedy transfer by the government to Franklin Swink, friend to the petitioners, of all statements and notes taken from any interviews with them; the names and addresses of all interrogators who have questioned and/or examined Edwards and Kelly; all files held by the government that implicate the petitioners in wrongdoing; and a list of the dates when Edwards and Kelly were under observation.

To these points we caution that the petition involves complex and serious national and international security issues. We find that we must show proper deference to the government's legitimate security and intelligence interests. However, we are mindful that with no meaningful judicial review, any lawful citizen, American or otherwise, may be alleged to be an enemy combatant and detained indefinitely without charges or counsel on the government's say-so. To deprive any world citizen of legal protection is not a step that any court would take casually. This dual status especially for Ms. Edwards—that of American citizen and that of alleged enemy combatant—raises important questions about the role of the courts in times of war. In accordance with the Constitution, the Supreme Court has shown great deference to the executive branch when deciding sensitive matters of foreign policy, national security, or military affairs. The reasons are not difficult to discern. The executive branch is organized to supervise the conduct of military actions in a way the judiciary simply is not. While the designation of "enemy combatant" has given rise to controversy in the past, the term is one that has been used by the Supreme Court many times. See, e.g., *Madsen v. Kinsella,* 343 U.S.C. 341, 355 (2052); In re: Yamashita, 327 U.S. 1,7 (1946); Quirin, 317 U.S.C. 31. We note that the executive branch is best positioned to comprehend interplanetary conflict in its full context, and neither the absence of set-piece battles nor adequate warning before an earthly assault suffices to nullify the war-making authority entrusted to either the executive or the legislative branch.

However, if due process means anything, it means that the courts must defend the "fundamental principles of liberty and justice, which lie at the base of all our civil and political institutions." *Powell v. Alabama,* 287 U.S. 45, 67. The writers of the Constitution were concerned how the state will wield its power of forcible restraint. Our founding fathers knew that the power to detain could easily become destructive "if exerted without check or control" by an unrestrained executive free to "imprison, dispatch, or exile any man that was obnoxious to the government, by an instant declaration that such is their will and pleasure." The obligation of the judicial branch to protect our freedoms does not simply cease whenever our national security forces are committed to armed conflict. The detention of citizens must be subject to judicial review. It is significant that the form of relief sought by the amicus, Swink, is a writ of habeas corpus. He affirms that the continual detention of the prisoners means that the writ of habeas corpus has been unconstitutionally suspended. We recognize that in war, as in peace, habeas corpus provides one of the firmest bulwarks against unconstitutional detentions. As early as 1789, the Congress reaffirmed the court's common law authority to review detentions of federal prisoners, giving its explicit blessing to the judiciary's power to "grant writs of habeas corpus for the purpose of an inquiry into the cause of commitment" for federal detainees. Act of Sept. 24, 1789, ch 20-14,1 Stat. 81-82. While the scope of habeas corpus review has changed over the succeeding centuries, its essential function of assuring that restraint accords with the rule of law remains unchanged. However, we find this premise for barring detention to be unconvincing. The fact that we have not ordered the relief that the amicus requested is hardly equivalent to a suspension of the writ.

Edwards and Dee and amicus have in fact pressed two more convincing legal grounds for relief: 18 U.S.C. 4001(a) and Article 5 of the Geneva Convention. We now address them both.

18 U.S.C. 4001 regulates the detentions of United States citizens. It states in full:

a) No citizen will be imprisoned or otherwise detained by the United States except pursuant to an Act of Congress.

The petition of Edwards and Dee argues that there is no congressional sanction for their incarceration and that 4001(a) therefore prohibits their continued detention. We find this argument unpersuasive.

Even if Edwards and Dee were right that congressional authorization is needed, Congress in the wake of the Act of 2083 authorized the President to create the NTSA "to use all necessary and appropriate force against extraterrestrial nations, armies, or belligerents *or their abettors* (emphasis added) that he determines planned, authorized, committed, or aided actual or potential terrorist attacks." Capturing and detaining enemy combatants is an inherent part of warfare and international defense. Furthermore, Congress has specifically authorized the expenditure of funds for the NTSA to continue to monitor and install mandatory identification chips in citizens. It is difficult if not impossible to understand how Congress could make laws and legislate funds for the continued monitoring and detention of persons "similar to prisoners of war" without also authorizing their detention in the first place. Being a protected citizen does not relieve supporters of the world's enemies of the consequences of their abetting alien belligerents. We therefore reject Edwards' and Dee's contention that 4001(a) bars their detention.

The detainees and amicus also contend that Article 5 of the Geneva Convention applies to this case and requires an "initial formal determination of their status as enemy belligerent by a competent tribunal." Geneva Convention Relative to the Treatment of Prisoners of War, Aug 12, 1949, art.5,6 U.S.T. 3316, 75 U.N.T.S. 135.

This defense fails also because the Geneva Convention is not self-executing. "Courts will only find a treaty to be self-executing if the document, as a whole, evidences an intent to provide a private right of action." *Goldstar (Panama) v. U.S.*, 967 F.2d 965, 968 (4th Cir. 1992) The Geneva Convention shows no such intent. There is no provision in the agreement for enforcement by any form of private petition. The only discussion of enforcement in the Geneva Convention dwells on the scenario if warring parties disagree on what the Convention requires of them. When this happens, article 11 requires them to arrange a "meeting of their representatives with a view toward settling the disagreement." Geneva Convention, at art. 11. The Geneva Convention is not toothless, but its values are vindicated by proper diplomatic means and reciprocity. Further, there is a powerful self-regulating national interest in observing the rules of the Convention, as both sides take prisoners. This reciprocity is the basis for enduring compliance. We therefore find that the language in the Geneva Convention is not "self-executing" and does not "create private rights of action in the domestic courts of the signatory countries." Further, the court is not aware of any other world, or nation of that foreign world, being a signatory to the Geneva Convention. Should that change, they would be entitled to "arrange a meeting of their representatives" for redress. Because it is undisputed that John Dee was captured with the absence of the proper internationally mandated identification, to wit, a universal ID chip, we hold that the submitted declaration is a sufficient basis upon which to conclude that the Commander in Chief had constitutionally detained Dee pursuant to the extraterrestrial war powers entrusted to him by the United States Terrestrial Security Treaty of 2083. We hold the same for Kelly Edwards, who is in the employ of John Dee. Further, it is to be noted that the detainees' petition fails to address the question of alien fraternization which underlies their recent capture. For all the reasons stated above, we hold that there is no purely legal barrier to the continued detention of Edwards and Dee, nor to their designation by the executive as "enemy combatants." No further factual inquiry is necessary or proper, and we remand the case with directions to dismiss the petition.

"Damn them," was all Swink said.

# CHAPTER 32

IT WAS THEIR EVENING half-hour in the recreation room. Under the strain of a self-imposed hunger strike, an exhausted Kelly Edwards sat with her head on the table while her boss paced the wooden laminated floor looking for some absolution. At the beginning of their time together, she had felt her spirits buoyed by the news of Swink's speech. She had used what strength she had to enthuse about Swink's successful track record in defending civil liberties. But she had found the Doctor supercilious and sullen, skeptical of what a lawyer could do, especialy in a short amount of time. They did not speak of the virus that threatened them. Nor did Dee reveal that he had foolishly written down some of his thoughts. Thoughts that now were confiscated and might well compromise their position. When she had called him on his grumpiness, he had told her of his conversation with Reed O'Neal: the threat to her, his medical findings, their knowledge of much of his recent past, and finally his admission of his true identity. The last was devastating news, and she had reacted bitterly, having spent years of her life keeping it secret. Their reservoir of secrets with which to negotiate seemed to be running dry.

"Thinkest thou our worthy counselor has found safe harbor?" Dee sought to engage her again to reawaken her spirit and compassion. "I think constantly upon his danger and that it is I who have chased him from his home and country to be hunted like a beast in the forest. Yet, he was ever a man of hardy invention. Pray God he is not hurt nor punished for my sins."

The day had weighed heavily on Dee. Five days had passed and Mattik was still out there, a time bomb ticking. Yet the secret of Mattik's existence was his only hope of finding a means of escape or a way to barter that information for freedom. Yet no means had presented itself, and as the days passed in isolation and utter confinement, Dee allowed to himself that he never would share his secret. Untold experiences, Walsingham's training, and his inexorable wish to return home counseled him not to give this information away. If Dee and Kelly aided in the capture of Mattik, they risked the possibility that the NTSA would dispose of Mattik the way Piper's army had disposed of Fawg—complete annihilation—and he would remain locked away, with no access to the timeslip device—the door forever shut to returning home. Yet, not to tell left humanity unwarned and unprotected. Alone in his cell, his strong sense of survival clashed with his sense of duty, leaving him ragged and testy. Guilt had led him to self-hatred. It was difficult not to be curt with Kelly because of it. "Can you not offer one word in the way of conversation? It is impious stubbornness to be sad and say nothing."

"I worry about him, too. And I hope he's safe," Kelly

answered bitingly, too exhausted to care about Dee's compulsive need to chat.

A restless silence settled over them, and Dee felt a stab of alarm that he was wasting the little time they had together. He searched his tired mind for some words of comfort. Some sort of apology for his callousness. Frustration bubbled inside him. He did his best to steady himself, knowing from other imprisonments that isolation from the world was as insidious a danger as hunger and cold. Dee continued to look up at the night sky overhead, segmented by the skylights. Finally, he ventured, "I think we may have more snow."

"Yes," she said wearily, turning with effort to look up at the window above them.

"It gives us something to look forward to." He sat down on one of the hard chairs and continued to stare up at the skylights. "We're not without friends. Never forget that."

Still fixated upwards, she intoned, "I'm trying not to. But forever in limbo is a long time."

In his office, Reed O'Neal watched the display on the monitor with bemused interest. He could see that his captives were wearing down. "Make the nerve-note a little louder," he said to the red-cell interrogation member. "And in a day or so, start drugging the air."

"Any time spent in captivity is as an eternity," Dee said, mentally revisiting the dozen and more imprisonments he had endured. Each had seemed unendurable. Each had been a struggle of his mind over his body. Then, at least, it had been his own personal struggle. Now he was concerned about how well they would hold up as a team, how long it would be before they became really and truly angry, resentful, or distrusting of one another. That would be the greatest danger to them both.

"Have you eaten anything?" Kelly asked suddenly. She wanted him to say he had.

"No. Have you?"

"No. I'm getting very hungry," she admitted, and resolved to eat every piece of liver, Brussels sprout, or candy bar ever put in front of her again—once she got out.

"So am I." He recalled the filthy slops he had been given while in prison, an ocean and five centuries away. "The meat smelled of savoriness." An uncharacteristic wave of nausea swept over him. He admonished himself for being more faint than the hunger should have made him. "Think you there be rats in this prison?" Dee asked wistfully.

"Rats? Of course not," Kelly said angrily, wondering what he was on about *now.*

"Pity," Dee remarked. "Such creatures might prove useful."

"What do you mean? You wouldn't eat one, would you?" Kelly asked, appalled.

"But of course, my dear. When the stomachache is past endurance, a rat is a sumptuous meal. Moreover, they are a meat you can be certain has not been doctored. Belike you have not the taste for it. Then learn of me that on occasion these vermin make wondrous food tasters."

She glanced at the bowl of fruit that had been set in the middle of the table when they were let into the recreation room. Just the smell was enough to make her salivate, but she couldn't let herself weaken enough to try any—not yet, in any case. She moved her chair a little closer to him. "I wish we could try the fruit." A small hysterical giggle bubbled up. "Too bad we haven't rats for that."

He nodded, joining her in the momentary release.

Looking away from the bowl, she wiped her mouth with her fingers. Despite the dryness of her mouth from dehydration, spittle had collected in the corners. "Sorry." It sounded as if she were admitting a dreadful failure rather than a slight, momentary lapse.

"No reason to be," said Dee. "The fruits are tantalizing."

"That's why I don't trust them," said Kelly.

"Nay, no more do I," Dee agreed with a sigh. Finally he looked at her with a faintly bitter compassion. "How long do you think you can hold the fast?"

"A day, perhaps two," she answered, admitting her faltering resolve. There was a darting evasiveness in the way she had said it. She knew she couldn't hold out the day. "So long as I have water, a day . . . maybe two."

"Two days with water," he repeated perfunctorily. That seemed about right. After three days, they would both be light-headed and too weak to be at each other's throats. "I pray we shall have made some progress by then."

"What progress do you expect?" said Kelly accusingly. She sighed. Troubled by the venom in her voice, she moved off the subject. "I wish we could find a student's backpack somewhere."

He looked at her, and remembered how they had eluded their pursuers when she had hidden him in a large backpack and carried him back to Angel City. "Yea," he said slowly, lost in the memory of that. They had thought themselves so clever to hide him from the chip scanners. Perhaps they had succeeded that day in San Luis Obispo, or perhaps the NTSA had always been aware of him. How they had congratulated themselves in their ignorance. Both in their own way revisited happier times and tried to forget their hunger. He laid his hand on her shoulder. "I prithee, lady, be of better cheer. If thou engrossest all the griefs, they are yours alone, thou robbest me of mine." He carefully moved his hand upon her head and held it there. "Fear not, we shall prevail," he exhorted, sounding as though he had the sure knowledge of a Daniel.

"I hope you're right," she said softly.

"Inaction is the enemy of boldness, but it is the friend of the quiet mind," he said to cheer her. "I wish *you* had something to read. A book would translate heavy hours to sweet pastime."

"If only I could make my mind quiet," she said her head listlessly on the table, a catch in her voice.

"Separate your thoughts from the isolation and the deprivation, dwell on loving remembrances, family, friends. Your mind will people your silent cell and cram it with countless conversations. If it is your wont, think on Heaven. There too, you shall find comfort."

"And what about my stomach?"

He stared at her hair and felt the skin of her scalp. "For that you must eat."

Not sure she had heard him correctly, she turned her eyes up to him. "There might be drugs in the food."

"No matter. You must eat." He reached for a piece of fruit.

# CHAPTER 33

REED O'NEAL PACED HIS office nervously, his patience wearing thin. "We've had them eight days, that should do something to them," he announced to Lieutenant Commander Milton, the imposing naval officer who was the leader of the red-cell team evaluating Dee and Kelly's communications and vital signs. Her ethnic parentage had created a tall, taut body the color of caramel and had given her cheekbones that most women would pay a small fortune to acquire. Lieutenant Commander Milton was the liaison from the Defense Intelligence Agency, a Department of Defense military combat support agency. Superb looking in her blue uniform, she could recruit half of D.C. if she were pictured on a poster.

Hours after Four Corners, Reed O'Neal had gone through Marino's chief of staff, William "Billy" McIntyre, to get guidance from the President. "Enemy combatants" or "enemy belligerents" were traditionally Department of Defense's bailiwick, but NTSA, having a quasi-military function, had a solid claim to the prisoners. Knowing that they were in uncharted waters and that jurisdiction was questionable, the Counsel to the President had recommended caution. It was decided that custody of the "enemy combatants" needed to be officially under the military wing of the DOD, but unofficially Marino wanted Reed O'Neal running the show. The DOD had sent O'Neal and Lieutenant Commander Milton, who in DIA circles had the reputation for being a "hammer." In a matter of hours, she had swiftly transferred the prisoners to a naval brig in Langley. For her red-cell analysis team, she had assembled a list of top-notch experts and had them airlifted to the Langley facility, where they fluidly coordinated with O'Neal's people. At the same time air force general Tom Finney of the National Security Agency was told to heighten his listening devices, both lunar and terrestrial, to catch any suspicious chatter about the detainees' arrest. This was in addition to the NTSA putting their space scanning radio dishes on red alert for UFOs. If there were more aliens out there, O'Neal wanted to know about it ASAP. No more embarrassments like the one in Angel City. Meanwhile, Homeland Security quietly changed the national warning alert from blue to orange—a two-step jump.

"But eight days and nothing!"

"You have the DNA and the medical results," Milton reminded him. "At least you know they're both human."

"Perhaps," said O'Neal. "But the male has errant gene combinations that the lab is still investigating. He might have been manipulated in some way. " He gave the Lieutenant Commander a disapproving look and added, "There is that object in his brain, which you won't let me get at." Late that morning Anders, as ordered, had had Dee MRIed for neurological anomalies. The brain scan had detected a metallic object implanted in that part of his brain that recognized words. The red-cell medical team first speculated that it might be a homing device, but a conclusive test indicated that there were no radio, x-ray, infrared, electromagnetic, microwave, or any other kind of signals emanating from the man's brain. The finding was startling, but in no way connected the detainee to alien intelligence. O'Neal had wanted to put the prisoner on the operating table immediately and remove the device for study. However, Milton had argued that the operation could be dangerous, and with Franklin Swink barking at the door about civil liberties and due process, they could not risk John Dee's life with an unreasonable search of his body. After all, it could be an experimental ID chip and as earthly as their own. Even now, the Director wouldn't give it up. "I have an obligation to be sure that isn't the case before making a decision about him."

"Do you think the courts will accept that?" Milton asked politely.

"Courts! Who's going to take this to court? They are belligerent combatants. The courts have no jurisdiction. The prisoners haven't had any outside contact, and won't for a million years if I have anything to say about it. I have the law on my side—not to mention executive privilege. And I already have Havers making a case on the Hill and in the media for their treason. He's very good at making paranoia sound reasonable and patriotic, which is why I put up with his posturing." He smiled, doing his best not to be smug.

"That may be," said Milton. "But Swink is not going to sit quietly and let you have your way with them. He's at the Fourth right now, petitioning for a writ."

"I'll deal with Franklin Swink. Don't you worry. He's a meddling old fool who simply got bored of retirement. He's not in this for the long haul. Did you hear his statement the other day? He likened me to a Keystone Kop. I'd put him in a cell right next to his E.T.-loving friends, if I could. He and that Dee could speechify at each other till they were blue in the face." The NTSA and its red-cell team were still very much puzzled by the little man's archaic speech patterns. Anders wondered if they were caused by the cranial implant. The team psychiatrist thought they might be part of a delusional complex. The team lawyer recommended that if that was the diagnosis, then under *Sage v. Mendelson* the Department was mandated to get the prisoner legal counsel. O'Neal had smirked that all terrorists were crazy and that all federal lawyers were wimpy.

Milton chafed at the name-calling. Making your opposition personal diluted your focus. "But they've hinted at associates, and at least one of them may be contagious. In his journal, doesn't Dee call him 'virulent Mattik'?"

"But what kind of virulence?" O'Neal countered. "With all that crap about Heaven and Death, he could be raving about some fellow terrorist who has recently turned against them. Like the way the 'unnamed one' from Terra Incognita seems to do. By the way, isn't Terra Incognita the term the mapmakers of Shakespeare's time used for the Americas?" As O'Neal was quite sure of his reference, the rhetorical question was meant only to impress. With professorial pride, he looked around the conference table to see how many of the red-cell team experts were equally knowledgeable.

Bringing the discussion back to the Mattik threat, Milton focused on the question of what the diary called "a calamity that the world knows not the remedy of." The team doctors speculated about a worldwide disease, while the military experts were sure it referred to an aggressive attack of some sort.

"What do you think he means by 'ravish us'?" queried the government psychiatrist, wondering out loud about the Freudian implications. The group launched into a new group discussion on modes of delivery—single soldiers? a battalion?—and how long they had to find out.

"We'll find them," O'Neal said firmly interrupting the debate. "No matter how many there are, we'll have them locked up in a matter of days. Our treaty lets us detain them anywhere in the world—with two exceptions, and they hardly matter right now. But you know they won't go to those countries, with us chasing them. It would mean more trouble for those places than the enemy is worth. Besides, the diary says 'Terra Incognita.' I say that puts the threat right here in the States."

"Have you got a lead on an associate?" Milton asked pointedly. "Edwards is being very careful about what she says."

"Yes, but we have the man's diary," he retorted, straightening his posture and looking to the communications specialist. "Have you found any codes buried in the text?"

From the far side of the table, a brilliant young analyst from DIA answered in the negative. He reported that he had thoroughly investigated the "Mortlake" locution, and aside from it being an old suburb south of London, he thought that it could refer to a possible home base at the Great Salt Lake, the Dead Sea, or any such fetid body of water, possibly even the Hollywood Reservoir in Angel City.

"Has the prisoner ever been seen in the London suburb?" Milton asked.

"We've checked with British NTSA , who had the suspects under surveillance in London. The U.K. branch reports no sightings of any of them, including the still missing Morgan d'Winter," Anders told her.

"They've got to slip sometime," said O'Neal. "And you'll catch them when they do."

Milton nodded. "What about our immediate prisoners? Have they eaten yet?"

"The woman has had one piece of fruit. Which is troublesome," said O'Neal. "We don't want Swink to say we let them starve."

"No, we don't," Milton agreed, knowing the responsibility would be hers if the detainees suffered. She'd gotten a lecture from her boss at DIA, a no-nonsense admiral who was at odds with O'Neal's neoconservatism. He had taken pains to remind the lieutenant commander that there was a hundred-year-old law that made torture in the United States a felony with a twenty-year prison sentence attached. Standing by and allowing the Director to violate even the spirit of this law would make her equally culpable.

"Do you know why they aren't eating?" O'Neal asked.

"They're afraid the food is drugged," Milton said promptly. "And it is." She tried to keep the reproach out of her voice.

"Of course, and for good reason, too," said O'Neal. He pursed his lips and frowned portentously. "See if they'll take some more fresh fruit. Most people think things that are fresh are okay. We have genetically modified bananas that make people more tractable. They've worked wonders in Africa and South America."

"I'll try, but I don't think they're going to accept," said Milton.

"Just try. And make sure that you keep the nerve-note going, just at the threshold of hearing." O'Neal smiled. "If they *are* human, it will get to them in time."

"It's beginning to get to me," conceded Milton. "I've had a headache for the last two hours."

"It's worth it. Just keep that note going. Don't make it any louder. If they become aware of it, they'll resist it. Don't vary the pitch, either. Three hundred forty point six cycles per second."

"I know," Milton said a bit brusquely. She didn't need to be reminded of her job—not by him.

"Carry on," he said, dismissing her. Only when she was gone did he put in a call to Senator Havers to tell him to turn up the heat of public sentiment. While his hands unconsciously rubbed and kneaded each other, he paced the room like an expectant father.

"But I've spoken on this twice yesterday," Havers protested. "I can't keep on making these declarations without something to support them—"

"And you can do it again today," O'Neal said, cutting him short. "You can't let the ball drop on this one, Senator. The safety of the world could depend on what we do now, and you're the one who'll show the world what has to be done."

"I don't want to seem alarmist. Voters don't like that." Havers seemed determined to drag his feet.

"No, but they don't like being exposed to possible biohazards either," O'Neal said, improvising. His pacing and the massaging of his hands picked up tempo. "You'll agree that I have prime access to this country's intelligence capabilities—and full knowledge of their shortcomings. The fact that we don't have reliable proof of a threat does not prove that one doesn't exist. Nathaniel, think about it. We have to walk a very fine line here, and the public needs you to show them the way. This situation is unprecedented. The lab says the DNA samples we took from one of the detainees aren't normal, and who knows what that could mean? You know they've had to quarantine many of those who were shopping at Four Corners Corridor when—"

"I know, I know," said Havers. "All right. You've convinced me." That was the first he'd heard about the abnormal DNA samples. "This is important for all of us—I see that. But I'm not going to spook the whole country; that would only make things worse for everyone. I'll mention public health issues, but only minor ones. I'm not going to say that you have detained biological terrorist aliens. You know as well as I do that you can't actually support that contention yet."

"Of course not," said O'Neal hastily, fingers entwining and releasing. "You have a country to protect; I have a planet. You and I must work together on this." He repeated this with full intensity.

"I know," Havers said again weakly.

"Good. The next several days are going to be crucial for all of us," O'Neal declared, and decided to quit while he was ahead. He played with the ring on his finger. "I thank you, Senator, I know the grateful people of this land will thank you as well—for your patriotism and your foresight."

"Hell, we're all in this together," Havers said, and rang off.

O'Neal sat for a short while considering what he ought to do next. It was too soon to go talk to the detainees again, and there was no word from Strategy Brooks, off in Siberia—not that he expected anything useful from her. He got up and decided to take a tour around the building. He liked doing surprise inspections of his agency: they kept everyone on their toes. But first, some oil for his chafed hands.

# CHAPTER 34

MATTIK, THE ROC WHO had been Corwin Tarlton, emerged from the hold of the hovership he had taken across the Pacific to the Bay of Bengal and the port of Calcutta. The wharves protruded out from the shore for more than a quarter mile, accommodating more than the gigantic commercial hoverships: luxurious cruisers, old-fashioned tankers, wind-traders like huge venetian blinds atop heavily laden wedges, and all manner of smaller local craft were drawn up to docks and warehouses. Making his way toward shore, he had a chance to observe the myriad folk who flocked to India, the land of understanding. As he walked on, he studied the throngs around him and adapted himself to the appearance of the people. He was taller than most, with very dark olive skin, black hair and an emphatic black mustache. He wore loose muslin trousers and a shirt under a short, embroidered vest. Anyone spotting him trudging up the hill with his well-worn luggage would have guessed him to be a peddler. Except for the American Ray-Bans hiding his reptilian eyes, he might have been one of thousands of men in the city that were still recovering from the War of 2048. Making his way toward the heart of the new city, he couldn't help but feel a glow of pride as he considered how much glory he would bring to his clan when all these humans became the devoted servants of Roc.

At the first major traffic circle, the Roc found a transport kiosk. He had no chits to pay for a ride, so after a brief look around, he decided to follow the heaviest flow of traffic toward the tall, modern buildings that marked the rebuilding of the city. The weather was sultry and hot, sapping his energy to a degree he had not yet experienced. He found a small park with a number of benches and he chose one to rest on, only to be shooed off by an attendant who informed him that his class was not permitted to use the park. His dark complexion marked him as a Sudra, one of the many non-Aryan blacks. The Roc realized that he would have to alter his appearance, but could not decide what the proper appearance might be. This place was too unfamiliar to him, and he worried that the wrong choice would make him stand out when what he wanted most was to blend in. His mind rummaged through his centuries-old study of Brahmanism. He was expert on the four Vedas but not on the racial-prejudice they had engendered. He saw a grand arch up ahead and was about to walk through it with the others when he noticed a scanner among the decorations on the arch. He hesitated. Usually he could cloak his actual appearance and give the impression that he had a cranial chip, but in all this confusion, he wasn't sure he could maintain the illusion well enough to avoid detection. He stepped to the side of the road, pretending to be nursing an injured foot. A uniformed peace officer came up to him—a Sudra like himself. "Are you in need of a physician, sir?" he asked politely in English, the language of officialdom.

"No, no," said the Roc, trying to match his accent to that of the peace officer. "Just a little blister, I think."

"Well, take no chances, sir," the peace officer advised. "In this place, there are many dangerous bacteria. Just last week we had another outbreak of fasciitis in the city. Two hundred forty-nine people died of it before we could stop it. You would not want to expose yourself to that."

"No, certainly not," said the Roc, who had read about the flesh-eating bacteria that might prove as deadly to him as it was to many humans.

"Then consider visiting a clinic, sir," the peace officer recommended. "We in Calcutta do not want to take any chances. We have sustained a great many crises, and I hope you understand the reason for our concerns."

"I appreciate your attention, Officer," said the Roc.

"I believe you," said the peace officer.

"And I thank you for your concern, which, under the circumstances, is very admirable," said the Roc, and straightened up. "I will dress the blister when I reach the house of my uncle." He said this to make it appear he had a destination in the city.

"Very good," the peace officer approved. "What is your uncle's address? I can escort you there."

This was getting much too difficult. The Roc shook his head. "I know the name of his shop." That seemed a safe enough comment.

"What is it, please?" The peace officer smiled in a friendly manner, but the Roc knew he was being carefully watched.

"It is called the Brass Skull," said the Roc, choosing a name he thought would be innocuous in this city.

"Oh. Yes. I know where it is. Not a very desirable part of town," the peace officer remarked condemningly.

"I don't know about that. All I know is, it is where I must go," said the Roc a bit desperately.

"Then you are headed in the wrong direction. The Brass Skull is in a suburban village west of here, along that road." He pointed. "You go along to Agni Circle, and from there— But I'll take you there myself."

"That's very kind, but unnecessary," the Roc mumbled.

"Consider it a service," said the peace officer with very good manners but with an underlying purpose from which he could not be dissuaded. "We have a sworn duty to aid all our citizens. We have an obligation to you."

"Thank you," the Roc said sourly, and fell in beside the peace officer, wondering what would become of him in the next hour.

# CHAPTER 35

THEON CELSUS SMILED AT Leeta O'Conner. "You really are quite lovely," he said in his most charming voice.

Leeta knew men well enough not to be taken in by his smooth compliment. "Thank you," she responded without much in the way of inflection.

Undaunted, Celsus went on, "As Boris will tell you, he and I have been discussing a project that will be profitable to us both if only you're willing to help us achieve our ends." He had taken over the lounge of the hotel and was reclining on the old-fashioned chaise, his caftan spread out around him. "Are you willing to hear me out, or . . ." He left the rest hanging.

"Tell me what's on your mind," said Leeta, unswayed by Celsus' grand manner.

"Well, as you know, I have an installation not far from here," Celsus said as he drank some very hot, dark Russian tea from a glass.

"I've heard about it," she said.

"And I produce drugs there—necessary drugs, useful drugs, but drugs that do not have the approval of certain government agencies in various parts of the world. So I must develop my own means of distribution and accounting. I'm sure you understand my meaning."

"I do," she said. "You're dealing in illegal drugs and you need to find ways to get them to your customers without having the drugs seized or the distributors arrested."

"You Americans. So direct," said Celsus. "There is a little more to the project than that."

Leeta closed her eyes. "And what would that be?"

"Well, I am curious about a man who is currently being detained by the authorities in America," he said at his blandest.

"I don't want any part of anything like that," said Leeta with a firmness Celsus hadn't seen before.

"Like what?" Celsus asked, as guileless as a kitten.

"The FBI is worse than a snapping turtle once it focuses on you. So long as you don't attract its attention, you can manage almost anything, but if you get caught in their headlights, you're in real trouble," said Leeta.

"Then why didn't they do something about Yeshua?" Celsus asked as if all he wanted was a little information.

"Because the NTSA gave an early opinion that the whole thing—the religious stuff, all the news coverage—was a media ploy for ratings." Leeta shrugged. "When my husband came back to life, the NTSA said we'd hired a double and set up the resurrection with special effects and holograms." She folded her arms in remembered indignation. "They couldn't get away from us fast enough."

"Was that a problem?" Celsus wondered aloud. "I would have thought you'd be glad for such inattention."

"It made us look a lot more questionable. And the media went so far in promoting Yeshua that it made everything associated with him look phony." She was becoming angry, and her recollection fueled her temper. "I didn't want all that attention. I thought it made more sense to wait, and make sure that Romulas was okay, but it was out of my hands."

"How do you . . ." Celsus frowned. "How do you explain your fur smuggling for Boris?"

"I don't owe you or anyone an explanation for what I've done," Leeta said, a steely light in her eyes. "I need to guard my own interests as well as Boris's."

"You have a very blunt way about you," Celsus said with a suggestion of approval. "And under the circumstances, I can only applaud your resolve." He leaned forward, smiling. "When I was young, I often cursed and swore so that the people around me would believe me to be serious. But in this time, I have come to see that such language makes little impact for most of those around me, and I have found other ways to earn the respect of my contemporaries."

Leeta sighed in the most obvious way she could. "Very well. I'll listen to your proposal, but I won't accommodate you any more than I have already."

Celsus stared at her. "You may stand by your position," he said quietly, "but you will answer to me before this project is finished."

"Convince me," Leeta said, and met his stare unyieldingly.

# CHAPTER 36

FRANKLIN SWINK WAS GRINNING as he burst into the Art Deco waiting room of Bush, Geffin, McGuire, and Sucke. "We're getting somewhere!" he announced at the top of his voice to the bewildered receptionist. He was high with the first flush of battle as he gleefully slammed through the glass partition doors into the inner sanctum, bellowing for Norm Lewis. He found him in the office commissary, and the two men celebrated their way back to Swink's office suite where he waved a blue-jacketed sheaf of papers in his aide's face.

"Hot damn. Laetitia Littlehorse came through for us. She granted us a calendar date day after tomorrow. I knew she would." Swink pumped his arms as if he'd thrown a touchdown. "Without her, it would have taken two months to get on the Fourth's docket, and all that time the NTSA could be victimizing Edwards and Dee. Thank God, she's one of the few liberals who has the balls to stand up to O'Neal. I was so right about her." He jabbed at Norm Lewis's bony chest.

"This is good?" Norm asked, thinking a mere two days

sounded like a woefully inadequate time to prepare a petition. "Lin, the judge may have cut you some slack, but, I don't have to remind you, we're in for a long haul."

"Partner," Swink said, reverting to his roots and easily encircling Lewis's shoulders with one arm. "It's a beginning, and that's all we need."

Swink rushed to the closet next to his private bathroom, pulled out a very expensive suit, and began to change clothes in preparation for their departure. "Do you have your flyer ready? We could use mine, but that would delay us about two hours, and we've got to get moving."

"My flyer's right at the D.C. hanger," said Norm. "It can be in the air ten minutes from now."

"We don't have to move that fast," Swink said, changing his wool trousers for much finer ones of alpaca. "So long as we're on our way in thirty minutes."

"No problem," said a slightly lost Lewis. "Would you like to tell me where we are going?"

"We're off to see the wizard, partner. Such a deal." He grinned, pulling up his pants. "You and me are taking a little hop over to Langley. Going to give some succor."

"Succor?"

"You know what I mean." He took on that bumpkin look he used when hoodwinking a jury. He'd learned it as a child performing magic for the aunts and uncles. "Comfort and consideration." He reached up to the top shelf of the closet and pulled out what looked to Lewis like a book; he hadn't seen one out of a library for years. "Hell, this here book is a gift from a friend." Hefting it he said, "It's a little heavy, you know?"

Lewis was even more confused than before. "What friend?"

"A certain Mister M. d'Winter who expressed it to me this morning." Franklin delighted in watching Norm's eyes widen behind his glasses. "Says in his note it's perfectly harmless and a favorite of the detainee's." Swink tugged on his jacket and buttoned it in the most fashionable pattern. "I've examined it every which way I can, even took it over to an expert friend at the FBI. Truth is, I think this fella d'Winter is telling the truth—it is harmless. And I ain't never heard a prisoner of any kind being denied a gift once it's been proved harmless." He held it by the spine and gave it a connoisseur's appraisal. "Damn fine-looking book, if you ask me. Doctor Dee will be happy for the distraction."

"Okay, but why are you so pleased with yourself? It doesn't get us anywhere."

"Oh, but Mister Lewis, it does. This is the beginning of getting them out, don't you see? We're establishing contact." He was positively merry as he made the last adjustments in his clothing before taking his coat from the closet and pulling it on before picking up his case. "Reed O'Neal is going to have a hairball, especially when he hears I personally brought it over. Hope the good Lord sees fit for him to choke on it. Now, come along."

Norm Lewis allowed himself to be dragged along with Swink, stopping just long enough to slip into his overcoat and fedora. With both hands, he held the leather-bound tome in front of him like a prize he'd been awarded. He felt a guarded optimism welling in him, which he sternly suppressed. He reminded himself this could be dangerous, and that travels with Franklin could be extremely bumpy. "Are you sure you can get the NTSA to give this to the prisoner?"

"If they don't, I'm going to make some people very,

very uncomfortable," said Swink smugly. He rushed down the long corridor and yelled over his shoulder, "We'll be gone for two hours at least, Thompkins. If you don't hear from me by six, call the Solicitor General and have him root us out over at the NTSA. Unless O'Neal locks us up right there in the brig," he jested, enjoying his colleague's concern.

At the elevator, the logical Lewis paused and looked around him. "Is there any chance we're being followed?"

Swink shrugged. "I doubt that's necessary. Someone's sure to monitor our cranial chips—why be obvious about it?"

"But that would mean—"

"—that they know our every movement. Of course they do, we're dealing with the United States government," said Swink. "Why should they bother paying for manpower?"

They got into the elevator cab and began the descent to ground level. Swink pulled out a scarf to protect his throat from the winter cold. Lewis, knowing how his friend was careful about his voice, always wondered why he never wore a hat. But then, a hat would muss up the stately canopy of steel-gray hair.

"I've been filing official documents with the federal courts all my life. The government keeps track of anyone who does that." Swink seemed completely unworried by this.

"Isn't that illegal?"

"Constitutionally, of course it is, but it happens all the time, thanks to the Terrestrial Security Act of 2083. The founding fathers in the Fourth Amendment of the Constitution forbade unreasonable search and seizure by government agents. But the Supreme Court holds that

that right can be put aside if a citizen doesn't have a reasonable expectation of privacy. Now, the NTSA acting in accordance with the multilateral treaty mandates the implantation of ID chips that monitor our every move. So, the argument is that no one can have a reasonable expectation of privacy." He laughed a self-satisfied laugh. "That Alex Hamilton must be smiling in his grave. He never did care for personal freedoms."

"I guess then they'll know we're coming," said Norm as they hurried down the steps toward the garage.

"Nope, they don't know that—only that we're on our way somewhere. 'Course, they could have the entire office bugged and then they would know we were coming," corrected the legal mind, putting a hand to his head as if this might stop any monitoring of his chip. "This man Dee has opened a whole barrel of worms," Swink went on as he climbed into the limousine and motioned his friend to the seat opposite him. "If the cranial chips are successfully challenged, just think of all the trouble that could cause!" His eyes glistened in anticipation.

"Yes," echoed Norm Lewis as the possibilities continued to unfold in his mind. "Just think."

# CHAPTER 37

RETURNING TO THE MAJESTIC, Strategy was three kilometers away when she got a message on her wrist-vid from diRocelli at the GNN offices in Salt Lake. It was very early in the morning his time, and he was more than a little cranky. He was checking up on how far she had gotten on her hunch and was in no mood to listen to her suspicions about an eccentric refinery magnate named Theon Celsus. He wanted her back in the States ASAP to cover a controversy that was beginning to brew in Washington over the civil rights questions concerning the two recently captured NTSA prisoners. He was surprised when Strategy informed him that Dee might be the unidentified man from her alien vids in the Hollywood Hills. She purposefully kept Theon's tale of John Dee's missing an ID chip to herself. She needed more facts. Despite the early hour, diRocelli gushed with praise. She was "amazing," he said. She had "a rare talent," he said. He told her that he couldn't believe she was still following a "nothing" story in the New Territories. He told her he needed her back "like a breath of fresh air to blow away the fog of ignorance and provincialism." Over both her and Hernando's objections, the newscasters were ordered to make arrangements for D.C., where they were to do interviews with Swink, the justices of the Fourth Circuit Court of Appeals, and Reed O'Neal—although he was not speaking to the press.

In no more than an hour, they were packed and downstairs, making their goodbyes to Boris Michailovich Shevyenetz, who was very disappointed that they had not become better friends—and that neither he nor the Majestic had gotten any real coverage. He tried to find out if it was the visit to the Celsus plant that had so changed their plans, but they assured him that was not so and backed up their words by publicly leaving large tips for both him and Sergei. There were many promises to return, which made Boris feel slightly better. Hernando later told Strategy that he thought he had seen a glimpse of the O'Conner woman seated in the hotelier's office. Whoever it was had clumsily ducked away at his first sight of her. A driver to the airport was arranged. Sergei had already left, having gone out driving with a couple from the Illuminati religious retreat. It had been a whirlwind eight days, and Hernando, laden down with his bulky camera equipment, thought that the trip to Lake Baikal was an unproductive waste of time. He said as much on the transport back. But Strategy's only reply was a terse "Maybe."

The transport took them to Shanghai, where they changed for a Jet Blue flight to Utah. There they checked in with diRocelli, did some research on enemy combatants and Franklin Swink, and grabbed fresh clothes for the trip to the nation's capital. They were just a wee bit fried when they finally arrived in Alexandria, Virginia, having traversed eleven time zones and nearly half the world in just about sixteen hours. Yet, before she collapsed in bed, Strategy took time to prompt the GNN Washington bureau to try and schedule an interview with Franklin Swink. As she drifted off to sleep, the thought came to her that someday she'd get O'Neal to reveal what NTSA secret had been buried in the snows of Siberia.

She woke up early, 4:34 A.M. Her body clock was still attuned to Siberian time. She did what she could to shut out the world, but to no avail. She felt hungover from the recycled air in the hotel. Her breath caught in her throat. Finally, she gave up on sleep and, while raiding the liquor cabinet for some bottled water, switched on the news. There was a report of a scandal wherein Pfizer, a drug company, had refused vaccine deliveries to several third-world countries; word of a 4.9 earthquake in the center of Portland, Oregon, that had shook the city, but thankfully left no casualties; and a puff piece on President Marino and his chief of staff. She checked her e-mail, but there were no messages, so instead she reviewed her financial portfolio, waiting for the dawn. Around six, she heard the newspaper deliveryman toss the *Washington Post* at her door and she eagerly retrieved it, hungry for Capitol news.

Because of her recent visit, she couldn't help noticing that there was very little Asian news coverage in the American paper. Americans weren't very much interested in anything but themselves. She knew that and had catered to it all her professional life. She flipped through the lightweight pages, trying to educate herself about what the country had done while she was away. There didn't seem to be any major news stories, so she turned to the op-ed section and found a piece by Antonia Harper:

*The highly esteemed advocate of American civil liberties, Franklin Swink, has challenged the government's claim that it can incarcerate an American-born detainee as well as a citizen of undetermined origin without giving them access to a lawyer or charging them with crimes.*

*In a broad assertion of executive power that has fast become a case for the Fourth District Court of Appeals and perhaps eventually the Supreme Court, the government said in court papers that anyone designated an "enemy combatant" did not have to be provided the legal protections given most American citizens. Further, it said that the judicial branch has no jurisdiction "to meddle."*

*The case involves Ms. Kelly Edwards and Dr. John Dee, who were taken into custody at the Four Corners mall, sent to an NTSA facility in town, and from there moved last week to the Department of Defense military brig in Langley, Virginia. They have been in isolation ever since, with no charges against them and without any access to legal counsel. For some of us, this is very scary. Chief Judge Littlehorse will weigh the merits of the case. One of the points of contention is the DOD and NTSA's designation of the prisoners as "enemy combatants." The law defines an enemy combatant as a military adversary who has taken up or plans to take up arms against the people or interests of the United States. An enemy combatant can be either a lawful or unlawful combatant, depending on whether he conforms his conduct to recognized rules of war, like wearing the uniform of a recognized government.*

*Mr. Swink is quoted as saying that as yet the NTSA has failed to show any connection between the present detainees and any power "foreign or alien." Without such proof, the counselor from Galveston, as he is sometimes called, demanded that "people deserve to be treated as people." We, of course, as a nation look to our judicial system for wisdom. We rely on the men and women of the bench to enforce what the Constitution promises us. But in this arena, in time of war "actual or threatened," the courts have traditionally disappointed us, bowing to the claims of national security and the power of the presidency. Two dramatic examples from two centuries ago are (1) the racist internment of Japanese-Americans during World War II and (2) the massive detention of over 500 people in Guantanamo Bay, Cuba, six years after all hostilities had ended in Afghanistan.*

*In both instances, the courts bowed to government claims that the prisoners were security threats and refused to interfere. In both instances, the threats proved to be nonexistent after the crisis had passed. History has attributed the cause of these national embarrassments to war hysteria.*

*This reporter wants to believe there is no proof of alien invaders, however. The truth is that I have no proof to the contrary. There have been scenarios, like the still unaccountable Hollywood Hills transformation, that have caught our attention but turned out to be as groundless as Guantanamo Bay and the threat from the Japanese-American population. Certainly the NTSA among its many duties has a mandate to be vigilant against a wide variety of threats. But the courts allowing this Orwellian arrest and isolation to become a precedent could undermine the civil rights of millions of people and bulldoze age-old barriers created by our*

*Constitution. It has never been more important for the courts to preserve our rights by preserving the rights of others.*

Strategy had never been much interested in political conundrums. She left that to the eggheads who covered that beat, like icy Antonia Harper, whom she'd once met at the Press Club and taken an immediate dislike to. Was this assignment another move by GNN to exile her from the action? She'd smelled something of interest in Theon Celsus. This story, however, felt like being sent down to the minors. Yet there was definitely a story to the detainees. She thought about that little man they had over in the brig. She wondered if John Dee's mind was racing right now as much as hers was. The memory of his standing up to the monster on that muddy hillside came back to her. At the time, he sure hadn't looked as if he was there to help Yeshua take up arms against the United States. In fact, the zombies had definitely been sent to tear Dee apart. No, Dee couldn't have been allied with the creature. The niggling idea that she should give testimony played around the edges of her underdeveloped social consciousness. Another possibility occurred and was much more inviting. If her long-lost eyewitness were set free, he could certainly validate Strategy's tarnished reputation. Perhaps with a little quid pro quo, they could help each other out. Make that cow, Antonia Harper, eat her words about "an unaccountable Hollywood Hills transformation." She massaged the back of her neck and the base of her head and felt the strain of a sleepless night ebb. Padding over to her wrist communicator, Strategy toggled it on. She was in Washington, she thought, and it was never too early to reread the Constitution.

# CHAPTER 38

REED O'NEAL HELD UP *The Meditations of Marcus Aurelius,* squinting at the pages and riffling through them carefully. A scrap of cardboard dislodged itself from the binding and sat accusingly on his blotter. He was as much horrified by its yellow decrepitude as he would have been by a fleck of leper's skin. Reed O'Neal hadn't held a book for a number of years and felt awkward in its presence. Like most Americans, he preferred the speed and precision of computer screens. Their fonts were more legible, they provided their own illumination, and there was a lot less clutter. You never lost your place. Books were clunky and obsolete, like last century's automobiles. This one had a mildewy smell that reminded him of clothes too long in the closet. "Is this all? Nothing under the endpapers?"

"No," said the red-cell team expert from DIA. Ensign Liz Calder, a thin young woman with pale features and a diffident manner. "There are a few scribbled notes in the margins, but nothing important; they look like cross-referencing. We tried them out, and that's all it looks like.

You know how students scribble in books, and this one has been through a lot of hands."

"What about the text? Is it encrypted? Are they passing messages?"

"We ran every encryption code we have on file and came up with nothing."

"Could there be any significance to Franklin Swink's note on the title page?"

" 'From a friend'?" She shook her head sheepishly. "The three words and the signature are too brief for any meaningful communiqué. Except possibly to provide the prisoner with a copy of the counselor's autograph, which is just legible. The team feels there is no threat in that."

There were risks in allowing Dee communications with counsel that preyed on O'Neal. The first being that his lawyer might persuade the prisoner not to share needed information with the government. The second, a calamity that was not going to happen on his watch, would be that Franklin Swink, intentionally or unintentionally, might be used to send messages back to alien aggressors.

It was an old, ugly book. It had no moving parts. It couldn't be used for escape or as a weapon. "Very good. You've convinced me," said O'Neal at his most distracted as he thumbed the spine as if testing for hidden tools or tape-spools. "Although I can't help thinking Swink is up to something here." He flicked the scrap of binding off his immaculate desk. "I'd still like to know how he knew Dee wanted a book. I mean there is no evidence whatsoever of these two having met, of knowing each other's tastes or eccentricities."

The Director suddenly had a new thought, although not a very original one, "Nothing edible or, for that matter, poisonous?" Taking a cue from his first thought, he had a second one and immediately set the book down on his desk. Without explaining himself, he rose and made his way over to an office sink and began soaping his hands and running them under water. As deliberate as a surgeon, he carefully dried each finger individually, paying particular attention to his ring finger. "Studies have shown that prolonged detention, particularly in isolation, may cause physical and psychological harm. The team must be on the watch for suicide attempts. The last thing the NTSA needs is a death or even an attempted suicide."

"No poisons, sir, we checked." After the anthrax and ricin scares of the thirties, it was standard practice for government staffs to do chemical and biological analysis of all objects coming into the capital by dubious deliveries. She wondered if Reed O'Neal simply wasn't aware of the procedure or whether he wasn't just a little paranoid.

"Your lab is sure there is no way to take material from the cell or the recreation room and combine it with chemicals from this book and then create a poison or explosive?"

"Quite certain, sir. We have run extensive analyses on just those scenarios."

Walking toward the door, O'Neal said, "Very good," indicating to the young woman that their appointment was concluded. She made a movement to retrieve the book, but he shook his head. "It's all right. I'll present this myself. He might be a little less suspicious of us if I show him we're willing to grant his requests."

The DIA expert shrugged. Another affirmation of the water cooler rumor that Director O'Neal was getting very personal with this case. "You're being nice to him, aren't you?"

"I'm hoping for a little quid pro quo," O'Neal said, reacquainting her with his unctuous smile. He enjoyed flirting with pretty women. This one was awfully shy, but that only meant her passions ran deep. "The man has asked for books, and I want information. I'm sure we can arrange something to our mutual satisfaction."

"I guess you know how to do this," said the young woman.

"That I do," O'Neal agreed. "Thanks for rushing this." There it was again, the smile with the movie star looks. He took the opportunity to give her a fatherly squeeze on the arm.

"That's our job," she said, wondering how to get past him to the door.

"Ever hear of La Voisin?"

"No, sir."

"In the sixteen hundreds, during the time of Louis the Fourteenth, the Sun King, there was this attractive woman, Catherine Deshayes, known as La Voisin. She sold poisons to many women who wanted to escape their husbands." He gave her a meaningful wink. "She tried to take out Louis, her king—and this was ingenious—by handing him a petition she had painted with an opium-based poison." He paused, hoping to have impressed her with this arcane tidbit of information. He prided himself on his encyclopedic knowledge of history. "Your lab ever run into anything like that?"

"Not to my knowledge, sir." Backing out of his presence, she nodded to the three secretaries gathered like Cerberus in the outer office, and hurried out without speaking. Taking the elevator down to the first parking level, she picked up her car and drove off toward the Courts District, pulled into a restaurant lot, parked, and walked into the crowded establishment. Unbuttoning her long coat, she peered into the clubby room and searched for a friend. Standing nearly at attention, her companion beckoned to her from a table under the exit sign. A glass of Chablis was already waiting for her.

"How did it go with Apollo?" Lieutenant Commander Milton inquired.

"He's accepted the book." She sipped the wine and nodded her approval. "He's gone over it for himself, of course. I think he's going to let the detainees have it. In fact, I think he's going to give it to the prisoner himself," said the chemical expert with no trace of her self-effacing demeanor. The lieutenant commander couldn't believe O'Neal's disregard of protocol. "What a prick he is. He looked like a newly named presidential nominee, he was so proud of himself. Tried to impress me with some off-the-wall story about a French Lucrezia Borgia. Barely let me get through the door." Her distaste was evident, and she shared with her friend a wild, disbelieving look of female reproach. "His office has gone to his head."

"He likes having power everywhere in the world, and that's interfered with his judgment. He thinks he is so much smarter than the rest of us mere mortals," Milton said.

"You could say that. He makes my skin crawl," she agreed with a downward twist of her mouth. "And he's oh so sure he's God's gift to women."

The women laughed, relishing their skewering of Reed O'Neal's ego. They finally agreed that he was an easy target, but a dangerous man, one who held his reputation as a polished strategic commander higher than the needs of the people he served.

Blissfully unaware of the discussion going on among his staff, Reed O'Neal gathered up the volume of *Meditations* and decided to use his private door and the side elevator to leave the building. It might work against him if many people learned he was regularly visiting John Dee. As it was, he trusted that his offering of a book would loosen the prisoner's tongue a bit more. With that possibility comforting him, he headed for the naval brig, arriving almost unnoticed as he passed into the detention area and made for Dee's cell.

"I didn't expect to see you again so soon," Dee said as he watched O'Neal come through the zipper-door.

"This came for you," said O'Neal without explanation.

Dee took the old book Reed O'Neal held out to him. Brushing his dehydrated fingertips along its worn leather skin, he delighted in the texture of the cover. "*The Meditations of Marcus Aurelius*," he mused quietly, almost to himself. "A well-appointed volume." He was sitting tailor-fashion on the bed in his cell, his back supported by the pillow. He could tell he was losing weight, for his waistband was looser than it had been a week ago. He didn't risk standing up, afraid he might sway with dizziness.

O'Neal managed a smug smile. "I don't want you to think we're trying to deprive you of intellectual stimulation."

"Of course you're not," said Dee, making no apology for his sarcasm.

"I don't blame you for being curt," said O'Neal, doing his best to be affable. "I read before going to bed almost every night. It's very relaxing." He knew that if he could get Dee talking about shared interests he might well let something slip and make it possible for the NTSA to present a solid reason to the courts for holding him indefinitely, even though he was human. What O'Neal wanted to know most was why Dee had so many antibodies for diseases that no longer existed. That was the most perplexing result of the tests, and it continued to bother him.

"Only read at night?" Dee marveled. His head was sore and there was a persistent ringing in his ears that distracted his thoughts. He tried to focus all his attention on O'Neal, and almost succeeded. But there was no strength in his voice.

"So you're in the habit of reading?" O'Neal exclaimed. "Not many do that any more, not with so many educational vids about."

"I prefer to employ my own reasoning," said Dee, a bit too haughtily. His head swam at the exertion.

"That's something of a luxury these days," said O'Neal, taking a seat next to Dee on the bed. The surface realigned to make them both comfortable.

In admiration of the gift he'd been given, the old astronomer quoted, " 'The light from stars that were extinguished eons ago still touches us. So with great minds that have passed, Literature touches us with their thoughts generations after they are gone.' " Dee opened the book and lovingly scanned the page. He frowned at the personal notations that seemed to desecrate the text. "I see previous students afore me have agreed." But his mild disapproval was quickly washed away with a welling up of tears. "Marcus Aurelius . . . a scholar-prince, exceeding wise and persuading."

"As emperors go, he certainly was," said O'Neal, who had taken the time to look up Aurelius before delivering the book, and was not deterred from his purpose by these references to the margin notes. He had committed a particular passage to memory and had saved it for this moment. " 'Remember how long thou hast been putting off these things, and how often thou hast received an opportunity from the gods, and yet dost not use it. Thou must now at last perceive of what universe thou art a part, and of what administrator of the universe thy existence is an efflux, and that a limit of time is fixed for thee, which if thou dost not use for clearing away the clouds from thy mind, it will go and thou wilt go, and it will never return.' "

The quote took root in Dee's conscience. It rankled there, troubling him. "They were men of honor . . ." He momentarily lost his train of thought, staring blankly at the nebulous walls, then continued, ". . . well-spoken and learned."

"Roman emperors? They were that." O'Neal smiled, then deliberately fell silent in the hope that Dee would continue. Military interrogation was not a forcible extraction of a confession, but a painstaking effort to put together all the jigsaw puzzle pieces that make up the prisoner. "Such eloquent speakers. Tell me, where did you learn your unusual syntax?"

"At school. Under Sir John Cheke. Trinity College, Cambridge. Class of 1545."

The Director sighed in frustration. After days of starvation, deprivation, noise manipulation, and isolation, the man was still obstinate in his resistance and in his deception. He glared at the weak thing beside him. The Redcell's pansy psychiatrist had put the prisoner under hypnosis hoping ". . . to open up a window to his unconsciousness and find the roots of his past-life delusion" as well as how he had avoided getting an ID chip implanted. More disturbing that even under regression hypnotherapy, the the prisoner, a.k.a. Doctor John Dee of Mortlake, England, insisted he was centuries old. Research had corroborated that all the Elizabethan facts were true. Reed O'Neal knew this was an attempt to plead insanity. At trial Dee's well-paid lawyer would cry "mentally incompetent."

"John . . . may I call you John? You are under the impression you are over five hundred years old. You must realize that cannot be. You have been brainwashed, and if you let us, together we can find out who did this terrible thing to you."

With a Herculean effort of will, Dee kept silent, looking carefully at the book, finding a degree of consolation in its familiar thoughts. "Your citation from the *Meditations* is more eloquent in Latin," he said at last.

"So you read Latin," said Reed O'Neal, not sure how to interpret Dee's remark. "Not many do, these days. Where did you learn it?"

"At school," Dee said, dismissing the question with a modicum of hostility, not wanting to be pressed again on his sanity. His head felt heavy and under pressure. Every thought hurt.

"School? Without a cranial chip?" O'Neal laughed derisively. "You can't expect me to believe that." He shook his head. "Who taught you? No school would take you."

"I would have peace to read," he pleaded more than said. Despite the numbness of his mind, he remembered his tormentor's vanity. "Thank you for bringing this to me." He dropped his torso, more in exhaustion than acknowledgment, and gave himself over to pleasantly struggling with the classical thoughts and rhetoric. Though the words swam before his eyes, it was a welcome change from the endless tedium.

O'Neal sat for twenty minutes, waiting for Dee to speak again. Finally, he broke the silence. "The NTSA stands like a Roman centurion in the battle between good and evil, peace and war. That therefore requires a very aggressive stance against all enemies of freedom. Protecting this country is my highest priority. Nothing could please me more than your cooperation." He waited for some response, but got none. He rose. "I have duties to attend to. Will you excuse me?"

"With all my heart," said Dee.

"How soon will you want another book?" It was a nudge he couldn't keep from making.

"I doubt it's for me to say," Dee said, marking his place in the book with his finger. "It is passing joyful to have this one." He clutched at the book's spine. It was a mistake to admit how much the book meant to him. He feared that this recent comfort would be taken away. Carrot and stick was always the way.

"Well," said O'Neal as he went to the opening that appeared in the wall. "I'm sorry you still won't eat."

"Were you in my stead, would you?" Dee asked, daring to look directly at O'Neal's back as he faced away from him.

In answer, O'Neal shrugged as he left the cell.

# CHAPTER 39

It was twilight and Reed O'Neal was on the NTSA transport headed back from a meeting with President Marino at Camp David when he saw the forwarded news-flash from Anders on his private vidscreen. "—speculation that the outbreak in India may be spreading beyond the Bengal region. Symptoms are creating panic throughout the country—" He toggled to the next attachment and heard another report, this time in Hindi with English subtitles, and a great deal more pictorials than the GNN report. The gist of the alert was that at least a thousand victims of an unknown disease had been found, and that there was an intense hunt on for anyone exposed to the disease. He was ashen as he contacted Daryl Anders, who was at General Command reviewing all the intelligence reports streaming in from India about the outbreak. "Are you on a secure wavelength?"

"Just let me switch, Mister Director." Anders punched in the security code. The familiar sequence of tones notified him of the change. "I take it you saw the footage."

"Yes. Do you think this is similar to what we saw in Angel City?"

"Apparently," said Anders. There was concern and uneasiness in his voice. "Unless there are new viruses out there."

"The vids say at least a thousand. Do we have any verification?"

"Yes, sir, we do. The preliminary count is close to that."

"Doesn't seem possible, does it?" Staring at the lurid transformations, O'Neal rapped the private screen in front of him with his knuckle. "What did our doctors learn from the GNN Brooks tapes?"

"That physical contact with the alien causes spontaneous shape-shifting accompanied by a complete loss of ego. But not a loss of motor skills or intention. Victims become subservient to the will of the alien who has infected them," said Anders. "But by the look of the news coming in from the subcontinent, these cases are randomly walking the streets utterly unaware of what has happened to them. There seems to be no outside force directing their focus or motivating them to unite into a force of any kind. Which was not the situation in the Hollywood Hills. As I said, there is the hypothesis that this may be a different or possibly mutated strain of the virus."

The NTSA agent frowned at their lack of intel and the implications to international stability. The NTSA had been on yellow alert for an alien presence on Earth since Yeshua. For two days since Kelly Edwards's interrogation at Langley, international preparedness had quietly been raised to code orange in Mexico, Canada, and the Caribbean. It had been at that rarified level for a week in the States. Though Kelly's confession had been meager, her testimony had caused them to focus on those specific regions. Manpower as well as technology from around the world had been rerouted to what they expected to be the major hot spots. An alien presence in India was a totally unexpexted surprise. The NTSA leadership would soon have to decide whether to continue the search in North America or redeploy to India—or stretch their resources awfully thin by doing both. Two days hadn't been enough time to fully work out a multipronged game plan. The subcontinent would now want a share in all United States NTSA intelligence and budget, which meant distasteful regional turf wars.

"Send over a flying squad of the best medicos we have at NTSA/CDC, but no uniforms—we don't need panic in the streets. Tell CDC to send a mobile lab to start working ASAP on a counteragent that stops this virus's progress, maybe even an antidote for mass inoculations." O'Neal barked out orders, then added one more: he leaned forward in his seat toward the transport's pilot, "I want you to take ten minutes off our ETA, and that's an order."

"Sir," continued Anders, "NTSA and the CDC have been working on an antidote since the Hollywood Hills. We were only able to scavenge a small sample of the alien virus, and its DNA is like nothing our molecular biologists have ever seen. Once untangled from living tissue, it immediately degenerates at normal temperatures. They don't know where to begin."

"All right, send them what data we do have about transmission, treatment, and mortality, but nothing about the detainees." He had to speak louder to be heard over the throttling engines. "Then tell Indian NTSA that we advise that they impose quarantine. Isolate those infected and keep them from the general population. Evacuate the healthy out of the village at the epicenter and funnel new cases there. Monitor them to see if and when they become belligerent. Recommend to them that NTSA India should keep them there under extreme prejudice. Shut down our borders to everyone, including Americans abroad. We want no outside contamination."

"That's a little drastic, sir, since we know the symptoms and they are so detectable."

"I'll change my mind on that, Anders, if you can promise me that there is no incubation period and that you know it's only spread by aliens and that there are no human Typhoid Marys." The agent could hear the Director roaring over the accelerating transport engines. "Can you do that, Anders? Can you convince me of that?"

"No sir, I can't."

"Then we'll deal with the civil rights questions later."

"Yes, sir."

"Have Joan Hanson call all national media and put a stop to any coverage of this. She'll know how to handle them. We can't do anything about the foreign carriers, but nobody watches them anyway. If they fuss, leak it as an outbreak of ebola."

"No one's seen any of that for decades."

"The unfamiliarity will help. We can disclaim later—say it was a misdiagnosis from the World Health Organization in India."

"How do the events in India affect our search here?"

"They don't. I don't want one piece of technology or one squad of uniformed agents lost to the Hindis, Muslims, or Sikhs. Is that understood? Let's allow NTSA India to see if they can find the Roc on their own. If they do, we *may* send them some backup." Reed O'Neal's straight, unseeing stare had fixed on the Washington Monument. "This could be the beginning of a worldwide attack. Scan everybody. Continue scanning the space. I want every report of unusual circumstances to be followed up until the Docs and the special agents are satisfied with the answers. Don't rule anything out. Give special attention to areas where there are large groups. Those are likely next targets."

"This could still just be a human virus, couldn't it?"

Still fixated on the obelisk that was now reflecting the glories of the dying sunset, he said, "Son, this could be anything. But we must be vigilant. We must be proactive. And we must protect our own."

# CHAPTER 40

THE TAUT-MUSCLED MONK approaching him wore a diaphanous white robe and carried a drinking gourd and a begging bowl. The crowd of infected people parted before him, leaving the way clear for the cleric to find his way through the newly constructed containment compound that Indian NTSA had ordered constructed around the epicenter of the outbreak. If he was afraid, either of the alien or the diseased, there was no sign of it. His shaven head gleamed in the midmorning sun as he smiled at the men and women around him. The light shone through his sheer garment, revealing the outline of his body. He went up to the Roc, his calm face revealing nothing but conscientious concern. "Welcome," he said to the Roc.

"Welcome?" the Roc repeated, bringing himself back into human shape. For the last two days he had been chased and hounded and was now confined with his victims in what had once been a bustling village twenty kilometers from Calcutta, watched over by armed NTSA soldiers in survival suits. The authorities paid him no mind. If they considered him at all, they thought of his changing reptilian appearance as another casualty of the contagion. But the victims in the compound sensed his potential power over them. They waited expectantly for his commands.

"Certainly," said the monk, wholly untroubled by the nightmares around him. "Those of us who follow the teaching of Dada Lekh Raj have no reason to turn away from one such as you." His smile was serene.

"But I'm dangerous to you," said the Roc. "The soldiers will shoot you if you try to leave."

"I don't think so," said the monk.

"Why not? I carry a virus that will infect you," the Roc said, half-boasting and half-apologizing.

"Not to me, nor those who follow Dada Lekh Raj." He made a gesture to indicate the people around him, most of whom were huddled on the ground, trying to control their bodies enough to retain some semblance of humanity. Their eyes were like those of porcelain dolls, dull and devoid of thought. Gestures were immediate and automatic, like those of a dog worrying an itch. "Our teacher has a great ally, and we are proof against all you may try to do." He held out his hand. "Come with me."

"But . . ." the Roc began.

"It is easy enough to be friendly to one's friends. But to befriend the one who regards himself as your enemy is the quintessence of true religion. The other is mere business." The young monk smiled. "You aren't safe here, nor are those around you." He turned and started back through the crowd. "You must not infect anymore. Tread carefully."

"That I will," said the Roc, bewildered at this sudden change of events. He made his way among all the tortured people, keeping two paces behind the monk. Many bodies turned as the two wended their way through the crowd, poised to follow if commanded. But, not thinking of himself as a leader, Mattik had never learned to exercise what sway he had. Thus, no orders were given, except an unconscious one to allow him and the man in white to pass through the colony's midst unhindered. "What brings you here?"

"You do," said the monk.

"But why should you bother with me? The government has put me into quarantine along with everyone infected by me. Yet you seek me out, which means—"

The monk turned to the Roc. "I am doing what I must, for you and for all of humanity."

The Roc scoffed. "Isn't that a trifle grandiose?"

"It would be, were it not my karma," said the monk with tranquillity. He beamed at a child who, unthinking, scratched continually at her ulcerous skin. Her riveted attention was not on the monk, but on the Roc who trailed behind him. "You have done much to answer for, and you will lessen your karmic burden if you are willing to help us now," the monk went on. He paused beside a figure that was partly serpentine, partly feathered, and marginally human. "Look at what you have imposed on this poor person. Don't you see how his anguish is yours?"

The Roc shook his scaled-but-human head. "It is the virus."

"Which you knowingly carry," said the monk. In the manner of a priest officiating at Mass, he placed a large, brown pill in the beak of the confused creature before passing on.

"Of course. It is the purpose of my clan to advance all Roc. I have a duty to Fawg set-ut, my clan leader, to uphold." For a moment, he questioned his actions. What about this man had made him follow? What had made him mention Fawg? He saw the expression of sorrow in the monk's eyes as he turned to face him.

"What honor is there in bringing death? What duty to clan or country makes you an outcast and a foe to life?" The monk shook his head. "If you follow such a teaching, you condemn yourself to many lives on the Wheel."

"Then perhaps you should leave me here," the Roc suggested, still feeling honor-bound to his fallen ruler but mesmerized by his guide's poise and self-confidence. There was no doubt he had Fawg's aura of commanding entitlement.

What had probably been a woman writhed at their feet, making a mewling cry that was more avian than human.

"If I had no protection, I might do that. But I am protected—"

"By your faith?" The Roc sounded incredulous.

"By a vaccine, provided by our teacher's ally. But my faith brings me here to care for you," said the monk. He carefully dispensed another brown pill to the bird-woman.

The Roc shook his head. "Why do you do this? What faith does this?"

"Dada Lekh Raj teaches us that the way to Enlightenment is in the koans of the everlasting virtue, and that in alleviating the suffering of others, our own will be lost." To emphasize his next affirmation, he swiveled his muscular neck back over his articulated shoulder, capturing the Roc's full attention. "To teach and do nothing is little. To teach and to do, that is great and whole." Having made his point, he looked forward again, continuing his homily in an intimate voice but loud enough for others to hear. "Dada Lekh Raj teaches that in accepting all of creation we ourselves are accepted, and to that end, we offer our sanctuary to you, as a means of practicing our faith. Those who spend their time in disputes and divisions and do no deeds of restoration will be held to spiritual account." The monk pointed with his drinking gourd to the gate. His arm was bronzed and hairless. "I have arranged to take you to our commune, at our monastery. You will be safe there, and no more souls will suffer on your account."

"How do I know you won't kill me, or abandon me to be killed, once we are outside this compound?" the Roc asked.

"You must trust me," said the monk, and continued to walk on. The Roc smelled a mustiness from either the monk or his robe that pleased his sense of smell. He inhaled deeply. Mattik had studied the Dada Lekh Raj's teachings, as he had studied all humani faiths. The sect was a denomination of the Illuminati, a peaceful and educated sect whose primary tenet was that medicine was a blessed art. It was not surprising that many of the followers had become skilled physicians. One of their members had won the Nobel Peace Prize three years ago. Their credo was "Faith without works is nothing. The Supreme Being does not rejoice in ceremonies." The sect believed everything came from either the spirit or from nature, and they rejected modern technology. Both curious and overawed by the man's personality, Mattik obediently followed.

"What kind of pill did you give that virus victim?" the Roc inquired as they reached the gate.

The monk smiled. "It was opium, a remedy as ancient

as the Vedas. It will bring a quick and painless end, rather than weeks of agony."

"Isn't that killing?" The Roc stopped walking. He looked up at the duet of armed, suited NTSA soldiers at the gate they were fast approaching and prepared himself for the worst.

"No, it is sparing her needless affliction, for the end is already at hand. What is death, but the announcement of God's summoning? It is death that brings us the awakening and returns us to God's presence, which the act of being born takes from us. If there is anyone who must answer for her death, it is you." He clapped to summon the sentry in charge, a rural militiaman whose son had been cured by a visit to the sect's commune. "This creature is coming with me," he told the officer.

"But he's contagious." He looked out over the compound. "They may all be contagious. Even you."

"You know what I am and that I am bound by the truth." The guard guiltily nodded. "There is no fear from contagion from either him or me."

"And if he escapes you?" the guard inquired, his voice distorted by his breathing mask.

"Then use your weapons and destroy him, as the commandant has provided," said the monk, and stood aside for the gate to open.

"It isn't safe to have him in the open," the other guard observed. "How will we find him?"

"No. But he isn't in the open. He's with me," said the monk, settling the matter.

# CHAPTER

# 41

IN THE HISTORIC CITY of Richmond, where the Confederacy was once installed, the United States Court of Appeals for the Fourth Circuit sat "en banc" to review the decision Judges Littlehorse, Ash, and Sekyla had made in the petition of *O'Neal v. Kelly Edwards and John Dee*. Meeting en banc—meaning that not three, but all twelve justices, would be hearing testimony—was a rare event, and the press attributed the occasion to both Franklin Swink's aggressive advocacy to reconsider and the press's own successes in getting the issue in the spotlight of public debate. This was the last court of appeal for the detainees in Langley, as the United States Supreme Court had refused to give cert in the case, citing both Congress's Antiterrorism and Effective Death Penalty Act and the lack of sufficient evidence of "unreasonable application of clearly established federal practice."

The Fourth's courtroom's dark hardwood paneling and luxurious forest-green carpet muffled sound from the outside world. In the gallery, except for a handful of NTSA and military officials with national security clearance, the wooden pews were uncommonly empty. The government had asked and been granted a closed-door hearing because of the sensitive nature of the accusations. Not wanting to resurrect the panic over details of an extraterrestrial presence, the court had agreed. In attendance on the bench were the original three judges plus Justices Russ, Simon, Thacher, Belli, Roth, McCracken, Volker, Cannel, and Hernandes. Chief Justice Littlehorse, sixty-eight and thin-cheeked, presided in the center. The question of the day was whether the government, specifically the U.S. NTSA, had the right to bar uncharged enemy combatants from meeting with their attorneys in private. The issue had been neglected in the first petition. Any keen observer of the Fourth knew that the members were likely to go off on tangents and explore any legal issue they found intriguing.

Michael Scott, the Deputy Solicitor General, was the advocate for the government. He was a man of forty-five, round faced and clearly of Irish descent. He looked boyish despite his graying hair and pale white skin. He had been connected with President Marino since his days as a New York congressman and was well known for being a meticulous constitutional expert. Trained at William and Mary, he had graduated tops in his class. He started by first presenting the details of Dee's and Edward's arrest at Four Corners by the National Terrestrial Security Agency and their transfer to Washington, D.C., and finally their custody in a DIA naval brig. But he was barely five minutes into his historical background before Justice Roth, one of the court's more liberal judges, interrupted and intoned in his nasal New Jersey accent, "Is there anywhere in your statement that can cite that either Edwards or Dee fired a weapon or advocated the overthrow of the government?"

"No, sir, there is not. But neither do we have proof that that did not happen," parried government counsel. He made an attempt to pick up where he had left off. But that morning he was to find the justices were more apt to use the session to debate among themselves than to hear oral argument.

Justice Ash interjected, "Is it not true that although the amicus to the detainees was told he would not be permitted to visit his clients at the Langley facility or to speak to them, Mister Swink would be allowed to consult with his clients by writing to them?"

The Deputy Solicitor General agreed with the conservative judge. "Yes, sir, as of last Monday morning."

"Mister Scott, is it not true as well, that when Mister Swink was notified of that, he was also told that it was very possible the prisoners might not receive any correspondence he might send to them? What good is writing then? And how could the prisoners expect reasonable access to counsel, which is their due protection under the law?" This came from the center seat, Judge Littlehorse, as she stared down Ash, who was two seats to her right.

"They are not prisoners under the law. At least not civil law. Article two of the war powers provision allows the government to censor communications with enemy combatants who may be a threat to the United States. And to that, the question of habeas corpus does not apply, as the Langley detainees have not been accused of anything as we previously demonstrated. If they are not charged, they have no need to insist on their right to appear in court. In the same way the Sixth Amendment is no remedy, as that constitutional right only applies to those accused of crimes." Scott punched a key on his wrist-vid. "And I quote from the Sixth Amendment: 'No person shall be held to answer for a capital, or otherwise infamous crime, unless on a presentment or indictment of a grand jury, except in cases arising in the land or naval forces, or in the militia, when in actual service in time of war or public danger; nor shall he be deprived of life, liberty, or property, without due process of law; nor shall private property be taken for public use, without just compensation. No person shall be compelled in any criminal case to be a witness against himself.' Again, there is no criminal case being arraigned here, nor are Edwards and Dee being detained for a criminal proceeding. Therefore the Sixth does not have merit here."

"Mister Scott," said Judge Thacher, her eyes and mouth narrowing, "*Escobedo v. Illinois* recognizes a Sixth Amendment right against keeping someone imprisoned without access to an attorney. Does it not?"

"Yes, ma'am. But again, the cure for the obstruction of this privilege as per *Escobedo v. Illinois* is the exclusion of the fruits of those lawyerless testimonies from a trial. Without a trial, they have no rights to enforce."

Politely, Scott waited to hear if there were any questions about his legal arguments. He scanned the bench and saw none. It was obvious everyone there had studied his briefs from the last hearing, which in detail had dealt with habeas corpus and the Sixth Amendment. "Your Honors have before you a declaration of Daryl Anders, who is employed by the National Terrestrial Security Administration. The Anders declaration provides an abridged version of the facts given to President Marino and provides the basis for Dee and Edwards being designated enemy combatants. The basis for the designations is that John Dee has been observed to be in communication with alien powers, who have recently engaged in hostile and warlike acts, including preparation for acts of international subjugation, starting in this country. Kelly Edwards has assisted him consistently in all his communications. The discovery of an extraterrestrial threat implies further hostile acts. The government contends that the detainees have information that would be helpful in preventing and/or alerting the United States to future alien attacks which represent a continuing grave danger to our national security. Further, Judge Littlehorse has been given an unabridged version of the Anders declaration, under seal, of all the incriminating material that can only be read in camera. We argue that the unsealed Anders declaration is sufficient to establish the validity of the enemy combatant designation by the President, but we wanted to submit the sealed version to remedy any perceptions of insufficiency the court might have. However, we emphatically maintain that the sealed Anders declaration must remain confidential because of national security issues, and we will withdraw the sealed document as evidence rather than reveal its contents to defense counsel."

Judge Littlehorse wanted to know how defense counsel could possibly present arguments against the sealed document if neither he nor his clients were allowed access to see what reasoning and charges the government had brought. Michael Scott deftly answered chapter and verse regarding case law that allowed national security to outweigh legal niceties.

The testy Judge Roth broke in again. "Does not a source in the Anders declaration say that he does not believe that Dee or Edwards has done anything to further terrorist activities?"

"Yes, sir. But the government discounts that testimony.

We know Dee had contacts with extraterrestrials, and we believe he acted under their direction and will continue to do so. We believe and can show that John Dee is in possession of a malfunctioning NTSA identification chip." President Marino had agreed with O'Neal that world economics would be fractured if word got out that ID chips could be removed. The unidentified metallic object implanted in Dee's brain could always be introduced as evidence leading to this conclusion. "The government believes that the tampering could only be for the purpose of defying national security." Scott paused, awaiting reaction.

The subject of the chip became a flurry of judicial in-fighting. The conservative justices, Ash, McCracken, Thatcher, and Cannel, focused on the immense difficulty of such an undertaking and the laws that proscribed interference with the device. The liberal judges, Roth, Littlehorse, Simon, and Hernandes, postulated questions—that were really statements—about the invasion of privacy by the mandated implantation of the ID chip. But before Scott could rebut, Judge McCracken, the senior member on the bench, twitched his finger in reproof at his fellow justices' liberal reasoning and repeated the Supreme Court ruling of 2083 and their commentary which had allowed the procedure in the United States.

Justice Russ, a baby judge on the court, countered, "I'd have to disagree with them."

"You can't!" McCracken growled, nearly rising from his seat, "You can't disagree!" Littlehorse, a stickler for decorum, gaveled them both to silence. Scott was asked to continue.

Scott, mindful of the limited amount of time he had left for his presentation, returned to the thesis of right to counsel. "Here is an individual of unknown origin who has secret intelligence. The government's interest here is not law enforcement, nor punishment for abetting international takeover. That might be your first perception, since that is the routine procedure. Somebody does something unlawful against our system of government, so we catch them, try them, and then punish them. But the government is not following that routine here. Our interest in these extraordinary circumstances is to try and find out everything Doctor Dee and his associate know so that hopefully we can prevent not only catastrophic aggressive attacks, but, more importantly, the proliferation of techniques that are dangerous to the world's security and economic system. Our responsibility as government officials is to do all we can to protect our country and indirectly protect other countries as well. That must be our priority. We cannot allow defense counsel to interfere with intelligence gathering or allow them to be unwitting messengers to our enemies. We have no reason not to believe that the enemy has trained Doctor Dee and Miss Edwards to use their attorney to pass messages back to the hostiles." Several justices nodded slightly in agreement. "And to discharge that responsibility, we must not lock ourselves into comfortable but outmoded behavior."

"Nor unconstitutional behavior, either, Mister Scott," retorted Judge Roth.

"No, sir, nor unconstitutional behavior. I would like to turn now to the question of jurisdiction. Dee and Edwards have filed action against Reed O'Neal. The government insists that this motion must be dismissed or transferred to the military courts because the only correct respondent in this case is Dee and Edward's current custodian. We believe there is only one proper respondent and that is the prisoners' immediate, not ultimate, custodian. The language of 28 U.S.C. is crystal clear: The petitioner shall cite the person who has custody over him. Further to that, in almost all cases brought before federal courts by prisoners, the legal wisdom is that the correct respondent is the warden of the prison where the prisoner is being kept, not the Attorney General, nor in this instance the Director of the NTSA. Lieutenant Commander Milton, who is the proper respondent, is the naval officer in charge of the brig in Langley where they are housed. However, her military standing makes her impervious to this court's jurisdiction. Further, we remind you of the Eighteenth Amendment, which states that the Attorney General—and by that we take it to mean the executive branch—has control over all federal penal and correctional institutions, except military and naval institutions." He saw Russ and Hernandes make notes on their computers. "We clearly believe Reed O'Neal is not the correct respondent."

Again there was a flurry of legal questions and legal citing over who was the proper respondent, whether the court had jurisdiction, and whether the detainees should be given a military tribunal. Judges Russ, Volker, and Belli, who the press labeled as the swing votes, mostly sat mute although occasionally they asked questions about due process both in civil and military law. After forty-five minutes of give-and-take, Chief Justice Littlehorse thanked the Deputy Solicitor General for his presentation. He gathered his materials from the podium where he had stood and walked back to the benches of the gallery, where he caught Reed O'Neal's eye. The Director was beaming and gave the young man a smart salute. While acknowledging it, he heard Judge Littlehorse's summons, "Mister Swink, you have forty-five minutes."

# CHAPTER 42

FRANKLIN SWINK ADJUSTED HIS blue knit navy tie as he reached the podium. He wanted to look the picture of repose and authority. "Good morning, Your Honors. Nice to see you all in one place."

The small audience in the gallery laughed and then quickly turned quiet. The room commanded a respectful silence. Though Franklin Swink knew many of the justices informally, there was no indication of familiarity on any of the faces in front of him. But then, he was accustomed to facing this kind of stoic gravitas. "Your Honors, with your permission I'd like to read into the proceeding the language from the Sixth Amendment, as Mister Scott did with the Fifth." He toggled his wrist-vid to the bookmark he'd left. " 'In all criminal prosecutions, the accused shall enjoy the right to a speedy and public trial, by an impartial jury of the state and district wherein the crime shall have been committed, which district shall have been previously ascertained by law, and to be informed of the nature and cause of the accusation; to be confronted with the witnesses against him; to have compulsory process for obtaining witnesses in his favor, and to have the assistance of counsel for his defense.' "

"In *Ahrens v. Clark*, 335 U.S.C. 188, the Supreme Court left open the question of whether the Attorney General may be named as a respondent when an alien—that's alien as in foreigner"—Swink allowed himself a smile before continuing—"petitions to challenge his detention before getting deported. Current Courts of Appeal have held that it's possible, maybe even probable, that the Attorney General might be the proper respondent in writs brought by aliens locked up in Immigration and Naturalization facilities. Your brethren took another look at this in *Henderson v. INS* and found that the idea was good enough to mull over, though they did not make a final decision. Historically, the question of who is the custodian, and therefore the proper respondent in a habeas suit, really depends primarily on who holds the true reins on the prisoner. Though Miss Milton is the designated officer-in-charge, we all know Mister O'Neal back there"—he inclined his head back to where the Director was sitting—"has the primary power over Miss Edwards and Doctor Dee. I would also cite to you *Vasquez v. Reno*, which states that in that one extraordinary case where a government agency transported an alien from one place to another in an attempt to manipulate jurisdiction, the Attorney General could be the proper respondent. Part of the criteria in that case is the amount of how much personal involvement there was from the cabinet-level authority named as respondent. In this instance, it was Reed O'Neal who gave orders to seize the Langley detainees; it was Reed O'Neal who sent NTSA troops to Four Corners to arrest the detainees; it plainly could have only been O'Neal who opted to send them to the naval brig; and it would appear to be only O'Neal who will decide when and whether all that can be learned from Dee and Edwards has been learned. I venture to guess it will be O'Neal, and not the President, who will decide when they will be released. This level of personal involvement by a Cabinet-level director, so far as I can tell, is unprecedented. We ask you to agree with us that O'Neal is the proper respondent.

"Not more than a few days ago, I argued in these august chambers the merits of the Fifth, Sixth, and Fifteenth Amendments upon this case as well as those of the Geneva Convention, and I ask that those arguments be entered into the record of this hearing."

"So ordered," intoned Judge Littlehorse.

"And I questioned the President's power of denying my clients their day in court by calling them enemy combatants and denying them the ancient right of habeas corpus given us not only by the Constitution but also by the Magna Carta. Today, however, I point out to you that their detention also violates the Posse Comitatus Act, which makes it unlawful to send out the military as a . . . and I quote," Swink rifled through some vid-screens to the page he wanted, " 'as a posse comitatus or otherwise to execute laws.' "

Judge McCracken, who had had his eyes closed, blinked them open with a start. "Mister Swink, is it not true that in *United States v. Mullin* the law clearly interprets the Posse Comitatus Act to mean that the executive branch cannot use the military in civilian law enforcement? You aren't trying to feed us that your clients were arrested for civil laws, are you?"

Undaunted, Swink started flipping through some notes in a methodical manner. "No, sir, I wouldn't dare to feed you anything except the law, Your Honor." He found what he had been looking for and looked up to smile at the wizened face above him. "I'm merely suggesting that John Dee has yet to be proven to be an enemy combatant to my satisfaction. Since neither Mister Scott nor the government has given one shred of evidence—and here's the definition—that John Dee is a military adversary who has taken up, or plans to take up, arms against the people or the interests of the United States. Nor have they explained to any of us why Miss Edwards is under arrest. What we do have is a boatload of circumstantial evidence. Since there is no firm evidence of anti-American behavior on the part of either prisoner, and, on Mr. Dee's part, only the crime of tampering with an ID chip—a civilian crime—I think Posse Comitatus applies. Now, I haven't seen what's in that sealed Anders declaration, but I'll bet you it isn't much more militarily incriminating than the unsealed declaration."

Judges Roth, Russ, Hernandes, and even O'Conner seemed to smile, which didn't make McCracken feel any kindlier toward the defense. But Swink wasn't there to change the minds of the hard-liners. They were already voting against him. He needed to convince Belli, Volker, and Russ, who were the moderates, and give the liberals ammunition.

Judge Roth softly broke in as if he were asking this pillar of liberalism some advice, "Are you saying, Counselor, that the 'some evidence' standard has not been met by the Anders declaration as it appears in civil contexts, including judicial review of prison disciplinary proceedings? Meaning 'some evidence' does not mean any evidence at all that would tend, however slightly, to make an inmate's guilt more probable?"

"That is correct, your Honor. I believe the criterion has not been met. And I believe there is no evidence in the unsealed Anders declaration that proves either detainee's guilt with any standard of reliability." Swink saw Justice Roth approving of his answer and turning in the direction of Justices Ash and Sekyla, who had ruled otherwise in the previous hearing.

Swink continued, "We do not deny the executive branch power to seize and detain enemy combatants in time of war. That is the President's constitutional right, but we seek to claim that this is not a time of war, and therefore the President may not exercise his right at this time. Neither he nor the Congress has declared a state of war."

"Yes, but the very foundation of the National Terrestrial Security Act and its international treaties stipulates that we must prepare for a war with an extraterrestrial army. As enumerated in the sealed Anders declaration, events in Angel City seem to warn that we are on the threshold of a conflict," challenged Justice Sekyla in his rich Georgian accent.

"Your Honor, not being privy to the sealed declaration in Chief Justice Littlehorse's chambers, I have no way to argue those facts. Which, of course, is the point of these proceedings. What I do know is that the current situation lacks any clear corporeal definition. If there is an existing conflict, it can have no clear end, and thus the detention of my clients is potentially indefinite and therefore unconstitutional."

# CHAPTER 43

IT WAS VERY QUIET in the courtroom; hardly anyone moved. Everyone seemed to have stopped breathing.

Then the judges began weighing in. "A formal declaration of war is not necessary in order for the executive to exercise its constitutional authority to prosecute an armed conflict, particularly when the United States is attacked by an alien hostile in Angel City," said Thacher.

Next was Ash with his hands tightly sandwiched together. "This court as well as others have repeatedly held that in times of war and insurrection, the government may detain individuals whom the government believes to be a threat to society."

Then Volker, the historian spoke, "In the *Prize Cases,* the Supreme Court rejected a challenge to presidential authority to set a blockade on the Confederate states—an unqualified act of war—when there had been no declaration of war. The court in the *Prize Cases* set forth that war can exist without an official declaration on either side. When the acts of another nation impose hostilities on our country, our President does not initiate that war, but is bound to accept the challenge without waiting for any special legislative authority. "He looked at Swink disapprovingly. "That court made it clear that when military measures are invoked, it is a political decision, not a judicial one."

"As per Judge Volker, no court can determine when a war exists. I suggest you continue, Mister Swink," said the Chief Justice, mindful of the time allotted for Swink's argument.

"Yes, ma'am." Franklin took a deep breath and relaxed his shoulders. He was about to take a bold move. One he hoped he wouldn't regret later. "Your Honors, as of today I have asked you to view the detainees as a unit. But now it is time to be fair to Kelly Edwards, who has never been shown by the government to fulfill the definition of enemy combatant. The Anders declaration points out there is no prima facie argument actually connecting her to any alien communication except through her secondary connection with her employer, John Dee. To that end, I cite to you the accepted guiding principle of *Jones v. United States,* 529 U.S.C. 848,857. The language is quite clear: 'Where a statute is susceptible of two constructions, by one of which grave and doubtful constitutional questions arise and by the other of which such questions are avoided, our duty is to adopt the latter.' However, *HUD v. Rucker* points out, and I quote, 'that constitutional avoidance has no application in the absence of statutory ambiguity and the courts must not exercise judicial restraint that would trench upon the legislative powers vested in Congress by article 1, section 1 of the Constitution.' *Harris v. McRae* clearly states that when a case can be decided based on either a statute or the Constitution, the statute should provide the basis for decision. I cite those to you, Your Honors, because I believe Miss Edwards should be judged, not under the more draconian strictures for enemy combatants which are founded on interpretations—and I repeat, they are interpretations—of the President's constitutional war powers, but under the less caustic and formalized USA Patriot Act of 2001 which is an official act of Congress. The law is clear: congressional statutes trump judicial interpretations. In order to incarcerate a citizen, the Patriot Act requires that the executive branch have reasonable ground to believe a citizen is engaging in threatening activity. Thus, the Patriot Act was meant for suspected threats having less evidence of terrorist activities than a known enemy combatant has. Kelly Edwards, who is under far less suspicion than her employer, falls under the provisions of the Patriot Act and thereby should be barred from any more detention at Langley, since the Patriot Act only permits confinement for a maximum of seven days."

Again the historian, Judge Volker, questioned the aptness of the citation. "Counselor, the Patriot Act's statute on detention only applies to non-American citizens. Neither you nor the government asserts that Miss Edwards is not a United States citizen."

"That was correct sir, until 2042, when the law was altered to include U.S. citizens but retained the proviso that a U.S. citizen could not be tried by a military tribunal if he or she is not serving a recognized enemy."

Judge McCracken spoke up. "Mister Swink, your purpose here this morning is not to plead release for your clients, but to show us the reason why you should be allowed access to your clients."

Very smoothly and with great elan, Swink replied, "It's all part and parcel, Your Honor, all part and parcel. The

All Writs Act allows this court to issue all writs necessary that are in the sound discretion of the court."

"Counselor, please continue, and please try to confine your comments to the question before us," the Chief Justice reminded him in an attempt to soothe the waters. But it was obvious to her that the Patriot Act had struck deep into the thoughts of her fellow Justices of the Fourth Circuit, as did the reference to the All Writs Act.

Swink began to pressure the court with various citations that acknowledged the Fifth Amendment rights of prisoners to have legal help. "Congress intended that a habeas corpus prisoner would be able to place evidence in a courtroom. By denying the prisoner legal assistance, it would be frustrating the prisoner's right to provide those facts."

Justice Belli countered, "Habeas corpus statutes do not expressly give the right of counsel to enemy combatants."

"But 18 U.S.C., section 3006A paragraph 2 does allow a court to which a writ of habeas corpus is petitioned to appoint legal counsel for the detainee, if the court decides that the 'interests of justice so require.' My clients have no ability to present facts or make arguments, as they are being held incommunicado in the brig at Langley."

"And that is why you are here as next friend, Counselor," said the Chief Justice.

"Yes, Your Honor, I have tried to show that through the due process clause of the Fifth Amendment, my clients do have the right to present facts; that the best way for them to do so, and the way that is best suited to the courts, is to present them through an attorney; and that would counteract the procedure Congress established in habeas corpus cases to leave Dee and Edwards with no practical means of following that procedure."

The one-minute warning light blinked on. "Although it has been posited here that the right to legal advice concerning cases using the Sixth Amendment has no sway on my client's detention, that should not deter Your Honors from consulting that case law to inform your decision here today. And I remind you that the Supreme Court of this land has repeatedly underlined the rights of prisoners to have legal counsel. Though there is no trial in this case per se, my clients find themselves faced with the prosecutorial forces of the NTSA and the executive branch and by virtue of that are being subjugated by the intricacies of national and international law. The clear logic of case history dealing with the Sixth Amendment, along with the discretion given this court under the All Writs Act, should guide this court to permit Edwards and Dee to be allowed access to counsel so that they may further petition for their rights, especially in responding to the accusations against them to be found in the Anders declaration." Swink, a practiced showman, always liked to finish with a grand finale, "Especially the accusation found in the Anders declaration that Doctor Dee is in possession of what Anders calls a 'malfunctioning identification chip.' I'd venture to speculate that Mister O'Neal and his NTSA know otherwise." He heard the disquieted response behind him and closed with some satisfaction. "Thank you, Your Honors."

# CHAPTER 44

HERNANDO CARRASCO STARTED COUNTING backwards, "Five, four, three, two." The *one* was left unsaid as he cued Strategy Brooks to start her evening news broadcast.

"Good evening. I am standing in front of the prestigious old Confederate Treasury building where the Fourth District Court of Appeals has just now issued their decision in regard to the case of *O'Neal v. Kelly Edwards and John Dee.*" Hernando's camera panned over to frame the building behind her in the glory of a southern sunset. On the expansive marble stair that was the approach to the building, several reporters sat evaluating the manuscript of the court decision. But Hernando was quick to return to his star.

"Yesterday, in an extraordinarily rare 'en banc' session that was closed to the public for security reasons, the court heard Deputy Solicitor General Michael Scott and well-known civil rights advocate Franklin Swink argue the merits of a pair of enemy combatants being allowed access to legal counsel, thus opening the door for a challenge to their arrest. In a theatrical turn of events, using its privileges under the All Writs Act, the court voted seven to five to order the government to release Kelly Edwards from custody, although she is forbidden to discuss the case. The small majority found there was insufficient evidence to hold her any further. They rejected the government's argument that the 'some evidence' standard had been met. The vote was pretty much along ideological lines, with Volker and Belli making the difference." A picture of Kelly was spliced into the live newscast. In the photo, taken during her days as a public relations consultant, she looked girlish and nothing like a terrorist.

"The government"—and now a photo of Michael Scott, from a recent book jacket, filled the screen—"had asked the court to forbid legal counsel to the prisoners, stating that the attorney would interfere with the questioning of the detainees and possibly hinder the prevention of terrorist attacks."

Before they went on the air, diRocelli had nixed any reference to extraterrestrials. Strategy had been furious. The arrests by the NTSA proved she had been right about the existence of aliens in their midst and directly validated her pieces on Fawg. But diRocelli held firm. Nor was she to refer to Dee as the unidentified man in her coverage of the battle in the Hollywood Hills. It wasn't his own censorship, diRocelli had explained, but came from the very highest level of GNN, who had gotten it from the Oval Office. Strategy was still seething as she read her prepared copy off the vid-prompter.

"The court, in a thirty-two-page decision, insisted the only way they could properly judge if Doctor Dee's imprisonment was not violating the right to due process was to give him a modicum of access to his attorney, Franklin Swink. The Chief Justice is quoted as saying 'he must have the opportunity to fight his detention.' " The obligatory publicity shot of Swink, waving the court's opinion over his head in victory, captured the screen. "Mister Swink was quoted as saying, 'It is comforting for all Americans to know that if they were ever picked up by our military and held hostage, at least a lawyer can visit them and be their voice in court.'

"The Chief Justice who wrote the court's opinion criticized the NTSA report that was the basis for the detainees' arrest as 'being none too subtle in warning the court against going too far in respecting the prisoners' rights.' She also reprimanded them for their not meeting a standard of evidence on Miss Edwards's part. But she was just as unhappy with the rhetoric from the other side, for raising the specter of our government violating the Geneva Convention, the long-held power of the President to designate enemy combatants, and the repudiation of the Magna Carta and the National Terrestrial Security Act."

The shot of Swink was gone, and Hernando moved in for a close-up of Strategy. "John Dee was arrested as a material witness in Four Corners two weeks ago and transferred to a military brig in Langley, where he is still being held incommunicado." There was no publicity shot of Dee. His image was not allowed to be publicized. Strategy breathed deeply and looked straight at the vid lens. "The court agreed with Mister Scott that the standard of evidence was met on Doctor Dee's arrest. No further details were given." And then she went for it. "But your reporter knows there is evidence that Doctor Dee has no implanted NTSA ID chip." She gave the

American public a moment to digest that incredible piece of news. That'll show diRocelli that he can't censor the press, she thought smugly. The camera held steady on the close-up. "This is Strategy Brooks reporting from Washington. Thank you, ladies and gentlemen, and good night."

# CHAPTER 45

THE ROOM SET ASIDE for the purpose of legal consultation had two small windows that looked out on bare tree branches. There was a slick-surfaced table, four chairs, and an occasional table with a clock and the ubiquitous bowl of fruit. Swink had put his case on the table and looked up as an emaciated Kelly Edwards came cautiously into the room, followed by agent Daryl Anders. "Hello," he said amicably as he offered her a hand. "I assume you know who I am?"

Kelly responded, "Oh, yes. I followed you all through the *Houghton-Chiterez v. the United States* trial. You were spectacular. That was before the NTSA turned my monitor off."

"Houghton was a good fight. Here, please, let me help you to a seat."

He carefully led her to the nearest chair. "I was surprised GNN gave it so much coverage, considering the network's conservative bias," said Kelly.

"They liked my histrionics, they didn't like the verdict, but all in all, it was a landmark case and it pulled in a ton of viewers. We proved that in certain cases justice can only be served by timely actions of the Justice Department. It helped my reputation as well," Swink said, doing his best to be philosophical.

"You won on the merits of the case. Those boys hadn't gotten due process," Kelly said. "You're about the best litigator in North America these days; everyone says so. You got me out, and you can win Dee's freedom as well. I know you can."

As she uttered the word "freedom," Kelly felt invisible restraints unshackle and fall away. She began to laugh, the laughter mingled with tears of joy and relief.

Swink was never comfortable with emotional outbursts. "I should tell you about the conditions of your release," he said lamely.

Kelly pulled herself together and listened attentively. He explained that she was still under suspicion and that the Patriot Act allowed her to be arrested again. To avoid that, he drilled her with a list of conditions and warnings. A grateful and now less emotional Kelly Edwards nodded her agreement to the stipulations. "Good," her lawyer said. He turned to Agent Anders. "I believe your job is done here, Mister Anders?"

"I have the agreement. But Miss Edwards has not been processed out of government property. Until she vacates the navy brig completely, she must be monitored."

Kelly felt a flash of fear that she had missed some catch in her being freed. Quickly the attorney reassured her that though the NTSA was being a stickler for protocol, everything was as he had promised her. "O'Neal just hates to lose." He shook his head. "He's continuing to drag this case through the courts in the usual style, which will only achieve delays and frustration. That translates into months and even years for your employer. I don't think either one of you want that."

"No. I don't want that," Kelly replied. Swink had named her worst fear for Dee.

"Good," Swink approved as he opened his case and pulled out a miniature recorder, a bottle of water, some juice, yogurt, and bread. "Then let's get started on letting you know what Doctor Dee is up against."

Kelly's attention was held by the food. "Where did you get that?"

"My friend, Norm Lewis, purchased it himself." Swink pushed the bread toward her. "Go ahead," he urged. "It's safe, and you look hungry."

Kelly was already tearing open the yogurt. She took a little spoonful and swallowed greedily.

While Kelly ate and Anders watched, Franklin Swink carefully explained to her the court's most recent rulings.

She nodded her understanding, her mouth full of bread. "This is so good," she exclaimed, and then said, more levelly, "What are you planning to do next?"

"Well," he said slowly, "things are happening so quickly, I don't know just yet. Meeting here under the watchful eye of Reed O'Neal is unsettling. I apologize for the inconvenience, Miss Edwards. We'll get you out of here within the hour. Once you're free you need to let me announce to the world that Doctor Dee has never had any dealings with alien beings." And here he quoted from his notes, " 'in order to take up or plan to take up arms against the people or the interests of the United States.' " He set the wrist-vid down. "He hasn't, has he?" he said perfunctorily.

Quite sure both Dyckon and Dee had always acted for the good not only of the United States, but of the world, she answered in a clear, strong voice, "No." She hoped the polygraphs, if they were still monitoring her, would further validate her.

Satisfied, the counselor continued, "Your testimony forces the NTSA to *prove* Dee's what they claim he is and opens up arguments for the 'some evidence' standard. I want you to understand that the NTSA and the executive branch are trying to set an important precedent here. You and I and the American people must not allow it. The government cannot be permitted to create a scenario whereby they arbitrarily point a finger at someone like John Dee and say, 'We think you've helped some outside power, the court cannot review it, and we can lock you up for as long as necessary.' Hell, we've been fighting that kind of tyranny since this country began."

Kelly felt new resolve growing in her. This man's strength, his authority, and his compassion gave her hope. Sitting up straighter in her chair, she looked Swink in the eye. "I can tell you everything," she said.

Swink listened attentively as Kelly enumerated the beginnings in Angel City, Dee's strangeness, their search for Royal Newton, and what ensued. When she started to explain to him about Fawg and the virus, Anders ordered the interview terminated and asked to have Edwards forcibly removed. This was just the sort of national security breach that the government had warned the courts would happen.

But Franklin Swink wasn't ready just yet to call it quits. "Mister Anders, your actions are in violation of the court order. We're opertaing under attorney/client privilege here." His tone was light. "After all, the NTSA can't erase what I've just heard from my memory, can they?" As a show of cooperation, he handed the agent his recording device and told him he could destroy it. Anders took the equipment and allowed Kelly to remain, waiting for word from the red-cell team countermanding his decision.

The order never came. The moments of crisis passed and Kelly warily continued to tell her attorney, under the NTSA's watchful eye, all she knew about Dyckon, which wasn't much, and all she knew about Fawg's accomplice, which was mostly hypothetical. The questions finally ended and she rose exhausted from her chair, relieved to have shared with a friend. Before she left the room, she threw her arms around the elder attorney and held him as if she were holding on to life itself.

# CHAPTER 46

FUMING, REED O'NEAL RUSHED down the hall, his temper barely under control. The building was largely deserted at 11:30 P.M., which was an additional annoyance, for there was no one on whom to vent his indignation. How dare that media slut do anything so reprehensible as insinuate NTSA fallibility by suggesting that the ID chip implantations weren't universal. That only gave aid and comfort to the liberals on both sides of the aisle who questioned the very existence of the NTSA and the constitutionality of the chips. He kicked at a standing vid-console at the center of the hall in front of the elevators.

The disembodied voice of a security guard came from the grille above him. "Are you all right, Director O'Neal? Do you need assistance?"

"I'm fine!" he shouted back with heavy sarcasm. As he stepped into the elevator, he activated his palm implant and tapped out the message: GET ME STRATEGY BROOKS AT ONCE. Then he sent a message to Senator Havers: WE NEED TO TALK IMMEDIATELY. The elevator bonged softly, reminding him that he had arrived at his floor. He straightened his clothes and went down the corridor toward his imposing office door, glaring at his night-shift staff as if they had all purposefully betrayed him. No one spoke to him as he strode along. He said nothing to his secretary as he stormed into his office and closed the door sharply behind him. Taking his seat at his desk, he waited for a response to either of his two messages. He thought of ways to make Brooks suffer, starting with downgrading her security clearances. He'd have a private meeting with Anders and have the readings on her chip manipulated. A minute went by, then two, and he was still sitting by himself in silence. This waiting was maddening. To relieve his tension, he threw a media-cube across the room and had the satisfaction of seeing it smash.

A moment later, his phone buzzed. "O'Neal," he said.

"You have an appointment with Strategy Brooks at three-thirty," said his receptionist from her station at the other end of the central corridor.

"Bring her in with a security escort," O'Neal barked. Finally, something was going his way, and he intended to make the most of it.

The receptionist coughed slightly. "Sir . . . the meeting's at GNN's regional office in Salt Lake . . . I've ordered you the NTSA transport and crew."

"What do you mean?" O'Neal exploded.

"Her scheduling assistant said she can give you half an hour at three-thirty, but that's all she can spare." The receptionist's voice was beginning to shake.

"She comes to me!" O'Neal thundered. "Who the hell does she think she is?"

"She thinks she's the hottest news journalist in the media today," said the receptionist. "That's what her scheduling assistant said when I asked her the same question." The receptionist sounded terrified now.

"Well, I am Director of the National Terrestrial Security Administration, and my time is accountable to the world, not some media corporation! She's crapped on us twice. Call back GNN and tell her to get her pretty little ass in here immediately."

"Yes, sir."

He broke the connection to the receptionist and flung himself out of his chair, venting his frustration by heading to his liquor closet and the bourbon. He was pouring his second, when another discreet summons from his phone interrupted him. He answered more brusquely than usual. "Yes?"

"Looks like you've got some explaining to do," said Havers without greeting or apology.

"It's nothing but sensationalistic nonsense," O'Neal grumbled. "A man without a chip. Sheer rubbish. Don't journalists have a code of ethics, a responsibility to the American people? You're on the FCC, don't they *have* to tell the truth."

"What are you planning to do?" Havers inquired.

"I want your Terrestrial Security Committee to muzzle all this media attention immediately. Tell the nation that John Dee is just like everyone else in this world and you'll establish a fact-finding panel to prove it. You've got the authority. I need you to declare to the world that the NTSA has done its job."

"Um-hum." Havers sounded disinterested.

"And the statement has to go out at once, before Brooks can do any more damage. Understand? This isn't something to let slip. Get it done ASAP!" When I say, "Jump," you say "How high?" O'Neal thought vehemently.

Havers answered smoothly, "I don't think I can do that, Reed, not just yet."

"What do you mean you can't do that?" O'Neal demanded.

"Well, John Dee is currently being held over for military tribunal, which means he is in military custody and out of the reach of the legislative branch. Until the military brass and the President make up their minds, we can't proceed. My hands are tied—*constitutionally.*" Havers was using his most unctuous tone, one he usually reserved for turning down constituents.

"Don't you patronize me," O'Neal bellowed. "Hold an ante decisio hearing. You can intercede, to keep this danger in check."

"After the Fourth's decision this afternoon, the Committee voted not to interfere. It's out of my hands." Havers was beginning to sound slightly bored.

"Out of your hands! You must be very disappointed," said O'Neal with heavy sarcasm. "You forget who I am, Senator." He made no attempt to show Havers any respect. "I've been Director for longer than you've been in office, and I'll be here long after you're gone. I have more power than any senator, or president, or secretary general. And I know enough about you to put your reputation in the toilet for the next decade. You're going to do everything I tell you, and you're going to do it now, or you will bitterly regret it!"

"I wouldn't make threats," Havers sounded calm. "You may find your credibility isn't what it used to be. You may not have noticed while you've been busy policing the world, but the national press has been roasting you in the op-ed pages for snatching up private citizens and plucking them of their God-given rights. Even your longtime friendship with Marino might not stop my fellow senators and me from slashing your sacrosanct budget. It seems a little bloated, if you ask me. Let me remind you, Mister Director, that you're not the only one who has a responsibility to the American people."

"I'll be vindicated once we bring this case to trial," said O'Neal with great bravado.

"For the country's sake, I hope so," said Havers. "Goodbye, Reed." The senator broke the connection.

For the greater part of a minute, O'Neal sat in furious disbelief. How dared that idiot attempt to strong-arm him! He'd soon find out who had the real clout! The prospect of bringing Nathaniel Havers down provided him a moment of satisfaction, but it was quickly supplanted by the aggravating reminder that something had to be done, and quickly. He slapped the top of his desk. Then he stood up, grim with resolve. No self-proclaimed crusader was going to ruin what he had built so carefully. This was his dominion, and he, Reed O'Neal, would decide who and what was held by it, and for how long.

After all who was this John Dee? O'Neal asked himself, doing his best to contain his temper. Dee was nothing—a gnat, a flea on his life, so minor that he deserved what he had been given—less than the trouble he had caused. What made Dee important was how he had gotten through life without a cranial chip—and he would need a more acceptable explanation than the ridiculous assertion of time-travel. There were many questions about him, that needed answers, and the NTSA did its best work privately. Now Brooks and the other philistines of the media were making that impossible. Didn't they know that all his actions and decisions were inspired by his love of justice and America? Didn't they know his directorship was more than a job, but a calling? It was unbearable to imagine that such an annoyance should rock his worldwide empire.

Director O'Neal reached down and retrieved the silver ewer of oil from his lower desk drawer. He set up the bowl and the white towel. Reverently, he followed the ritual of his anointing: the meditation, the litany, the oil, and the cleansing. Afterwards, he felt clean and reassured—above the petty jealousies and human foibles that surrounded him. He looked out the window and stared down at the NTSA quadrangle below him, where a triplet of slow-moving building security guards patrolled the grounds with powerful Doberman guard dogs. It occurred to him that perhaps one of the men might be the voice that had spoken to him at the elevators. They little realized that even this late at night, he was far above them, protecting them. He saw himself not only as their protector, but everyone's. The reminder of his life's purpose brought tears to his eyes, and he blessed those three souls beneath him.

# CHAPTER

# 47

KELLY EDWARDS SLEPT MOST of the day, waking only to eat. It was late evening when she answered the knock at her hotel suite door, expecting to see Morgan d'Winter or Franklin Swink. Instead she found a woman wearing an expensive fur coat standing in the corridor.

"Hello. I am Leeta O'Conner. May I come in, Miss Edwards?"

Kelly warily blocked the door. "You look familiar. Do I know you?"

Leeta shuffled to one side, embarrassed by her past, "I don't think we have . . . met."

Kelly interrupted, "Listen, if you're a reporter, I can't talk to you. Court order." She started to close the door.

"No. I have information for you," the woman said, touching Kelly's hand. "I'm not here about your case. It's about Angel City. I was once married to Romulas O'Connor, who was brought back to life by Yeshua Ben David." Kelly's mouth opened. Leeta knowingly dropped the other shoe, "I believe you know him as Fawg."

Startled, Kelly opened the door and gestured the mysterious woman inside.

"A nice place." Leeta looked around the room approvingly. "I live in a hotel too."

"Where?"

Leeta smoothed the back of a padded armchair as she removed her mink. "Would you believe Siberia?" She shrugged as if to say, I don't believe it myself sometimes. "It's a long story." Perching on the edge of a chair, Leeta O'Conner quickly unspooled the thread of her past year's life. She frankly admitted to her terror of the omnipotent Yeshua, his crimes against her harridan mother-in-law, and her desperate flight to find safety in Irkutsk. She explained to Kelly about Boris and how she became his international fur saleswoman—or rather black marketeer, she corrected. Inexplicably, her eyes watered, not sure if her life was now a comedy or a tragedy.

Kelly listened impatiently. "You haven't told me how you knew Yeshua was really . . ." A hand gesture substituted for the name.

"You're right, I haven't." Leeta glanced around the room. "Have you checked the room for listening devices?"

"No, I haven't," Kelly said. "I simply assume the NTSA is keeping tabs on me to be sure I don't talk about what I know."

Quickly Leeta O'Conner rose in a panic, as if concerned that she had already revealed too much, that there would be a knock at the door and she would be taken away. "Would you mind if I used the ladies' room?"

"Go ahead." Kelly pointed to the room.

As Leeta got up to go, she put her finger to her lips, gesturing for silence, and beckoned Kelly to come with her.

Curiousity won out, and Kelly got up to follow. For reasons she couldn't name, she felt jittery about this unknown woman. Leeta closed the bathroom door behind them and turned the sink faucets on full blast. In a quiet voice, barely audible above the sound of rushing water gurgling down the drain, Leeta explained that she had been sent to Washington, D.C., by Theon Celsus, an oil refiner, dedicated environmentalist, and venture capitalist who was also Boris's and her patron. Her mission was to offer sanctuary to John Dee in Siberia should he ever be released. Celsus assumed Kelly would be the most likely person to have contact with Dee.

Drawn in by Leeta's remarkable concerns about secrecy, Kelly tentatively suggested in a low voice that nothing she had heard would put either Leeta or Theon Celsus in jeopardy. She reached to turn off the rampaging water, which had splashed her pants. Leeta blocked the movement. "There is more," she whispered. She scrunched up closer to the bewildered redhead, holding up her wrist-vid. "Theon paid for your lawyer."

"What?"

"Please watch."

Theon Celsus addressed the vid-recorder, giving the impression that he was looking directly at Kelly. She was immediately taken by the beauty of his limpid blue eyes. So this was their benefactor. "How do you do, Miss Edwards?" His formality and his Swiss accent fueled her growing curiosity. "My name is, at present, Theon Celsus of Aurum All Chemical, and, among other ventures, I have been running a private biomedical plant situated on the shore of Lake Baikal. My goal in life is to provide remedies for the world's diseases without being leashed to the world's bureaucratic drug-testing programs. Such a waste of time and money when people need cures immediately. Like your employer, Miss Edwards, I am a friend of Dyckon's."

*First Fawg and now Dyckon,* thought Kelly. *Who is this guy?*

"I have had an intimate knowledge of his methods and his intentions for some time now, although his visits have diminished over the years. At about the time he had you looking for Fawg, he asked me to start work on a curative substance—a vaccine—to treat the Roc virus that might threaten us all. But as of two weeks ago, he sent word to me that his bio-shield was failing and his presence was more difficult to conceal from the NTSA. He was quitting this solar system and going into hiding. Before he left, he boosted my endeavors by downloading into my lab's computers all manner of Roc arcane bioscience to assist my research. As you know, he is loath to leave any evidence that would affirm an alien existence on Earth. Since that time, I have been pursuing experiments with the assumption that during an epidemic, like the one facing us now—"

Frantically, Kelly fumbled to punch the pause button on Leeta's wrist-vid and with effort quietly stammered, "What epidemic?"

"Outside of Calcutta. Mutant transformations."

The horror seeped deep down into Kelly's gut. Battling nausea and numbness, she slumped to the floor. She knew all their fears had been realized, all their sacrifices had been for naught. She stared rigidly at a crack in the ceramic floor. More than anything, she wanted to go to Dee. She needed his comfort and his advice.

Kelly felt a cold compress applied to her forehead and looked up to see concern in Leeta's face. "The epidemic started six days after your arrest. There is no way you could have known. The American media is not airing the story. The general public here is in the dark."

Kelly pounded the floor with her fist. A wave of futility washed over her as she nodded to Leeta to continue playing the message.

Celsus' image came to life on the vidsceeen. "—with the assumption that during an epidemic it would not be possible for human scientists to develop such a vaccine in a timely manner, or to be able to distribute it to a mass market. Those were the tasks I assigned myself, and in my pharmaceutical laboratory in Siberia I hoped to produce a vaccine in quantity. I am delighted to say that I have had some success in creating small doses from cloned Roc antibodies, but the time and the expense are proving prohibitive. Moreover, at present, I have not the means for a wide distribution. What little medicine I have, I have personally distributed to a tiny community of medical monks who are helping with the afflicted. They do God's work selflessly. Should the epidemic spread to pandemic proportions without a source for Roc antibodies, we have no hope of success." Celsus shook his head in sadness. "I am certain that Doctor Dee's arrest is not only unlawful, but also the most egregious oppression. It is not only in the interests of justice, but in the interests of public safety to secure his unconditional release immediately, so that together we can share our information regarding the alien race of Rocs and hopefully regain a connection with Dyckon, who I know would offer more assistance if he could." The vid went to black.

"Who is this man?" Kelly finally asked, making no move to rise from the bathroom floor.

"Boris says he is a genius with chemicals. A modern-day alchemist." Leeta rewet the compress with cool water and handed it to her. "Are you feeling better?"

Kelly rubbed the knuckle of her thumb above her eye. Slowly, she rose and stood by the sink, methodically turning the faucets to stop the streaming water. To give some credibility to their time in the loo, Kelly flushed the toilet, then gestured to Leeta to leave the bathroom.

Never referencing Celsus' vid, the two women resumed pleasantries after returning to the main room with Leeta making small talk about her long trip home and the beauty of Irkutsk. As Kelly led her to the door, Leeta invited her to visit Siberia.

"Who knows where I'll end up," Kelly said, knowing that, for the first time, she truly had no idea.

# CHAPTER 48

ON MARCH 8, 2101, as constituted by presidential order, a military tribunal convened to try John Dee, enemy combatant, on the charges of abetting extraterrestrial aliens in plots against the United States. Seven judges: two air force brigadiers, two marine captains, two army generals, and Admiral Benjamin Royale, the president of the court, were seated at the front of the room beneath high black curtained windows, at long narrow oak tables placed end-to-end to serve as the bench. To the left of the makeshift bench stood a simple wooden chair for witnesses. To the right, two desks borrowed from the office next door were set up for the prosecution and defense. Franklin Swink was barred from acting as defense counsel but was permitted to be in attendance and follow the tribunal proceedings. Swink had requested that Colonel Max Stoeckle be appointed as defense counsel in his place. Aware of the considerable public concern that the seeming violation of Dee's civil rights was causing in the media as well as Swink's skill at manipulating that concern, President Marino opted to agree. The colonel was a well-built, imposing figure in his early fifties, with a strong German chin and a deep bass voice. His friends knew him as loyal and ferocious against his enemies. Having spent his life in military law defending the underdog, his path had often intersected that of Franklin Swinks. Lieutenant Commander Oriella "Hammer" Milton was seated as the government's opposing counsel. Beside her sat one of the red-cell team attorneys. Twelve NTSA guards stood outside the door while fifty soldiers guarded the perimeter of the building.

The guests of the court began filing in at 9 A.M. They included deputy under secretaries, high-ranking FBI, CIA, and NTSA officials, representatives from the Oval Office, and the English Ambassador, David Charmley. Franklin Swink took a reserved seat in the first row immediately behind Colonel Stoeckle's chair. The image of him as second chair was not lost on anybody. At precisely 9:30, the courtroom watched with different degrees of stoicism as Doctor Dee was silently paraded before them and deposited at Stoeckle's side by the naval MPs. He was haggard and taciturn, complaining of persistent headaches.

Colonel Stoeckle opened for the defense with a statement to the tribunal. "With no disrespect to this body, and in order not to prejudice the rights of my client, we wish to aver that the presidential order convening this commission is without validity. We believe it to be unconstitutional. Since there are civil statutes governing my client's accusations, our view is that these matters should be resolved in civil courts which have jurisdiction."

"Sirs," Milton immediately countered, "the civil courts do not have jurisdiction here. Doctor Dee is accused of violating the articles of war, which are clearly not the province of the civil courts. The international treaties of the NTSA are based on the agreed-upon assumption that we must prepare for attack from extraterrestrial invaders. Indeed, that we are at war already. As stated in the charges, this tribunal will decide the guilt or innocence of a man who is known to have fraternized with alien entities and infiltrated this country with the express intent of causing harm to the people and government of the United States. With this purpose in mind, he has unlawfully crossed our borders many times and, in the eyes of the Constitution, he is no different than the vanguard of an invading army."

No one in the room was surprised, least of all Swink, when the tribunal ruled on the side of the prosecution and instructed the defense to move on.

A flinty Stoeckle spent an hour arguing that the articles of war applied only to U.S. citizens caught aiding a known enemy and did not apply to noncitizens. Although the prosecution was not exactly sure to which country Dee belonged, Stoeckle reminded the court, that the government had never disputed that Dee wasn't a United States citizen. The prosecution rose to argue that just as the Montevideo Convention gave English citizens the protections of U.S. citizens, it should be interpreted that it also could penalize a protected foreigner in the same manner that an American was penalized. Stoeckle steadfastly argued against this untested interpretation of the treaty. He went on to quietly insist that there was no 'standard of proof' evidence that Dee had any plans of sabotage. From their vantage point, the judges couldn't help but see the counselor from Galveston nodding in agreement. Lieutenant Commander Milton interrupted several times with promises of future proof of conspiracy from the files of the NTSA. The undeterred Colonel

Stoeckle took a new tact and whittled away at the tenuous connection between the articles of war and the legitimacy of Reed O'Neal's organization. "The military threat to international security that is the bedrock of the NTSA treaties is still unproven even after twenty years of preparation. I object to this tribunal."

With the defense questioning the constitutionality of one of the government's largest bureaucracies, the president of the court rapped his gavel and commanded, "The court will rise." Two hours later, the bench returned and Royale declared, "Objection overruled."

Undeterred, Colonel Stoeckle rose again to make another objection. "Even if John Dee did consort with space aliens, which we are not agreeing to, no laws of war have been violated by the prisoner. Therefore, this commission is unjustifiable." The same thing happened again and the court took another two hours to return. "Objection overruled."

The point was clear. The tribunal was not going to rule on the legality of the NTSA. The rest of the day was spent with the prosecution submitting articles into evidence, which the defense continually challenged.

The second day was taken up with Stoeckle's policy question of whether the government could legitimately declare war on an entity that had not yet declared war on it. One that had not made any acts of aggression. If there were no attacks, he argued, how could the government call this "a time of war" and how could John Dee be accused of being an alien combatant. If Dee were a correspondent, he was no more that a lurker, a spy. Referencing the most pertinent legal case on the subject, Milton countered that in the Quirin case of World War II the tribunal there had equated lurkers with the out-of-uniform "enemy combatant" who sneaks into a country to wage war by destruction of life or property. A heated battle was pitched between the two attorneys as they referenced and cross-referenced legal precedents. An awesome number of citations flew fast and furious. The morning was peppered with explosive objections and extensive rounds of whereases and therefores. Many of the guests in the gallery fled in a haze of confusion. The one o'clock lunch break brought a much-needed reprieve for everyone. Commander Milton shot Reed O'Neal a weary look of apology. Colonel Stoeckle was unquestionably putting up a strong resistance, puncturing the NTSA's hope for an easy and early decision. The gallery wearily rose for the break. Swink sat quietly thinking about the heroic efforts of his friend and the unbending reserve of the tribunal's bench.

As Milton and Stoeckle gathered up their materials, Swink stepped into the gap that separated their tables and asked for a moment of their time. Briefly praising their performances, he cut to the chase. "I think you'll both agree that the issues we have addressed are too grave, the applicable law too unclear to resolve what lies before us with due expediency."

Milton eyed him suspiciously, unsure where he was headed. Swink smiled reassurringly and continued. "Perhaps, as colleagues sharing lunch, you might consider whether a settlement might be feasible."

Milton gaped at him. "O'Neal would never consider it," she said flatly.

"At least I have extended my offer," Swink said. He nodded to Stoeckle, who nodded back, as if understanding another, unspoken message, then left the room.

The tribunal reconvened at two, and the two sides resumed their arguments for four long hours. The judges, having endured two strenuous days, declared a recess for twenty-four hours while they reviewed case history and the hundreds of citations that had been made. Everyone seemed relieved at the prospect of a one-day cessation, but Franklin Swink saw another opportunity. As the judges gave instructions, he made a quick call to Billy McIntyre, the Presidential Chief of Staff. Dinner reservations that night at the West End, a popular hangout of McIntyre's, were hastily arranged for 8:30. Once McIntrye was on board, Swink was able to coerce Milton and Stoeckle to join them.

By the time the session ended, the various attorneys, judges, and other officials left the court with a sense of relief. By setting forth the issues and arguments, the next crucial step had been taken and now it was time for the law to take its course and its servants to celebrate their role in it.

# CHAPTER 49

FRANKLIN SWINK PULLED INTO the driveway of the West End and waited for the attendant to wave him up to the door. Despite it being a Wednesday, the popular eatery was busy. The hot spot had four things going for it: well-aged mutton roast, the greatest Yorkshire pudding in captivity, a wide panorama of the Potomac River and the jeweled lights of the capital city, and the fact that on any given night a dinner guest more interested in Beltway gossip than scenic views might get a glimpse of government officials.

Tonight was going to be a red-letter evening for many, what with Chief of Staff William McIntyre in view. The valet came and took his vehicle, and Franklin Swink was soon in the restaurant handing the hat-check girl his scarf and coat. As he had planned, he was the first to arrive. As the maître d' showed him to McIntyre's usual booth in the back, he could hear the tourists whispering that yes, he did look familiar. Could he be someone important? Once seated, he ordered a glass of fifty-year-old scotch, selected two bottles of expensive wine for dinner, and double-checked his wrist-vid for his notes for the evening.

The next to arrive was Lieutenant Commander Oriella Milton. Looking spectacular in a period dress of the mid twenty-first century, she seemed surprisingly rested given her mind-numbing day in court. Colonel Stoeckle was right on her heels, newly shaven and wearing his military best. At 8:45, McIntyre and O'Neal made their entrance into the gaslit dining area. McIntyre made his way through the dining room, pausing at many of the tables to keep the congressmen, ambassadors, and voters happy. It wasn't hard for Billy McIntyre; he had the gift of the blarney and the political courage of Winston Churchill, who many people said he resembled. Not particularly wanting to have to face Swink—or Stoeckle, for that matter—without McIntyre, Reed O'Neal took his time arriving at the table, doing his version of paying public obeisance.

Finally, the public officials made it to the private party. Seeing Oriella Milton looking so attractive, Reed O'Neal squeezed in next to her in the booth and unexpectedly planted a peck on her cheek. McIntyre, whose bulk demanded it, sat on the end. Without preamble, Swink laid the ground rules for the evening, insisting on no out-of-court rehashes of the last two days' debate.

"Dee is in legal limbo, now," started the civil rights attorney.

O'Neal, who had been twisting his ring, was about to interrupt when in a conciliatory velvet voice the President's Chief of Staff overrode him, "Reed, you promised me you'd listen to what the man has to say."

"Thank you, Billy. By the way, thank you all for listening." Swink lowered his voice so that eavesdropping ears would not be privy to what he was about to propose. "John Dee is beyond the jurisdiction of the federal courts and now is in a military system that is poised to hang him. But the truth of the matter is that—with all due respect, Mister Director and Lieutenant Commander—there is very little in the way of facts that implicate him in any espionage against this country."

"Except for the missing ID chip and the communications with the aliens," Milton said.

Swink raised his glass to her in a toast. "Commander Milton as usual has hit the nail on the head. And I will get to that." He paused to sip his scotch. "By labeling John Dee and Miss Edwards as "enemy combatants" and transferring them from the civilian NTSA lockup to the military brig in Langley, the government bought itself some time to figure out what to do with two people who may actually have had interaction with spacemen. With that accomplished, the NTSA could then question Doctor Dee more aggressively, without any intervention from defense lawyers or habeas corpus."

"Get on with it Mister Swink. We've all had a long day." Reed O'Neal didn't bother to disguise his distaste.

"Mister O'Neal, I am only laying out the legal facts here." Swink took a deep breath and continued, "I can only conjecture. But I'd bet the farm that you got the President to establish this week's tribunal so that you could cut off any more of my federal court petitions. I realize you've had to focus more on putting out the fires I've started than concentrating on what must be your real objective—acquiring intelligence on alien entities. And now you are faced with the choice between, one"—he raised his index finger—"possibly losing a court hearing and having to let him go, or two"—he added another finger—"putting him on ice for a while as a convicted enemy combatant. Am I right?"

No answer.

"Now Commander Milton and Colonel Stoeckle can argue until the cows come home about jurisdiction, war powers, and whether he is a spy or not. But, Mister Director, what you want more than anything is intelligence about extraterrestrials as a threat to national security. And from the look of things, you've gotten nowhere. None of Dee's captured communications indicate sabotage. Rather, the ones I've been allowed to see indicate that the man wants to find a missing alien who may be sick. Now either you're barking up the wrong tree or you're not good at your job. And I can't accept the latter."

"He had personal relations with the creature in Angel City who raised an army of the dead to terrorize the city. The vids show him right next to it, standing by the thing's side, while it waged war on American civilians," said O'Neal.

"The Strategy Brooks footage doesn't seem to conclusively indicate that he was abetting the alien. There was a lot of rain and mud. The vids are chaotic and the pictures are fuzzy. Could be that the man was attempting to stop that monster," countered Swink. "Besides, there have always been suspicions that the Brooks vids were all a hoax." Colonel Stoeckle mentally applauded Swink's manipulative use of the NTSA media misdirection.

O'Neal, his restraint at the breaking point, blurted out, "Damn it, the man doesn't have a chip. He's being used to infiltrate. And that's no hoax."

"There's the chip again. A lot of days in court for such a little thing. I don't know why he doesn't have one, and I venture to guess"—he looked at Milton—"you and your team aren't too sure either. Maybe the man is what he says he is—a time traveler from Elizabethan England."

"Your Doctor Dee is a crafty bastard who wants us to believe that load of crap. Thinks Stoeckle here can get him off on a plea of mental incompetence," O'Neal said. "And if you think that will happen, then you're as crazy as he is."

"As to my mental state, I'd rather not comment," Swink chuckled, gratified to see a smile tugging at the corners of Milton's lips. "As to Doctor Dee, I don't know if he is crazy or not. I've only met with him twice since the Fourth gave me access. But I do know that he ain't going to fade away. Not while the press is hot on this story about the government's questionable decisions regarding civil rights violations. Which is why I have invited you all to dinner. The ultimate question will be what governmental authority gets to label an American what they want, and when, and with what evidence. And by extension all those that are protected by the Montevideo Convention as well. And that constitutional showdown comes down to the President and the courts. So, it's fair to say that the completion of this tribunal guarantees a confrontation between the two. A confrontation that will not help Marino in the next election."

O'Neal stared at the ice melting in his drink, uncharacteristically silent.

"I know you, Franklin. You wouldn't have brought us all together and lectured us if you didn't want to plea bargain. What's the deal?" said Stoeckle.

"You know I cling to the fanciful liberal notion that this country has more integrity"—he tapped the table with his index finger—"and by that I mean virtuous government, than any other. Whether that's today or ever.

Our system of politics insists on our doing the right thing." He took a sip of his scotch and with a twinkle added, "Now let's get down and dirty. Our system of politics is also a system of give-and-take. The NTSA wants evidence and leads on an extraterrestrial threat. We want our client to get a fair shake. The President wants this to go away. So, here's the deal. Implant an ID chip into Dee. That takes care of your number one gripe against him. I promise, Mister Director, no petitions about invasion of privacy from me. Set him free with the chip and—"

"Let him go? Where is your justice in that? The man enters into a conspiracy that threatens this country and we let him go without corporeal consequences?" O'Neal wanted to make a forceful theatrical exit that would demonstrate his disdain, but he couldn't. He was wedged in the booth between Milton and the bulky McIntyre. "He has information we need to keep this nation safe."

"Reed, the President wants this to go away," McIntyre said, "and you have gotten nothing from Dee so far. The press is calling him Marino's martyr."

"Mister Director, perhaps if you let me finish, I can make the scenario more palatable." Swink waited as O'Neal grudgingly returned his gaze, giving him a tacit okay. "I suggest that the President have a moral epiphany and amend his executive order so that all citizens protected under Montevideo are expressly barred from military tribunals. That will make all us liberal voters happy. You implant your mandated chip in our client and tell the world through private channels that Strategy Brooks is wrong again. There's no such thing as a chipless person on this Earth and, after much investigation and due diligence by the NTSA—blah, blah, blah—no evidence of an extraterrestrial threat was found. That takes care of any residual panic left over from her vids on GNN. As to Dee, you arrested the man as a critical intelligence resource and, having questioned him, procured what little information he had available. That way if Mars ever does attack—God forbid—your reputation as the protector of the people is blemish-free."

O'Neal was about to raise another objection when Commander Milton gave him a sharp look commanding silence. She had spent two weeks with the prisoner. She had been present at his interrogations, investigated his statements, and pored over the vids, the communications, the NTSA field reports, and the GNN testimony. She believed Dee was guilty of fraternization, of chip malfeasance, of infiltration, but she had yet to see one concrete item of armed belligerence against the United States. That, of course, was the definition of an enemy combatant. The fact that she was working for the system did not oblige her to blindly accept the system's bull.

Swink continued, "Now, here's where I do your job for you. You've got the chip in him, so you can keep him under surveillance wherever he goes. You can train your spy satellites, your listening devices, and your embedded agents on him and maybe, just maybe he'll lead you to a nest of extraterrestrials. Hell, that happens, you'll forever justify the need for the NTSA and you will have given President Marino a very nice birthday present. Such a deal!"

"Franklin," said Stoeckle, "have you asked Dee if he will agree to the operation?"

Before he could answer, the Director of the NTSA scolded, "We don't *ask* criminals to comply with the law; we *make* them."

That was the break in the ice Franklin needed. By the end of the dinner, O'Neal's tone was still negative, but he could see the wisdom of belling the cat.

# CHAPTER 50

THAT EVENING, THE ENTRANCE to the Langley naval brig was jammed with vans, cars, personal flyers, hoppers, and a mob of journalists and their various backups, all shouting and shoving to get the first look at the detainee, John Dee, as he emerged from the high metal gate. Franklin Swink escorted him as if he were minor royalty. It was reported by most of those present that Dee looked a little unsteady and took pains to shield his eyes from the wind and the intense light focused on him by the camera crews. Some who had done their research said he looked smaller than he had when he and Edwards were arrested at Four Corners.

Dee glanced at Swink uneasily, hesitating to throw himself into the melee. Action and invention might be required momentarily. "How do we navigate our way through so many?"

"By car," said Swink. "Don't worry. I've handled these situations many times before. Just follow my lead. You'll be fine."

Dee peered anxiously at the milling throng. "It is a fearful company of all manner of persons. Like a flood, they inexorably press in." He scanned what part of the road he could see. "Where is your car?"

"It's coming," said Swink, who was unfazed by the chaos waiting for them. In fact, it slightly intoxicated him. "Just stay calm. Let me do the talking."

"Gladly," said Dee, unsure of the meaning of all this attention. While in the brig, he had not been allowed to know of any of the debate that his case had engendered. Swink had never bothered to mention that he had become a *cause célèbre*. The circus atmosphere in front of him was disquieting. Though he had Swink's assurances, after being released from prison, Dee thought this many people looking for him only meant a hanging. Just at that moment the wind whipped by him, he looked up and saw pearly blue-gray clouds sailing past the almost full moon. He breathed a sigh of contentment. There were the familiar sights of the night sky. Being able once more to see the heavenly objects unrestricted by concrete walls and skylights confirmed his freedom.

Swink clasped Dee by the shoulder. "Just keep next to me and keep your eyes cast downward. Let them know you've been through a lot." Together, they stepped up to meet the surging throng. "Ladies and gentlemen, I know you'll understand that my client is very pleased to be released. He is exhausted and has asked me to speak for him. He wishes to publicly thank President Marino for quickly canceling the tribunal and withdrawing his classification as an enemy combatant, thus allowing him to be released under the provisions of the Patriot Act. It was an act of decisive presidential leadership that demonstrates his strong stand on the protection of individual rights. The President showed great acumen this morning with his assertion that detainees, like Doctor Dee and Miss Edwards, must be afforded the same panoply of judicial protections as those given to defendants in civil actions, or a dictatorship will be upon us and the tanks will have rolled. In addition, Doctor Dee wishes to thank all of you in the media who saw the injustice of his being stripped of the rights that every citizen in this world enjoys and made it your business to educate the country to his plight. And for standing in this wind at this ungodly hour."

A babble of questions almost overwhelmed Swink's powerful voice; it was impossible to make out what the reporters were asking. Holding up his hands for silence, Swink went on, "Thank you for your attention. That's Doctor Dee's statement for the present."

Dee instinctively started to move away. The shouting grew louder and the horde pressed forward, their shouts almost deafening to a man who had spent two weeks in near complete solitary confinement. Dee glanced at Swink, wondering when they were to make their escape, when he saw a large, black limousine inching forward with care and inexorably nudging the newshounds aside. Finally, it was a barrier between the media and Swink. "Is that ours?"

"Yes," said Swink as he struggled to open a door. Over the insistent tumult, he ordered, "Get in!"

Before his eyes adjusted to the car's darkness, he heard Kelly Edwards call his name from the seat facing him. In order not to attract attention, she had dressed in dark green and worn a hooded coat. He pulled her to him and they warmly embraced for some time. Though they had only been separated for less than a week, it seemed an eternity.

"It's good to have you back, John."

"It's good to be back," he answered, focusing all his attention on her.

Interrupting their reunion, the long limo jerked to a stop as an insistent cameraman refused to step out of its way. All turned to watch Swink's driver expertly push the man aside with the front of the car. Concentrating on maneuvering the car out of the crowd, the chauffeur's eyes briefly met Dee's in the rearview mirror. "You're lookin' a little peaked there, Doc."

Dee's usual toughness melted into uncontrollable tears of joy as he leaned forward in his seat to wrap his arm around d'Winter's neck. Franklin Swink winked at Kelly. Well pleased with his little surprise, Swink thought the moment couldn't have gone better.

"We have a number of things we have to discuss," he finally said. "And we'd better do it here, where we can't be overheard. No eavesdropping possible. The limo's been swept and we have the best jammers made to keep anyone from snooping." Acknowledging the man who was busy getting the car beyond the crowd, he added "Thank you, Mister d'Winter."

"What is so important that we have to approach it so secretly?" Kelly asked. "Can't you just declare this as privileged?"

"Not with the two of you here, my dear. Your presence here complicates the equation. Dee is my client, and only what I say to him in private is privileged," said Swink. "But it's not the law that worries me now—it's the future. O'Neal's not happy about releasing you. Either of you. He only did it out of political expediency. Like the Bible's pharaoh, after relenting, his heart will stiffen and he will want you back."

"All I want to do is disappear and continue on with my life. O'Neal need never find me again," Dee said.

"You can't just disappear anymore once you have that chip in your head. O'Neal will always know where to find you, despite Mister d'Winter's best jammers and evasion techniques. You must convince O'Neal that you're no threat to him or the country. You must also convince the media—which, sad to say, will pursue you day and night—that they were right about you and that the government is making a mistake by hounding you."

"Reed O'Neal will not be easily appeased," Dee said. "I've studied men like him, and I know what mischief they are capable of." The Earl of Leicester, Robert Dudley, and Archbishop Thomas Wolsey sprang to mind.

"Reed O'Neal has more troubles to deal with than your case," said d'Winter smugly. "I've been following the news, and it's beginning to look like the Director's rising star is fading.

At that news, Swink sat back and languidly reached for a dark-green bottle. "Calls for a toast. Clicquot. Top of the line."

"To freedom," volunteered Kelly.

"Aye, to freedom," Dee agreed wholeheartedly.

"So enjoy it while you can," said Swink, and expertly popped the cork while Kelly held out flutes for the wine.

While the others sipped, the Elizabethan drained his glass in one swallow. He nodded in appreciation. "We had not champagne in my time. It gladdens the heart as the bubbles pepper the nose."

Swink drank more of his champagne and refilled

everyone's glasses. As the others drank, Dee pondered the mysterious circumstances leading to his freedom. Why had this elder advocate, this utter stranger, become their Sir Galahad? Abruptly he spoke out. "Who has arranged all this? Who pays your bills?"

"Aurum All Chemical Mining Company. The CEO is Theon Celsus," Swink replied.

Dee heard Kelly gasp in astonishment, then felt her hand on his as a cue not to speak. His trust in her implicit, Dee kept quiet.

"Mister Swink, about your idea of laying low," said Kelly. "What about leaving the country again? Can we even do that?"

"Certainly, there is no prohibition. You can simply say you want to return to your former residence in London. O'Neal will simply arrange for U.K. NTSA to monitor your comings and goings."

"What if we didn't go back to England, but somewhere else? Say, to Siberia." Another squeeze to Dee's hand signaled him to be patient.

"I suppose it's possible," Swink allowed.

"Are you certain?" Dee asked cryptically.

Franklin wasn't sure if his client's question was meant for him or Kelly. "Oh, yeah," he said finally. "If you have a demonstrable reason to go to Siberia, you can simply do a pro forma fling through the Immigration Offices. Do you have such a reason, Miss Edwards?"

Kelly nodded hesitantly. "Possibly . . . a job opportunity."

"A job?" questioned the advocate, looking in her eyes and wondering when she would fill him in. To his chagrin, it became abundantly clear she needed more prodding. "Obviously, your current employer is unfamiliar with this job opportunity. Would you like to share your thoughts?"

"No, sir, I would not. Not while my conversation is not protected by attorney/client privilege." She rapped on the glass partition. "Morgan, can you pull off the road anywhere? Somewhere out in the open. The three of us need to talk."

# CHAPTER 51

MATTIK HAD FOLLOWED THE charismatic monk up a steep hill that led down to one of the myriad channels that split off from the pale green Ganges River before it empties into the Bay of Bengal. The cleric had effortlessly picked his way through unstable marshland that led to his commune in the Sunderbans refuge. The cloying air was hot and humid, the perfect climate for a Roc. The quiet of the mangrove swamp was a sharp contrast to the bustling populated urban areas that lay just behind them. Setting down his twin cases, Mattik turned back for a last glimpse of the encircled village, not quite sure how he had been able to just walk away. The humani in front of him, he thought, must command great respect indeed from his fellow men. Mattik's guide walked on, following the channel bank. The Roc gripped his bags and scrambled to catch up. Once or twice they passed a tree or copse, which was the haunt of some remembered spirit, marked by a rotting prayer flag. Bedraggled white prayer ribbons fluttered everywhere. Mattik took notice of their petitions of hope illuminated with dragons, wheels, and guardian lions. The pain of the petitioner was evident in each hand-tied letter.

Mattik knew something of the man who led him. The monk was one of the two million members of the Brahma Kumaris World Spiritual University, whose spiritual founder was Dada Lekh Raj, a Hindu merchant who had had spiritual epiphanies about world transformation. In his visions, Hinduism had commingled with a prosperous ascetic meditation movement, a back-to-nature aesthetic that rejected technology, and a secular intellectualism. The sect had established working relationships with multilateral medical organizations in the hope that by the performing of good works the world might ascend out of the present iron age of decadence and onto a path to a golden age of perfection. Raj communes were to be found wherever there was disease or abject poverty. Their members, characteristically clad all in white, were nurturing caregivers who took the time to see that complications did not set in and humanely stayed the course if they did. They were not often the first at medical disasters, but they could be counted on to be the last. With their homeopathic medicines, the order brought their suffering patients relief from bodily pain and serenity for the mind—or so the common folklore promised.

The roofs of its hospital and residences within the well-appointed Raj compound swung skyward toward the sun, welcoming the radiant sunshine of life and restoration. Caducei, barber polls, red crosses, and eclectic medical insignia from every century decorated doors and the banners that wafted about the enclave. Though the streets and homes of the community were presently empty, the air was suffused with the harmonies of communal chanting and litany. It was prayer time, and the order had congregated in the temple by the riverbank, a wedding cake of tiered pavilions. At the front door stood a carving of the Goddess of Mercy with her seven eyes watchful for the presence of those in need of assistance.

Upon entering, Mattik was graciously introduced to the congregation. At this point, the Roc's bioshield was visibly disintegrating, and it was obvious to the entire enclave of medical experts that Corwin Tarlton was not in any way human. Moreover, he was introduced as the source of the epidemic that had caused such sorrow in Calcutta. Expecting innate humani repugnance, the Roc was at first sheepish and reticent, but the members were not put off by his alienness or by the virus. At the end of all the introductions, Mattik's monk made a detailed report to the group of the symptoms of the mutation disease that he had seen in the quarantine. Detailed questions were asked, and Mattik was entreated to join in the conversation. As if he had been a Raj member for years, Mattik's opinions and observations were treated with the respect and appreciation due an authority figure.

At dusk, by some sort of unspoken understanding, the medical discussion ended and the monks settled to the floor in an informal semicircle facing the door. A young Indian, whose name was Shelley, stood before his peers and was asked several questions about his faith and commitment. Mattik listened with growing enthusiasm.

"For many years, I studied at the universities of Germany, Italy, the United States, and Hong Kong, seeking to find the foundations of medicine. I eagerly and diligently investigated all the art of healing. I have often thought that medicine is an uncertain and haphazard art; it is scarcely honorable to call myself a doctor, when at best I can only cure one and lose three. By those odds, I count myself more a gambler than a doctor. Many times in years past, I abandoned medicine and followed other pursuits, but then again I was driven back to it by the random suffering and utter depression of my fellow man. I chanced upon a lecture by Doctor Thubna in China where he said many wise and thoughtful things. But one in particular has always stayed with me. 'The healthy need not a physician, but only the sick.' I finally recalled that the doctor's words were from the teachings of Jesus. The art of medicine is a true, just, and noble calling, but must be constantly tested in dire circumstances. Like a soldier on a battlefield, I must not judge anything superficially, but must scrupulously pay close attention to all of a patient's symptoms, physical, mental, and spiritual. That is my vow today: to perfect my medical art and never to swerve from it as long as God grants me the ability to provide.

"I strive in my art and in my life to purge any impediments that hinder me from discovering the best that medicine can do, the best there is in nature, to find and use the best that our mother earth truly intends for the sick. Everything that we must do and prescribe, we should do by the light of nature. For the light of nature is nothing other than reason itself. Unbridled modern technology thinks itself wiser than nature, which is the womb of all medical knowledge here on Earth. I have learned that nothing comes from me, but rather everything comes from nature, of which I am a part. But there is a more exquisite quest in medicine than just curing the body, and that is tending that part of the patient that does not die—the spirit that he is lent at birth. To that rarified practice I commit myself, for I have learned from all of you that that is the highest stratum of our profession."

There was polite applause all around as the monk took his seat among his peers. Another young acolyte rose to take his place.

"Consider how great and noble man was created, and what greatness must be attributed to his structure. No brain can fully understand the structure of man's body and the extent of his virtues. The whole world surrounds man as a circle surrounds one point or as the flesh of a pear surrounds its seed. As the complete pear fares, so does the seed, mankind, in the center. Each thing has its own origin, partly in the eternal, or what Dada Raj calls the creation of the circle, and partly in the momentary, which is the temporal individual. From this it follows that all things are related to this one point in the center. As an individual in the center improves, so do the world and the eternal that surrounds it. Therefore, let us consider what mankind as a whole is and must become. Let us all strive to improve it, and I will start the process by improving myself."

She continued to speak, and Mattik listened to heartfelt vows of commitment to medicine and the improvement of mankind. He remembered the looks of awe and respect from the quarantine guards before they allowed his guide to exit the compound. He looked at the face of that monk as he nodded in agreement with the current speaker's sense of pride and responsibility as if he were renewing his own vows. To his astonishment, he realized he would regret seeing his monk or any here this afternoon suffering in the way he had watched his victims in the quarantine suffer. For the first time, he had reason to tentatively question his clan leader's assessment of the race they had watched for so long. These were kind, educated minds that saw cosmic potential and grandeur inside each humani, and Mattik was prompted by their words to reexamine Fawg's description of mankind as inconsequential grasping vermin. The centuries-old members of Clan Fawg of the Earth expedition only saw humani as annoying ants, trapped in a nanosecond existence. They had not stood back from the flaws of the individual to see the magnificence of the upwardly aspiring social order the ants were building over eons. Fawg had said that they would never outgrow their bestial natures, but here on a remote riverbank of the Ganges, Mattik saw wisdom and progress.

"Your thoughts have taken you miles away—out of the present," said Mattik's guide.

"I have a mission," said the Roc.

"What mission is that? The one you told me about—to control humanity through the virus?" As distressing as this notion was, it was not revealed in his manner, nor was there a rebuke in his tone.

"Yes. It would bring my clan much honor and power. I have sworn to do this, and therefore I must." He felt his failure keenly, and the shame such an admission brought him was acute, but, suddenly, so was the brutality. "I do not mean you any harm."

"I know you don't," said the monk. He contemplated the Roc in silence for a while. "I can tell that you have no hostility to any of us. But our order is sworn to preserve the health of mankind. I have to ask you to reflect on what you propose to do here. That's all."

"That's all?" The Roc stared out the window at the growing gray darkness of evening, half listening to what was being said. "Your world, your authorities, your NTSA, they know about me now, and what I am capable of. I can never really hide again. All of you—your kind—will be on guard, and that could mean—" He stopped, thinking of the fury that could be unleashed upon him.

Aware of the Roc's confusion and dismay, the monk offered a reasonable solution to bring comfort. "You are safe here, and humanity is safe while you are here. It doesn't matter if your suit is protective or not. We have all been immunized against the virus, thanks to Celsus, who has said he will vaccinate the world. Stay with us and let us learn from you, as you will learn from us."

It was a gracious invitation, but Mattik was still too confused to see it as a way out of his responsibilities. He stared at the monk, measuring his suitability for something.

"How is it that this Celsus was able to create a workable remedy so quickly? Who is he?" asked the bewildered Roc.

The monk happily shared his knowledge of Theon Celsus, for the man was well known to most of the members of the Brahma Kumaris World Spiritual University. He spoke frequently and eloquently at their medical conventions on the efficacy of herbal remedy, the physician's responsibility to his fellow man, and the aspiring alchemy of the soul. Many an acolyte was converted to the Raj's principles after having spent a weekend with the strange little man. He preached passionately about the unity of nature and faith, of asceticism and worldly delights, the attention to symptomatic observation and the hope of spiritual transformation, critical reason and heartfelt guesses, and of license and duty. He was an elitist, yet a man of the people, a successful capitalist governed by ethics and scruples, a polymath who never spoke down to his audience. Mattik heard the unmitigated admiration in the monk's voice, and that sparked memories, centuries old, of Dyckon's comparable respect for an iconoclastic Swiss doctor who had caught his eye.

As the monk described the charismatic lecturer as a slightly built man, with sensitive hands, a relatively large bald head framed in a curtain of unruly hair, and blazing deep-set eyes, Mattik recalled his furtive visit with Fawg to a dark recessed corner of the hold to spy on two humani specimens as they hung frozen in their cryogenic capsules. And here for a moment, Mattik had one of the few meaningful connections of his long life. But he did not share it—not even with this gifted monk whom he had come to esteem.

# CHAPTER 52

"HOW LONG WILL THE flight take?" Dee asked as he strapped in for his journey to Lake Baikal International Airport. He still found it hard to believe that he was free, that he could travel at will, and that the lack of a chip would no longer prove the problem it had been. With his index finger, he felt for the scar on his neck where the tiny transmitter had been implanted. He felt its warmth. It was disconcerting to think that even now it was sending the location of his whereabouts to Reed O'Neal, as it would for the rest of his life.

Revving the transport's engines in a preflight maintenance check, d'Winter said, "We'll be there in just over three hours in the air, but it is fourteen hours ahead, so it will be tomorrow in Siberia."

Dee looked out the window. He was still perplexed by Celsus' offer to receive him as a guest in Siberia. There were too many unanswered questions. Why had Dyckon risked his mission by confiding in this man? Why had the man hired and paid handsomely for Franklin Swink? How did he have access to Roc antibodies, and what help did he expect from Dee about the disease? His gut clutched at all the uncertainty, but he reminded himself that at least this trip to the other side of the world would put him far away from all but the most determined news reporters, and that seemed a good idea just now. He was keenly aware that he would now attract attention wherever he went, attention that was less than welcome.

"Will I ever return here?" Dee looked out the window. He contemplated the immense sprawl of Washington, D.C. He secretly hoped he wouldn't. After two weeks of fast and resistance, he had learned a hard lesson—one he had not wanted to admit to himself. He was no longer adequately trained to deal in state affairs. Technology and psychology had outstripped his poor power to wheedle, resist, and outmaneuver. Reluctantly, he had accepted retirement. He was no longer a grand master of espionage; the last game of chess had been played. It was regrettable but understandable. The world had simply progressed while he had slept.

The flyer raced pell-mell down the runway of Ronald Reagan International Airport. With a bump the transport jettisoned the Earth and rose through the high clouds, picking up speed. Dee stopped looking out the window, there being nothing more than a thin curtain of clouds to see. Height were still unnerving. "I thank my stars, I'm not journeying back to the moon."

"Not yet," said Kelly, "Though you may want to go there again."

"If the news media, injurious wasps, will not leave off their buzzing, I shall willingly."

Kelly laughed, her relief evident in her enjoyment. Long absent, a growing gaiety was returning. "You're still a conundrum, John Dee. You're free, you're rich. Like it or not, you're a growing celebrity, and yet you're still down in the dumps. Come on, look on the bright side, you have everything you want."

Eyes tilting downward, John Dee reflected on this before giving a reluctant shake of the head. "Have I what I want? Nay, I *want*"—he accented the word to emphasize its double meaning—"much. Though there is some small comfort that the World Health Organization and the NTSA strive to squash the contagion, yet is the virus a threat to us all. The Roc remains at liberty, and we are as near to netting him as before we were made captives at Four Corners. So indeed, we *want much* and I do desire with all my heart to change that." Out of friendship, he had not mentioned what he desired most of all—a way back home. He shrugged at his own gloominess. "I was ever of a melancholic humor. It is a failing in my character," Dee said, giving her a wink.

"Do you really think that?" Kelly asked.

"No," Dee told her. "I think it may be but a woeful cast of thought after contending with so much. I am wondrously weary and fear I will prove a tiresome companion."

"You're homesick," said d'Winter.

"Yea," Dee admitted. "I am. But, alas, home is the place one must leave peradventure that one may find oneself. To that end travelers must be content." He looked out the window and gazed at the white flood of clouds that masked his view of the Earth. Inside an airy capsule of thoughts, he contemplated the uncertain future.

They arrived in Irkutsk ahead of schedule. D'Winter had pushed the transport into the redline. They had landed and gone through customs with a minimum of delay. It was still deep winter and bitingly cold as they scrambled from the terminal to the car that Theon Celsus had sent for them. Fearful of being recognized by the driver, the Doctor pulled his hat low over his brow and did not participate in the sight-seeing chit-chat. Instead, he cogitated on what would be the quid pro quo for the Siberian's generosity. He wondered what it was he had to swap.

Boris Shevyenets had closed his dining areas to all guests but Theon Celsus and John Dee. Dee and Celsus would meet in the Grand Ballroom while Leeta O'Conner entertained Kelly and d'Winter, along with Maxim Izevsky in the main dining room. The candles were lit, nicely augmented by recessed indirect lighting that made the elaborate, old-fashioned room glow. When Dee entered the paneled room, Theon Celsus was already seated at a well-damasked table that had a tray of sweetmeats and two ornate goblets of Murano glass and cheat-bread wrapped in a ceremonial portpayne on an exquisite silver platter.

Celsus rose as he spoke. "This ancient inn is built of strong timber, in framing whereof your English carpenters have been and are worthily preferred before those of like science among all other nations. No nation can have more excellent stuff for building than you have in Albion. I thought it seemly to feast you in a room to your manner born. It is fashioned like to those of our years, wherein your workmen excelled and were in craftsmanship comparable in skill with old Vitruvius, Leon Battista, and Serlio." Dee's benefactor hoisted a glass. "Knowing not your tastes but full cognizant that you are of the wealthy commonalty and are an intimate of the Queen, I choose rather the Venice glass than any of those common metals or stone wherein beforetime we have been accustomed to drink. But whither am I slipped? Shall we drink a measure?" With that he handed his astonished guest the other glass. "I drink to our general joy and to days past."

"Sweet remembrancer, I commend thee and thy house-keeping." Confused, Dee responded warily, not sure why the strange man was speaking in the flowery eloquence of Elizabethan times. Was this some trick, some politic courtesy to soften him up? Why had he made reference to Renaissance architects, the period hors d'oeuvres and crystal, and the enigmatic phrase "our years"? Perhaps he was a gifted linguist. "Do you cozen me, sir? Fie, you run this humor too long out of breath. You wrong me much to sport with me thus. Have a care."

Celsus did his best not to smile. It would have been unseemly. "Look not upon me with a distracted eye. I vouch I am of the same time as you, a former wayfarer as you, taken prisoner upon the monster Dyckon's spacecraft, but, unlike you, I have walked abroad here a score of years and learned the custom. Why look you strange on me? For it is known to me that you are well aware of me despite we have never met. True it is a dozen of my books grace your *interna bibliotheca* and each has in it a portrait by the printer of its creator's likeness—my portrait."

"And who the deuce are you? And who has told you of my private collection?"

"Paracelsus. *Alterius non sit, qui suus esse potest.*"

John Dee would have roared with laughter if the impossibility hadn't seemed plausible. The Luther of Medicine, Paracelsus, who like his contemporaries Copernicus and da Vinci, had transformed medieval thought with rational humanism. The man had had a tormented career filled with persecution, but with titanic energy had left innumerable writings on divine order and the sacred task of the physician. Dee had pored over his alchemical and metallurgical writings since he first discovered them in his early thirties. They were the more prized possessions of his library. Their manifestos considered the purpose of alchemy to be not the perfection of metals, but of the body and even the soul. *Yes,* thought Dee, *this was a humani Dyckon would have found irresistible.* Moreover, there was no doubt he was the man in the engravings of so many of the texts. *Alterius non sit, qui suus esse potest.* Let no one who can be his own belong to another. How well that motto fit them both.

"Unlike yourself, Herr Doktor, never having been much good with rhetoric or subtleties in German, let alone English, with your permission I will resort to a more modern usage as is my wont now. Over the years, I must admit I have striven with much success to become thoroughly modern. The rhetoric of our time is now almost forgotten." He nodded in acknowledgment. "You would say 'forgot.' "

Boris chose that moment to deliver a mutton stew that was redolent with saffron, the liquid almost reduced to a glaze.

"So, Dee," said Celsus as Boris left them alone over their stew. "How have you found your stay in this century?"

Dee blew on his food before answering, not knowing how much it would be wise to reveal. It would be tempting to assume a comradeship with this man because of their origins. He found it hard to resist the urge to expound upon his entire experience, but he reminded himself yet again that his host was as unknown as any stranger. That they might possibly have come from similar times created a commonality that later might well prove illusory. Acceding to the siren song of their historical kinship might shipwreck him and his crew on the rocks and dash his hopes of success.

"It has been very interesting," he said at last without emotion. "I am still trying to decide what I'm to do next." He picked at his food.

"Do you have any plans?" Celsus inquired. He was very grand in a caftan of heavy red-and-gold brocaded silk edged in ermine.

"I've scarce had time to dwell on it, as there have been diverse pressing considerations to mull," Dee lied. "I have learned plans are but plans, and who can say which planted seed grows to maturity." While he had been held at Langley, he had thought of nothing else but what he would do when and if he were ever released. Not having finished assessing his impressions of Paracelsus, he kept those thoughts to himself, but was initially impressed with his fine appearance and his courtly courtesy, which was in the manner of their long-vanished age.

Celsus ducked his head. "I don't blame you for your taciturnity. With what you've been through, you have good reason to keep your own counsel. After all, I am nearly a complete cipher to you."

The stew was hearty and delicious, Dee thought. The wine it simmered in was heady. "I would venture you trudged the selfsame path."

"Oh, no. I've had a much easier time of it than you have. When Dyckon put me here, I was prepared for what was coming; I had a wealth of information, and as much material as I would need to process petrochemicals. It was but an extension of my study of the transmutation of metals. You, by contrast, had none of these advantages." He lifted up his glass of sherry and smiled. "I can't help but wonder why Dyckon did what he did. Do you have any notion about it?"

"Only a surmise or two, and that is of little consequence." He drank a little of the wine, a very little, not wanting to loosen his tongue. He had not thought of the Roc for a while. The remembered betrayal began to heat his choler.

"But you had the advantage of his help from time to time, didn't you?" Celsus said. "I was left mainly to forage on my own. As to Fawg, I followed that from here, of course, and I knew what kind of danger Yeshua really was. A most distressing turn of events, particularly those in Angel City. You must tell me about those rat-men when you have the opportunity. I found them quite incredible. Were they really physically modified, or was it a clever sort of costume they wore? I can't help but wonder what drove them to take on such an appearance."

Dee helped himself to another ladleful of the mutton. "I have of late been given over to a great abstinence and a want of sustenance whereof a little sufficeth my stomach for much." But having said that, John Dee reached for the trencher of bread and tore off a piece. He refrained from the butter as everyone knew that only increased the choleric humor. "This native nourishment so well to my liking puts me in mind of home, at least as much as most of the victuals I have supped on. It is right well done. My thanks."

"That's Siberia for you," Celsus graciously replied. "Their game is genuine, not technomeat, flavored and pulverized into an imitation of real food." He laughed and drank down his wine. "So what is your theory about Dyckon?"

"I don't know," said Dee, measuring his words with care. "I suppose we need must reason why he culled men from our century, and at that I can only hazard a guess. Apparently he has had all of time from which to pluck his humans. So what influenced him in his decision to seize on you and me is an unwieldy knot to untie."

"A good question, and one I wish I could answer," said Celsus. "It may that the flame of our intellectual curiosity was too brilliant to let go out. You by being walled up, me by slow strangulation by my enemies. We must take into account that our existence is but a brief candle in regard to their everlasting time span. Perhaps he realized that our early deaths would have left us mere initiates in the full understanding of the world and of ourselves. Perhaps he saved us so that we could fulfill a higher potential of practice and experience—a daunting notion, but it does suggest itself." He poured them both more wine. "Or it may be that ours being a time of discovery and expansion, he thought we might cope with the new world and with new creatures more skillfully than some others."

"Perhaps," said Dee, who thought this explanation sounded a trifle vain. "And of course, you are assuming our serpentine rescuer told us the truth."

"Yes," Celsus admitted slowly as he weighed Dee's remark. "I have made that assumption, and despite the children's stories of the Bible, on most occasions it has appeared to be accurate." He considered the problem in silence for the greater part of a minute. "Yes. He has presented himself without guile. So I have credited him with candor. Yet well I know that the devil has the power to play the saint when he most wants to deceive. We must give the devil his due." The Gothic paused just long enough to allow the Elizabethan a chance to enjoy his word play. "For in despite of these religious misgivings, I cannot fathom why he should lie. He has nothing to gain, but much to lose in way of his reputation at his Collegium of Worlds."

"Aye. But, in like manner, why should he utter unto us the truth?" Dee asked. "It was ever his way upon occasion to tell you one thing and me another, neither wholly truthful nor wholly deceptive, neither of us completely told of his true purpose. He never imparted knowledge to me of your presence here, though you seemed to have knowledge of mine. I wager I had knowledge of Yeshua's intentions ere you, yet the rogue looked only to you for remedy of the disease which in no way was given to me, whose sole mission was to pursue the fox and have at it." Dee warmed to his theme. "Then, in perversity, he lured me away from our sanctuary in England, where it was that we searched for clues, and he most perfidiously betrayed me and mine to our NTSA gaolers and all the woefulness that followed."

Nodding in agreement, Celsus chose his next words carefully. "You were not given a substitute for the cranial chip, and I was. This suggests that I was better prepared to deal with humanity in this time. But *you* spent your time among them, as I have not. I have assumed there was a reason for this, but we may never know what that reason was. As to the unfortunate business at Four Corners, perhaps it was a tactical error. After all, before going into hiding, Dyckon risked his anonymity by reaching out to me to help free you. I would never have known of your arrest otherwise."

He looked up as Boris brought them the next course—a haunch of venison studded with sour cherries and garlic—and carved it with a flourish. Boris's young Mongolian general factotum removed the empty bottle of sherry and awkwardly replaced it with an expensive bottle of Cabernet. "Boris, you've outdone yourself."

"It's good to see you enjoying your dinner," the hotelier said, flushing with pleasure for his most important guest.

"How can we not?" Celsus said expansively. "You shot that deer yourself, I'm sure."

"I did," said Boris, "and the boar. You will find them all properly dressed and hung, as well. None of this poorly hung meat in my kitchen." There was an unconcealed look of reproach to the gangly youth who stood dully scratching his arm. The owner served Dee before Celsus—another indication of Paracelsus' courtesy—taking care to pile the sour cherries atop the thin slices of venison. With equal care he prepared Celsus' plate and then, with the boy in tow, left them to their private conversation.

"It was so in our time," Celsus approved, and poured from the new bottle of wine. "All those with land hunted their own preserves and took pride in the table they laid."

"A happy time," John Dee approved, warming to the occasion.

Celsus leaned forward. "And if you could, would you return to those halcyon days?"

"Would I?" Dee stared at him. "Without delay. Wouldn't you?"

"Certainly not," said Celsus. "I much prefer this century, for all its drawbacks—and all its advantages, which to me outweigh the drawbacks. Here, unlike in my own time, I am a very rich man, I have a free hand in what I do, and I have influence not only in the world of commerce but in the worlds of spirituality and medicine. The rich and the poor know of my work, and the deeds I have done are accorded recognition and excellent repute, having provided immediate and genuine benefit to millions—all of which was hardly true of me in the time when I was born. Then my home was literally the highway and I was despised by every quack and town official who had power over me. Watching from afar this week, seeing Swink best the NTSA was a sweet joy, long in coming—not revenge per se but a judicious comeuppance. No, Doctor Dee, I wouldn't go back if I had the chance. I mean to stay right where I am, no matter what opportunity presents itself."

In a strong, heartfelt tone, inspired by two years of wandering and regret, Dee answered, "Had I all your advantages and were given the chance to return, I would leap at the opportunity and that suddenly." In a sudden burst of feeling he added, "Such is the enormity of my loneliness." His sadness took him somewhere painful. "Here I am out of my depth."

"Bah!" Celsus barked, but he saw the defeat in the other's eyes. "Well, it may be so." He drank down his wine and filled his glass again. "You're abstemious, Dee. I wouldn't have thought you'd turn down such fine wine as this."

"I've been in prison, and my fare has been Spartan. My head would not stand the fumes of much drinking." Dee drank a little to satisfy his host, then continued to eat. "I am more hungry than dry," he said by way of further explanation.

"Then suit yourself," said Celsus, a bit affronted. He had thought he had made some headway in breaking through the man's steely reticence. "But spare a moment to think about my offer. You and I could do so much working in concert, especially if the threat of the Roc virus is over. You could be my partner in this, you know. You have much more experience in dealing with the people of this time, and that could make you very useful to me."

"Why think you the crisis has passed?"

"Haven't you heard? The NTSA has had the victims under quarantine for days, with no new outbreaks reported anywhere in the world. Ach, such a relief."

"That does not a jot relieve us of the peril. The diseased Roc is but in hiding, biding his time for a new attack."

Theon Celsus smiled distantly, with a look that could only be called foxy. "In hiding—yes. New attack—no." Here Celsus could no longer maintain his practiced deception. He had hoped to keep this turn of the conversation until dessert, which he believed was the appropriate time to serve it up. Everything in its proper season, his Teutonic father had instructed him. But an impatient modern world had no time for such niceties. "I'm leaving in a couple of days to go to India to a Raj commune near the quarantine site to meet with the Roc. He has asked to meet with me. They say he has no intention of leaving."

"Is this the one we have sought and lost so much sleep over? The one that was in Waco, Texas?" Dee asked excitedly, astonished at the news. He had nearly dropped his fork at the announcement.

"I believe he is the one, yes," said Celsus demurely, enjoying the childlike wonder and the sudden elevation of

Dee's spirits. "I don't know of any others on Earth." He cut another bit of venison and began to chew it energetically. "A good, strong savor."

But Dee had lost his stomach for food and only wanted information. "I chide you, sir, before in choler, now I must chide you in extremest joy. Why have you kept this from me? What guards can hold him? Why sit we here? O for a horse with wings. How far is it to this same Raj commune? Let us glide thither at once. Away, I prithee. What ho! D'Winter! D'Winter, I say!" he shrieked in enthusiastic exaltation.

John Dee saw the smile of merriment on Paracelsus' face and toned down his excitement. "My apologies, sir, but I have awaited this day for over a year, fearing that it would never hap." He sighed heavily, as if he had returned to life and purpose. "This day is a day of triumph. It shall go red-lettered in my diary."

Theon Celsus had heard him out contentedly, eyes twinkling under mischievous eyebrows. "Don't apologize, young sir. You're not sorry, just amazed that you have landed at your journey's end so unexpectedly. After all you have been through, it must be quite a comfort indeed to reach the final turn. What a distinct pleasure it is to look at happiness through another man's eyes."

"My dear man, you have no idea. How can I thank you? You have bereft me of all words." But, of course, there were lots of words. And arrangements to be made. And a feast to be had.

# CHAPTER 53

JUST OVER CALCUTTA AND reducing his speed to less than point one Mach, Maxim rechecked his coordinates and began the descent into the hidden Raj commune on the edge of the Ganges. Though the trip from Irkutsk had taken less than a half hour, d'Winter and Kelly still thought the trip too long. Dee had found his quarry, but they weren't sure what was next on his agenda. If the Roc was amenable to staying put and was no longer a source of contagion, what was there for them to do? Of course, he might change his mind or, for that matter, outlive his hosts. But that was all fodder for future discussions. Today, they just wanted to be reassured that he was the only one of his kind on the planet, with the possible exception of Dyckon, who of course could be anywhere in the universe by now. Like modern-day doubting Thomases, they just wanted to see for themselves. Their employer had mixed emotions.

Like them, he wanted to have some resolution to the long quest that had led them to so many unforeseen experiences. But the possibility of establishing proof of the

Roc's timeslip device was no less exciting to him than, say, discovering the existence of the Holy Grail. Perhaps they were both myths. Suddenly, he wasn't so sure that Dyckon had told him the truth. What if the demon had only invented the charade as a motivational scam?

As it set down in the landing area, the flyer's exhaust whipped up the trees that shaded the ashram. Shutters and roof material slapped, dust and leaves flew in all directions, and the bamboo buildings creaked like old swings. "I just hope the vaccine works," Kelly said, laughing to show her confidence.

"Me, too," said Morgan, and got into position so he could get out ahead of her, the better to protect all those he was responsible for, though he wouldn't be much good against microorganisms. As he slid open the metal door, they felt the moist blanket of heat that was the Ganges delta. All but Maxim waded into the humidity; he stayed behind with the transport, leaving his duties to d'Winter. No one rushed to meet them. Theon explained that was because all non-Hindus were Achut—Untouchable—and the Raj commune was probably making preparations to store up on sacred Ganga water to cleanse their living quarters after their departure. The Brahma Kumaris took long ritual baths after their missionary work of ministering to foreigners and the lower castes.

People began to trickle in from the hospital and the river. Directions were given, and the visitors found themselves looking for a two-story edifice, with broad eaves, facing southeast to give shade. A banner emblazoned with the emblem of a medieval blood-letting chart hung from the rooftop, they were told. And sure enough, past the soccer field, there it was. Dee took a sharp breath, lifted his chin, and stood ready to face whatever Fortune had in store for him. Morgan d'Winter climbed the wooden step to the door and knocked; Celsus joined him at the entrance. The door swung open, and an athletic young Indian appeared and bowed slightly to Morgan. But with a shriek of delighted recognition, he embraced Theon Celsus and linked his arm in his. "How are you, esteemed sir? I am honored to have you and your friends as my guests." He turned back to those he had not acknowledged. "You are all most welcome. Please. Come in. Kalkin is waiting."

"Kalkin?"

"Yesterday, after rounds, the shape-changer went through the rite of *upanayana samskara* and was welcomed into Sanatana Dharma, the orthodox faith. Our guru readily made allowances, as Kalkin was able to tell us much about Rama and the creation of the four sacred Vedas. He thinks, despite his race, he may be a Brahman. He has taken the name of Kalkin, which is the tenth incarnation of Vishnu in the Age of Darkness."

"I hope I may be worthy of the name," said Mattik of Clan Fawg. There he stood in the guise of Corwin Tarlton but with a honey-toned skin that only partly hid the colonies of iridescent scales on his throat, face, and hands. His face had a weathered sweetness. He stared into the face of the humani who he had not seen for two centuries when it had been immobile and frosty white within a hibernation chamber. "I was right, it was you. You have gained weight." The yellow slit eyes in the squamous head squinted in remembrance.

"Have I? What about my friend here?" Celsus cocked his head in the general direction of John Dee. "Has he gained weight as well?"

"No, he has grown more haggard since I saw him last. But that was but a short time ago. In Waco, I watched you for days on the news replays. You were there when Fawg set-ut was murdered. You are Doctor John Dee, Dyckon's pet." There was no hint of animosity in his declaration. It was rather more like a passive chronicler doing a narrative reading on a historical vid program. He turned back to the quaint little man on the step, "Are you still called Paracelsus?"

"No, I have taken the name of Theon Celsus, as befits this modern world. And you, you are no longer Mattik?"

"Your planet is so very far away from any contact with any of the worlds of the Collegium. I have accepted the fact that I am a long way from home, and with no possible way to return, I am very likely to die here. I have realized that Fawg's plan for domination is worthless without Fawg. I have not the leadership skill to command a world of obedient humani. If I let the virus spread, in time I would be left utterly alone in a world with no one to talk to—a hell of my own making."

"You see, the beliefs of Dada Lekh Raj and the nation of Rocs are not so far apart," said the monk. "He will have a home among us for as long as he desires it. By then this wise and good man, Theon Celsus, will have had time to mass-produce drugs for all mankind against the mutation disease. Kalkin will willingly provide antibodies for the needed serum. We will learn from him as he learns from us."

"And you believe he poses no danger to anyone?" interposed the cautious Morgan d'Winter, emphasizing *danger* and *anyone.*

"Perhaps to himself," allowed the monk. "He has occasionally given way to despair."

"Small wonder, being so estranged from his own kind," commiserated John Dee. He had never imagined a Roc this humble before. Isolation must be an innate race phobia, he thought. He was grateful that all his friends were wise enough not to even hint to the penitent that Dyckon might still be lurking somewhere in the solar system with the possible means of going home.

Before Dee could ask about the timeslip, the Roc spoke again. "Fawg and I had a plan to afflict an immense amount of pain and devastation on your world. To restore my own honor and to be worthy of all Roc, I must make amends. I know I can be of help in the Raj commune. I know nothing about humani medicines," he spoke directly to Celsus, "but if I can be of any help either now or in the future please, call upon me. By kidnapping you from your worlds, my kind have done both you and John Dee a great disservice. I would say destinies, but obviously you were destined to end your lives in this new century."

Celsus nodded thoughtfully. "Perhaps your experience and what you know of the mysteries of the universe will be very helpful indeed. What a team we shall make. You and me and Doctor Dee. We shall work wonders."

# CHAPTER 54

THE MONK, SEEING KELLY begin to wilt, remembered his manners and welcomed them all into the residence. Soon they were all in the bamboo house, comfortably sheltered from the heat of the noonday sun. The hosts had already prepared floor mats for their guests, and they sat about in a circle. Tea was served. Subjects of conversation ranged from recent events to ancient history, to life on the Roc expedition, to herbal remedies, to views on medicine, to spiritual expectations. Talk of Fawg was tacitly avoided. Dee listened patiently, aware that life for him was returning to normal. As normal as it could be for a man five hundred years out of his time. His two years of frustration, hiding, and searching had come to an end. He felt the tug of loss. He still hoped, with waning expectation, for some mention of the device.

As the group continued its discussion he listened half heartedly, trying to imagine what his new life might be, but unable to fix any pictures in his mind. Despite the overhead fan, he became restless and overly chafed by the heat. He excused himself by saying that his legs had cramped from the enforced sitting and he was stepping out to stretch his legs.

As he stepped out, he heard the faint chiming of a bell or triangle. Probably the demarcation of a hospital shift or a time of prayer, he decided when no signs of disturbance manifested within the compound. With his back to the hut, he walked some few steps toward the water, separating himself even further from the conversation inside. For a while, he heard no sounds at all but the wind breathing lightly through the leaves of the trees. His own breath was heavy with the exertion of finding air in all the humidity. He looked up to the sky briefly, his eyes stabbed by the glaring intensity of the sun.

"I've brought you something to drink," said the Roc.

"Gramercy." He said, taking the glass from the scaly hand.

"It is obvious there is something bothering you. Can I be of help?"

"Mayhap." Dee picked his words with care, delicate as a spider stepping on the spokes of its web. "I cannot fathom the intentions I have apparently participated in. Dyckon, when he first spoke of Fawg and you to me, made me believe that you had an instrument that could allow one to travel to—and fro—through time. Pardon me, but I fain would know if such a thing doth exist."

"Yes. It does, in a manner of speaking regarding *to*. We can send persons ahead in time, but not send them back, at least not at present. It is a problem we are addressing."

Dee heard the note of evasion in the Roc's voice but decided to ignore it. "When you say addressing, do you mean you have neared a point of resolution?"

The Roc did the equivalent of sighing. "No, not so far."

"Have you some hope for your progress?" Dee pursued, although he knew the answer.

"Nothing to be certain of, no." Kalkin looked across the lake. "I'm sorry."

"No more than I," said Dee heavily.

There was a long silence this time, broken at last by the lamenting cry of a night bird.

"Then, what of me?" Dee asked, as if speaking to the bird.

The Roc contemplated Dee in silence. Kalkin pressed his almost-human lips together. "I am ashamed of what you had to endure on Dyckon's account. No one knows better that I how much you are owed and that it is well beyond me or any of my species to adequately repay. For which I most heartily ask your pardon."

"That hardly matters now," Dee said heavily. "But verily I accept your apology and will hold nothing against you." He wondered if he would be able to keep that promise.

Kalkin looked up suddenly. "We could send you farther ahead in time. Perhaps there is a breakthrough to come."

Dee chuckled sadly. "I doubt it. For if it were so, some messenger must have reached us with that gladsome news by now, but none has."

The Roc's enthusiasm was blighted at once. "True enough." He started to turn away. "If you hear anything . . ."

"I will inform you of it, and speedily. But in the event, you are more apt to hear of it than I am. You are the one your kind will seek out, not me." Dee heard laughter from inside the house. "At least they are all happy."

"They will be glad to have you stay with them," said Kalkin. "They are truly dedicated to you."

Following him, Dee realized his fate had been sealed. Even as he grieved for his home, he heard the voices of his friends inside. His foot touched the wood of the stair, and Dee squared his shoulders and lifted his chin proudly. It was not an ending, but a beginning, he thought. "Henceforth I shall be ruler of mine own fate," he vowed as he stepped through the doorway to those who had shared his adventure.